"A beautiful and timeless tale of family and loyalty, friendship and devotion."
—Mette Ivie Harrison, author of the *New York Times*
Notable Book *The Bishop's Wife*

"Powerful and heartbreaking, *The Passion of Dolssa* shows us that the voices of dissent can only be silenced for so long. Their echoes carry down the centuries, sounding warnings for our own time. Julie Berry writes the past as if she lived it."
—Jennifer Donnelly, *New York Times* bestselling author of *These Shallow Graves*

"Julie Berry's sweeping tapestry of friendship and belief is both epic and intimate, both sweet and painful."
—Elizabeth Wein, award-winning author of
Code Name Verity and *Rose Under Fire*

"Two unique girls, thrown together in a time of change and danger. One transcendent reading experience."
—Nancy Werlin, National Book Award honoree and
New York Times bestselling author

"The slow build reveals . . . a compelling, admirable young woman in a gorgeously built world that accepts miracles without question . . . Immersive and mesmerizing."
—*Kirkus Reviews*

"[A] powerful and beautifully written novel."
—*VOYA*

OTHER BOOKS YOU MAY ENJOY

the
PASSION
of
DOLSSA

A NOVEL

JULIE BERRY

PENGUIN BOOKS

PENGUIN BOOKS

An imprint of Penguin Random House LLC
375 Hudson Street
New York, New York 10014

First published in the United States of America by Viking,
an imprint of Penguin Random House LLC, 2016
Published by Penguin Books, an imprint of Penguin Random House LLC, 2017

THE LIBRARY OF CONGRESS HAS CATALOGED THE VIKING EDITION AS FOLLOWS:

Names: Berry, Julie, 1974– author.
Title: The passion of Dolssa / by Julie Berry.
Description: New York : Penguin Group, [2016] | Summary: In mid-thirteenth century Provence, Dolssa de Stigata is a fervently religious girl who feels the call to preach, condemned by the Inquisition as an "unnatural woman," and hunted by the Dominican Friar Lucien who fears a resurgence of the Albigensian heresy; Botille is a matchmaker trying to protect her sisters from being branded as gypsies or witches—but when she finds the hunted Dolssa dying on a hillside, she feels compelled to protect her, a decision that may cost her everything. | Includes bibliographical references.
Identifiers: LCCN 2015020814 | ISBN 9780451469922 (hardcover)
Subjects: LCSH: Albigenses—Juvenile fiction. |
Inquisition—France—Provence—Juvenile fiction. | Christian heresies—Juvenile fiction. | Faith—Juvenile fiction. | Provence (France)—History—13th century—Juvenile fiction. |
France—History—Louis IX, 1226–1270—Juvenile fiction. | CYAC: Albigenses—Fiction. | Inquisition—Fiction. | Christian heresies—Fiction. | Faith—Fiction. | Provence (France)—History—13th century—Fiction. | France—History—Louis IX, 1226–1270—Fiction. |
GSAFD: Historical fiction.
Classification: LCC PZ7.B461747 Pas 2016 | DDC 813.6—dc23 LC record available at
https://protect-us.mimecast.com/s/1dmaBqSXVApmFE

Penguin Books ISBN 9780147512963

Printed in the United States of America

1 3 5 7 9 10 8 6 4 2

For Teofilo Ruiz and Mark Gregory Pegg,
with deep gratitude,

and for Phil,
who makes all things possible

CONTENTS

FRANSA

TOLOSA

PROVENSA

BAJAS

BARCELONA

anno DOM
1241

DITERRA AN

"Sin is the cause of all this pain, but all shall be well, and all shall be well, and all manner of thing shall be well."

—Julian of Norwich, fourteenth-century mystic, and the first woman known to write a book in English

From *Revelations of Divine Love*, Chapter XXVII

Whatever we inherit from the fortunate
We have taken from the defeated
What they had to leave us—a symbol:
A symbol perfected in death.
And all shall be well and
All manner of thing shall be well.

—T. S. Eliot, twentieth-century poet,
quoting Julian in his poem "Little Gidding"

1290

FRIAR ARNAUT D'AVINHONET

The Convent of the Jacobins, Tolosa

must write this account, and when I have finished, I will burn it.

Mine is the historian's task, to record the events of the last century, showing God's mighty hand in ridding these southern lands between the Garona and the Ròse rivers of the heresy of the Albigensians.

I am asked to show future generations how God's justice was carried out by the crusade against these so-called "good men" (*bons omes*), "good women" (*bonas femnas*), and "friends of God" (*amicx de Dieu*), and how the inquisitions that followed, wrought by my brother Dominicans, finished God's holy work. The collected records of more than half a century of inquisitorial toil are mine to examine: transcripts, testimonies, and confessions from a generation now all but extinct.

When searching out a history, sifting through a thousand facts and ten thousand lives, one often uncovers pieces that do not fit. The prudent choice is to cast those details aside, like chaff into the fire. The story must be understandable. The moral should be clear.

Perhaps I am not a prudent man. I found pieces that haunted me, voices echoing from parchment leaves that would not let me sleep at night. I could find no rest until I searched out the truth, studied what I could learn about those involved, and found a way, with, I pride myself, a minimum of invention, to make the pieces fit. If only for me.

There are those who would say this record casts doubt upon the righteousness of the Church's work. Which is why this book, written for my private satisfaction, must not outlive me.

I myself have never been an inquisitor. I was, I confess, not cut out for it. But I was a patient laborer in the fields of knowledge, and so to Tolosa's archives I was sent after my university studies in París. Here I have spent nearly thirty years.

It was in the days when Count Raimon's daughter Joana still ruled as Comtessa de Tolosa, before Provensa came under the rule of the king of Fransa, and when I, myself, was new to this vocation, that the bishop of Tolosa, himself a former inquisitor of renown, came home to the Convent of the Jacobins to spend his final days.

It happened that I served in the hospice one evening. The ailing bishop began to speak to me. He seemed impelled to tell his

tale. He confessed to a secret doubt that had plagued him throughout his life—unease over whether he had done God's will in one
particular case. I reassured him with all my heart that he had done
his best to serve the Lord. He thanked me with tears. In the morning, he was gone.

Some months after, I found papers belonging to a priest in a
seacoast *vila*, a priest known for composing sacred songs of great
beauty. The papers made it clear he was not their author. A woman
had written them, and with them, a curious and troubling account
of her own spiritual journey. Names and places in the woman's
account reminded me of the old bishop's testimony. And so I wondered.

Later still, a lengthy narrative from a friar in Barçalona fell
into my hands, painstakingly recorded. The pieces of my mystery
at last began to fit. I puzzled over its connecting threads. Finally,
and perhaps, rashly, I decided to stitch the pieces together, however
clumsily, and record it. The gaps and errors in the sewing are my
own; of its overall completeness, however, I feel certain. These
voices from the past had arisen like ghosts demanding to be heard.

This, I will confess, is one of the secret thrills of my historical
work. But listening too closely to those voices, in these times in
which I live, may also be its most terrible danger.

1267

BOTILLE

I swear to tell the full and exact truth about myself and others, living and dead. Why keep secrets? There's no one it would help. The dead are all I have to talk about, anyway. What harm can there be in telling their stories now? They are safe, beyond reach.

There was a time when my name was Botille, when I lived with my sisters and our old Jobau. We lived by our wits, and great buckets of nerve, and anything—*anything*—we could steal, or sell.

Like most in Provensa, we'd seen hunger and illness. We'd grown up in Carcassona, a city broken by the crusaders before we were born. But what was yesterday's war to little girls? We'd lost our mother. That was all we had room for. She left each of us her love, her reputation, two sisters, and Jobau. And one silver crucifix to share.

We begged for our dinner and stole washing from peasants to clothe little Sazia. We huddled together to keep warm at night. Jobau's drinking and his temper harried us from town to town at the hands of the *bayles*. We were wanderers, survivors, always searching for a home.

We thrived upon it. Greedy little urchins, foolhardy little thieves.

Now I see we were magic, my sisters and I. We laughed at ourselves, at Jobau and the world. Nobody's ever made me laugh like my cynical little Sazia could. You wouldn't think it to know her now. We gave Plazensa, the eldest, fits of rage with our cheek.

Life was sweet, though I doubt we realized how much. Home was each other. Not walls, but the adventure of the search to find them.

Our wanderings led us to a small seaside town called Bajas, and there, among vintners and fishermen, we saw an opening and decided to seek a home. We washed our faces and combed our hair and tried to make something more of ourselves. We swore we'd give up thieving. We'd grown old enough to know it was safer to be inside the law, and the arms of the *vila*, than out of them. We took over an old derelict tavern and dared to run it.

Plazensa's brewing, our scrubbing, Sazia's fortune-telling, and my hustle brought customers in. We began to feel that we might belong, and others counted us among their neighbors and friends. Finally and forever, I believed, we could be safe.

Then I met Dolssa.

1241

DOLSSA

The summons came from Dominus Roger, him who'd baptized me and taught me to reverence the body and blood. Our own parish priest came to lead me to the cloister of the abbey church of Sant Sarnin, the great cathedral of Tolosa. The inquisitors wished to speak with me.

My mother turned pale. She pulled me into her chamber under pretense of wrapping a scarf around me.

"Daughter, hear me quickly," she said. "Answer as little as possible. Don't upset them. Say nothing about your preaching, and certainly nothing about your beloved."

I would have none of this. Who were they, that I should fear them?

"Speak only as you are," was her warning. "A modest and true Christian maiden. Be humble. Be still."

"But Mamà," I said, "why would I be otherwise?"

"My darling," she pleaded. "You don't fear them, but you should. Inquisitors have made Count Raimon send hundreds of heretics to the fires. Their verdicts—not even he dares resist them. Not anymore." She rested her forehead against mine. "You were too young to know all that happened during the war years, and even since. Your papà and I shielded you from it as best we could."

I was aghast. "What has that to do with me, Mamà? I'm no heretic! Is that what you believe of me?"

"Hush!" Mamà glanced at the door. "Of course you're not. You know how I feel. But you *are* different. You are . . ." She hesitated. "Your words give you authority. You have believers. This is something the inquisitors can't ignore."

"My beloved does not fear them, nor keep silence," I told her.

The waiting priest tapped at the door. We both felt caught. Mamà's whisper became an urgent breath in my ear. "Youth makes you bold. Love makes you trusting. But it is madness to provoke these inquisitors. They will not like what you say about your love. Not when you're so young, and a girl."

I waited for her to finish. There was no point in vexing her. But she knew she had lost.

"God knows I will stand by you, come what may." Her grip upon my arms was tight. "For my sake, guard your tongue to guard your life, my daughter."

DOLSSA DE STIGATA,
THE ACCUSED

Testimony recorded by Lucien

THE CLOISTER OF THE ABBEY CHURCH
OF SANT SARNIN, TOLOSA

You wish to speak with me, Friar Lucien? Prior Pons? My priest said you wished to ask me questions.

I have seen you, Friar, in the street. You pass by our house often.

Tell me, what is it like to live in a convent? To take holy vows along with others? I've often wondered.

My mother prayed and planned for me to enter the cloister. The thought was sweet, in a way. But my beloved told me my path was different. Silence does not serve his purpose for my life. He asks me to tell others about our love.

All right. You shall ask the questions, and I will answer.

Oc, I reject all heresy and false belief, and cling to the true Catholic faith.

Oc, I swear to tell the full and exact truth about myself and others, living or dead.

Non, I have never seen a heretic. I do not know any of the *bons omes* nor *bonas femnas* that are called heretics. I have lived a very sheltered life in my parents' home. *Non*, I have never listened to their preaching, nor helped them, nor fed them, nor carried gifts for them. How could I? I rarely even leave my house, Friar.

I am eighteen years old.

My name, as you well know, is Dolssa de Stigata. My father was Senhor Gerald de Stigata. He was a knight. He died five years ago last spring. My mother is Na Pitrella Braida de Stigata. I live with her and our few servants in my father's ancestral home here in Tolosa.

I, preach?

In my home, *oc.* I have shared my thoughts with relatives and friends on a few occasions.

That is where you heard me? Through a window. You saw me.

I preach that my beloved Christ is the ardent lover of all souls. That he stands beckoning to all God's children, to come taste of his goodness. To be one with him, as he is one with me.

Why do I preach this? Good friar-preacher, you who wear the mantle of Blessed Dominic the Preacher, I could ask the same of you!

Oc. In this room, questions are yours to ask.

I preach because my beloved calls me to. My one desire is to shine his love into the world.

What?

Oh!

Oc, since you ask, I'm laughing. How can I not? You wondered, how do I know the devil hasn't tricked me? I can only answer, if it is the devil who teaches people to trust in the love of Jhesus, then what, I wonder, should we call men of the cloth like you?

Far less impertinent, good friar, than you calling my beloved a devil. Remember who my beloved is.

Plainly, friar, I am a *femna*, and yet I speak. I do as my beloved urges me to do. Who shall forbid what my beloved commands?

Oc, Sant Paul said it was a shame for women to speak in church, but I do not speak in church. I worship in church, and I speak in my own home, as a Christian woman is free to do.

But *oc*, you guess rightly. If my beloved bid me to speak in church, I would do it. My beloved is greater than Sant Paul. Surely, you would not argue that an apostle's words are greater than the Lord's? The apostles didn't listen to Santa Maria Magdalena, either, though she was right when she told them she had seen her Lord risen from the tomb.

You accuse me of heresy.

Oc, I am listening. I'll give you my answer.

I can no more retract or deny what I have said about my beloved than I could choose to stop breathing. Against my will, breath would flow into my lungs; against your will, speech will flow from them also. If you seek to silence me, I will only cry more urgently. My beloved's praise will not go unsung, not so long as I have breath.

Oc, I know who you are. I know what you claim you can do to me.

How can I fear you with my beloved beside me? His arm is mightier than all flesh, and I know he will protect me.

BOTILLE

---

struga picked, of course, the worst time possible to tell
me.

We wore our hair dandled up in rags to keep it off our hot
necks, allowing the sun to burn our sweaty skin. Our oldest, flim-
siest skirts we had pulled snug between our legs and pinned to our
backs. There we were, thigh-deep in juice, stomping, squashing,
mashing the cool, slimy grapes under our heels and deliciously
through our toes, while the harvesters clapped and laughed and
sang to Focho de Capa's *fidel*. It was a party. A frolic. And a bit of
an exhibition. Astruga's thighs—purple, even—were nothing to be
ashamed of, and as for mine, skin was skin, wasn't it? The sky was
blue, the air was hot, the sea breeze stirring our little *vila* of Bajas

was playful, and the splashing new wine was sweet on my lips, its perfume rich enough to knock me over and drown me happily in the old winepress.

And that was when Astruga told me she was pregnant.

Not in so many words, of course.

"Look at the buffoons." Sweat rolled in rivers off her wine-red cheeks. Jacme and Andrio had linked their beefy, sun-tanned arms and were now swinging each other in idiotic loops, bawling out their song, while the other men slapped themselves and howled, and the married women shrieked with laughter. Jacme and Andrio were great laughers, those two.

"They're a pair, all right," I said. My thighs ached from all the stomping, but the music compelled us onward. I'd waited ages for my turn in the press. I wasn't about to flag now.

Astruga showed no signs of slowing. She leaped like a salmon through her sea of sticky wine. Always a restless one, Astruga. "I need one."

Maire Maria! She needed a man. Today, not tomorrow. I sighed. Harvest frolics were known for this. All those *tozets* with their lusty eyes upon her, her buoyant chest bouncing practically into her eyeballs, and her skirts tucked up and pinned over her bottom . . . Of course she would feel herself in a mood to pick one of these young men, like a grape off the vine, and crush him against the roof of her mouth.

Across Na Pieret di Fabri's neat vineyards, chestnut trees blazed with fall color, while dark, narrow cypress pines stood sentinel. Past the trees was the village proper, Bajas, crowning its round hilltop like a bald man's hat, and beyond it, the brilliant blue lagoon of the sea, my sea, that cradled and fed tiny Bajas, and connected her to the entire world.

Paradise had stiff competition in our corner of Creation.

Jacme chose that moment to scoop a handful of pulpy juice out of the vat and pour it down his throat. Purple dribbles bled into his stubbly beard. He winked at us, and old Na Pieret de Fabri, whose vineyards these were, whacked him harmlessly with her hat.

I looked at all our sweaty purple *tozęts*. Great overgrown boys they were, though I supposed I must call them men. "After we're done, you can take your pick of *omes*."

"Botille," Astruga said, her smile still as bright, "I need to speak with you."

I lowered my weary leg and caught my breath. I knew what those words meant.

Astruga capered like a baby goat, kicking up her heels and splashing wine into the open, leering mouths of the *tozęts* dancing around the vat. And now I knew why, why she'd bribed Ramunda, whose turn in the winepress it ought to have been, to give her this chance to bounce and spin in her purple skin for all Bajas to see. She needed a husband, and fast. Perhaps, she had reasoned, if she played today well, she could find herself one.

Or I could. For that was my job in Bajas. Most *tozas* helped the family business of catching fish or harvesting salt. Some spun wool or silk; others wove baskets, or helped their papàs and mamàs fashion clay pots. Countless others grew vegetables and tied and trimmed grapevines.

But I, I caught suitors, harvested bridegrooms, wove dowries, fashioned courtships, grew families, and tied and trimmed the unruly passions of our hot-blooded young people into acceptable marriages. I brought them all to Dominus Bernard's altar in the end. Only sometimes, as now, with a baby on the way, I did not have the luxury of time to plot and plan.

I watched Astruga's eyes linger on Jacme's broad face.

"Jacme?" I whispered.

She shrugged. "He'll do."

I danced a little closer to her. "Is it he?"

She looked away, and shook her head.

I danced in a circle around her. If she wanted my help, she'd best not turn her eyes away from me. "Who is the father?"

She turned the other way, like a naughty little *toza* who won't confess to stealing the honey.

"Tell me," I pressed. "I have ways of making the father marry you." And I did. My sisters and I—we had ways all our own.

The high flush in Astruga's cheeks cooled. "Not this time, Botille."

Ah. He was married already, then. Well, no matter; Astruga was young and fresh. Weren't all the *tozęts* adoring her even now? This would be easy for me.

"Are you working on another match right now?"

"Maybe."

"If you marry off that cow Sapdalina before me, I swear, I'll claw her eyes out."

It *was* Sapdalina's troth I was working on, and while I wouldn't call her a cow, per se, she was a challenging case. At least she wasn't pregnant.

"That would hardly be fair to Sapdalina," I observed.

Her angry face fell. "Oh, please, Botille. I'll do anything. You've got to help me."

Astruga's skirt came unpinned and sank into the wine. She squealed and snatched it up, then thrust the soiled cloth into her mouth to suck out the blood-dark juice. Just then the church bells rang, and she let the skirt fall once more.

I looked toward the village, with its white stone walls, its rising houses ready to teeter and topple one another, and the brown square bell tower of the church of Sant Martin.

She'd shown me what, if I hadn't had a head full of wine and *fidel* tunes, my instincts should have smelled before Astruga had even spoken a word. The fruit growing in her vineyard was planted by a handsome rake, a delightful talker, a charmer if ever there was one, and the source of all my best clients. I owed him, really. Already a growing list of roly-poly babies had him as the *papà* they would never know.

Dominus Bernard, Bajas's priest at the church of Sant Martin.

"*Acabansa*! Finished!"

Focho de Capa, self-proclaimed lord of the revels, scooped a ladle of syrupy juice from the vat and drank it with great flourish. "*Bon an!*" A good year, good for the grapes.

We climbed out of the vat. Itier pulled us each out by the wrist onto the platform next to the press and planted wine-stained kisses on our cheeks. We climbed down the ladder. Astruga let herself be seized about the waist by frizzle-headed Itier and led off to the table that had been set up, spread with bread, cheese, salmon, and roasted vegetables. I lingered behind to wipe a bit of the juice off my arms with a rag Na Pieret di Fabri handed me.

Widow Pieret's eyes were still as blue as *la mar*, though her face was brown as carved chestnut and creased with as many deep grooves. Her husband, related to the lords of Bajas, had been a vintner, but his death, five years back, left Na Pieret to manage his great vineyards alone. It had been a terrible blow. Still, Na Pieret, who had never been weakened by childbearing, had borne up under the burden admirably. But today, though she smiled, she seemed tired.

"What is it, *ma maire*?" I genuflected, a courtesy owed to a great lady of advanced years, then I rose and kissed her cheek. All old women were "my mother," but Na Pieret was someone I could almost wish were my mother.

"Ack! You are covered in *viṇ*." She patted my cheek. "Smart Botille. Not a thing happens in this village but what you have a hand in it, is there?"

"Oh, pah." I unraveled the damp rags from around my hair. "I won't take the blame for everything."

Na Pieret leaned against the handle of her cane. I noticed her head quiver slightly. "I need your help, Botille." She spoke quietly. "I can't run the vineyards anymore."

I saw how much it hurt her to speak these words, though she said them simply and without self-pity.

"But your hired help, surely. They do the work for you, *non*?" I looked over to the feast table, where half a dozen of her hands lounged, stuffing their faces. "Are they lazy? Do they steal from you? Sazia and Plazensa and I can put a stop to that. We'll teach them a lesson—"

"No, no." Na Pieret squinted her eyes against the rays of the setting sun. "They are only as lazy as any other laborers ever were. No, they are kind to me."

"Then what is it?"

"I need a strong back, and eyes I can trust. I need someone who cares about the grapes like they are his own. But you know I have no children to entrust them to."

The wine on my skin had dried to a slimy, sticky sheen, and I began to itch. Hot breezes from the south did nothing to help.

"My mother had two daughters," Na Pieret went on. "My younger sister died last winter, leaving her two sons orphans, seven leagues from here, in San Cucufati."

"Oh?"

She nodded. "I want you to bring them to me. I will give

them the farm, and they shall become my sons."

Seven leagues? I pictured myself traveling seven long leagues with two quarrelsome little *enfans* in tow. What did she think I was, a nursemaid?

"How old are they?"

Na Pieret pursed her lips. "They were sturdy, useful children when I met them last," she said, "thirteen years ago."

I smiled, and looked over at Astruga, busy stuffing a piece of bread into Itier's mouth. "Is either of them married?"

"Botille!" Na Pieret laughed. "You haven't become one of the desperate *tozas* yourself, have you?"

"*Non*, Na Pieret." I took her by the elbow and steered her toward the table. "But there are always plenty of them about, and now I have two more husbands to offer them."

Na Pieret tapped my forehead with her swollen knuckles. "Only see to it you don't marry off my new sons to any of the silly *tozas*."

I shoved a half-drunk Andrio aside to make room on the bench for Widow Pieret to sit. "That, *ma maire*," I said, "is a promise I doubt I can keep."

DOLSSA

was a young girl when my beloved first appeared to me. Just a girl of no consequence, the child of pious parents who were much older than most. Mamà used to say I was her miracle *enfan*, the fruit of prayer, just as the prophet Samuel had been. I was happy in my home, and much loved.

Mamà dreamed for me the heaven of the cloister. Nothing would have made her happier than to see me take a nun's vows. Papà, however, envisioned the joy of family. He wanted grandchildren, and a legacy for his home and name. Poor, gentle Papà would not live long enough to see such a dream. He died not long after my visions first began. I don't know how I would have endured the loss, were it not for my beloved's secret visits.

We mourned Papà many days. Kinsmen and neighbors came to grieve with us, and condole with my widowed mother. Already they began to speak of me, in whispered voices, as a holy maiden, because I went so often to church. They cupped my cheeks in their hands and spoke blessings upon me. Some were faces I knew, but most, I didn't. It took me by surprise, seeing so many people claiming Papà's friendship and commemorating his life. Where were they during that life? Why didn't I know them? Of course, I'd only known him in his later years. He'd lived a full life before I came along.

I knew Papà had gone to God. But I would miss him so.

"See how she does not cry," a cousin of Mamà's whispered to her sister. "She's serene as an angel."

I was only shy.

"*Oc*, see the pious sweetness of her gaze," said the sister. "Like one of the blessed saints."

I watched my mother, wishing she'd stop talking to all these family strangers.

There was a man there, tall and grim. He spoke to my mother in a low voice. I went to her side and slipped my hand in hers.

"Bound for the church," my mother was saying. "It's out of the question."

The man's eyes examined my face. "She is very young."

I inched back behind Mamà.

"She will be a nun," my *maire* said firmly. "It is already settled."

The tall man tipped his hat to my mother. "My sorrow for your loss."

I didn't understand then what he must have been asking. I only knew that I would never be a nun. A bride of Christ, *oc*, but the cloister could never enclose all my love. It was too vast, too deep for such walls, such silence, such seclusion.

I left my *maire's* side and went and lit a candle for Papà. How I would miss his step in the hall, and his laugh at dinner. I was thirteen, and now Mamà and I were left alone.

Not long after *mon paire* died, the fires began. What once were sweet visions now burned in my soul, in my brain, in my blood. My beloved, pouring his presence over me, consumed me with his love. I couldn't sleep. I could scarcely eat.

Mamà thought I mourned Papà. It was easy enough to let her think that.

The world grew dull to me. Tolosa, the vibrant pink city, the *trobadors'* own rose of Europe, became dismal, tired, and brown. My will to remain in it grew slack.

My beloved was my great romance, and—impossible miracle!—I was his. He caught me up on wings of light, and showed me the realms of his creation, the glittering gemstones paving his heaven. He left my body weak and spent, my spirit gorged with honey.

There are no words for this. Like the flesh, like a prison cell, so, too, are words confining, narrow, chafing, stupid things, incapable of expressing one particle of what I felt, what I feel, when I see my beloved's face, when he takes me in his arms.

There is only music. Only light.

And no one may take it from me.

I told no one what was happening to me. My beloved was the most private secret of my soul.

Mamà began to speak of the abbey for me, and I refused to go. We quarreled bitterly, and grew cold with each other. At length she relented, with a heavy heart, and began to speak cautiously of me marrying. If I would not fulfill her dreams for me, I supposed, she was willing to concede that Papà's hopes had been honorable. There was a kinsman, she said. A goodly man, well respected. He had asked Papà about me once, and Papà had been pleased. In a panic I told her my heart was already taken. At this she became sick with worry that I had sinned. So, at my beloved's urging, I told her the truth about us.

She believed me. Relief made it easy for her to believe. Her maternal pride thrilled to think of me as being touched by divine grace. The next evening, she brought a cousin over to hear my tale. I wasn't happy, but I was glad enough to have the anger between us abated that I told my story anyway.

The next evening, Mamà brought another friend, and her cousin brought two others.

I was troubled, so I went to my love for guidance. He asked me if I would, for his sake, tell many about the loving kindness he'd lavished upon me. Within a week our house was full to overflowing. I found myself, against every instinct—for I would far rather have remained in my room, in the solitude where my beloved could find me—speaking to houses full of listeners, night after night.

I began to venture out of doors more, not to preach, but merely to taste the world, see the city bloom in high summer. I smelled fresh breezes blow across the winding Garona River, and watched larks flit about the porticos of Our Lady de la Daurada.

But I also saw a city still bruised and bleeding from years of crushing war. I saw souls darkened by loss and bitterness in the crusades. I saw faith destroyed after the brutality we'd endured in its name. Then I understood why my beloved had sent me.

So I opened my mouth to teach the only lesson I knew. Of love everlasting, of mercy reaching beyond the prison walls of death, of the bliss that awaits us when we die.

What a feeling it was, after a lifetime lived in my parents' house, to be part of the world and make a difference in it. To do something, however small. To speak, and be heard, if only in my own home. I thought I would speak in the city squares, but Mamà forbade it. "You do not dare do such a thing," she said. "This city is full of inquisitors, combing through the people for hidden heresies. To preach on the street is to arouse their alarm."

It didn't matter. People came. People sat outside and listened under windows. Just so, I later learned, did one eager young inquisitor and his elderly companion sit and listen. I didn't know it at the time.

I preached almost daily. One day, I remember, I saw the tall man who had come to our home when Papà died. He sat and listened to me speak. His face was so grave, he frightened me. Afterward, while the other guests mingled and broke bread, he approached and thanked me for my holy message. He offered me a pair of apricots. They sat so temptingly soft in his hand— did he know I couldn't resist apricots?—but I said no. A storm cloud moved across his eyes. He bowed and walked away.

Not long after, Friar Lucien de Saint-Honore began to preach in the square closest to our home. His voice was musical, but his accent was French and northern. He had keen dark eyes that missed no detail. Were he not a tonsured friar, he might have been a comely man.

Day after day he returned, raising his voice of warning. I could hear him from the upper window where I sat. We must flee the treacherous heresy, he said, that entwined itself around our way of life—the false beliefs that slithered through the grasses of our fair Provensa, with false teachers leading people away from the true faith and toward unholy rituals and vows. Lucifer's enticements, he warned, were no less beguiling today than those he'd planted in the Garden. The heretics, those false teachers of no authority, were serpents, and we ignorant Tolosans were Eve, deadly fruit poised upon our lips.

Upon *my* lips.

In our Father's house, I told the believers, there is never alarm, but only gladness, love, and peace.

Not long after that, the interrogations began.

BOTILLE

I made my first match when I was thirteen, but it was so easy, I don't know if I should even claim credit for it. Make no mistake, I charged a fee. I never let qualms get in the way when money is involved.

We had only just moved to Bajas, my sisters and Jobau and I, and taken over the derelict tavern on the skirts of town, near the water but not too near, for Plazensa required an ale cellar. The villagers still looked at us with some suspicion. We weren't local. We spoke Oc, but our accents were different. We came from the city of Carcassona, and we weren't a fishing family. And then there was Jobau. Mamà had charged us to look after him, keep him out of the way, and prevent him from provoking others. Plazensa grew skilled at fermenting just about anything, and we followed Mamà's orders by keeping Jobau drunk.

The fishwives especially distrusted Plazensa, who at sixteen stood tall and buxom, with the thickest head of long black curls this side of the Pirenèus Mountins. I didn't attract much notice, but Sazia did. At nine, she wore boys' trousers and wandered up to villagers offering to tell their fortunes for a penny. She made people wonder. They wondered all the more when Sazia's predictions about where the fisherman would net the greatest haul proved right again and again.

Plazensa said we should call the tavern the Three Skylarks. Sazia suggested the Three Pigeons, and it stuck. "After all," she said, "you might bake a pigeon into a pie, but never a skylark." All that summer as we patched and painted the tavern, and Plazensa scolded me for not doing enough to help, I watched out the window as the goat-cheese man's daughter, Lisette, sat in her parents' back garden, uphill from us, eating plums and stitching something in her little cloth book. To this day I can't think of her without picturing her sticky mouth and stained embroidery.

I wasn't the only one watching her. A goosenecked young *ome*, Martin de Boroc, spied on her daily through the shrubs that divided her gardens from ours. How she never saw him says much about her great stupidity, but as I say, matchmaking is nothing more than paying attention.

Martin de Boroc's father died at the end of that summer, leaving him his fishing boat, ensuring Martin would starve neither himself nor any future wife to death. So finally, one day, when I could no longer bear the suspense of wondering whether he would, for the love of Santa Sara, show his face to Lisette through the trees, I knocked on Lisette's parents' door.

Paul Crestian, Lisette's papà, kept his flocks of goats in an enclosure that stretched behind both of our homes. He stored his cheeses in his damp cellar. It is a fattening occupation, tasting every batch of creamy cheese to make sure it is just so. He answered the door and frowned at me over his round belly. "*Oc*?" he said. "You are the new girl from next door? The plain one, with the pretty older sister and the little duck of a younger sister."

I bowed. "That is right. Do you want to see your daughter married?"

Paul Crestian made the sign of the cross, then glared at me. "Why are you asking?" His brows lowered. "If your old *paire* thinks he can wed Lisette, he can think again."

I worked hard not to laugh. "No," I said. "Jobau doesn't want to marry your daughter. But Martin de Boroc does. Do you have a dowry for Lisette?"

"What kind of a father do you think I . . ." His eyes bulged at me. "Why am I telling a little *toza* my affairs? Off with you!"

"Martin de Boroc will make a fine living now that he has his father's boat," I said.

"Fish," growled the shopkeeper. "They're a slippery business."

"I will negotiate the marriage," I said, "for ten silver shillings, and a leg of *moton*."

"Ten silver shillings!" roared Paul Crestian. "I don't need help from a little—"

"Don't forget the *moton*." I ran to the waterfront.

The tide had come in, and Martin de Boroc had just finished mooring his boat. He carried a net of fish slung over his shoulder. Most had given up the struggle, but one still flopped desperately against the cords.

"Martin," I said, "do you want a wife?"

His mouth hung open. "Not one your age!" He tried to push past me.

I planted my palm against his chest. "What would you think," I said, "of Lisette, the goat-cheese man's daughter?"

He went limp. So did the fish.

"What would I think of Lisette?" he whispered. His eyes grew cloudy, like a fish's once it's been dead a few days. "Maire Maria!"

I wondered what he saw in that sticky face, but it was no concern of mine. "For ten shillings, and a pair of fat red *mujọl* fish, I will speak to Paul Crestian for you, and tell him he should be thankful to you if you were to ask for his daughter's hand."

He gulped. "Ten silver shillings?"

I held out my hand. "Payable in advance. If Lisette has a dowry, you owe me ten more."

He shifted his dead fish to his other shoulder. "I haven't got ten shillings on me."

"I'll follow you home."

I instructed Martin to present himself at Paul Crestian's home the following evening, bathed and brushed, then went home with his ten shillings jingling in my pocket, and a gleaming red *mujọl* clutched in each hand. The first fish, I gave to Plazensa, who eyed it hungrily and ordered Sazia to find more fallen wood for the fire. The second, I took next door to the shopkeeper. Mimi, my house-cat, followed me, mewling at my dangling prize.

"Martin de Boroc sends his regards, and your dinner," I told Paul Crestian. "He plans to come visit tomorrow evening to discuss Lisette's dowry. Make it a generous one, for a handsome, promising bachelor like Martin de Boroc can have his pick of wives."

"To discuss Lisette's dowry!" sputtered that girl's father. "I've not given my consent. Why should I give my only daughter to a bony fish man?"

Mimi lunged toward the fish. The goat-cheese man snatched it high out of reach. "Daughter," he cried, "can you cook well enough to get married? Prepare me this *mujọl*."

Lisette wandered into view, sucking on a plum. She wrinkled her nose at the fish but took it away dutifully. That night I smelled roast fish coming from both of our ovens, though Lisette's house had a slightly different aroma. I think she stuffed her fish with plums.

The next afternoon, I snuck a jug of Plazensa's special ale out of our cool cistern and carried it over to Paul Crestian. "A present," I said, "from our cellars, bought specially for you by Martin de Boroc. He's a generous soul, isn't he?"

The shopkeeper uncorked the jug and sniffed it. Its rich, malty scent filled the room. He took a foamy sip and tried to protest, then took another sip. Bajas was strictly a wine town, but Plazensa and her ale would soon change all that.

That evening I spied Martin de Boroc walking stiffly toward Lisette's house. He'd attempted to smarten up his appearance. Lisette's papà, I knew, would have finished Plazensa's ale by now, and if it could lift Jobau out of the doldrums, it could soften up the cheese man.

Half an hour later we heard loud laughter from the Crestians' *maison*. Plazensa looked up from caning the twine seat of a broken chair. "What's going on over there?"

Martin de Boroc burst through the tavern door and poured ten shillings into my lap. Plazensa stared at him. Mimi rubbed against his ankles. Even with a bath, he still smelled of fish.

"What was that for?" my sister cried, when he'd left.

"Couldn't say." I then pulled the first ten pieces Martin had given me from my pocket and presented them to Plazensa.

"What are you doing?" my sister cried. "Robbing the church? Stealing from merchants?"

"Such a suspicious nature," I tutted. "Martin de Boroc paid me of his own free will."

A smiling Paul Crestian sailed in and presented me with coins and a leg of *moton*. He planted a wet kiss on Plazensa's ruddy cheek, patted my head, and twirled out the door.

Plazensa leveled a pointing finger at me. "You've put a hex on the village men," she said. "You've bewitched them into paying us for no reason. Teach me! Tell me how you did it!"

"I did nothing of the kind," I said. "Pass me more twine. If we're ever going to open this tavern, we can't sit here gossiping."

"Who's next?" Plazensa wondered aloud, peering out the window. "Any other people coming to fling money or meat at you?"

"I don't know what you're talking about."

But half an hour later the door opened, and in came Azimar de Carlipac, the shipbuilder, jingling a little sack of coins.

"Which of you is Botille?" he demanded. "I've got a daughter who's due for a husband."

And so my career began. Along with Plazensa's enterprises, it fed my family. It kept me busy and needed by the entire village. To be needed is one way to be safe. The other is to have money. Given time, I'd have both. We'd uprooted and moved enough, we three plus Jobau. We'd found a new town every time he lost his head and his temper, or our petty thefts were found out. No more wandering. I would build a safe home for us, here in Bajas, with reputation and money to spare, one bashful bridegroom and one blushing bride at a time.

LUCIEN DE SAINT-HONORE

The balding priest, Dominus Roger, ushered the young heretic a second time into the questioning cell at the cloister of the abbey church of Sant Sarnin, where Lucien sat waiting. The prior of his order, Prior Pons de Saint-Gilles, watched him from behind a table, while a notary waited nearby to copy every word. Lucien hoped his agitation didn't show. An inquisitor must be calm, with the peaceful composure of Christ himself.

The priest's thick hand rested heavily on Dolssa de Stigata's shoulder. The other hand gripped the heretic's elbow. Had she needed to be forced to come in? Lucien imagined himself performing that same task. She was slight of build; she wouldn't weigh much. The priest met Lucien's gaze, relinquished his captive, and sat by the wall. He looked nervous. A relapse such as this reflected badly on him as a shepherd to the fold.

The young woman stood and gazed directly at Lucien without any show of shame or embarrassment.

"Please sit down." Lucien gestured toward a chair.

She did not sit.

Must he now stand?

"Donzęlla de Stigata," he said, "I have asked you to sit."

She watched him.

Prior Pons's languid gaze upon him made Lucien squirm inwardly. This was a test, and he was failing it, beaten by this maddening young woman before he'd even had a chance to ask her his first question.

If she could ignore his requests, he could ignore her defiance. He shuffled through his papers.

"Dolssa de Stigata," he began, "we hear reports that you've disobeyed our orders."

Her long dark hair flowed out from underneath her white cap. It caught the muted light coming through the panes in the dusty chamber.

"Is it true, Donzęlla Dolssa"—Lucien winced at a catch in his voice—"that you still claim to speak with our Lord, and to receive replies from him? That you persist in claiming a special intimacy with him, such as between a bridegroom and a bride, and that, despite our express orders, you continue to teach a group of followers these unsanctioned and unholy falsehoods?"

A small smile moved the heretic *femna*'s wide mouth. Lucien found his gaze drawn to the small mark over her upper lip. The devil's mark, he had more than once thought of it. Which would explain its dark fascination.

Lucien retreated to his papers. "We warned you," he said. "We attempted to correct you through merciful instruction. And yet you persist. Why such rebellion?"

The priest, Dominus Roger, mopped his brow. The damned girl—for she was surely that—only blinked lazily at Lucien. Brazen. Insufferable.

"Donzęlla," came Prior Pons's crackling voice. "It would fare better for you if you answered."

"Would it, then?"

He spread his hands upon the table. "Naturally."

She seemed mildly amused. "I have never spoken anything other than the truth. And I speak the truth now when I say that whether I answer you *oc* or *non*, you will burn me either way. So I see no reason to speak to you any more words than I wish to."

"And yet you have plenty of words to use elsewhere," said Lucien. It was peevish of him, and realizing so infuriated him.

"I speak more elsewhere," she said, "when I have the ears of people capable of listening."

All the while this damnable heretic's lips smiled inwardly, as though she alone were in possession of a delightful joke. As if she and someone else behind where Lucien sat conspired together in some droll jest.

Lucien rose. "It rests with the Holy Church to obtain audience with the Most High, and with him who holds Sant Peter's keys, to receive divine revelation for the Church. It is not and has never been the province of childish, silly *femnas* to speak in the name of the Lord."

"I will notify him, when next we speak, that he is in violation of your rules."

"Insolent creature!" Lucien turned to the prior to seek his outrage. But his spiritual superior's eyes were full of silent warning. *Control yourself.*

Lucien regulated his breathing and turned back to the heretic.

"We have shown you mercy," said he. "We spared you with a warning. I pleaded for you myself, in consideration of your youth. And this is how you reward our charity?"

"Donzęlla," said Prior Pons, "I beg of you not to force our hands. We have fought a painful war over just such threats to the faithful as you. You are a poisonous flower in the Lord's vineyard. Some find your youthful bloom attractive. Protecting the innocent and the gullible from such venom is our mission. We find no pleasure in your destruction, but we will do what we must."

A strange light burned in Dolssa de Stigata's eyes. "You must do what you must," she told him, "and I must speak the words my beloved bids me speak. He is more than recompense for whatever you may do to me."

"Your defiance," answered Prior Pons, "by its very nature, is sin. It is heresy."

"If you choose to, you may label me a heretic," said Dolssa. "But God in heaven is the judge of such things, and to him I plead my case."

"You will be excommunicated." Lucien's voice rose. "Your soul will burn in hell, and your body will burn in a heretic's pyre."

But still the infuriating, devilish girl only watched him. She was well practiced at prying her fingernails into the cracks in his composure.

He'd lost. But so had she. "You cannot win," he told her.

"I have already won," she said. "I dwell with my beloved, and when you slay me, I will dwell in his arms forever."

"Then before they spread your influence further," said Lucien, "we will make sure that those already infected with your poison will also be cut off."

Dolssa pulled in an anxious breath. At last. Lucien could almost feel the rise of her chest as her heartbeat registered his meaning.

"My words are my own," said she. "I claim their punishment, also, as my own. Surely, you can't construct a crime from associating with me."

Triumph was sweet upon Lucien's lips. He selected his next words carefully.

"As our inquiries into the faith of your countrymen has demonstrated clearly, association is how the devil impregnates the weak with his damnable fallacies. Association is life, and death—eternal life, and eternal death."

Her eyes smoldered. But there was fear in them now. Not even *her beloved* could banish it.

"Your mother, your kinsmen, your maid, your cook . . . your devoted followers . . . One can never be too careful, Donzella, in choosing one's associations. Not in Provensa."

DOLSSA

hey led us, my mother and me, bound like criminals, past reeking tanneries and slaughterhouses, through La Porta Narbonesa, and outside the city walls, where shameful deeds belonged. At least they didn't drag us through the streets by our ankles.

We came to a field near the river at dusk. Torches flickered in the two towers of the Castęl Narbonesa abutting Tolosa's wall like disapproving eyes. Wind rushed along the river reeds, sounding a warning of my beloved's anger.

Count Raimon's *bayle*.

Soldiers.

Executioners.

Begging lepers who rejoiced at finding a rich audience.

Behind them, singing holy songs, the friars, and Tolosa's bishop, also Raimon, dressed in state.

A crowd of watchers. Faces I once preached to. Treacherous neighbors and disloyal kin, blurring together in the smoke. The same relations who had called me pious, and praised my virtue. What had I done, that they should abandon me so?

Before us all, the fire raged. An animal, hungry for its prey, it snarled and snapped at me.

My life unwound before me like a spool of thread. Never in my darkest dreams could I have imagined this was how my days would end. That I should die so shamed and so utterly without help.

That my beloved *maire*, pure as linen, should suffer and perish for my sake. For my reckless pride. For her devotion.

Lucien de Saint-Honore read out a little sermon, then Count Raimon's *bayle* read the charges. Count Raimon! Our lord in Tolosa, who once greeted my father warmly in the streets, now ordering his daughter's death at the inquisitors' request!

I blessed the friar's words for delaying our deaths. Every living moment let me gaze longer into Mamà's loving eyes.

Preach on, preacher. I have no more pride to wound.

God and righteousness had triumphed over Mamà and me, he said. Heretics. Disobedient, unruly, unnatural women, he called us. The *femnas* de Stigata, mother and daughter.

Ma maire. How she loved me! Her soft eyes, full of comfort.

Beautiful in the firelight. She kissed my lips.

"God could give me no greater token of his love for me than you," she said. "Remember, my daughter. I go first."

The Holy Virgin, she'd said, had whispered to her and told her to trust in God's deliverance. All would be well. She should walk without fear all the way to the pyre. But she must go first.

She walked bravely. I trusted in that promised deliverance. My beloved would rescue us. I stood still to behold our salvation. Then the *bayle*'s foul hands seized my sweet *maire* and thrust her in the flames.

I prayed. I screamed to my beloved. *Come! Come and spare her!*

She died choking in the smoke, calling out my name.

Maire Maria, grant me a vision of her soul escaping into your arms, to blot out the sight, the heat, the smell of her burning skin. Her arms, consumed like greenwood, that once caressed me.

My *maire*. My good and gentle *maire*. My truest and only earthly friend.

Was it hours? Was it an eternity in hell? The churchmen watched me watching her.

She sank at last against the pole to which they'd tied her arms. She was gone. My time had come.

Something struck my ankles, then my wrists, bound behind me.

"Run."

So soft was the word in my ear that I didn't believe it.

"Run."

Hands plucked the cords from my wrists and ankles and steadied me.

"Run," said the voice again. I saw no one. Hands seized my arms and steered my body away from the flames, from the friars and the *bayle*'s constables. Hands pushed me on my way, so to keep from falling, I ran.

Smoke and darkness. Noise and confusion. They were all I had.

The rushing Garona barred my escape to the west. Open fields to the south would offer me no shelter. To the east lay the Roman road. More wall, more gates. Trees. People.

Darkness, be my cover, I prayed. *Jhesus, hide me well*. Back past La Pọrta Narbonesa. Back around the angry bulk of treacherous Count Raimon's *castẹl*.

Past the shouts of the friars, past the outer suburbs, until the countryside swallowed me in oblivion. Along a path joining the road. On and on, though my legs trembled and my belly burned. I walked when I must, to gather strength to run again.

He had come for me, but not for my mother.

It is a sin to question his unsearchable ways.

But I wished he had chosen otherwise. I, who longed to be with him, and Mamà, dearer than all that is dear—why not preserve her and bring me home?

He came. Just when I could no longer call on him, he came.

And just in time, if I must live, for the hounds were massing for the hunt.

LUCIEN DE SAINT-HONORE

Lucien de Saint-Honore paused outside the prior's door in the night-blackened corridor of the convent. His habit swished around his legs, reminding him that he was truly there, and not a mere specter swallowed by the dark.

He knocked on the door.

A canon, the prior's companion, opened it and stood silent as Lucien passed into the study. Prior Pons de Saint-Gilles stood before the fire with his hands clasped behind his back. He turned to face his visitor.

"What news, Brother Lucien?" asked the prior.

Lucien opened his mouth to give an answer he dreaded giving, then caught Prior Pons's gaze as it moved to a brocade chair facing the fire. Lucien swallowed. Of course, Bishop Raimon would still be here. After tonight's debacle, he wouldn't budge until justice was served.

Raimon de Fauga, bishop of Tolosa, rose from his seat and regarded Lucien. Even in the dim light, the elegant material of his robes set him apart from Pons and Lucien. His bishop's ring gleamed.

"I see by your eyes that you have not found her." The bishop shook his head and glanced at the older prior. "Tonight is a blot upon the record of our order, Pons."

Prior Pons warmed his hands at the fire. "We are here to heal Christendom, not to hunt runaways in the dark."

Raimon's robes swished as he turned away. "It's a disgrace. An affront to the Church, and to law in Tolosa. If she makes it out of town and into the countryside, the *bayles* will wash their hands of her, while she infects some other corner of the Lord's vineyard." His servants entered, bearing fragrant baskets. "Ah! Dinner."

"The *bayles* are looking for her even now," Lucien blurted. Bishop Raimon turned to him, and he lowered his gaze. "Lord Bishop—"

"As they should." Bishop Raimon beckoned to one of his servants, who sliced a slab of roast duck onto a waiting plate. The bishop gestured to the other to move his chair to the table, then sat and seized a delicate pair of ebony-handled knives and applied them to his meat. Lucien had never seen such graceful little utensils. He found himself staring at them in doped fascination, while the rich red scent of the meat wet his tongue.

"Sit, Pons, and eat," the bishop said. "There's plenty." When the prior hesitated, the bishop poked a knife laden with meat in his direction. "Even our moderation needs moderation, Pons. I declare it would be a sin of ingratitude for you to refuse me."

Prior Pons took a seat, and the bishop's servants carved him a plate of food. They must have carried the bishop's dinner all the way from his palace.

Lucien's stomach writhed. The friars had dined on bread and thin soup hours ago. Would he also be invited to sup? No. He made himself look away. Oh, for but one slice of fowl! There was never meat for the lesser friars. Even when Lucien was a boy, there had been only hunger. His father, a candlemaker, always seemed to have more mouths to feed than customers.

Bishop Raimon spoke without looking up. "Senhor Hugo."

"My lord."

A figure appeared out of the shadows, making Lucien jump. He was dressed as a knight of rank in a velvet cap and an emblazoned surcoat displaying a family coat of arms. Lucien recognized him from the execution. He'd stood with Count Raimon, watching the proceedings through grim, angry eyes. It seemed like days ago, instead of hours.

"Hugo, are you sure you didn't see anyone close to the heretics tonight?" The bishop chewed a morsel thoughtfully. "No one who might have cut the younger one free?"

The knight's gaze took in Lucien in a sweep. The scabbard at his side shimmered as if it had a murderous will of its own.

"I saw no one but ourselves, my lord," said the knight. "Count Raimon, your retinue, the inquisitors, and the executioners. I would have said it was impossible for anyone to reach the women unseen in such an audience. They were well surrounded."

The bishop swallowed a dripping bite. "What does the count intend to do now? Wash his hands of the girl?"

Senhor Hugo's stance shifted, slightly, but with power. "That is why I'm here," he said quietly. "I will track the girl myself."

Lucien thought the bishop looked momentarily impressed, though the elder churchman was much too smooth to show it.

"Examine the executioners," the bishop said, with a wave of his little knife. "Inquire into their characters. Learn whether one of them might have been bought by friends of the family. Or whether they deliberately freed her in defiance of our work."

Lucien blinked. The executioners, defiant?

"Lucien," the prior explained, "we've only just had our permission to conduct inquisitions restored earlier this year. Three years ago the city of Tolosa rose up in such protest that Count Raimon petitioned the pope to halt our work, and was granted it." He sighed. "They did the same, six years ago, and I traveled with Bishop Raimon myself to petition the pope for relief. To be an inquisitor is to be like one of the holy martyrs. Wickedness will always try to stop us." At the word *wickedness*, his gaze fell upon Hugo, but the knight showed no reaction.

"The Count of Tolosa comes from a long line of heretic

lovers," muttered the bishop darkly. He turned to Lucien. "Young friar, understand this: these suspensions of inquisition were mere delays. We shall be wiser this time. Some of the inquisitors among our order were, shall we say, a little too quick to convict, hence the outcry. But we can't trust the loyalty of the people of Tolosa. The executioners could be conspirators. You'll see to the investigation, then, Senhor Hugo?"

The knight stirred. "I will."

Lucien was glad not to be one of the executioners.

"Use what force you deem necessary," the bishop added.

The knight nodded. "I will speak to the officers."

"As will I."

The knight shot an annoyed look at Lucien, whose stomach, just then, groaned loudly. He blushed hot.

"I will speak with them, my lord," Hugo repeated, "but I doubt the executioners were in league with the prisoners."

Raimon plucked a tidbit of duck from the point of his knife with his lips. "Then somehow she must have brought her own blade and concealed it." He licked grease off the blunt edge of his knife. "The heretics often display a most diabolical will to survive."

"Men on the field of battle behave no differently, Bishop," said Hugo. "The will to cheat death is not confined to heretics."

This comment earned Hugo a wrinkle of the bishop's upper lip. "This one," the bishop said, "will not cheat me."

"I will bid you *bon ser*," said Senhor Hugo. "I have a runaway to find."

Prior Pons beckoned for Lucien to approach for a private conference. He spoke softly in his ear. "Where is Brother Humbert?"

"Resting," Lucien whispered. "Tonight's chase exerted him uncomfortably."

It wasn't the first time Prior Pons had inquired about Brother Lucien's older, less vigorous companion. By their rule, Dominican *socii* ought always to be together, but Brother Humbert's age and ailments often worked to prevent this.

Bishop Raimon waved, and his short-haired attendant produced a parcel full of dark, moist cake. From the fragrance of it, it was made with apricots and soaked in red wine.

"Let the girl slip away," the bishop said between bites of cake, "and she'll light a fire throughout Provensa. She's as unrepentant a heretic as any *bona femna* or *bon ome*, and a defiant, unnatural female, which is worse. And she's not the only one." He chewed. "I hear reports. In Bavaria, in Flanders, these women gather without orders or vows. They form private religious houses. Some claim to speak with God themselves, as yours does. It's clear where that will lead."

Prior Pons murmured his assent.

Bishop Raimon laid his utensils on the table and leaned back in his chair. "You must find the girl alive," he said. "The little slut must be caught by morning."

Lucien blinked. *Slut?* He pictured, for a moment . . . "Of course we'll find her alive." His words earned him a look of warning from the prior. "Why, Bishop, would she not be alive?"

The bishop chuckled. "Dolssa de Stigata has lived a soft and comfortable life in her parents' home. She has never exerted herself more than to pluck a chestnut from her father's tree. If she makes it through this night, she could well die yet of thirst or exposure or injury."

"Then we leave it to God," said Prior Pons, "to execute his own justice."

"You are an indulgent fellow, Pons," said the bishop. "The people must witness her end. She herself no longer matters. She's beyond all hope of salvation. But let her die on the road, and she becomes a martyr."

Slut. The impossible image of Dolssa de Stigata trying to entice a man would not leave Lucien. He thrust it from him with effort. "We will find her, Lord Bishop. If I must find her myself."

"I know you will," Bishop Raimon said. "The Lord requires it of you." He dabbed at his lips with a napkin, then rose and made his way toward the fire, where he leaned against the mantel.

"Go prepare yourself, Lucien," said Prior Pons. "Friar Humbert would slow your journey, I fear. Let him remain, and you go, but if you haven't found her in a few days, return. Be safe." Friar Lucien nodded and left the room.

Bishop Raimon watched Prior Pons's thoughtful expression as the young friar left.

"I really thought she would recant when they brought her mother to the pyre," the bishop said. "That's why I ordered them to take the mother first. My little gamble went awry. It was never the mother who mattered. If we had burned the daughter first and let the mother live, she'd have found her grief hotter than our flames."

Prior Pons sipped his wine. "All for nothing, then?"

"Oh, no," Bishop Raimon said. "An execution is never wasted." He chuckled. "Attendance at mass soars after a burning."

IZARN DE BASIÈJA

Witness Testimony recorded by Lucien

VILLAGE OF BASIÈJA

> Izarn de Basièja: peasant farmer in
> the village; resides on the outskirts, near
> the highway; age thirty-one; married,
> three children; grows cabbages, radishes,
> parsnips, and the like

Good day, Friar, good day. You honor us by coming here. Can we offer you our humble food? My wife, she is very talented with *sopa*. You will like it. Come sit. I will pour for you.

A young girl? A child? Ah, a *donzęlla*. Many people pass by on the road, and we do not notice them all. When?

Oc, Friar, there was a *donzẹlla* who came through. Very early in the morning. We found her in the straw with our goats. She was asleep, with her hands folded as if she prayed.

Of course you would be looking for her. She was a holy woman. Not a religious, no, not a nun. No! Not a *bona femna*. I have nothing to do with them. But one could see she was pious. My wife gave her food, and she prayed before she ate it. Our goat, she had gone missing, but she returned that morning and nuzzled up to her. It was a miracle. That goat has never liked people.

Two days ago. We urged her to stay, but she would not.

She went south and east from here, along the valley. Toward Castèlnòu d'Arri.

You will bring comfort to her, Friar. I know it. My wife, she prepares a pocket of *fogasa* bread and cheese for you. Perhaps when you reach *la donzẹlla*, you can share it with her.

BOTILLE

I entered the Three Pigeons as the sun was setting. I found Sazia curled up in a corner, with a drowsing Mimi draped over her shoulder, and Plazensa leaning over the bar, talking to a customer. Jobau's snores drifted down from the loft above the tavern.

"Botille." Plazi smiled at me. "I saved you a dish of roasted onions."

"Look at you," Sazia said. "You're filthy."

Plazensa's customer eyed me slantwise as I passed by in search of a bucket. His cap sat low over his thick-whiskered head. He hunched his large body over the bar as if to go unnoticed. He looked like a sailor, just in port. His gaze didn't linger on me long, and I was accustomed to that. When a man met Plazensa, then learned she had younger sisters, his mouth would begin to water. Until he met us. Sazia and I were perfectly acceptable-looking people, I believed—or Sazia would have been if she'd wash her hair—but we were nothing next to Plazensa.

Peddling as I did in the marriage trade, I was often asked why I hadn't found a husband for Plazensa. A rich merchant's son, they would say, or a minor noble from Narbona would happily carry her away. But Plazensa wanted a husband about as much as Jobau wanted to toil in an honest trade—though there never was such a one to fuss over weddings as she. Plazensa preferred to run the tavern, boss Sazia and me to death, and amuse herself—and supplement our income—with a few customers on the side. She kept a room in the back. We didn't ask questions.

I wondered if this great bushy behemoth at the bar would end up buying entry to the back room. I hoped not, as that would leave me in charge of the ale, and I sorely needed a bath.

The door opened, and in came Felipa de Prato, a farmwife. Her face was brown as a hazelnut, and her eyes were old and tired, though she couldn't have been thirty yet. She nodded absently toward Plazensa, then dropped herself into the low cushions before Sazia and held out her palm. In her other hand she carried a small basket of radishes and carrots.

Sazia pawed through the basket. She had a sweet tooth and preferred a bit of fruit, perhaps a cluster of grapes, but the de Pratos barely scraped by, so she got on with things, and began kneading the outstretched hand between her fingers. Felipa's eyes rolled shut, and she sank in her seat. I'd seen that look before. When Sazia touched their hands, her clients' worries floated away. Her hands were magic on their tired bones. I wondered whether Sazia's palm-reading customers came to her for her prognostication, or for the massage.

Soothsaying was as natural for Sazia as matchmaking was for me. She listened to what she knew. I paid attention to what I saw and what I felt. Sazia woke up with visions of what would befall villagers; I woke up with wedding plans.

Sazia and I had inherited these gifts from our mother. I don't remember her, but I know she had the old magic. She was a *devina* herself, I believed. A sorceress. Jobau said so. Sazia and I got her powers, and Plazensa got her beauty. The way Plazensa wore that beauty was a magic all its own. We were the Flasucra sisters. Add us together, and we made our mother.

I filled a bucket with water from our barrel and dunked a rag into it. It felt cold on my skin, but the late afternoon was so hot, I welcomed it. I stood in the corridor behind the bar, where I could listen and watch Sazia without Plazensa's customer seeing me. I rolled up my skirt, dunked a foot in the bucket, and began to scrub.

"Don't worry so much," Sazia told Felipa de Prato. "The wheat will do well this year. So will the *legums*, but that husband of yours needs to get off his *aze* and water them."

Felipa's face relaxed, and she nodded in relief, but when Sazia mentioned her husband, she pursed her lips. Joan de Prato would get an earful tonight, I'd wager.

I dunked my other foot in the water. The smell of grapes filled my nose once more.

"Also, you are having a baby," Sazia went on matter-of-factly. The poor farmwife's eyes flew open. "It's early still. You will need to eat melons, peas, leeks, and garlic. Milk and cheese, and fish when you can get it. They will be good for the baby."

Felipa's chest rose and fell rapidly. A single tear streamed down the side of her nose.

"No fear," said Sazia. "This baby will be joyful and full of health. Your husband will love the child, and love you for bearing it, and stop sneaking over to— Never mind."

"Who?"

"Never mind who." She patted Felipa's hand and rose from her seat. "Remember. Water the *legums*. Eat melons and leeks. Your husband will come around."

Felipa rose to her feet, looking unconvinced. I scrubbed the last bit of wine off my shins and wrung out the cloth. The rest of the lingering purple would probably take days to fade.

"Don't worry," Plazensa called to her as Felipa headed for the door. "Sazia is never wrong."

The door shut, Plazensa turned to Sazia. "Who's Joan de Prato sneaking around with?"

Sazia waved the question away. "You bore me, sister."

Apparently, Plazensa also bored the sailor at the bar, or else he bored her, because he rose at that moment and left. I unpinned my soiled skirt and replaced it with my usual one. Then I sat in the seat vacated by Felipa and began devouring the soft, creamy onions Plazi always made on baked-clam days, scooping them up with a crust of bread. Heaven. There is nothing in this world like a well-cooked onion.

"You're mistaken, anyway," Sazia said. "I have often been wrong. There was the time with the donkey, and the matter of the de Grava baby."

Plazensa wiped the sailor's mug with her apron. "It is not your fault if you tell a farmer to buy a donkey and it drops dead on the way home from market. It was probably the work of demons, and anyone knows the work of demons can't be predicted." She frowned at the mug, spit on it, and wiped it some more. "As for the baby, you said the de Grava wife would birth *un filh*. Probably the farmer wished so hard for a son, it confused you. So they had *una filha*, so what? She's growing as big and strong as a son. You're young, *sǫrre*. Give yourself patience."

"My turn, Sazia." I scraped the plate with bread. "I haven't had my fortune told in ages."

Sazia pushed her thick hair out of her eyes and made a face. "That's because nothing ever happens in our boring lives, pah."

"Maybe," I said, "your fortune can tell me how to find a husband for Sapdalina."

Sazia stuck out her tongue at me. "I don't tell you how to do your job. You don't tell me how to do mine."

"Poor Sapdalina." I sighed. "I can't find a man to take her for love or money. Flat, blotchy, dull, and weepy. And she never stops sniffling."

"She's not so dull," Sazia said. "I read her fortune once. She had me laughing for ages."

"That's a sight I'd pay to see," Plazensa said. "Cheer up, Botille. Some wife will die, leaving an old widower desperate. If you're lucky, he'll be half blind. Voilà, Sapdalina."

Sazia snapped her fingers at me. "Give me your hand, or no fortune for you."

I sat down, offered the hand, and then settled back into the soothing motions of her strong fingers rubbing and rolling my hands. Sazia didn't read palms. She found the future embedded deep in the flesh and bones. Too bad she couldn't find a fortune in my back.

"Ah," she said. "Maybe you're not so boring for once. You are to take a trip."

Na Pieret di Fabri's nephews! I smiled. Who couldn't help being proud of such a sister? My little *sorre*. I could remember when she was no bigger than one of Paul Crestian's baby goats.

Mimi slid off her shoulder and slipped onto my lap. She clawed my legs and flopped down. Outside, gulls cried over the lagoon, which grew darker blue as the sun sank behind Bajas.

Now Sazia scowled at her own hand. "It appears I am to come with you."

"Oh no, you don't," Plazensa howled. "You're not going away and leaving me to run this dump all by myself! Leave me listening to Jobau's rants alone?"

"Will I be successful in my errand?" I asked.

"Yes, yes." Sazia's face was troubled. "But you will meet someone . . ."

"Ooh," Plazensa teased. "Finally the matchmaker meets her own match!"

Sazia set my hand down on her low table and began drumming her fingers. "That's all."

I knew when she was lying. "No, it isn't," I said. "What's this about meeting someone?"

"Yes, Sazia, tell us," said Plazensa. "Will he be rich or handsome? Too much luck it would be for Botille to find both." She handed our sister a cup of ale.

"It's nothing," Sazia insisted.

"Wrong," I said. "Tell me what you see."

Sazia took a sip of ale, then looked straight at me. "You will meet someone," she said. "You have to take the trip." She rubbed her temples as though they ached.

"Tell more," Plazensa demanded.

Sazia reached for my hand. Instead of rubbing it, she placed it against her cheek and cupped it there, enclosed by her own. Late summer sweat beaded on her skin. We waited.

The door to the tavern swung open, and a thirsty-looking farmer appeared, but Plazensa halted him with an imperious thrust of her arm. Her jangling bracelets told him to leave—now. He wasn't a fool.

Sazia let my hand fall. She downed the rest of her ale. "I see only sorrow."

Plazensa pursed her lips. "It is a *tozęt*," she declared. "It is always the young men who sow sorrow. Stay home, and none of this will befall you. If I must, I'll lock you in the cellar."

"Who said anything about a *tozęt*?" Sazia was indignant. "You can't go hiding from fate. It's on its way to you, no matter what you do."

"Sazia," I said, "do you have any advice for me? Anything I can do to shield myself?"

Sazia sighed. "Bring a whip," she said, "and some cheese, and wear Mamà's crucifix."

We never wore Mamà's crucifix. We kept it safely tucked away. It was a gift to her from one of her lovers. One of the few things of hers we'd managed to keep.

Plazensa opened the cupboard and pulled out what was left of our lump of farmer cheese. She stuffed it all into her mouth and chewed defiantly.

"Don't be silly, Plazi." I went in search of something else to eat. "I can get more cheese from the de Borocs, next door."

"You're not leaving here."

Sazia rose and stretched. "Her only hope is to go out and meet what is coming," she said. "If she waits, greater sorrow will find her. Fate punishes those who try to cheat it. When do we leave, Botille?"

I looked out the window at the rolling waters of the lagoon. I would miss them.

"I have to talk to Sapdalina," I said, but my mind was not on Sapdalina. "We leave in the morning."

WILLIAM DE LAURAGUÉS

Witness Testimony recorded by Lucien

Village of Vilafranca de Lauragués

>   William de Lauragués: stonemason;
>   age forty (he thinks)

ood day to you, Friar Inquisitor. Have you come to preach? My men will not mind listening to preaching after we break for the day and for dinner. We must seize the daylight. Count Raimon's *bastida* will not build itself, and these stones, they do not cut themselves, either. We'll be a fine town here before too long.

If you're hungry, the cook has some nice fatty coneys, and turnips, and bread and cheese. Probably some wine, too, if he hasn't drunk it all himself. He's over there by the fire.

I go to mass, Brother Preacher, on holy days. My wife, she makes me. My soul is good enough with God. Eat some food, and save your words for those who need them more. If you will return in the evening, the men will be glad of some preaching to pass the time.

A *femna*? That's the other way they like to pass the evenings. Ho! Ha!

Friar Inquisitor, I have one hundred and forty men here under me, building this *bastida*. I can't concern myself with every wench who wanders into this camp.

How was this one different, then?

And when would that have been?

Hm? Oh, nothing. Are you related to her?

What has this *donzęlla* done, to have a preaching friar searching for her? Does she have a father or uncles or brothers looking for her? I ask, because a man came through yesterday seeking a girl. A lordly man, I should say a warrior. Likely no connection.

I haven't seen a young *donzęlla*. But I will tell you this, Friar. You'll recall the rainy morning, a few days back. My men huddled in tents and waited for the storm to pass. I came out in the rain to examine a section of wall. When I approached, I saw a figure get up and scurry off. Man, woman, young, old. I don't know. Vagrants do pass through. If this person thought the wall would offer shelter from the wet, he—or she?—was mistaken.

Here's the odd thing. I reached the spot where the person had been. All around it was mud, thick and black. Wet as eels, the day was. But in the spot where the person had been, it was dry as salt. With grasses spread in a hollow like blankets. Dry as holy relics, yet surrounded by all that wet, like Gideon's fleece.

My wife said the person must have been a true saint for God to keep the water off like that. She said it's a miracle.

My wife is a faithful Catholic, Friar Preacher.

It may have nothing to do with the *donzęlla* you're looking for.

You asked if I'd seen anything, and that's what I saw.

DOLSSA

lways I avoided the towns. I made my way around them at night. The days were warm, but the nights chilled me.

I starved and hid and slunk across the countryside, keeping close to, but off of, the Roman road. I slept in barns, curled against animals. I drank from streams and ate apples from trees.

When I had the strength, I cried for Mamà. And for my life, for all I ever thought it could be. My mother was dead. My beloved seemed deaf to my cries. My name, my home, the little world of kindness that once surrounded me. All were gone. And Mamà, gone most cruelly.

I came to a larger town than any I'd seen since leaving Tolosa. A child told me it was Castèlnòu d'Arri. I didn't dare hide here to sleep. Too many people coming and going, too many who might notice me and report me to a *bayle* or a cleric.

Lord, save me, I cried within my heart. *Carry me past this place*. But my feet were leaden. The friar's fires began to sound like a way of keeping warm.

The smell of smoke drew me to the smoldering remains of a supper fire. There was no one near, and nothing close but a small darkened *maison* on the outskirts of town, so I lay down beside the coals. Cinders pressed into my cheek, but the warmth on my body was heaven.

"What's this?"

I sat up. It was a woman's voice. By the embers' glow, I saw her filthy clothes and hair tied in a rag. She stood with her fists on her wide hips and studied me.

"You don't belong here." I didn't belong anywhere. "You look like a ghost. Hungry?" My stomach would not let me deny the offer of food.

The woman disappeared into the *maison* and returned with a clay bowl. *"Caçolet,"* she said. Beans, swimming in grease, and bits of meat, served with a slab of stale *fogasa*.

She saw me staring. "Too fine for my food?"

I dunked the flat-baked *fogasa* in the brown sauce and bit off a bite. It burned my tongue. I didn't care. Once, I would never have eaten such foul fare.

"I'm called Jacotina."

I barely heard her, for chewing and swallowing. Then I realized she wanted my name. Should I lie? She had fed me.

"What do you call yourself?"

I swallowed a burning lump. "I don't have a name anymore."

She nodded. "Lots of us get here that way. Here. Come in. I've got a cot you can use."

I rose on shaky legs. My dish tipped, and I almost lost a morsel of *caçolet*. I cried out.

"It's all right," Jacotina said. "There's more. Don't be afraid."

I followed her into her little *maison*, ducking low through her door. She lit two candles, and I looked around. It was small and dirty, and a rose perfume smell mingled with sweat and mildewed bedding. She had, indeed, an extra cot, separated from her own bed by a threadbare curtain on a string. Even such a simple cot beckoned to me. To sleep on something other than the damp, frosty ground!

She handed me a bucket and a cloth.

"You're a sight," she said. "Clean yourself up a bit. They'll be coming soon."

I froze. "Who's coming?"

She cocked her head to one side. "Not the *bayle*," she said. "Least, not usually. I keep outside the walls and don't trouble anyone. Who are you hiding from?"

I gulped down more *caçolet*.

She fished inside a small wicker trunk and pulled out a peasant frock like her own. "It'll be a sight too big for you. We can lace it up. It doesn't need to stay smart for long." She pulled sashes and a belt and ribbons from her trunk and draped them over her shoulders.

It was growing on me, this peasant food. It wasn't half bad once it stopped burning my mouth. "Why do I need to change my clothes?"

She paused. "Here's as good a place as any to disappear, my girl without a name," she said. "You're not from Castèlnòu d'Arri, that's plain. And you don't know how to get by. I'll help you. Start you out on the young, timid ones. But you've got to earn your keep."

I fingered the dress she'd thrown down on my cot. The fabric was thin, transparent as calfskin vellum, and trimmed with flimsy lace.

"Most people's working day is done; ours is only just begun," she said. "I'll call you Rose. Eat up, and get that face washed, Rose, before the men come."

I realized then what she'd offered me. A bite of food stuck in my throat. I should have refused any more food, but I didn't know when I'd eat again. I gulped another bite, and another, and another still.

"I can't do that," I cried, said, with sauce dribbling down my chin. "I won't! Lie here, with strange men? I'll die first."

Jacotina laughed. "Not with your belly full of my *caçolet*. You make your maiden protests, and still you gobble like a baby pig." She untied her skirt and replaced it with a red one from her trunk.

"Do you have money to pay for it? No? Of course, no. Yet you ate it. Too noble to pay, just noble enough to take."

"I accepted your food as given in charity," I cried. "I'll trouble you no more."

Jacotina sat upon her mattress. "You're on the run, aren't you?" Her eyes grew afraid. "Are you a *bona femna*? The kind they call heretics?"

The taste of *caçolet* grew sour on my tongue. "No," I said, "I am not one of the friends of God. Not a *bona femna*."

How many times had Lucien de Saint-Honore asked me the same question?

"Then what if I were to let the *bayle* know I'd seen you?"

Fool to rest, to eat, to warm myself by anyone's embers! "Then they will find and kill me all the sooner."

Jacotina's black eyes studied me.

"I have made a holy vow of chastity," I said. "I dare not break it, in fear for my soul. My Lord will provide for me."

Jacotina eyed me as though I were a waste of space. "You *are* a *bona femna*," she said. "I do not honor you. I do not bow. But I can give you pity."

"I'm not one," I said. "And what use have I for pity from a sinful woman like you?"

The words. They landed on the packed dirt floor. Next to the clay pot of beans and meat.

She's a prostitute! I told myself. *With the gall to think that I,*

Dolssa de Stigata, would stoop to her base and wicked sins. What claim has she upon my courtesy?

My anger, my mortification at what she'd suggested I do, burned hot. Yet my insulting words! My beloved, I knew, would not be pleased with me. I looked back at her face, ready to submit to her anger.

But there was none. When I'd flung out my hateful words, she had chosen to ignore them.

She rose and opened the door. "Here comes someone," she said. "Time to go. Duck out and follow the stream around the town. I must get ready now. May the *bon Dieu* provide for your soul as you hope he will. It has never been so for me."

I touched her hand in parting. Then, in haste, I swallowed four more urgent bites of *caçolet*. I had no more shame left. Only enough to resist her profession.

I stooped through the doorway of the tiny *maison* and out into the black night. I ventured forward as fast as I dared, but I could barely see my hand when I extended my arm in front of me. Soon I heard a hearty voice greeting Jacotina, and the sound of her voice in return. I tried not to think of what would happen next.

I reached the stream and followed its sounds along the bank. *La luna* swam behind the clouds all night, until it finally peeped through, and by its light I looked about to see that, to my surprise, I had left the town well behind, and rejoined the river. For the first time in days, my limbs had strength for the journey. My body was warm with the vigor of movement and the memory of the *caçolet*.

Help had not come from my beloved, but from the vilest of sinners. Friendless and alone as I was, hunted by the Church I'd once called home, the wicked might now be my only safety. Safety! She wanted me to be her paid whore, and she, my procurer! Thank *Dieu* I'd escaped.

Yet, I could not deny, there'd also been sympathy, help, and patience in Jacotina's greedy eyes.

JACOTINA

Witness Testimony recorded by Lucien

Village of Castèlnòu d'Arri

Jacotina: *meretrix publica*; age forty-six;
residing outside the city walls

ou want to talk to me? Talking's not usually what they have in mind when they come here.

Oc, I'll talk with you. Come to my place, where we can talk more privately.

Take a seat. Make yourself at home.

You're young for this, aren't you? Not too young. Your beard wants to grow faster than you can shave it, and so does the hair on your head. That's a fine head of hair you'd have, if you'd let it grow. Stay with me a few days, if you like, and let it.

It's hard work, preaching the word. A man's got to have some release. Just like he needs food and water and sleep. He needs other things. That's why I'm here. Isn't that why you're here? Oh, now. Don't fret. There's no shame. No shame at all. The tales I could tell you—but of course I never tell tales. Let's just say that men of the cloth are some of my best customers.

Well enough. If we must talk first, we'll talk. Have some wine. Wine helps with talking.

When was this?

A young girl?

Oh, I see. Too old for you, am I? Just how old do you think I am?

Don't be fooled by youth. You're old enough to know what experience is good for.

All right! I hear you. Not that kind of young girl. A young girl just passing through? Traveling alone? Why would she have passed my way?

What would make her wish to avoid the town?

Isn't that a curious thing? A young girl without a mother, an aunt, or a companion, fleeing through the countryside. Traveling by night? She must be trying to die. What has she done to make you want so badly to find her? Is she your mistress? Your dainty young *enamoratz*?

Never mind. Don't take on so; it's a fair question. Many a holy brother like you has a concubine.

Tell me this. When you've found her—this person—what will

you do with her? Is she to be restored to her family?

Of course it's none of my affair. I'm curious. You haven't told me all, that's plain. But your business is yours to keep. I can't help you. I have not seen a young gentlewoman come passing through by night and all alone. You've wasted my time and cost me tomorrow's dinner.

You don't mean that.

You do mean it.

Monster! You knew what I was when you came here.

You would threaten me with this, a poor woman, all weak and alone? I don't do any harm to anyone. There's not a judge nor a priest in the city who doesn't know I'm here.

I have told the truth. Upon my honor, I have.

Please, good sir, forget you met me here. Are you hungry? I have *caçolet* in my pot.

I only meant to help.

Help you. That's what I mean. Help you. Not help her. How could I help her if I never even saw her?

If all you say is true, she's probably already long past helping now.

BOTILLE

knocked at the door of the small stone *maison*. No one answered. I knocked again.

"Wait here," I called to Sazia, who stood with Garcia and his son, and the mules.

I headed around to the back. Sazia called after me, but I was in no mood to wait.

It was the afternoon of our second day of traveling, and after several wrong stops, we'd reached San Cucufati, and found what several nearby folks assured us was the *maison* we wanted. Plazensa hadn't let us depart without first making Sazia swear on our mother's grave that she wouldn't leave my side, so Sazia never let me out of her sight. This charge to protect me had turned my baby *sorre* into a tyrant hovering mother, and I don't take kindly to mothering. I'm not used to it.

Na Pieret had sent Garcia, her trusted hand, to safeguard us on our journey to San Cucufati. He was old enough to be no threat to two unmarried girls, but not so old that he couldn't still make a bandit think twice when he wielded his club. His son, young Garcia, was fourteen and scrawny, without a whisker to his chin. The only threat he posed was driving Sazia to distraction with his idiot jokes. Me, I found young Garcia funny, so to pay Sazia back for smothering me, I egged the young jester on.

We'd rattled along over dusty roads in Garcia's cart, which Na Pieret had provided for hauling her nephews' belongings. I was surprised to discover, on the road, how much I missed *la mar*. I wasn't native to the seacoast, but she had become my own—her colors, her moods, her rolling waves, her breezes, and her quarrelsome birds. Not since we'd first come to Bajas from Carcassona years ago had I traveled this far. I enjoyed seeing the world pass by, but I missed the call of the water. My feet and my bottom were glad to have found our destination at last.

Two days we'd traveled to get here. We began with lauds prayers in the strangers' chapel of the Abadia at Fontfreda, which made us feel like pilgrims instead of mere messengers. The abbey monks avoided us, but we felt their holiness. I sent up a prayer to ward off whatever worried Sazia, just in case. We spent the night sleeping under stars. By day we strolled along, drinking in the autumn colors of trees reflected in glassy streams and watching blackbirds slice their way through the glorious blue sky.

Two days we'd watched travelers wend their way—some in cleric's robes, some toiling under packs of wool or vegetables. Merchants in the larger villages, with curious shingles advertising their wares, wondered if we'd come to buy. I saw strong lads I could easily find brides for in Bajas. It set me wondering whether I couldn't expand my trade a bit beyond our village.

Now nothing but a few well-chosen words barred me from procuring two new husbands for my maidens back home. With luck, one for Astruga, the other for Sapdalina. All this fretting of Sazia's! Sunshine and success. That was what I smelled in the pastures of Na Pieret di Fabri's dead sister's farm.

There was no one in sight. A stand of grapevines grew behind the house, neatly tied and trimmed. Na Pieret would approve. A small field of ripening vegetables—including plenty of onions— spread over the rough, rocky soil, and beyond that a thatch-roof shelter serving as a barn overlooked a plot where a pair of goats foraged. I headed for the shelter.

"Oo-ooh," I sang out while I was still some distance away. You never want to catch farming peasants by surprise. They might be butchering, with knives in their hands.

A loud sound escaped the makeshift barn, followed by a burst of swearing and shouts of raucous laughter. I hitched up my skirts and hurried forward.

"Bonjorn!" I cried.

A head popped out from between the beams supporting the

thatch roof. The thick body to which the head was attached seemed scooped out of clay rather than grown in the usual fashion. Man? *Tozęt*? Monster? I couldn't be sure. His hair, which hung low and thick over his protruding forehead, was filled like a hen's nest with dozens of chicken feathers, sticking every which way. Even out his ears.

His smock was smeared shoulder to belly with ripe green chicken dung. More of it clung to the stubble on his chin and cheeks, which he attempted to wipe with a greasy rag.

Blame it on my mother, who was never around to raise me better: I shrieked with laughter. Cackled, straight to his face.

His bushy eyebrows lowered. He looked at me as if *I* were the feathered stranger reeking of chicken *męrda*, and not he. Pray God this was not the stalwart nephew on which poor Na Pieret must place her trust!

"Aren't you a feast for the eyes? And the nose," I said by way of greeting.

He turned and stomped back inside.

I followed. Odd cases like his intrigued me. Perhaps he was the village idiot, just wandering by.

Inside the shelter, the feathered troll and another young man sat around a makeshift enclosure for poultry. The other young man, unfeathered and unsmeared by chicken mess, wiped tears of laughter from his eyes. At the sight of me, he doubled over, clutching his guts lest they spill out. I liked the set of teeth I saw on him, strong and wide and white. His laughing displayed them well. Without even trying, I could think of three girls who'd marry him for those teeth alone.

The other one, the village idiot, glowered at us both, rose to his feet, and peeled his smock off over his head, then turned it inside out and scrubbed his face with it. He was a strong one, from the bare looks of things, and not just in his odors.

"*Bonjorn*," I said, seizing an opening. "My name is Botille, and I have traveled here from Bajas at the request of Na Pieret di Fabri. Your *tanta* on your mother's side."

The chicken-dirt idiot stopped his scrubbing, then flung his dirty smock at the other one.

"Dead?" he barked at me.

So he knew of her. Not the village idiot, but the nephew after all? Or, saints forbid, both nephew and imbecile? Poor Na Pieret! Poor grapes!

"No, *Dieu* keep her," I said. "How did you get . . . your feathers?"

His face, when he scowled, which was apparently always, bunched up into surly thickness—thick lips mashed between a jutting chin and a wide nose with furious, flaring nostrils, all presided over by bushy eyebrows and black menacing eyes.

"Feathers," I repeated, and pointed toward my own hair. Then he understood. He attacked his hair with his hands, savaging his scalp until the feathers fled in terror, leaving his hair looking like an ill-kept shrub.

This set the other one off laughing again. With someone less handsome I might have grown annoyed, but attractive people are easier to forgive.

"Which of you is Na Pieret's nephew?" I still clung to the hope that Senhor Chicken Stink was not included in the pair of brothers I'd come to find.

"Which one of us is not?" said Laughing Tooth.

"Shut your mouth, Gui," said the idiot. To me: "Who are you?"

I bowed. "I am called Botille, as I already said, if you'd been listening." I opened my mouth to begin my little speech, the one I'd spent two days rehearsing in my head. Instead I said, "What happened to you? Why are you covered in *merda*?"

"None of your business," said the first.

"He slid on a pile of chicken shite," supplied the other. "Landed face first. It was beautiful, *oc*! Never till I die will I forget the sight."

"You'll die now if you don't hold your tongue." Village Idiot shifted his glower in my direction. "What do you want?"

"I've come here from Bajas, on the seashore," I said, "as a favor to your *tanta* Pieret, to ask you to dispose of your property here immediately and go live with her. She asks you to share with her the management of her extensive vineyards and farmlands, as her heirs."

They looked at each other for a stunned moment.

Laughing Tooth knocked over his stool and left it there. He looped a length of rope over the neck of a placid heifer that stood watching them both with a bored expression.

Village Idiot dumped a bucket of water over his head. With water still streaming over his chest and back, he began chucking tools into a canvas sack. Then he paused.

"The harvest," he moaned. "All our work, all year. My aching back, all so someone else can eat our chickpeas and carrots and onions?"

"Symo, who cares?" whooped the one called Gui. "Maire always said Tanta Pieret was rich, rich, rich. Leave the harvest for the next poor fools." He tethered the cow to a post, then began to tie up their mule. "*Oc*! I have it. Old Maynart's son. He's marrying Fabrissa the Fat. We can tell them the cottage is empty, and they can move right in."

Symo still frowned.

"If it makes you feel better," said Gui, "have her fill up some baskets with whatever's ripe now." He gestured toward me.

"Always room for onions," I said. "But I'm not your farm wench."

Both turned to look at me. "What kind of wench are you, then?" demanded Symo.

"It's not that I'm too good to pick vegetables." I felt a bit sheepish. "But if you want my help, ask me right."

Gui grinned. Those teeth. "What kind of help are you offering?"

Symo boffed him on the ear. "Leave off, idiot." He turned to study me. "What are you to Tanta Pieret? Daughter? Daughter-in-law?" I smelled sweat mingled with chicken shite wafting from his skin. "We should abandon our farm on the word of some strange *toza* from nowhere?"

It's just as well that old Garcia and Sazia chose that moment to venture under the shade of the thatch enclosure, for I was about to tell Symo the Stupid precisely what I thought of him.

"*Bonjọrn*." Garcia wiped the sweat off his brow and smiled amiably at the two brothers. "Has Botille straightened it all out, then? You'll come with us?"

"*Oc*, we're coming!" sang Gui.

Symo ignored his brother and addressed Garcia. "You know my *tanta* Pieret?"

Garcia nodded. "Been attached to her twenty-five years now."

"She wants us to run her vineyards?"

"I already told you that," I said. "Why should you believe Garcia more than me?"

Symo frowned and stuck a thumb in my direction. "Who is she to Tanta Pieret?"

Garcia looked nonplussed. "Nothing."

"We're friends," I said. "La Domna di Fabri sent me because she trusts me."

The chicken man, still shirtless, ignored this. "And my *tanta*'s vineyards, they prosper?"

The greedy dog.

Garcia's eyes narrowed, and Symo realized his blunder. "You appear, strangers, and tell us to leave all we have and go." He appealed to Garcia. "If my aunt has four sickly grapevines, we are lost."

"Four sickly grapevines!" I fumed. "You think your *tanta* could afford to send all four of us here to collect you, baggage and all, from the fruit of four sickly grapevines?"

Sazia flopped down onto a pile of straw and closed her eyes. "Leave off, Botille," she said. "They'll come. You might as well take some rest while they pack."

Gui took notice of Sazia then. He brandished his smile and a basket at her. "Are you the wench who'll pick our vegetables so we can go sooner?"

Sazia regarded him coolly. She was a girl on whom toothy smiles had little effect.

"Young Garcia," Sazia called to her comical tormentor. "Come here. The men have some *legums* for you to pick. Don't eat them all as you go."

Na Pieret had packed us plenty of *fogasa*, dried fish, *pomas*, *viṇ*, and cheese—and for all this, I still heeded Sazia's warning and brought my own supply of cheese—so we had no shortage of food, but to humor the brothers, we built up a fire and stewed a pot of chickpeas with onions. Big fat beauties they were, too. Symo himself picked and ate much of the produce on the spot, shucking and gobbling chickpeas as if they were to be his last meal.

That was it, then. The gallant and the imbecile would both be coming back with me. I'd hoped for two worthwhile bachelors. I could settle for one plus a spare. No matter; I'd find someone for the idiot. Marrying him off would be interesting. I smiled to myself. A test of my abilities. Not even pregnant Astruga, I'd wager, would welcome the thought of a chicken-stinking curmudgeon like this one sharing her hearth and her bed. Whom did I have in my arsenal who was truly desperate? Besides Sapdalina, for I was fond of her. I wouldn't be able to sleep at night knowing I'd saddled her with this lout.

ABRAHE IUDIO

Witness Testimony recorded by Lucien

The River Port at Carcassona

Abrahe Iudio: a Jew; age thirty-three;
wine merchant from Aragón; trading
at the port on the Aude River

ood evening. I take it you are not here to trade in wine, but in souls, yes? I will listen, if you like, though I am not from Carcassona, nor France. *Sí, sí,* Carcassona is the French king's now. I've traded here since I was a boy with my father, and he, since he was a boy with his father. What he'd say to see the mighty towers of Carcassona fall from the hands of the Counts of Trencavel!

Sí, I am a Jew, but I can listen to your preaching. Any learned man is worth hearing, and who needs enemies? Aragón, she is becoming a place where no Jew can afford to annoy his neighbors. You are one of the Dominicans, *sí*? And Dominic, he was a Castilian. That makes us all neighbors.

It is only a joke. Of course no inquisitor could be neighbor to a Jew.

You come from Tolosa? Can I offer you a pitcher to quench your thirst? You must be weary after your travels. No, put your money away.

I? I have been here four days now, this trip. Two more, and I depart for home.

Certainly, I have my licenses and papers. The port master knows me. I pay my tariffs.

Have I seen a young lady?

Good Sir Monk? Preacher, then. Good Sir Preacher, hundreds pass by every day. Young ladies in great state, and poor girls in rags. Carcassona's towers beckon to them all.

I am a newly married man, Sir Preacher Monk. My young wife is *la niña de mis ojos*.

A girl alone, of gentle birth? A runaway? Poor creature. Her family must be very much afraid. She has no more family? May the good God keep special watch over the poor frightened stranger, and may those she meets be kind, and think of their own sisters.

Is she one of your Albigensian heretics, as the French call them? No. A Catholic? How, then, a danger to believers? She is young to have offended God. God is patient, and with the young, always patience is needed.

The river? My lodgings are by the riverside. I take my raft along the Aude from Narbona.

If I gave wine to every beggar who couldn't afford it, I wouldn't last long in trade. Bread? Do I look like a baker? Who said I gave her bread and wine? If it was Pedro Rodrigues, he can stick his head in a barrel. He's so drunk, he can't tell waking from dreaming.

Who told you?

My wife told you.

She is quick-witted, my wife. She remembers things I forget. Well, so it is, now that I recall it. A girl did pass by here. I took pity on her. She seemed so hungry, and thin. It was nothing to offer her some food. Any decent soul would. As I remember it now, my wife gave her an apple for her journey.

Which way did she go?

Now let me think. *That* way.

Sí, it was that way. South, along the river, toward the Pirenèus Mountains. And now, excuse me. Time I gathered up my crates and made my journey back.

Sí, I did say I'd leave in two days' time, but the weather's changing. The climate can turn treacherous in conquered Provensa, and when it does, I want to be far from here.

BOTILLE

t was morning by the time we left. Gui would have left immediately, but Symo lingered over every animal, every farm tool, each sack of seed, and each hanging ham. He and young Garcia drove the chickens, ducks, and a pair of geese to a neighbor's. Then he pored over each pot and scrap in their little stone *maison* before deciding whether to pack or leave it. We filled Garcia's cart full to bursting, and then filled the brothers' own small barrow.

After supper both brothers disappeared for a while, saying their good-byes about the *vila*. I imagined more than one local girl would shed a tear at watching Gui walk away.

We travelers slept under the stars once more. The night was clear, if cold. We were well bundled up together, Sazia and I, and the Garcias on the other side of our little fire. The sky was still fully dark as we rose and readied the mules for our journey.

There would be no riding in the cart now that it bulged with their belongings. The goats and the heifer trailed along behind, attached to the rear of Garcia's cart, while the brothers' mule pulled their smaller barrow.

Fabrissa the Fat arrived with her mother, armed with brooms, to take possession. This didn't cheer Symo any, but Gui laughed and plastered a kiss on the bride-to-be's round cheek.

We set out heading south along a trail that kept its side close to the river. I watched the Aude slither by us, its dark surface beribboned with rippling moonlight.

"How long do we follow the river?" I asked Gui.

"Only a league more," he replied. "You say we'll reach Bajas tomorrow?"

"By evening," said Garcia senior.

La luna hung beautifully bright over the horizon, in a sky still dark. Cold breezes blew over the river and ruffled the tall grasses along the bank, making them rustle and chatter. In their waving fronds I sensed small animals stirring. The pure song of a nightingale, a *rossinhol*, rang across the water, ending in a trill. It was an hour for sprites and fairies. What magic might lurk among the riverbank grasses? Anything was possible just before dawn.

Up ahead of me, alongside the mules, our traveling party walked in a knot, talking together and blowing upon their hands. I let my footsteps slow just enough for some privacy. A far cry this was from my lagoon by *la mar*, but still, the riverside was a feast, and I wanted no conversation to disturb my reverie.

We approached a bend in the Aude. Our path forged straight ahead, cutting a swath across the grass and leaving the bulge in the river blossoming out to our right. I hated to leave its shores behind.

I stopped. I heard something. A sough, a sigh. I turned back to the gleaming water. All around it was moving darkness and nothing more.

It must have been the wind. Nothing but the wind could have reached my ears.

But I'd heard it.

An animal, most likely.

But what if not?

If I told the others, they would think me mad.

I would take a moment, just one brief moment, to satisfy my curiosity. It would be nothing, and I'd hurry to catch up, and no one, not even Sazia, could sneer nor brood over my fancies.

For it must be fancy to think I heard anyone at so desolate a place and hour. I slipped into the tall grasses and plied my way through, my feet slipping down the incline toward the water. The tips of grasses and rushes shone in the moonlight. I saw nothing, nor did I hear anything but the wind and the grass and the water.

"Who's there?" I called out softly. Nothing.

I ventured about as much as I could, though the thick stalks prevented my going far. Closer to the water the ground grew soggy, and my feet sank deep into the muck. Any farther, and I might sink all the way, and would my party, still marching on, even hear me now if I screamed? I had been foolish to come. It was time to go back.

I stood breathing the damp sweet river air, and told myself to return. My feet would not obey me. I wrenched one out of the muck, and then the other, then turned for one last look back.

There.

A breath.

Nothing more than a breath, with the tiniest note of a cry.

I followed the sound, faint as it was over the gurgling river-bank, and pushed through more grasses. Some reached over my head. I could see nothing, but the voice was close.

My toes stubbed against it. It was no fairy, no animal. There in a mound of flattened grasses lay a body.

La luna shifted behind the clouds, lending me just enough light to see.

It was a woman lying facedown in the dirt. A young woman, I thought, from her thin build. Too thin. I'd swear she hadn't eaten in weeks. Her clothes sagged off her frame, and her arms lay wrapped over her head as if to hide it, or to cushion it from a blow.

I bent and nearly toppled onto her, losing my footing in the muck. I touched her back, and felt her ribs rise. She was alive but cold, frail and hollow as a wounded sparrow.

"Donzella?" I cried. "Can you hear me?"

I moved her arms to more easily roll her onto her back, which gave me my first glimpse of her face. She cried out, and her eyes flew open. Eyes full of fear.

They were wide, deep eyes. Her cheekbones protruded from her hollow, starved face. As soon as her eyes flickered open, they closed again. She wanted to see me, it seemed, but hadn't the strength.

"Please," she gasped. "Leave me be. Tell no one you saw me."

I slid my arm beneath her back and hoisted her upright. Her head lolled backward.

She had the strength and heft of a straw man. Her wrist, when I grabbed it, felt as weak as if she'd already bled to death. She was dying in my arms.

My companions would have gone far. I should run after them, but I feared if I took my eyes off this creature for even a moment, her soul would flee her body. I should cry out to Sazia, but it might terrify this poor bird. But there was no other option. I opened my mouth to scream, then stopped, as if a ghost had closed its hand around my throat. *Do not make a sound.*

I stared at the girl.

Footsteps above me on the slope caught my ear, and I looked up. I cradled the girl close to me, as if I could hide her, then saw to my relief that it was only Symo, standing in the moonlight, staring down at me. He looked about ready to skewer me. When I wouldn't rise, he skidded down the slope toward me.

He stopped abruptly and turned back. He'd heard something.

Some twenty feet away, a tall man cloaked in black stood on the bank. A thrill of fear went through me. He stepped forward into better light and pulled back his hood, and I saw he was one of the black-robed Friars-Preachers. An inquisitor, one of the Dominicans. His crucifix gleamed in the moonlight. *That's all right, then,* I thought. Some people feared them, but any man of the cloth would offer help, or at least perform last rites for this poor girl.

"You, young man," the friar called to Symo. His voice was preternaturally deep, like the roar of ocean waves on the beach. "What are you going down there for?"

At the sound of the cleric's voice, my frail charge roused herself enough to open her eyes and fix them upon me. She could barely shake her head. Only her dying eyes could tell me what she needed to say.

Surely, the inquisitor could help.

Her lips trembled. She pleaded silently for me to look at her. What was I to see?

Symo did not answer the friar. He turned toward me, and I gazed back. He saw what I held in my arms. I shook my head, then lowered the creature down into the grasses.

"What are you doing?" repeated the friar. "What do you see, my son, that arrests your attention?" Again his voice struck me. He spoke Oc, but his accent was northern. French. It was a delicious voice, one that would melt the most hardened sinner.

Symo made a small bow in the direction of the hilltop and

the holy man. "I am keeping watch over my sister," he said. "She is a half-wit, and she wanted a closer look at the moonlight on the water."

Sister. Half-wit! I rose unsteadily from my crouch and ascended the slope, where I bowed to the man of God. I was still at war with myself—why shouldn't I ask him for help? But the ghost hand had a muzzle grip on my mouth now. I mustn't betray the poor dying girl's secret.

"What were you doing, my child?" asked the friar, in a much gentler voice. His specially-for-half-wits voice, I reckoned. I'd give Symo a good kick later on. "What were you looking at down in the grasses?"

I twined my fingers together behind my back and twisted from side to side like a nervous little *toza*. If Symo would burn in hell for lying to a man of God, then I would join him in the flames. "A dying bird," I said slowly, softly, to play my infantile part. "Sad bird!"

The friar smiled. His tonsured head might mar his earthly beauty, as it was meant to do, but when his stern face relaxed, the inquisitor was a handsome man, younger than he sounded.

"Bless you, child, and may angels guard you," was the friar's answer. He beckoned me closer, and I approached, all innocence and trust, while Symo glowered at us both. The Dominican, who proved a good deal taller than I had realized, noticed the crucifix around my neck. He took the silver chain between his finger and thumb. "It makes me glad to see you wear this, as a Christian ought. Remember to pray every day, won't you?"

The friar draped an arm over my shoulder. Sweet incense perfumed his heavy cloak.

"What is your name, my good girl?"

"Botille." No other name came quickly to mind.

"Tell me, Botille, will you help me?" he said. "I am looking for a *donzꞓlla* who is lost. Did you see any footprints down by the river? Or any articles that might belong to a lost soul?" He gestured over the expanse of the great Aude and its dancing-grass basin.

The view to the west, as we faced it, was still fully dark, but behind us, a dim morning glow peeked into the eastern sky. Before long, darkness would no longer hide the girl.

I shook my head solemnly. "No footprints," I said. "Only the birdie's. Like this." I held up a thumb and two fingers, pretending to mark the shape of a bird's feet into imaginary soil. I caught a glimpse of Symo watching. I found some amusement in having baffled him completely.

The friar laughed. "Heaven bless you. You have a woman's form but a child's heart. Our Lord would have us all be so pure." He beckoned to Symo, who obeyed, trudging forward as nimbly as mud, all the while watching the friar balefully from heavy-lidded eyes.

The friar placed a hand on Symo's shoulder. "Now, you two. I can use your help. You are traveling, *oc*? If you come across this lost young lady—you will spot her as a runaway, and likely quite weak—you must send word. She needs God's help. I am sent to lead her back to God. Ask any priest or cleric to send word to Friar Lucien de Saint-Honore of the Dominican convent in Tolosa. That is my name. Will you remember that? Repeat it to me."

"Friar Lucien de Saint-Honore," we both chanted. Symo looked like he'd rather still be slimed in chicken *merda* than recite this strange catechism.

"That is right." The friar gazed into our eyes. "I know I can count on your help."

My conscience smote me. What had I done? Lied to a holy man, and one trying to help the girl? What if illness had addled her judgment and made her fear this man without cause? Who was I to hide her from a rescuer sent by God? Before long, hiding would no longer matter to her. She would leave this life for a place where no traveling friar could ever find her.

"Friar Lucien," I blurted out. Symo's eyebrow twitched a warning, and I remembered the role I must play. I tugged plaintively on the friar's sleeve. "Why is she a lost soul?"

"Ah." The friar nodded. "How to put it—she has strayed far. Far from home, and far from the truth." He looked to Symo for understanding. "The traveler I seek has not heeded the counsel of those who would lead her in virtue's paths."

Symo's left eyebrow rose. A remarkable trick. He seemed wholly unimpressed with Friar Lucien de Saint-Honore's answer.

Friar Lucien de Saint-Honore patted me on the head. "God shall correct the wanderer, though the ordeal will not be an easy one." He smiled sadly. "As Christ's preacher, my mission is to protect the lambs from the wolves of falsehood that enter in to destroy."

"You're up and about it awfully early in the morning," observed Symo.

The friar chuckled. "So are the wolves, my son," he said. "A good shepherd must always keep watch."

Symo, it seemed, didn't relish being called "my son" by a man who was only a few years older than he.

Young or no, pompous or no, Brother Lucien must be wise, it seemed, reciting scripture as he did without needing to consult a book. He could help the girl. His concern seemed earnest enough, though I couldn't imagine how a bird's skeleton like my poor creature from the grasses could harm the puff on a dandelion, much less a soul.

Morning larks called to one another from the shallows at the river's edge, and the sky began to silver behind the friar like a halo.

I opened my mouth to tell him.

Then I closed it so hard, I bit my tongue. My eyes, against my will, flooded with tears, and my mouth with blood and spit. In spite of myself, I made a little squeak of pain, and wiped my lips on my sleeve.

"What is wrong with the girl?" The inquisitor took a step back and looked at Symo in alarm. "Does she often dribble and foam at the mouth like this?"

Symo steered me roughly toward the cart. "Only when she

talks to people who frighten her," he said. "Come on, Botille." He dragged me forward. "The others are waiting for you."

"God speed you on your way," the friar called after us. "And remember, if you see anything, I'm Friar Lucien de Saint-Honore."

My "brother" shoved me along more forcefully than he had any cause to. "Let go of me, Symo," I hissed once we were out of earshot. "I've got to go back and check on the girl."

"Act docile, you lackwit," he hissed back in reply. "The friar's still watching."

I let him older-brother me along, all the way back to the others, but I wasn't done talking. "That girl is dying. She may be dead already. You had best hope you don't die anytime soon, or you'll burn in hell for eternity, lying through your teeth like that to a holy man. Sister, indeed!"

"You were no different."

"I had no choice. You made me do it. 'My half-wit sister.' I'll fillet you like a mackerel."

"I look forward to watching you try."

Sazia, by now, was running to me. She crossed the distance between us and the cart in seconds and took me by the hand. Symo finally relaxed his tyrant grip on my shoulders.

"Botille, where were you?" She smoothed my hair off my forehead. "Who was that you met? What did he say? Are you ill? Why was this one"—she wrinkled her nose at Symo—"helping you along like that? Are you feeling faint?"

"In heaven's name, I'm fine," I said.

Sazia struck her palm against her forehead. "I never should have let you out of my sight. I knew something would happen. . . ."

Symo watched us both as though he'd just discovered we each carried a horrid wasting disease. "It's true, then," he whispered. "You *are* the half-wit sister, and the younger one came along to keep you in her sights."

"Go eat your elbow," I snapped. Sensible Sazia's grip on my hand had cleared my head somehow. "Little *sorre*," I cried, "tell me, for I don't dare turn back. Is that man still watching us? The friar we were speaking to?"

Sazia clearly would have liked to ask more questions, but she looked over my shoulder. "He's well down the road," she said. "He grows smaller with each step. Who was he? Already, I don't like him. Look what he's done to you. Your heart is racing."

I ignored her questions and dragged her back the way we'd come, ignoring Garcia's shout from the cart. "You come too," I called to Symo over my shoulder. "We need your help."

I slid down the trail my footsteps had matted in the tall grasses, back to where the poor girl lay. Her eyes were closed. She was still.

In an instant I was six, finding my mother.

No.

I threw myself down on the mud and grass beside her. I rubbed her cheeks. I stretched myself over her body, not to crush but to warm her.

"Open your eyes," I cried. "Talk to me. Help is here, *galineta*, sweetheart, wake up!"

She was cold. But not completely. Her body shuddered, and she coughed.

I heard Symo ask my sister, from a dozen leagues away, "Does she know the girl?"

Sazia knelt beside me, and together we rubbed the creature's arms and trunk and face. There was almost nothing there.

"Don't stand there, you great ox," I told Symo. "Go get some wine and a blanket. If your goats have any milk in them, get us some. We'll need you to carry her too."

Symo started up the slope, for once without any protest.

"Don't tell the others," I called to him. He halted, turned, then shrugged and carried on.

"How's he supposed to not tell?" Sazia wrapped her coat around the girl. "They're waiting and wondering what's become of you. Garcia the elder is hopping to be on our way."

"I don't know. Give her to me." Forget Symo carrying her. I eased her into my lap myself and rocked her back and forth. The poor girl tucked her head under my chin. I could feel her shallow breath down my neck. At least she was breathing. I breathed along with her. In, out, in, out. *This is the way we stay alive.*

Symo returned quickly with a shallow bowl of foamy milk and a blanket. He knelt and held the bowl to the girl's face and tipped some in. Dribbles ran down my skin under my frock. The girl snorted and spluttered, then began suckling the lip of the bowl like a baby at the breast. My own full-size baby.

"What did you tell them?" Sazia asked Symo. She tucked the blanket around us both.

"That Botille had taken a fancy to having a little nap here by the river."

"You *what*?" I cried.

Symo shrugged. "Did you give me a better option? Not everyone has your gift for lying. It was the best I could do. I told them you asked for a comforting drink of warm milk before lying down."

The girl in my arms roused herself somewhat, and raised her head.

"I'll pickle you when we get home." I turned to my patient. "Are you alive, *donzęlla*?"

Her wet lips worked up and down as though she hadn't realized the bowl was gone. Swallowing seemed an altogether new experience. "Is there more?"

I wanted to cheer, hearing a voice come from that hollow body.

"Slowly," I said. "We'll get you some. But you must drink slowly, or you'll give it back to us, and we won't like that a bit."

She shrank. "Just a little more?"

Symo went to get some. The girl drooped against my shoulder. Overhead, the sky grew paler, lit with orange at the far horizon.

"Tell us your name," I whispered. "What do they call you back home?"

She grew so still that I feared she'd left us. I shook her slightly.

"No name," she murmured. "No home."

Symo returned with more milk. The girl's determination to drink it gave me hope.

"Botille," Symo said, "Garcia and Gui have no patience for this game you're playing."

"And whose fault is it that they think I'm playing it?"

"We're losing time," he said. "Let's bring the girl with us and be on our way. We can explain how we found her to them."

Milk ran down the invalid's chin and into her lap. She pulled away from the dish and turned toward me. It was an effort.

I could not say how old she was. I would have thought young, though her wasted appearance could have belonged to a much older woman. But her eyes—they were older than lifetimes.

"No," she said. "I won't."

Sazia, who stood frowning down on the whole proceedings, spoke up. "To stay is to die."

"In Christ's name, tell them nothing, unless you would murder me." This speech left her tired and coughing.

"Murder you!" I cried. "Weakness has made you mad. You are on death's very door. Come, and we will nurse you back to health. Our friends will do you no harm."

The girl didn't take her eyes off me. "Far better I die here," she said, "then follow and die at the hands of my enemies."

I remembered the inquisitor, and tucked the blanket more tightly around her. "They're looking for you, aren't they?"

She closed her eyes.

"The friar said he would lead you back to God," I told her.

"I never left God." She opened her eyes. "He means to lead me by the fastest route."

From higher up on the banks, we heard Garcia calling to us.

"Just a moment, Garcia!" I hollered back. "I . . . I've been ill. I am changing my clothes."

Symo's eyebrow rose, and I realized my mistake. "Run up and wait with them," I ordered. "I'm not changing my clothes around you."

"No one asked you to." Symo left.

"I barely escaped," the girl went on. "My mother did not." She sank in upon herself then. Her eyes grew dull, her face slack.

Sazia's face brooded darkly. *What do you see, little sorre?* I wondered.

"Blackness." My sister answered my thoughts aloud by whispering in my ear. "She is a storm cloud of sorrow. You wander in, you may never find your way out."

"So we leave her to die, then?" I whispered back. "I'm surprised at you, Sazia."

"Death might be a mercy for her." Sazia gazed at the girl's wan face. "I don't like it either. But listen to what she said. She must be a heretic, and sentenced to die. Somehow she got away. Do you think they will just let her go?"

My eyes smarted with tears. She was practical, always, and cool-headed. But still, I wouldn't have expected this of my Sazia.

"She can't be a heretic," I said. "Look at her face. Like a sad angel."

"What did you think, that heretics grew horns?"

I had heard words to that effect. Horns, and giant genitals, too.

"There won't be room in all Provensa for me to hide from Plazi if any harm befalls you."

Sazia's forebodings often went too far. Fortune-tellers are in the warnings business, just as marriage brokers are in the love business. We each have biases that follow our trade.

I made my decision. The girl's face made it for me. "There won't be room in hell for *my* wretched soul if I leave her here to die," I said. "We'll take her with us, and you'll help me."

Sazia pursed her lips and stood. "So be it, then," she said. "I've warned you."

Sazia climbed the slope and persuaded Garcia that all was well and that they should resume their journey, while Symo helped me wrap the *donzẹlla* in a blanket and hide her in his small cart, obscured by some bags of seed. She struggled against our efforts to bundle her into the barrow.

"I must follow the river to the sea," she said feebly. "North and east is my route."

"And that is how Friar Lucien de Saint-Honore follows you," I told her, "north and east along the Aude. We will take you to the sea if that's where you wish to go. But we will take you south and east, away from the river route. That will rid you of your pursuer."

She was too weary to protest any further, so she yielded herself reluctantly to our care.

Sazia and I walked with Symo's cart, which rattled along behind Garcia's. Symo walked with the Garcias and Gui, which suited me. Privacy was our best hope. We kept a sheet handy to drape over the girl's face any time other travelers came into view.

I jumped at hoofbeats and birdcalls. I worried that every shadow was the friar, come to snatch my poor bird. But no one wondered at our cargo. With each passing hour, I pictured the inquisitor's course veering farther and farther off from ours.

I'd armed myself with the whip Sazia had told me to bring, to use against anyone who had clever ideas about what to do with country lasses walking the roads alone. Already I'd been forced to brandish it once at a shrimpy pair of harvesters who wanted to tumble in the weeds, but we'd managed to fend them off with words rather than blows. Another time a man of high bearing and very proud countenance rode past us. He stopped to study me full on in the face, then pressed his heels into his horse's flanks and rode on. Not that I wanted his kisses, mind, but I was annoyed. That ugly, was I? That common? What else would I be, strolling along a country road at such an hour? Did he hope to find an heiress?

My little bird poked her head up from her blankets like a turtle emerging from its shell. "Do you have any cheese?"

Sazia rolled her eyes. "Next she'll want roast beef," she said. "Food's in the other cart."

"Leave off," I said. "She's been starving. And it just so happens, I do have cheese." I pulled a small brick of cheese, wrapped in a cloth, from my little pouch. "Remember? You told me to bring it." I broke off a section and offered it to the girl, then pulled my hand back. "A bite will cost you your name."

She turned away. "I can't trust anyone with my name."

I took a bite. "I can't trust strangers with my cheese." It wasn't my kindest moment.

"Fine," she said. "It's Braida."

"There, Braida," I said. "That wasn't so hard, was—"

"She's lying," Sazia said.

The girl's face grew pink. She scowled at my sister.

"My name is Pitrella Braida," she said more humbly. "Surely, you will allow me the privacy of my family name, given my situation."

My hardhearted sister shook her head. "She cares about someone by that name," she observed. "But Pitrella Braida is not her own name."

"What are you, a devil?" cried the girl. Up ahead, Garcia turned to look back at us.

"Plazi always said you were a little devil," I said loudly to Sazia. "But that's just Plazi for you." I turned to our prisoner. "You'd best shush if you don't want to be found out."

"You are devils, both of you," she whispered, and a tear ran down her cheek, "to torment a Christian maiden so. I've told you my troubles. You pride yourself with the thought of helping me, but you're helping me to my death. God in heaven! Would that I had died with my mother!"

"Maybe," Sazia ventured, "you should just give her the cheese."

So I did. As I handed it to her, a thought came into my mind. *Be patient with her.* Not my own impulse, surely. Patience never was my strength. But as I watched her eat her cheese, too quickly, too hungrily, and I remembered my own lean winters, I thought how this genteel young lady had probably never learned how to tighten her belt and get by. *All right,* I told the thought. *I'll try.*

She wiped crumbs off her lips with her fragile fingers, then settled back down in her nest to sleep. Before she did, she opened her deep-set eyes and looked at us both.

"My name," she said, "is Dolssa de Stigata. I am from Tolosa. With this information, you could betray me to a heretic's fiery death, though in the name of God, I swear I am no heretic."

I glanced at Sazia. She nodded slowly.

"Good to meet you, Dolssa de Stigata de Tolosa," she said. "I am Sazia Flasucra, and this is my sister Botille. We are both of the fishing town of Bajas, at present. We have an older sister, Plazensa. We will take you to our home and hide you there. We will never betray you."

Dolssa closed her eyes. "I am in your hands, and you are in God's, so I remain where I have always been." In minutes she was asleep.

Dolssa de Stigata, I learned, was a girl of miracles. There is no other way I can account for how we made it back home to Bajas without the Garcias or Gui discovering her. Granted, Symo's cooperation was vital. But cooperation from Symo, the surliest, most uncooperative pig I'd met in a long history of meeting pigs, could also be logged as a miracle.

An example: at dinnertime on the first day, we passed through the village of Fontcobèrta. A gang of overgrown *tozets* swarmed our carts and asked where we were bound. We told them, Bajas. They then demanded "trade." They poked at the parcels in Garcia's larger cart, then descended on Dolssa's little barrow. These ruffians ignored our men's threats. I was about to make the colossal blunder of using my whip, when the ringleader of the band, pawing close to Dolssa, let out a howl and pinched his nose shut. His comrades did the same, and one by one slunk off, telling us they weren't interested in trading in pig *merda*, thank you very much.

"What was that about?" wondered a baffled Gui.

"Your farts scared them off," Symo said. "At long last, a good use for them."

"Oho," bristled Gui, "if you want to talk of farts—"

"I don't."

"Your wind could knock over a barn."

"Your farts aren't exactly honeysuckle vines. You talk like there's a turd in your throat."

Fame of our stench spread. No one would sell us dinner in that village, so we had to make do with our provisions. I tiptoed over to the barrow and sniffed, but I smelled nothing strange at all. Dolssa needed a bath, but no more than young Garcia did. It had to be a miracle.

Ghost odors notwithstanding, we sailed right under the noses of people passing by on the roads. I wondered if Dolssa would take her leave of us in the night, but she didn't. Under cover of darkness, we pulled her off the cart so she could stretch her legs, but she returned to us and slept on the ground, tucked and bundled between my sister and me.

But not before another miracle. It lingered with me long afterward. We girls stood concealed in a small copse of trees near the road, having just passed water in preparation for sleep. Two shadowy figures, a man and a woman, stepped out from behind the trees. I feared bandits, but their hollow faces, gray hair, and poor, frail shapes clad in somber black clothing made them seem more like ghosts.

"What do you want?" Sazia whispered.

"Bow to us?" came the old man's plaintive voice.

I turned to my companions in confusion.

"Bow to us," pleaded the woman. "Ask us to bless your souls. We are friends of God."

Time stood still. My skin tingled. Almost, I confess it, I wanted to bow.

"Make no bow," whispered Dolssa into my ear, "and give them

no honor. It is a *bon ome* and a *bona femna*. Once, great *cortezia* and *onor* were shown to these *amicx de Dieu* in Tolosa in all the villages in these lands. That is what Blessed Dominic called a heresy, and that is why the crusaders came."

The poor, thin pair was on the verge of tears. The man bore up the woman with his arm.

"Do you have any bread?" The man's voice crackled with his plea. "A morsel for the friends of God?"

They smote my heart. "Wait here." I guided Dolssa back to where we would all sleep.

Dolssa took my wrist in her weak grip. "If you feed the heretics," she said, "you could be punished as one of their believers." She covered her eyes with a trembling hand. "The same is true of feeding me."

I had no bread. Our stores were all in Garcia's cart. Even the cheese I'd brought at Sazia's cryptic request was gone.

"Were it not for these *amicx de Dieu*, there would be no inquisitors hunting for me," whispered Dolssa. "Yet who am I, now, who shares their fate, to judge?" She released my wrist. "Feed them if you will," she said, "and may God protect your foolish generosity."

As she released her grasp, my mind went to a sack in the little barrow. I opened it. I knew it contained seed, not food. But there before me was a full loaf of bread, and the cheese cloth I had brought, full of fresh, soft, white cheese.

"God bless your soul," the *bon ome* said to me when I gave

them the meal. I began to thank them, then halted, hating myself. Twice blessed I was that night, or twice cursed, by two different kinds of heretics, two different sets of damned believers. But the miracle of the cheese and bread, I was certain, was Dolssa's.

As she slept, and then took milk and bread and vegetables, Dolssa was, herself, the chief miracle. In two days she returned from the grave. There would be weeks of healing to come, but her improvement filled me with reverent joy. I had never been holy, but God and I were partners in mending this girl. I watched over her, tracking her every breath, as if she were my own sleeping *enfan*. Each sign of healing made me want to sing.

Years before, I had found Mimi, our cat, as a starving kitten, no more than a few weeks old. She was frail and nearly bald, with a belly swollen full of worms. Sazia would have ended her life mercifully, but I refused, and insisted on nursing the kitten with drops of milk and bits of mashed chicken meat and fat. That which you tend, you come to adore with the kind of love that bypasses sense and reason. So it was for Mimi. So it came to be with Dolssa.

She slept day and night, like Mimi, but there were times, when I walked near the barrow, when I heard her speak. Soft whisperings, as though she carried on a heartbroken conversation. Madness could do this, but she did not seem insane. Grief might make one mad, and if any had cause for grief, it was she. I heard her plead over and over, "Where are you? Where are you? Why have you left me alone?" Poor soul. She must be speaking to her mother.

I was only six when I lost my mother. Is there a best age for such robbery? Was I better off for Mamà's death being long ago, tucked behind the hopefulness of youth and the forgetfulness of time? Was Dolssa the lucky one to have had her mother longer? Or was she the more bereaved for being old enough to understand and remember all that she had lost?

Night was fully dark when we arrived back in Bajas, but *la luna* revealed to us the town. For some distance, salty breezes off the sea had filled me with longing. Now, as we climbed Bajas's round-domed hill, the lullaby of *la mar*'s gentle waves called to me. We were home.

Na Pieret di Fabri's house was one of the grander, taller ones in town, toward the top of the hill, near the church. We went there first. We made enough noise for all sorts to poke their heads out their windows to complain and ogle the newcomers. In Bajas, with all the holes in our walls connecting one house to the next, a sound heard by one was a sound heard by all (as newlyweds often learned to their chagrin), so in no time we had a full audience.

I'd had two days of watching Gui and Symo's *azes* swagger across muddy roads and fields like they owned it all. To hear them talk, their *tanta*'s vineyards had already made them rich as counts. I enjoyed watching them shrink a bit smaller now with all our curious Bajas eyes upon them.

Astruga leaned out her window, bosoms and all, and called to the *tozets* to notice her. Dominus Bernard exited a front door and made the sign of the cross, the outrageous faker. I'd bet my inheritance if I had one that he wasn't there comforting the sick or counseling the sinful. Correction: with the sinful, yes; counsel and comfort of a special kind. It was the home of the frisky Rixenda, whose husband, Peire, was a sailor often away at sea for days on end. Astruga saw Dominus Bernard, scowled, and retreated behind her shutters with a bang.

Then Na Pieret di Fabri appeared in her candle-lit doorway to greet her new sons. She stared at them, and they bowed to her. She raised her trembling hands to Gui's face, and kissed each of his cheeks. Symo next received this affectionate welcome, though given, I thought, with perhaps a little—a very little—less warmth than his handsome brother had found.

"In a day soon to come," the good *domna* proclaimed, "we will feast. My sister's eyes have returned to comfort me in my old age, here in the faces of these, my new sons. But now, home, each of you, to your beds. I will keep my sons to myself. We have a lifetime of catching up to do. Garcia and his son will stable the animals, and we will deal with the luggage tomorrow."

So swept up in this reunion was I that I failed to see the mess we were in. While Garcia steered Pieret's mule down the narrow tunnel leading to her stable below, Sazia tugged on my sleeve. "Dolssa," she whispered into my ear.

Symo turned and met my gaze. "The *donzellas* have much luggage in our little barrow," he told his newly met *tanta*. "Like princesses, they packed too much. But since they might want it before morning, I will take it to their home tonight."

"Great *cortezia* has my new son." Na Pieret beamed. "Like a true knight, he places the comfort of the fair *donzęllas* first."

True knight, indeed.

I heard a familiar voice calling out my name. Plazensa ran up the hill, her skirts clutched high to her knees, her black hair streaming behind her. She plowed into me, knocking me right into Symo's barrow. Only by purest luck did I not hit Dolssa and crack her head open.

"So you're back," Plazi scolded. "How dare you worry me so much, and then come back without even a scratch on you?"

"*Bon sęr,* Plazi," I squeaked. "Can you get off me?"

"And you, Sazia!" Plazi's fury rose. We both knew it was only a cover for her worries, and we didn't mind a bit. "Some truth-teller you are. To twist a poor girl's heart like a dishrag, all soaked in fear, and for what?"

Sazia submitted to Plazi's furious kisses. "Sorry to disappoint you, *sǫrre.*"

"And to leave me alone with Jobau, moping around like the devil with a toothache!"

It was then that I noticed Gui eyeing my older sister apprecia-tively. This wouldn't do. I couldn't have Gui favoring my harlot goddess of a sister. She'd never have him. I needed to marry him off to someone else. Those teeth of his were shillings under my mattress.

Na Pieret di Fabri's laugh rang out. "Forgive your sisters,

Plazensa, and take this to drink to our health. They have brought home my prodigal sons." She handed Plazi a large pitcher from her own vineyards.

Gui stepped forward in his most gallant way. "May I have the pleasure—"

"No, you may not." I seized Plazi's arm. "It's late, and we must get home to bed. And, Gui, before you think of charming our sister, remember, we've traveled two days with you, and we've watched how you eat."

Symo apparently inhaled a puff of feather down at that moment, for he began coughing and choking so hard that Gui had to whack him on the back.

"Leave off," croaked his victim. "I'll take them their things and be back soon."

"Plazi," I hissed into my sister's ear. "We are bringing home a surprise. Whatever you do, by your hope of heaven, when you see it, do not make a peep."

That night I lay in my bed next to Sazia, listened to *la mar*, and thought about all that had happened to me these four days. The trip and Sazia's warnings. The friar and the dying bird. What if I hadn't heard her sigh? What if I'd come along too late? What if I'd told the friar what I'd seen? Was she a heretic fleeing the pyres? Or was she somehow deceived, or mad and in need of a pastor's help?

I thought of Sazia's warnings. Darkness and danger, sorrow and pain.

But the miracles! The voices in my head. The signs that followed her. Was Dolssa de Stigata even flesh and blood?

I thought of the feeble pair in the woods, the *bon ome* and *bona femna*. Once there were many of them throughout the little *vilas* of Provensa. The war to destroy them nearly destroyed our homeland. Old-timers spoke often of its bitterness and blood. Whole towns and cities had been burnt to the ground, and their people with them. Once the "good men" and "good women" were revered as holy, but now they were more feared and hated than devils. Not for their own sake, but for what was done, in the name of Christ, to those who believed in them or helped them or let them live among them.

Dolssa de Stigata wasn't one of them. But what, then, in Jhesus's name, was she?

BOTILLE

f course we will help her."

"Hush, Plazi!" I hissed. Walls had ears. It was dangerous to discuss Dolssa aloud. She still slept in the back room where we'd hidden her, on a cot behind a curtain.

Plazensa chopped carrots and onions for the day's dinner, while I plucked a plump young *polęt*. I'd already wrung its neck and bled it, and now it was my job to preserve the feathers for a pillow, and the meat for the *sǫpa*.

Outside the Three Pigeons, sunlight sparkled off little waves of the lagoon. The sky glowed with sunrise, like a morning in heaven. Gulls called to one another from the shallows, where shellfish begged to be crunched between their beaks, while around the tavern our other, more fortunate *polęts* clucked and waddled over the packed-dirt streets, foraging for bugs. It felt wonderful to be home.

A fragile wail from next door penetrated the partition between the tavern and the neighbors next door.

"Oh!" I cried. "Lisette has had her baby, then?"

Plazi smiled. "The day you left. A *tozęt*. Big enough, and strong, but it will not stop crying. Didn't you hear it last night?"

I shook my head. We'd been tired enough to sleep through a war, after our four days' march. I eyed my sister's pile of *legums*. "You should add another onion."

Sazia slumped into a stool by the bar and stirred her bowl of porridge. "Dolssa is danger, Plazi," she said. "I keep telling Botille, but she won't listen. That girl is being hunted by an inquisitor. They killed her mother. You can count upon it, they will find her."

Plazensa frowned. "Why should they? Did you tell anyone about her?"

"Only Symo knows. He was there when we found her." The chicken's stubborn underwing feathers would not yield. What harm, I wondered, were a few tiny feathers in the *sopa*?

The harsh, barking bray of a dying donkey floated down to us from the loft. Jobau, waking up screaming. We were used to this. Provensa's long years when the crusaders came every summer, killing and burning, had never ended for him. His dreams, some nights, made him a madman.

Plazensa released a rope attached to a pulley, whereon a

bucket was tied. It rattled down, and from it she pulled an empty jug. She replaced the jug with a full one, and a hunk of flat *fogasa* in the bargain, then hoisted on the ropes to raise the bucket up to the loft. The pulley had been my idea, and I was rather proud of it.

Jobau's liver-stained hand fumbled for the bucket. Before long, a belch informed us that our lord and master was safely disposed of for another morning.

"You're only wasting the *fogasa*," observed Sazia. She poured honey over her porridge.

"Jobau," Plazensa called, "Sazia wants to know if you actually eat the *fogasa*."

"Plazi!" groaned Sazia. "Must you look for trouble?"

A rude gesture from the lip of the loft was our reply.

"What Mamà ever saw in him . . ." Sazia muttered.

Another rude gesture.

Plazi dropped her *legums* into the crock over the fire. "He was handsome," she said, to goad our sister. Sazia grimaced. Jobau's yellow skin, his haggard flesh, his long wisps of foul, unwashed hair . . . I didn't despise Jobau like Sazia did, but to see him as handsome took more imagination than I had.

Of course, Sazia's real problem with Jobau was that he was her father.

"Enough about Jobau," I said. "We have more pressing problems to think about now."

"The girl." Plazensa twisted sprigs of rosemary over the *sopa* pot. "Cut up the *polęt* for me, will you, Botille? I've got to chop parsnips."

Just then a huge figure emerged from the back hallway. I jumped. It was the fisherman from the tavern the day before our journey. I noted the brief glance he and Plazi shared. So. Another of her clients, slinking away. We pretended we hadn't seen him. This was the routine. Perhaps he was becoming a regular. But how much of our conversation had he heard?

I pushed the feather bag out of Mimi's reach, then shoved my fist up the bird's bottom and grabbed a handful of squishy entrails.

"We will keep her here safely," Plazi said. "We'll keep her secret."

"How?" said Sazia. "By locking her away forever? Some life that would be."

Plazi waved her knife. "We'll tell people she's our cousin, come to stay with us."

Sazia laughed. "She's obviously noble, Plazi. No one would believe she's our cousin."

Plazi chopped her remaining parsnips as if they represented all our problems. I hacked off my chicken's thigh in the same spirit.

Sazia shook her head. "She can't stay forever. You must see that."

"Marry her off, then," Plazi fumed.

They both stopped. They turned toward me slowly. Oh, no.

I took a step back. "You're joking," I said. "Impossible. And I only work for a fee."

The tavern door pushed open, and we all froze. Even Sazia pasted an artificial smile upon her face. We were just three innocent sisters having a harmless, amusing conversation.

It was only Sapdalina.

"Good morning, Plazensa, Sazia, Botille." Sapdalina wouldn't make eye contact if eye contact could save her immortal soul in Paradise. "Lovely morning, isn't it? I'm sure it is, for those who"—she burst into tears, and phlegm mushroomed from her nose—"aren't teetering at the brink of starvation. . . ." Here Sazia handed her a clean cloth for her face. "Or will be, as soon as their aged fathers die, which is bound to happen any day now"—a moist sneeze—"leaving them penniless and cold in an unforgiving world." She sank into a barstool, then leaped off it, yelping as though the stool had bit her buttocks. "Oh! I've no right to sit. The seats are for paying customers, and Santa Sara knows, I could no more buy an ale than I could marry a king's son. But I ask for nothing so lofty as a king's son!" She forgot the cloth, and wiped her facial productions onto her long, straight bodice. "Just a man, ever so common, and ugly, too, if it pleases God, and if he wants to beat me, I probably deserve it. So long as he doesn't get too violent, I won't complain."

"Sapdalina," Plazensa said severely. "You don't need a husband. What you need is help."

"Who says she doesn't need a husband?" I demanded. Sapdalina's fee would be small, but a fee, nonetheless.

"I do." Plazi's eyes blazed. "She needs lessons. In the art of catching a man."

Sazia groaned into her empty porridge bowl.

"You brought some men back home with you, Botille. I hear one is quite handsome." Sapdalina smeared her hand under her nose. "Could I have the other one? You can save the handsome one for customers with more money."

I pictured Symo and Sapdalina in each other's arms, and had to gnaw on my knuckles to keep from laughing out loud.

"Well, Botille?" Sazia teased me. "Shall we announce Sapdalina and Symo's wedding?"

"Ooh, Symo, is that his name? *See-moo, See-moo.* It's not a mouthful, at any rate. Some names would be unbearable to have to say over and over and over."

Like Sapdalina. Sazia, who could read our minds, snickered at me. I wrenched the *polęt's* other leg off, but only the bones came, leaving the fat and flesh dangling behind.

"Sapdalina. Child. You are unfit to win the love of a dog, much less a man," Plazi told her. "You need lessons, and I'll give them to you."

I silently gave Plazi one of the tongue-lashings she's famous for. Sometimes she reads my thoughts too, and I hoped this was such a time. *Now is not the time for a rescue project! We already have one, and she lies dreaming in the back room!*

"I'd be so grateful for lessons," Sapdalina said, "but I have no way to pay for them."

"Is there anything you can do?" inquired my older sister. "Besides sneeze?"

Sapdalina sat a little straighter. "I can stitch like anything."

I dropped my squashy chicken on the table and silently demanded that Plazensa look at me. Finally she met my gaze. Sazia joined the circle. We thought of Dolssa, and her tattered but once-fine clothes. I thought of finding her a husband. I thought of keeping her alive. Plazensa dared either of us to object to her new project. Even Sazia, reluctantly, agreed.

"Stitching," I told Sapdalina, "could help."

Thus I found myself leaving the tavern and heading along the slip for the docks, in search of Guilhem, our highest—and practically only—ranking bachelor in Bajas. A knight, the son of a knight, and nephew to a great lord in Narbona. He enforced the collection of taxes and rents heavily, but what nobleman did otherwise? He quitted himself bravely when roving *faidits*, those displaced nobles who'd lost their lands during the Crusade, came looking to stake new claims in small Bajas.

We liked him well enough. But even if we hadn't, he was single and not yet thirty. He still had a thick crown of hair. He was the only groom I could think of for Dolssa.

I knew I'd find Senhor Guilhem at the docks. I braced myself to spring upon him my most audacious matchmaking plot yet. There would be obstacles. He'd be hard to win over. These nobles of ours, here in the sunny south, were raised on *trobador* songs right along with their wet nurses' milk. Mundane, earthy, baby-making, *sopa*-eating marriage was a far cry from the elaborate love of poised and pretty ladies at court that they preferred. It was all a game to wrap up their greed for a dowry in an elegant package. And Dolssa would certainly have no dowry. How had I let Plazi talk me into this?

I slipped off my shoes and felt the wet sand squelch through my toes. My mutterings about Plazi disturbed a graceful pair of bright pink *flamencs* dipping their great beaks in the shallows in search of breakfast. They flapped off in protest, and I laughed at their dangling pink legs. A bit like mine had been, even a wash or two after my grape-stomping.

I reached the fishy docks, pink and white with their splatterings of shattered prawns and seagull *merda*. Past the docks, the shimmering salt pans lay. Soon the autumn sun wouldn't burn away water fast enough to yield our precious salt, and the workers would have to wait till next summer.

A small fishing boat was just coming in, clanging its bell for someone to come help with the tackle and tie the ropes. Already in port was a vessel I recognized.

"Botille, my beauty!"

Giacomo Arbrissi, a merchant sailor from Florença, waved to me from his dock. I was no more his beauty than he was my grandmother, but the stout and hairy salesman always let me have first look at the items he'd brought to sell because, he said, I knew more about the lives and wants of townsfolk than any *bayle* or priest.

I greeted him with a kiss on both whiskery cheeks. "*Bonjorn,* Giacomo!"

"Come away with me to Florença, Botille! Someday I'll take you with me."

I grinned. "I wouldn't mind."

Giacomo was our source for goods we could never find in Bajas. His trading route took him to Itàlia, Fransa, Provensa, and Aragón, but he always took time to enter the lagoon of *la mar* and peddle his wares to tiny Bajas and the other ports around its circumference. It was practically an act of charity. We were poor here. Only what we could pull from the sea or the soil was ours, and then, not for long.

"Come see what I have for you." Giacomo pulled me toward his boat. I climbed down a ladder into the stuffy hold. "Who needs what I have today? Exquisite olive oil—"

"We make plenty of our own," I said.

"Some beautiful knives—"

"Fishermen," I said. "Plazensa, but we can't afford them. The usual handful of people with money. Na Pieret, maybe."

"Take a deep whiff of these pungent spices, all the way from India!"

"Ooh, folks will like these, especially if you sell them by the pinch."

"Books, from Rome, treatises on theology—"

I shook my head. "In Bajas? Who here would want those?"

"Not even your priest?"

"Hah!"

Giacomo wiped the sweat off his shiny pate. "Will no one want my nice parchment and ink?"

I considered. "There's the notary," I said. "He's the only one who could use it."

Ever the optimist, Giacomo turned to another parcel. "Cloth!" he cried. "Good stiff English wool, beautifully woven in Flanders; and silks from Byzantium. Ever seen such colors?"

"Not since you were last in port." I smiled.

Giacomo pulled out a little stool and sat upon it. "Botille," he whispered. "Tell me. Who in Bajas is in love or courting? Betrothed, or soon to be?"

He shook two silver combs, tipped with carved and painted bone, from a velvet pouch.

I took a dainty comb and held it up in the one shaft of sunlight penetrating the hold.

"You know of secret lovers before they know themselves," said Giacomo. "Tell me. Who needs to see my pretty combs? I have ribbons, too, for the poorer *tozęts* to buy for their *tozas*."

I sighed. "I've fallen a bit behind in my work," I told him, "but I'll soon set things to rights. Then I'll bring you buyers."

"A buyer, perhaps," wheedled Giacomo, "who may buy a pair for you?"

I planted a kiss on his shiny dome. "Don't bet your silver purse on that, old friend."

"I'll carry you away to Florença!" he called after me as I climbed back onto the dock.

"My bag is packed!" I set off once more in search of Senhor Guilhem.

I found him in the counting house, leaning back in a wooden chair, in bored conversation with Lop, the *bayle*. I approached Senhor Guilhem and bowed.

"Botille," said my lord. "How fares your sister?"

Oh *no*. Not Plazi. I bowed again. "Which one, Senhor?"

"Your older sister. The alewife, and the beauty."

"My sister is in excellent health. *Grácia*." I bowed again. "I wonder, Senhor, if you would grant me the opportunity to speak to you?"

He waved his hand at the room as if Lop were not in it. "Speak on, then," he said. "My time is leisurely today."

Lop's eyes tracked my every move. There was something canine about our silent, gray-whiskered *bayle*. He was a man past his prime but not far past it, still able to strike fear into the hearts of drunken lads after a night's revelry.

"Bon Senhor," I said. "A *private* word with you?"

The knight's eyebrows rose. "Off with you, then," he told Lop. "The wench craves a *private* word." He made it sound like a joke. The *bayle* looked none too pleased, but he left.

"Well?" said Senhor Guilhem. "What will you have of me? Justice, I'll guess. Is there someone bothering your family? Stealing from your tavern?"

"No, Senhor. Something else." I gulped. Normally, I didn't worry about finding the right words. I just sailed right in and let the right words find me. But I fished in deeper seas this morning.

"Senhor," I began, "perhaps you are aware that one of the small functions I play in Bajas is that of a matchmaker?" Senhor Guilhem looked taken aback. "For marriages. I help people make good marriages."

He rocked his chair forward. "You make marriages?" he repeated. "So young as you are, and still a maid yourself?"

I bowed. "You might say I have a talent for it."

He smirked. "To what do you attribute this talent?"

I hadn't expected this. "I . . . pay attention," I said. "To people. I see who is shy, and who is lonely. Who is fussy, and who is patient. And so on. I put them together."

"And the people of Bajas," continued Guilhem, "are shy enough and lonely enough to need help from you?"

"Not everyone." More was the pity, too. "But enough fail to see the person who could please them, because they focus on the wrong things."

"But you focus on the right things." He stroked his beard. "Marriage, you think, should please people?"

I didn't like the sarcasm creeping into his voice. "Senhor," I said quickly, "have you ever considered marriage?"

His mood grew dark. "To what does this question tend? Marriage to you?"

I laughed. "No, Senhor! Never with me!"

He leaned forward abruptly. "To your sister?"

I swallowed a laugh. "Oh, Senhor," I said. "Your honor would not long remain satisfied with a wife like Plazensa. She is only a peasant, after all, and what a temper she has! You see her beauty, but I can assure you, she has a tongue like an adder's bite."

He rose and paced the counting house. This was not going well. If Guilhem began coming around to plague us at the tavern, Sazia would have a fit.

"Jealous sisters say things like this about each other," he muttered to himself.

"I'm not jealous!"

He laughed at this. "With a sister like Plazensa, how could you be anything but?"

A pleasant courtesy.

"I love my sister, Senhor," I said, "but I must speak to you about someone else. I heard"—*yes, this could work*—"of a noble *donzẹlla*. One of exceeding beauty and virtue."

Guilhem was unimpressed. "To hear their parents tell it, the land teems with such fair *donzẹllas*. Never is one of them described as ugly and dull. But many are."

I waited.

"Proceed."

So he *was* curious.

"This lady," I said, "will soon pass nearby this place. She has suffered a great sorrow."

Say something, you wretched man, and buy me time!

"She was betrothed," I went on, "to a most gentle and manly knight. . . ."

Guilhem sat a little straighter and thrust his shoulders outward just a touch.

"But he died." Maire Maria, I could think of no battles wherein he should have died. "Defending a bishop from assassins."

Guilhem frowned. A shocking story like this, he would have heard.

"In Lisbona," I added hastily.

"In Lisbona?"

I nodded solemnly. "All the way in Lisbona. So, this fair and virtuous lady is devastated with grief. Understandable, don't you think?"

He watched me out of the corner of one eye. "I suppose."

"And now she feels she must leave her homeland and travel far away to . . . Florença . . ." *Yes, why not?* . . . "to join a convent, and pass the rest of her days in prayer."

Guilhem rolled his eyes heavenward, as if this entire tale had been a great disappointment. "What is that to me, then?"

Was he made of wood, to have no curiosity? My best spinning, lavished upon this dunce of a nobleman, and utterly wasted!

Time for desperation. "My younger sister, Sazia, is the best fortune-teller along this entire lagoon."

Senhor Guilhem smiled at this. "So I've heard tell."

"You have?" I beamed for my little *sorre*. "How nice. When Sazia heard the tale of this poor, sad, beautiful *donzella*, she was seized by a premonition." I must remember to tell her about this when I got home.

"And?"

Now was the time for the kill. "And do you want to know what it was?"

Senhor Guilhem's nostrils flared. "Damn you! You lead me this far to ask me, do I want to know what it was?"

I bowed my head modestly.

He huffed out a breath. "What was it?"

I mustn't smile. "The premonition," I whispered, "was written in the stars. You were to be her true love, and she was to become your adoring wife."

It took Senhor Guilhem several swallows to work up the spittle he needed for a large, contemptuous laugh.

"True love," said he.

"True love." I nodded.

"Pah."

I waited.

"Old *trobador* nonsense," he said. "Died with the war. Not even a fool thinks of such things now." He was working hard to convince me of something. I decided to let him win.

"Undoubtedly," I said.

"Exactly."

We both nodded.

I sniffed. "I'm only repeating what Sazia said."

We were allies now. "Maidens' tales," said my new friend.

"Just so."

"I have no time for such things."

"Of course not." I examined my knuckles. "Even though, they say, Sazia is almost never wrong."

"Almost never."

"There you have it," I said. "There's quite a distance between 'almost never' and 'never never.'"

"I see why you're a matchmaker, Botille," said my generous lord knight. "For a wench, you have an uncommonly good brain."

I bowed. "Senhor does me great *onor* with such a compliment."

He patted me paternally upon the shoulder. "Who is the lady?"

Aha.

"Well," I began, "Senhor will forgive me if, just at present, I do not reveal her name. Her plans are secret, for if her family learns of her intentions, they will disown her."

Senhor Guilhem was deeply affected by this revelation, but not in the way I'd hoped.

"No family? No dowry, then, either?"

Sympathy. That was what I'd been hoping for. Not money lust. But what should I expect? Even we peasants married sometimes for pillows and pots. But poor as we were, we could afford to think about affection. These greedy nobles only wanted gold, jewels, weapons, and land.

The lord of Bajas snapped his fingers. "But if they approved of me"—he colored deeply—"if they approved of whomever she did marry, there would, of course, be a dowry."

I shook my head sadly. "None, I fear, but her great beauty and goodness. Her family lost everything when the crusaders came."

He blew out his breath in great disappointment. Lop poked his head in the door just then and examined us with one curious eye. "Pardon me, Senhor. Are you finished with the wench?"

"When I'm finished with a wench, you'll know it, and so will the wench," Senhor Guilhem said. Lop squiggled away like a bitten eel.

"I've taken your time." I bowed yet again and slipped toward the door. "For that I beg pardon. There are so many problems with this theory of my *sorre*'s, I never should have troubled you with it. I only thought"—another bow—"that you might be curious to behold—"

"Behold what?"

"That is to say, if your grace would condescend to a glimpse, just a glimpse—"

"A glimpse of what?"

"Such as might be arranged in the woods not far from the village, over against Na Pieret di Fabri's western vineyards, by moonlight."

"You're raving. Of what do you speak?"

"It could seem like a chance meeting. No need to take any special care or ceremony in your dress. Just a chance to behold for yourself whether the maiden lives up to the reports that are made of her. You could play the part of an absolute stranger, and she'd be no wiser."

"She *who* would be no wiser?"

"Tuesday," I said. "I have a feeling Tuesday is when she will arrive. Half an hour after dark." I reached for the door. "But only if you're curious. *Bonjọrn*."

"You're a slippery fish."

I bowed. "Others have said so."

I was halfway out when his voice reached me. "I suppose you think, Botille, that you'll get a fee from me for your services."

I allowed myself the smallest of smiles. "Only if you're satisfied, Senhor."

From the waterfront, I toiled up the hill toward Bajas proper, with sea breezes pushing at my back. The bells of Sant Martin's rang. Time for prayers. On such a busy workday, I didn't expect many people at church, and that suited me. I wanted a word with Dominus Bernard.

I passed by the street where Na Pieret lived, and met Symo coming around the corner, with Gui beside him. Sapdalina, I saw, came up the street behind the brothers, and watched them both with an expression of pathetic longing.

"*Bonjọrn*, Symo, Gui." I bowed in a friendly way. "What a difference a bath makes, no?"

"*Bonjọrn*, Botille." Gui grinned, then elbowed his brother. "What ails you, Symo? No *bonjọrn* for our only friend in Bajas?"

Symo's beetle brows bristled. "What do you mean, 'our only friend'?"

Late morning sun glinted off Gui's supernal teeth. Sapdalina, who had parked herself invisibly nearby, as only she could do, nearly fainted at the sight of his smile.

"I don't want to be your only friend," I told them. "So let me introduce you to some more friends. This is Sapdalina, the best seamstress in all Bajas."

Poor Sapdalina flushed salmon pink. *"Botille!"*

Gui gave her a good-natured bow, and Symo jerked his head stiffly in her direction.

"Sapdalina could stitch you some clothes better fitting your new position," I told Symo. "You're heirs to the vineyards now. You shouldn't dress like the lowest farmhand."

I was rewarded by a stare that would intimidate a rampaging boar. But Gui let out a loud laugh. "She's right, you great slob," he said. "It's time we dressed better." He glanced at Sapdalina. "You'll come by, then, and measure us?"

If Sapdalina could have bowed till her nose touched the ground, she'd have done it. "I shall come every hour," she said, "until I catch you at a convenient moment for the fitting."

Symo groaned. Gui had the grace to keep silent, but I saw his wish to unsay his request.

"Well, then," I told the merry group, "it sounds as though you have your amusements spread out before you for some time to come. *Bonjorn.*" I hurried off.

"Botille."

I turned back to see what Symo wanted.

He scrubbed his dark scalp with his fingernails. "How fares your, er, sister?"

"Which one?" asked Sapdalina.

"He means, of course, the sister who traveled with us," I told her. But he wasn't asking about Sazia. I understood him. "The journey has fatigued her," I said, "but she's resting well."

He nodded once and then strode off elsewhere. An odd fish was Symo.

I finished the climb to Sant Martin's, pushed open the old oak door, and stepped inside the sacred darkness.

A little light entered through the glass windows near the ceiling, beyond the reach of thieves. They were the only glass windows in all Bajas, and the way light rippled and fanned through them fascinated me. Like rays of glory from heaven, piercing the dusty gloom of the church, making each airborne mote shine like a star.

Dominus Bernard was nowhere in sight, so I knelt near a shrine to Johan the Evangelist. I fingered Mamà's crucifix, still hanging about my neck. It was a small bit of silver, very precious, worth more than its price, because it had been Mamà's. I wondered which lover had given it to her. When I was younger, I liked to imagine it was a great and wealthy *senhor*, and that he had been my father. Now I didn't bother with such fancies. I just thought of Mamà.

We, her daughters, weren't very holy, heaven knew, but that didn't mean we held no reverence for holiness. We were Christians, like anyone. With a savage like Jobau to care for, and our livings to make, piety was a luxury.

Mamà had been a courtesan. A beauty about the court of the counts of Carcassona. Moving from man to man is never an upward path. The last man was Jobau. It never bothered me to discover, as I grew older, that Mamà had been a fancy whore, an adulteress, and a sinner. Mamà loved us. She loved her lovers. She loved miserable Jobau. I remember her loving strangers and neighbors and even poor, starving lepers. She loved Jhesus, too. Wasn't it the Evangelist who told of the many times when Jhesus forgave sinful women? And our own Santa Maria Magdalena, of whom the Lord said that her sins were forgiven, for she loved much, the same who sailed across *la mar* to Provensa with Santa Sara?

I only knew one prayer. Mamà had taught me the Paternoster. The "Our Father."

> *Le nostre Paire que es els cèls*
> *sanctificatz sia lo teus nom*
> *avenga lo teus regnes*
> *e sia faita la tua voluntatz sicò el cèl et e la tèrra.*
> *E dona nos a nos oi le nostre pan qui es sobre tota causa.*
> *E perdona a nos les nostres deutes,*
> *aissí co nos perdonam als nostres deutors.*
> *E no nos amenes en temptacion*
> *Mas deliura-nos de mal.*
>
> *Our Father who is in heaven,*
> *May your name be sanctified.*

May your kingdom prevail,

And your will be done, as in heaven, so on earth.

And give us our bread, as we have true need,

And pardon our debts

Just as we pardon others' debts.

And lead us not toward temptation,

But deliver us from evil.

I felt my Mamà's peace as I spoke the words. Smelled her lavender-scented hair. Like the starry, sunlit dust, her love beamed down on me from heaven.

"What do my eyes behold?" A laughing voice from behind me sent Mamà's sweetness tinkling down like shards of broken glass.

I stood. "*Bonjorn*, Dominus Bernard."

"Botille, at prayer?" The priest's smile was almost as dazzling as his windows. "I'll make a good Christian out of you yet."

I smiled. "Do you make good Christians with sermons, or with kisses?"

The rogue didn't even have the grace to blush. "The kiss of peace, my daughter. I am generous with the kiss of peace."

He needed punishment for this. "Generous you are, indeed," I said. "I hear congratulations are in order. A new addition to your growing family."

His composure fell somewhat. "Astruga?"

"Bravo for your honesty."

He clucked his tongue sympathetically. "You'll help her, won't you, Botille?" he asked me. "See to it that she's safely situated?"

"What will *you* do to help her?" I inquired. "By rights, you should be the one offering help. At the very least, you should pay my fee."

"I," said our village priest, with an air of great injury, "will give her the sweetest wedding mass a pretty young *toza* could wish for. At my lowest possible price."

I shook my head and leaned against the wall. "Why did they send you to Bajas, Dominus Bernard?" I said. "A face like yours could have gone to Tolosa. Or París."

He laughed. "Who says it didn't?"

This was news to me. "Oh?"

"They sent me here," he said, "after a few unfortunate misunderstandings."

"With noblemen's wives?"

He winked. "A bishop's concubine, among others."

"For shame!" I wagged a finger in his face. "You tell me too much, Dominus," I said. "You ought not to trust me so."

"Why, Botille," he said, "you are the one *femna* I know I can trust."

Because I was smart, and because I was not beautiful. A man's good female friend, that was me. No matter. I was certainly not standing in line for Bernard's kisses.

I patted his hand. "Why did you ever become a priest?"

He looked affronted. "It's my calling," he said. "I was always marked for the clergy. Do I not minister to the fold? To the sick, to the dying? Am I miserly at dispensing comfort?"

It was true. In every respect except continence, Bernard was a model priest.

"Plus, I like to sing," he teased. "But what brings you here, Botille?"

I wondered whether I could trust him as much as he claimed to trust me. I decided to make a beginning at it. "You saw me return last night from my journey."

"*Oc*. Na Pieret's nephews. She is overjoyed," he said. "Go on."

I hesitated. "On my travels, I heard of friar inquisitors traveling in search of heretics."

Dominus Bernard's face darkened.

"Do you know anything about this?"

He shifted his weight. "Yes," he said slowly. "This Order of Preachers has gone *castrum* to *castrum* and *vila* to *vila*, interrogating people to see if they believed in and honored the old *bons omes* and *bonas femnas*."

His words echoed throughout the old church. They made my skin prickle.

"Have they come here?" I realized I was whispering.

He shook his head.

This silent, private conversation—even it was dangerous. That made me furious.

"Why should they care," I asked, "if we honored the friends of God? They're just quiet, pious old people—why would we *not* honor them?"

Dominus Bernard sat down upon a bench. "Because it was our way," he said at length. "Not Roma's way."

All our wars, and all our dead, for nothing but this? "We say *oc*, and they say *si*," I said, thinking of Giacomo. "That's our way too. Shall we die for that?"

"The Church decides, Botille," said our handsome priest, "what is holy and what is not. We decided the *bons omes* and *bonas femnas* were holy without consulting the Church. And look about you." He gestured to the empty chapel. "No one is here for prayers."

"What has that to do with anything?" I whispered. "The village is busy at work, fishing and brewing and working the harvest. Does the Church think the *bons omes* and *bonas femnas* are what keep good Christians from their prayers?"

"They need someone to blame." Dominus Bernard's youthful beauty faded a bit when he looked as pensive as now. "Dominic de Guzmán, the founder of their order, was convinced the Church had grown lax and stagnant from Tolosa to Narbona and beyond. Perhaps it had. But he looked about him, saw the friends of God, and decided they were the reason. That's where the trouble began."

"You are a man of the Church," I said, "and this is your native land. What do *you* think?"

He raked his hands through his curly hair. "I . . . I think these inquisitors vaunt themselves too much. The Crusaders did their work and leveled these lands. Soaked them in blood. But still a few friends of God remain. So now these inquisitors think to bring the war to each *castrum* and village in the region. Their inquisition will succeed where we village priests have failed, they say, since the Dominicans are so much smarter than us priests, with all their theology studies. They're forcing the *senhors* and nobles to do what they wouldn't do before the war: execute heretics and brutally punish those who were kind to them."

I turned over his words in my mind.

"They should abandon this mania," Bernard said. "The *bons omes* and *bonas femnas* are fugitives now. In another generation they will all be in their graves. Why punish people for bowing to them decades ago, when that's what everyone did?"

"You don't seem very worried about heresy," I observed.

He leaned in closer. "Don't tell the friars," he said, "but my own uncle was a *bon ome*. He feared God as much as the pope. Our family bowed to him hundreds of times. Thousands."

"But surely," I said, "that all lies in the past."

Dominus Bernard shook his head. "Not to the inquisitors, it doesn't. One fear enflames them: falsehoods destroying the faith. So where we see neighbors being neighborly, they see heresy spreading. We see a lad bow to an uncle; they see a sympathy forming that will damn the lad to hell when he's grown. 'Little foxes,' they call the heretics, 'spoiling the vineyard of the Lord.' What they don't understand, they destroy. And they believe they please our blessed Savior by doing so."

I shivered. How close I'd been to Friar Lucien de Saint-Honore. Thank God, he had believed Symo's tale about who we were.

Dominus Bernard clapped a warm hand on my shoulder. "Don't worry about them, Botille," he said. "We are small and poor in Bajas. They'll not trouble themselves with us."

"Why?" I asked. "Aren't the poor just as vulnerable to heresy as the rich?"

Dominus Bernard laughed. "Very amusing. The Dominican friars own no property, as other religious houses do. When they conduct an inquisition and convict a heretic, the nobles often confiscate their goods and wealth. They'll even convict the dead, dig up the bones and burn them, to shame their names, and sometimes to snatch property from their heirs. From this treasure, the inquisitors and their order are paid. They are performing a service, you see, for the counts and lords. Ridding their lands of falsehood."

I rubbed my arms. The chapel felt cold, but I was beginning to see.

"So, naturally," the priest went on, "they concern themselves mainly with inquisitions in places where there are offenders with goods worth confiscating."

For the first time since our conversation began, I took a deep, relieved breath. "Just as well."

"To be small and unimportant, Botille," said my priest as I bid him *bonjorn*, "is true freedom. That's why I like Bajas. When you're my age, you'll see what I mean."

MAURINDA

ust outside the town of Raissac-d'Aude, an old woman watched her grandchildren play on the grassy bank of the wide Aude River. Her name was Maurinda, and she had seen a great many things in her long life, many of which she would much rather not have seen.

But days like these offered sights more welcome to tired eyes, when autumn colors brushed the leaves, when cooler air meant grapes and olives and relief from August's oppressive heat. The blue of the sky, sharper than memory, bluer even than *la mar* itself.

The prettiest sights of all were her grandchildren. Five of them, through God's grace, and the tireless body of her daughter, Esquiva. Esquiva was all Maurinda had left, but she'd married a decent man, and God had blessed them with many children. Strange that after so many sorrows, so much loss in the wars, God should allow Maurinda these comforts in her later years. Her mother's generation had lived joyfully in their youths, in the old, colorful, courtly Provensa before the war, before the hated French crusaders came. Her mother, her aunts, her mother-in-law—their bitter cups came at the ends of their lives, but now, for Maurinda, sadness and loss were in the past.

For here they all were, these delicious children. Two *tozęts* and three *tozas*, brown and red, round and fat. Their cheeks, so full, their eyes, so bright. In all the world, Maurinda thought to herself, there were never such pretty children. She was too old to be much help in the fields, but this Maurinda could do for her daughter, to earn her keep: she could keep a hawk's eye upon the children. And she did.

Maurinda watched them invent games in the dirt and push each other about. She didn't mind. Children will argue, and if you stop them, they never learn how to fix things themselves. Much marital woe, she reflected, might be prevented by teaching little *tozęts* and *tozas* early how to properly fight with one another.

A movement down the bank caught her attention. A man in holy orders, all by himself, settling down to sit overlooking the river. Tall and lean, he was. A young man, dressed in white and black now dusty with travel, his shaven head curly with new hair.

Maurinda firmly returned her gaze to the children. Three, four, five . . . They were all there. The second to youngest, Garina, was slippery as a fish, and just as drawn to the water. Maurinda dared not take her eyes off her.

But now little Garina had caught sight of the man of God. She called to her siblings and wandered over to him on her chubby legs.

The other children, more inhibited than Garina, watched as their sister toddled up to the holy man and climbed right into his arms. He was so surprised that he did not resist, but supported her weight cautiously, as though she might break, while she stretched her brown arms around his neck and kissed his whiskered cheek.

Maurinda knew she should get up and intervene. But old bones prefer their rest. She watched to see what would happen. Some infants are gifted with special grace, and Garina was one of these. Maurinda hoped the man of God would see it.

Slowly, as if he'd once known how to but had since forgotten, the young friar gathered his arms around the child and patted her back. She pulled her face away and regarded his, then jabbered at him in that dear way she had, asking him questions without waiting for answers. *She'll be telling him about the dog,* Maurinda supposed, *though he won't understand a word.*

The young man answered, and the baby beamed and released another torrent of babble.

Then the child called to her siblings once more, and they crept forward one cautious step at a time. The youngest, smaller than Garina, lost her courage and ran to her *mima*, but the three older children made their way to Garina's discovery. They circled the seated young man and watched him watch their sister. Baudois, the oldest boy, dared to greet the holy man with a proper bow. Maurinda nodded. *That's right*. Bon eṇfan, *Baudois*.

The holy man rested his hand atop Baudois's floppy-haired head. The two other children nestled close to the young man on either side, like nursing pups to their mother. The baby in Maurinda's arms peeked at the scene, then buried her face in her *mima*'s neck.

"It's all right, *galineta*, my sweet," Maurinda told her. She rose with a creak and settled the *eṇfan*'s weight upon the hip that bothered her less, then headed over to the children.

With a closer view, she decided that she liked the holy man's face.

"A blessing on you," she said to greet him.

"And upon you, and upon these children," he said in return.

"Are you well?" she asked him. "Tired from travels?"

The holy man smiled. "I am well enough. *Grácia*."

But he wasn't, quite. Maurinda noticed him wiping a tear from under his eye. "What ails you, good brother?" she asked. "Have the little ones been careless and injured you by mistake?"

His face seemed to glow. "I am not hurt. This little one . . ." He shook his head. "Our Lord spoke truly when he said that of such is the kingdom of heaven. She has brought me heavenly peace."

Maurinda smiled. "What brings you to Raissac-d'Aude? I gather, from your speech, that you're not from this place."

"The Aude led me here." He settled Garina on her feet and rose to stand on his own. "I followed the river in search of a lost soul. But I have found no sign of the person I seek. I sat down here with great heaviness, and thought I now must return to Tolosa in disappointment. I have already been gone far too long."

"Tolosa!" Maurinda tutted in sympathy. "On foot? No wonder you're weary."

"You have not seen a *donzǫlla* pass by? A runaway? Thin and dark and travel-worn?"

Maurinda shook her head.

The friar swallowed his disappointment. "So be it. I will find her."

"Of course you will." Maurinda patted his arm. "Come refresh yourself and eat. My son-in-law, Gardoz, and my daughter, Esquiva, will welcome you gladly."

Maurinda was pleased that he agreed. Esquiva would be too. This guest would honor their house. Little Garina took him by the hand and chattered as she drew him toward their *maison*. Maurinda hefted the baby higher and shepherded the three other children along behind them.

"Don't lose hope," she told her new companion as they neared her daughter's small dwelling. "The river draws everyone to it sooner or later. The only thing that draws the river is the sea."

He stopped. His young escort tugged his hand in vain. "The sea," he whispered. "God has heard my prayer." He turned and smiled at Maurinda, and the beauty of it made even her cheeks blush. "I must send a letter."

BOTILLE

he sun was nearing its peak in the sky when I returned home from the church of Sant Martin. Fishing boats' bells called to one another, and to me, but I resisted the temptation of another walk along the water and went inside.

The tavern was empty except for Plazensa, and fragrant with her *pọl sọpa*. After making sure we had no customers, I asked her, "Has she woken up yet?"

"Once," was my sister's reply. "She ate a little porridge and went back to sleep."

"Poor thing."

"I heard her talking to herself for a long time," Plazensa whispered. "You'll need to speak to her about that. We'll have a hard time hiding her if she jabbers like a madwoman."

I wondered what it must have felt like for Dolssa to wake up alone in our small room. Her journey here in Symo's barrow must have seemed to her like a terrible nightmare.

"Have you taken some food next door to Martin and Lisette yet?" I asked my sister.

"Oh, would you?" she asked. "That baby fussed all night. Lisette probably can't see straight today."

I filled an urn with *sopa* and stepped outdoors, then pushed my way through Martin and Lisette de Boroc's front door.

The Lisette I knew would never have tolerated the mess that greeted my eyes. I pushed through a curtain to find her perched anxiously upon the edge of her bed, clutching her baby in one arm and trying to coax him to latch on and nurse with her other. She looked ghastly. It was not for lack of experience that she struggled. Her two-year-old daughter sat on the floor, banging a stick against the wall and watching me with large, serious eyes.

"Bless you for coming, Botille," she said. "This baby won't eat. Won't sleep, won't stop crying."

I set down the pot of food. "Give him to me," I ordered, "and eat something."

Together the babe and I paced their house, and I attempted to tidy up as I went, but their son wouldn't stop squalling in my arms. It took both my hands to hold him snug. To be sure, I felt badly for the poor mite, but it wasn't long before my sympathies were greater for his mother. No wonder she looked so tired and so worried. If this child didn't fill his belly well and soon, he wouldn't thrive.

We went outside, and I greeted the goats that wandered over to gently butt my knees, and picked Lisette some plums. Her father, the goat-cheese man, came up from their cool cellar. He eyed the baby with trepidation.

"I keep to my cheeses," he whispered to me. "The cellar is the only place where I can't hear the child."

I understood.

I bounced, I bobbed, I shushed, I soothed, I sang, but no matter what I did, the baby wouldn't settle. Even the goats ran off to avoid him. Finally I went back into the house with the child and the fruit, and handed both to Lisette. She thanked me, and I slipped away. I would return to bring meals, I told myself, and I would say a prayer for poor Lisette.

Back at the Three Pigeons, a sailor sat at the bar, finishing a bowl of *sopa*. Sazia washed tables, and Plazensa pounded on a dark mass of bread dough. She already had a pot of eel stew simmering for supper guests. Mimi would not leave the hot pot alone. She could never resist a fish. I took a bucket and went outside to fill it at the well several times, until I'd filled a pan on the coals and started filling another one.

"What are you about?" Plazensa wasn't pleased at my splashing.

"A bath," I whispered, "for Dolssa."

Sazia looked up. "Poor thing needs it," she said. "I'll help."
When all was ready, Plazensa locked the door to the tavern and
joined us.

We opened the door to Dolssa's room, armed with suds and
steam. Sazia carried a bowl of *sopa* and a mug of ale. I carried
two pans of hot water, and Plazensa's arms were filled with a dish
of soap, a vial of oil, cloths, a blade for trimming, and a lavender
concoction of her own. Mimi slipped through the gap just before
we shut the door behind us.

Dolssa knelt upon her mat, praying. She finished, then greeted
us with a worried look.

"What are you doing to me?"

"Don't fear," Sazia said. "We're helping you get cleaned up
after your long journey."

She edged away from us, toward the wall. "*Grácia*," she said.
"I'll tend to myself."

Plazensa placed her things on the floor and sat to peel off
Dolssa's stockings. "No one," she said, "refuses the help of the
Flasucra sisters. We're the helpfullest help you'll ever find."

I loved these moments, when we three worked together. The
sense of our mother, of her magic in our fingertips, tingled in the
air about us. Perhaps, it amused me to think, Mamà was Mimi today, or Mimi was Mamà. The gray cat sat primly in a corner with
her tail curled around her feet, watching the spectacle.

"Eat." Sazia held a spoon of hot broth up to Dolssa's mouth.
She looked reluctant, but she obeyed. I wasn't surprised. Strong

men melted under the influence of Plazi's cooking.

I got to work unbuttoning Dolssa's dress. I paused as I saw her eyes roll upward and close, her lips muttering silent words.

"Is she putting a hex on us?" Plazensa asked.

"She's praying," I whispered. "It's all right, Dolssa. You don't need to pray for protection from us. We want to get you clean so you can mend."

"Aiee!" Plazensa let out a cry as she peeled a wool stocking off our patient's foot. We crowded around to look.

The skin was black with filth and dried blood, but the toes looked waxy and yellowish under toenails grown too long. Burst blisters oozed with pink discharge. Rotten skin peeled away. The smell of sickly flesh assailed our noses. Mimi approached to sniff.

Plazensa ripped off the other stocking and looked away.

This was serious. Such wounds could take infection or abscess. She could lose a foot. "Into the water," I said firmly, and raised both Dolssa's knees to submerge her feet in my larger bucket. She winced at the heat of the water, then sank into a rest.

"I'm not an unclean person," she said weakly. "My maid, Monica, used to bathe me. . . ." Her eyes grew red, and she began to shake.

"Sopa," demanded Sazia, the tyrant. I was happy to have my little *sorre* distract Dolssa with food while I removed her remaining clothes. The rest of her body was not so frightening as her feet, but she was dirty everywhere, bruised in places, bitten by lice, and weakened by hunger.

"Poor child," Plazensa murmured. "Poor little bird."

We propped her up with pillows while Plazi sponged her sore skin. I dunked Dolssa's hair in my other bucket and rubbed soap and water through her long, draggled locks.

"We'll need more hot water," I told Sazia, and she went to refill the pans.

While Plazensa whistled and splashed, Dolssa's eyes met mine, though upside down, as I cradled her head over a bucket. "Why are you doing this?" she murmured. "You don't even know me."

Her sopping hair hung from her face, leaving her looking weak and pitiable. She reminded me of a bedraggled Mimi one time when she grew too adventurous, playing in the surf. I wanted to laugh, but it would be cruel. The poor girl was bewildered and terrified.

I remembered something my mamà used to say. "God knows you," I said. "God knows just what you need."

Dolssa's eyes filled with tears. Poor tired thing—even the least kindness was too much for her.

"What are you two saying?" demanded Plazensa.

I smiled at my sister. "We're discussing your beauty. I say you're the prettiest *femna* in all Bajas, but Dolssa here says all of Europe."

"Oh, pah." Plazensa busied herself with scrubbing and worked hard not to smile. Dolssa's face betrayed a rising sense of panic.

Plazensa removed one of Dolssa's feet from the water and rubbed soap into her skin. When it reached her wounded toes, she hissed through her teeth. Plazi carefully wiped away the suds and rubbed the poor foot with a rag. She worked her lovely fingers carefully around the mangled toes, then, with her knife, deftly pared away the offending nails.

Dolssa vacillated between flinching with pain, cringing in embarrassment, and sinking into the comfort of our ministrations. But every time she caught herself reposing in our care, she would jolt herself back to alertness and fear.

"Are you cleaning me up," she whispered, "for some particular use?"

"We don't plan to fry you and eat you," I said, "if that's what you mean."

Sazia returned and resumed force-feeding our charge, then helped me wash her body with wet cloths until it was time to re-fill our buckets with fresh water. There was no sound but the soft splashing and the sibilant shush of our breathing. Slowly, gently, we washed away the residue of her ordeal fleeing Tolosa. It re-minded me of when Plazensa and I would bathe little Sazia after Mamà first took sick.

Sazia worked a comb patiently through Dolssa's long, wet tan-gles. Finally we both joined Plazensa in rubbing her chafed and harassed skin with oil, anointing her hair and neck with laven-der. Plazensa wrapped Dolssa's cleaned and oiled toes in soft, dry cloths, then pulled some knitted slippers of her own over the ban-daged feet.

Dolssa finally seemed to have settled into a sleepy peace. She had ceased resisting our attentions, and gone limp. I was glad to see it.

"It's important that you know," she told us, "that I am a virgin for Christ."

Plazensa's lips twitched. "Good for you. Are you bound for a convent, then?"

The girl shook her head. "No. I . . . I just wanted to make sure you knew, in case . . ."

"Good." Plazensa nodded firmly. "Remain a virgin, then, until you marry. Men like to imagine that's how every girl—"

"Oh, but I won't marry," Dolssa said breathlessly. "I couldn't ever."

Sazia chimed in. "I don't blame you. Watch out, though. My sister Botille could persuade a eunuch to take a wife. No one's safe around her." She pulled a nightshirt over Dolssa's head and shoulders while Plazensa and I stripped her bed and spread fresh sheets for her.

My thoughts returned to Senhor Guilhem and the mystery lady I'd concocted. Dolssa's virgin pledge was an unwelcome twist. If she wouldn't marry, what safety was left for her?

"Finish your broth, and back to bed with you," ordered Plazensa. "You need sleep if you're ever going to return to strength."

Dolssa submitted to Plazensa, as most people do, and lay down upon the clean bedding. Plazi and I spread a blanket over her.

"I'm curious," I said, "why you're so concerned that we know about your pledge. It's scarcely our affair."

Dolssa pulled the blanket up to her chin and nestled down under the blanket like a child. Mimi claimed a space next to Dolssa's knees, prodded it with her claws, then cozied up beside her.

Dolssa's eyes were wide as she peered up at me. "I assumed you were . . ." She yawned. "Aren't you grooming me to be one of you?"

"Grooming you?" Plazensa laughed. "To be one of us, sisters! Why, you dear child . . ."

Dolssa's heavy eyelids closed. "Not a sister," she murmured. "A prostitute."

Plazensa carried Dolssa's clothes into the front tavern room at arm's length, pinched between her thumb and forefinger, as though she held a dead rat by its tail.

"To be a *prostitute*, like one of you," she fumed. "Of all the outrageous insults . . ."

Sazia coughed and glanced at me. I wouldn't meet her gaze for all the gold in Roma. If I laughed now, Plazensa would make me sleep on the muddy beach for a week.

"Ungrateful little wretch!"

She dropped the dirty clothes into a wash water bucket, and commenced pounding the clothes with a paddle.

"Oh, let be, Plazi," I said. "You know it's what everyone thinks about women who work in public houses." I took over her laundry pounding for fear she'd smash right through the pail. "Remember, she's not like us. She's from a wealthy family in Tolosa. One that can afford to keep their daughters pious and holy."

"Unlike the rest of us," said Sazia with a toss of her frizzy hair, "whose daughters must grovel in the gutter to earn their daily bread."

"Is that what you think?" Plazensa's eyes flashed. "That we *grovel* for our bread? Is *that* what others think?" Her voice rose a notch with each question.

"Well, we used to steal it. . . ." Sazia wrenched open the door to the cavity in the stone fireplace that served as our baking oven. The hot smell of Plazensa's black bread tantalized us.

"I'll grovel for a chunk of your bread right now, Plazi, if it'll make you feel better," I told her.

Sazia slid a board under the loaf to pull it out. Plazi shooed her away. "Get you gone," she said. "That bread's for customers. Who does she think she is? A nun without her habit? A virgin bride of Christ?"

We were distracted then by a tapping at the window shutters. I poked through the honeysuckle vines to see Astruga peering in at me.

"Oh, *bon*, Botille," she said. "It's you."

"So you see," I said. "I live here, after all. What is it, Astruga?"

"Have you found me a husband yet?"

I sighed. "Obviously not."

She thrust out her lower lip. "Well, get on about it."

"Give me time, Astruga," I whispered, for out of the corner of my eye I saw Plazensa growing inquisitive.

"I haven't got time, as you well know." Her hand went protectively to her belly.

"Astruga," I said, "be reasonable. I haven't forgotten you. But these things don't happen overnight."

Again, the pout. "Yes, they do."

She was beginning to annoy me. "And that's why," I said through smiling teeth, "people usually seek for my services *beforehand*."

She shrugged. No contrition from this quarter, not that I had expected any.

"How soon can you find me a man?" she asked again. "I need one fast."

I shook my head. "Astruga, you are going about this all wrong. Tell me. Help me do my work. Why should someone want to marry you?"

She took an affronted step back and held out both her arms, displaying her figure. When I said nothing, she favored me with a flourish of both hands, outlining the contours of her more than adequate womanly curves.

"So what?" I said. "You have bosoms. You haven't answered me. Why should someone want to marry you?"

Her nose poked the clouds, she was so indignant. "For this!" Again, her physique.

"What's going on over there?" Plazensa called. "In or out, but leave off with the window talk!"

"Never mind my sister," I said. "Astruga. When it comes to

marriage, the men of Bajas are more sensible than you suppose."

She was having no part of this outlandish notion.

"Yes, you're pretty enough," I said, "but what else can you offer? In a wife, a man wants a sound choice. Have you a dowry?"

"A bit," she said. "More than some girls from Bajas."

That would help. "Can you do anything?"

Her mouth hung open at the question.

"Cook?" I supplied.

Again with the nose. "Course I can."

"Hmm," I said. "I hear otherwise. Sew?"

She shook her head. "A little."

"Make wine?"

She looked away. "Papà does that."

"Tan leather?" I said. "Make soap? Keep bees? Spin wool?"

She thrust out her lip so far, I wanted to snatch it with my finger and thumb and give it a good twist. "I can make babies," she hissed. "And that's what matters most."

"Oh, *oc*," I said, "men like that in a wife. But a fair number like to think they discovered their wife's skill in that area themselves."

Astruga's face screwed up in fury. "You'd best find me someone quick, Botille, or so help me, I'll—"

"You'll what, Astruga?"

Her nostrils flared while she searched for just the right revenge. "I'll scream!" She turned and marched up the hill to her papà's house.

ESCLARMONDA DE MONSOS

Witness Testimony recorded by Lucien

City of Narbona

Esclarmonda: fifty-two; married wife; living
with her invalid husband outside the city

rom Tolosa? You've come a long way.

There was a time when I liked to roam about too. I used to visit my sister, south of here, along the lagoon. Her husband fished it, before he died. I haven't seen her in years. These aged feet of mine won't let me travel. She's still there, last I knew, eating what her son drags up from the sea.

You are looking for a girl?

I have seen no one of that description, Friar. Dolssa is a curious name.

Oc, yes, there are *tozas* aplenty, but local ones, all of them running about chasing the *tozęts*, priding themselves on their hair and their round, red cheeks. Their turn will come. A man will woo them, babies will delight them and break their hearts in turn. Like my son, Niot. What good is he to me now, dead in the wars? Such a curly-headed babe he was!

I have seen no one like the *donzęlla* you describe.

You want to ask my husband? Ask him if you like, but his wits are no longer his own. He keeps to his chair. He will have seen nothing, nor could he tell you if he had seen your *donzęlla*.

Oc, I might have missed her, but I watch the road and the river. Ever since the aching took hold of my feet. I sit here and watch the world pass by, since I can't go greet it myself anymore. I can't swear she hasn't been here, but I can say I'm fairly certain she has not. Are you sure she came this way? Might the angels already have taken her?

What will you do now? Keep looking?

There is a convent just up the road, in Narbona, Friar . . . Lucien? Friar Lucien. Listen! Those are their bells ringing, even now, for prayers. If you follow the river, you will come to it eventually. The Brotherhood of Sant Esteve. Perhaps they could help you there with your search. If nothing more, they would welcome and feed you.

Try the village, then, if you want to ask others.

Oc, oc. If I see any sign of a girl such as the one you seek, I will send you word at the convent.

God speed you on your errand, and may you find the girl you seek. God protects and keeps his own, does he not?

HUGO

enhor Hugo's horse picked its tired way up the winding, wooded lanes of the mountain where the Abadia de Fontfreda lay hidden from view. On either side of the path, peasant harvesters and lay brothers shouldered wooden crates of grapes through leafy vineyards. Hugo already knew he could count on a bed for the night, and information. Perhaps there would also be good wine.

If he looked behind him, acres of fertile countryside stretched down the mountain, bathed in blue sky and golden sun. Bees worked alongside the lay brothers, and all was peace. *To end one's days in such a place . . .* thought Hugo.

Finally a turn in the path brought buildings into view, and the walls of a grand abbey church. He passed fragrant herb gardens and flowers tended by silent, sweating laborers in the September sun. He reached the stables, and a lay brother hurried out to take his horse.

"*Bonjorn*," Hugo said to the brother, who bowed in reply and then led the horse away. Other brothers, Hugo saw, had taken note of his coat of arms. The abbot would be here before long to greet him. He'd better hurry.

For such a place of holy contemplation, the *abadia* swarmed with activity. Other travelers and pilgrims toiled up the path, as did brothers guiding donkey carts full of grapes. Stonemasons perched on scaffolding and chipped away at column heads. Dozens of lay brothers came and went, while from beyond the walls to their refectory, the voices of the monks in song filled the drowsy air with sweetness.

"Good friar." Hugo accosted a youthful lay brother, then bowed to him. The brother's soft face blanched at being so addressed by a noble knight, and he hastily bowed in return.

"Is there a place here where visitors may come to pray?" Hugo asked the young brother.

The quivering youth gestured toward a small chapel tucked against the hillside.

"And do you see many travelers stopping here for sanctuary in their travels?"

The lad nodded.

"Has there been, by chance, in the last few weeks, a noble

donzella, dark of hair, and slight of build, traveling alone?"

He frowned and shook his head at such an unlikely picture. His cowl appeared to itch his neck.

"Tell me," said Hugo, leaning closer to his ear. "I am also looking for information about a party of peasants passing through. They had one older *ome*, two hearty young *omes*, one youth, and two *tozas*. Two donkey carts, and some other animals. Have you seen them?"

The young brother's eyes lit up. He nodded solemnly.

Hugo dropped his voice to a conspiratorial whisper. "Tell me, my friend," he said. "It would be a blessing if you happened to know where they were going."

The brother shook his head sadly, as if regretting he could not be of more use.

"No matter," Hugo said. "Now, here is a curious thing. It was said of this party, by some, that they carried a foul-smelling cargo. Some horrid, offensive odor. Did you notice that?"

His companion took a step back and shook his head.

"No odor that you detected?" None. Hugo shrugged. "Not all tales can be believed."

The young brother began to show signs of wishing to be anywhere but here. The glow, it seemed, of conversing with a noble knight had lost its luster.

"One final question." Hugo spoke before his captive could escape. "Did this party, by some chance, have any wish to bury a body?"

The lay friar shook his head so fast, his chin wobbled. He bowed, pressed his hands together, and fled.

Hugo watched him go, and nodded. *Bon.* He intended to find her alive. This news held no guarantee he would, but he was satisfied. Then doubt set in. Was this party he'd seen pass, and later heard tales of, a waste of his time?

The abbot, flanked by monks, emerged from an arched doorway and made his stately way toward his noble guest. Best not to seem too inquisitive to him. Unsuspecting lay brothers to interview would be plenty. Moments would appear, and Hugo would know how to seize them.

BOTILLE

Pealing bells woke me before the sun had begun to peep over the lagoon. It was Sunday, but these weren't Sabbath bells. Someone had died.

I threw a blanket over my shoulders and stumbled through the dark corridor to the front room of the tavern. My sisters followed like haggard ghosts, wrapped in anything they could snatch. We threw the latch and ventured out into the street.

Autumn had come in the night. The air bit my throat, and my breath fogged before me. Leaves' edges had begun to turn, and the lagoon brooded quietly upon the prospect of approaching cold.

When no one opened the door next to us, I began to fear it was Lisette's baby, but of course they would not ring bells for an *enfan*.

Soon Lisette ducked through her low doorway with the child, quiet for once, in her arms, and tall Martin, who had to bend double to clear the door, hunching along beside them, carrying their sober little daughter, Ava.

Up and down the road the doorways opened as the bells still rang. We counted ourselves and counted one another. *Oc*, we were still there. We saw our neighbors and were glad they were not gone, but each revelation brought new fear. Who had left us?

Then the name slid along the strands of peasants roping through the streets of Bajas: Felipa de Prato. Young mother and farmwife. The one whose blessed and fertile fortune my little *sorre* had only just foretold.

Sazia turned away. Lisette reached with one arm to embrace her young daughter, and kissed the crown of her sleepy head.

Plazensa enveloped Sazia with her blanket-draped arm and held her close. Sazia hid her face in her hands. I wrapped my arms around them both. Plazensa met my gaze.

"Was it the pregnancy?" she whispered.

I shook my head. "No one said so to me." Did anyone even know about the pregnancy? Did her husband, Joan de Prato?

"Maybe she wasn't pregnant." Sazia spoke from the hollow of Plazensa's collarbone.

Plazi stroked her hair. "Hush. Of course she was."

"I must have been wrong." Sazia's breath caught in her throat, but my proud sister would not cry. "If I was wrong about her prospects, I must have been wrong about her child."

Felipa already had two young children, who were close to starving. I supposed that was why the news of this third arrival had not filled her with joy.

I steered my sisters indoors. Up and down the street, somber Bajas slowly returned to their homes. Inside the tavern, we sat down together at the bar, and I poured Sazia some ale.

"I am through with telling fortunes." Sazia's voice was flat. "What cruelty is it to give a dying woman false hope?"

"Oh, Sazia, you mustn't do this to yourself," I said. "Giving hope to the dying sounds like mercy to me, not cruelty. You believed what you said was true."

"And you were right about it. She died from her pregnancy," said Plazensa firmly, as if she could settle the matter. "She probably didn't follow your instructions."

"No, don't," moaned Sazia. "Are you saying it's her fault she died, for not following my advice?"

Plazensa chewed on this. "Not her fault, I'll grant you," she said. "Perhaps she was too poor to eat the foods you told her she needed. What was it? Leeks? Melons?"

"You don't die," Sazia told her ale, "for want of melons."

"But you do die," I said, "for want of food, if you're ill. Felipa was very thin."

"They had a farm," Plazensa protested. "It's harvest time! Remember the *legums* she brought us when she wanted Sazia to tell her fortune?"

Sazia took a mournful swig of ale. "Don't remind me."

"Maybe," I said, "they were most of the *legums* she could find. Remember what Sazia said? That Joan de Prato needed to get off his *aze* and water his crops?"

Plazensa rubbed Sazia's back vigorously. "It's a crime! For a mother to starve right under our noses!" She flexed her fingers, as if she were ready to tear justice out of someone's skin. "Maybe," she said on further thought, "Felipa wasn't so much worried about his cheating as about starving. And about her *enfans*."

Sazia was miserable. "She probably always fed them first."

"The *enfans*," I repeated. "Plazi, what's cooking today?"

She nodded, rose to her feet, and began poking around shelves. "There's *fogasa* left over," she said, "and some nuts, and plenty of cheese."

"Plums," Sazia suggested, "from Lisette's tree."

"Ale." Plazensa produced a pitcher. "At dinner we can take them something hot."

"Thank you." I kissed both of their cheeks. "I'll get dressed and take the food over, and see how the *enfans* are doing."

"If you need to, bring them here," said Plazensa.

Sazia and I looked at each other. "That's dangerous, don't you think?" I pointed toward the room where Dolssa still slept. "Hard to hide her from little children."

My older sister frowned. "Then arrange for someone else to look after them," she said. "No telling whether that man can look after his own self now, much less his little ones."

"I'll go look after them," Sazia said. "I owe poor Felipa at least that much."

And so, Bajas, all of us, we drifted to the de Prato home. The late September winds blew through our clothes, but we didn't feel them. We wandered in, and we wandered out. We listened to the low songs and prayers Dominus Bernard murmured for Joan de Prato's benefit. We listened, because the hollow-faced widower could not. His thoughts were somewhere else.

We left bits of food like offerings at a shrine. Felipa's two children, a boy and a girl who seemed nothing more than round faces on *flamenc* legs, watched us come and go, then dove into the food. The poor mites were too young and confused to know they'd lost their *mamà*. The one thing they knew well was hunger. Today, inexplicably, a feast had arrived, pot by pot, in their small home. I wondered if, in days to come, when the little ones realized what had happened, the rare memory of full bellies would confuse their hearts about what had truly happened in their lives this day.

We drifted home. We gnawed on *fogasa* we couldn't taste, and washed it down with wine. We drifted back up the hill to mass. Far more of us than usual went to hear Dominus Bernard that day. After the liturgy, he spoke of resurrection, and we cried for the poor sad babes too hungry to understand their *mamà* had flown.

BOTILLE

hat has happened?"

I brought Dolssa some food and found her seated, leaning against the wall, stroking Mimi and looking longingly at the weak light filtering through the doorway.

"*Una femna* has died." I set down her bowl of porridge, and Mimi slipped closer to investigate. "*Una maire*, with young *enfans*. *Un filh* and *una filha*. And another was on the way."

Her wide eyes held my gaze. A thousand lifetimes lay there, and somewhere, the maiden Dolssa de Stigata hid behind them, behind her torments. Could she venture out, I wondered, into our world enough to feel this loss?

"Was she ill?"

"Not that we knew." I sat down beside her. "Some illnesses, the eye doesn't see."

She closed her eyes for some time. Her lips moved.

She'd gone far away again. I wondered if she remembered what we'd been talking about, or even that I was still with her in the room. When she spoke, it surprised me.

"The poor little ones."

"*Oc.*"

We sat. Up front, in the tavern, customers began arriving, looking for Sunday's lunch. Plazensa's dulcet voice greeted them as ever, but in a somber hue today. Through the wall, Lisette's baby fussed, and his *mamà*'s footsteps paced.

"Do you have a mother, Botille?"

"I had one, of course," I said, "but she died when I was six. A wasting illness."

Dolssa's lip trembled. "I am sorry."

Was she crying for me? "Don't be sad." I put on a smile. "It was years ago now." I leaned back against the wall beside her. "Little Sazia was only three. Like Felipa's oldest *tozęt*."

Dolssa wiped her eyes on the nightshirt. Released from her dirty clothing, washed, and dressed loosely as she now was, she seemed a new creature altogether, as though some of her pain were bound up in the fabric of her old garments. She seemed younger and more frail. Her body, I considered, wasn't all of her that was starving and wounded.

"You should eat your porridge while it's hot," I said. "I put cream in it for you. If you finish it, I'll cook you an egg. We need to put some meat back on you before you disappear."

Her long lashes opened slowly as she regarded the food. "Was it a peaceful death?"

I was taken aback. "Felipa's? I don't know, I haven't heard—"

"Your mother's." She turned toward me again, and I felt the gaze of those eyes, like lanterns reaching both to me and through me. As though she could see me both today and that long-ago day, equally well.

"I wasn't there," I said. "None of us were. She faced her end alone. It was I who found her body."

After midday, Sazia went to the de Prato home to look after the children. I promised I'd look in on her when things settled down at the tavern.

"So Sazia plays *la maire* today," observed Plazensa as Sazia climbed the hill. "I wonder how she'll do."

"Well enough," I said.

Plazensa shoved a chair aside with her hip. "Have you ever seen her tend to children?"

I tried to think. Surely, I must have.

"She has no use for them," my sister said, "until they're old enough to not be boring."

"And what age is that?" I inquired.

Plazi winked. "Her own age, at the very least."

Less than an hour had passed after Sazia's departure when Joan de Prato entered the tavern. Or rather, his ghost did. His face was so sunken, and his back so stooped, I would have said he had thirty more years on his soul than the thirty-some he'd earned by rights. His elbows propped up a head too heavy to bear. Plazi poured him a cup of wine, no charge, and patted his hand.

He worked on that wine all afternoon. Men squeezed his shoulders. They embraced him. Some sat down and wept their sympathies into his ears. But Joan de Prato heard none of them. He couldn't.

BOTILLE

On Monday we buried Felipa. Nights may have grown cool, but days were still too warm for a long viewing season. Her abject husband could no more greet mourners in his home all week than he could afford to offer them food and drink. So Na Pieret's servants, Jacme, Andrio, and Itier, dug a grave in the churchyard, and we gathered around and listened as Dominus Bernard bid her keep company with the angels until the first trump should sound. He gave a very fitting homily, did our curly haired parish priest.

Sazia listened, with a child's hand clutched in each of hers. Felipa's stunned children, it seemed, had finally grasped what their *mamà*'s dying meant.

"I can't bear it," Sazia had confided in me earlier that morning. "It would be better if they would cry. It's the most piteous thing. They just sit and stare. Yesterday wouldn't end. I couldn't comfort them even if I were the comforting sort." She showed me her hand with a wry smile. "See how helpfulness is rewarded—their cat bit me."

I gave her hand a kiss. "I'll send someone else to relieve you, *sorre*."

Na Pieret came to the burial with Symo and Gui. They stood on either side of her like guardian soldiers. Like sons. It made me glad to see how proud of them she looked. Na Pieret had always been generous to our poor in Bajas. I hoped her nephews would carry on her legacy of courtesy when they inherited her place in the village.

Several times during our priest's remarks I caught Astruga peering intently at me from under her shawl. She had meaningful glances for everyone—for Dominus Bernard, who would not return her gaze; for me; for poor, helpless Sapdalina, my other client; and for Gui, who took no notice of her whatsoever.

After the family threw handfuls of soil into the grave, Jacme, Andrio, and Itier finished the job. Symo and Gui joined them. I sidled over to Na Pieret to inquire after her health.

"Never better, Botille," she told me in a low voice. "These *filhs* of mine have made me young, although"—she made the sign of the cross and glanced at the filling grave—"sometimes even youth is no protection."

I slipped my arm through hers. "Such a sad tale. The poor *enfans*."

"You'll look after them, won't you, Botille?"

I nodded. "I'll poke my nose in."

She squeezed my arm. "It's what you do best."

A sad commentary on my talents. "They are treating you well, then?" I asked. "These great big baby *filhs* of yours?"

She chuckled softly. "*Oc*. My sons are very good to me. Hard workers, too. My sister did a fine job with them."

"*Bonjọrn*, Botille." Gui of the Great Teeth returned to his *tanta* and greeted me. Symo the Troll only glowered from under his gigantic eyebrows.

"*Bonjọrn*, Gui. How do you like our little Bajas? Do you miss San Cucufati?"

Astruga appeared beside me and flicked her lashes at Gui.

"Won't you introduce me, Botille, to our newcomers?" she said.

"Gui, Symo," I said, "this is Astruga." I fixed a winning smile upon her. "The *tozẹts* have come here to help their tanta Pieret look after her vineyards."

All Bajas knew this, of course, but these were the courteous games we played. As matchmaker, I never stopped playing them.

More eyelashes. "How generous of you both." By *both*, she meant Gui, whose hand she took and held tightly.

Gui's eyes met mine in alarm. "How fares your sister, Botille? Is she in good health?"

I nodded toward where Sazia stood with the family.

"As you can see, if you look," I said, "Sazia is in excellent health. *Grácia*."

He coughed and extricated himself at last from Astruga's grip. "I'm glad," he said. "Ahem. And how is your other sister?"

Astruga's face bunched up in a fit of annoyance.

"You mean Plazensa," I said. "Bossy as ever."

"Plazensa," Gui repeated slowly. "An enchanting name."

"But you can't marry her," Astruga cut in.

We all stared at her. Symo cleared his throat noisily.

"Hsst," Na Pieret said, rescuing us all. "There goes the family. Now we follow."

Senhor de Prato shuffled away from the grave, following the measured footsteps of Dominus Bernard. Sazia took up the rear with the children, and the rest of Bajas followed in a somber clump behind. On we proceeded, with Astruga as determined to place herself beside Gui as he was to avoid her, and Symo scowling at the whole business, while the rest of Bajas wept all the way to the de Pratos' little *maison*, then dispersed to our homes.

Astruga dogged me all the way home from the burial that afternoon.

"Gui is very pleasing," she said brightly.

I would have none of her attempts at cajoling me. "Is he, then?"

"The handsomest man in all Bajas!" she gushed. "Excepting the married ones, and those who can't marry." A fitting little burst of honesty from a girl pregnant with a priest's child.

"High praise, from you," I said. "Is it old Plastolf di Condomio who makes your heart beat faster? Or is it our Jobau?"

"You're vexed with me," she said. She gave me her meekest, humblest gaze, complete with eyelashes. The eyelashes went a step too far.

Oc, I was vexed with her for her selfish pique from yesterday. What she didn't realize, because she was Astruga, and spoiled beyond all measure by her indulgent *papà*, was how livid I was for her cheek at Felipa's burial. To flaunt and flounce herself so at Gui, amid all those mourners! Had she no courtesy whatsoever? No shame? No respect for the bereaved, or for the dead? I shuddered to think of Felipa looking down from heaven upon such behavior.

Truth be told, though, I was surprised Gui had no use for her. Perhaps he had better judgment than I had reckoned. No woman alive can compete with Plazensa, but Astruga was right. If Gui wanted my sister, he'd be disappointed. Thus he would be harder to marry off than I'd guessed. Oh, this I needed, atop everything else. A fastidious wooer and more desperate women.

I didn't want to lead Astruga anywhere near Dolssa. So I let my footsteps follow the slope past our house and toward the water.

"I'm trying to find you a husband, Astruga," I said. "Be patient, and give me time."

"But time is what I don't have, Botille!" she whined. "What am I going to do? It won't be long before I'm fat, and everyone will know what I've done!"

I picked a spiral snail shell from the gritty sand and chucked it into the lagoon. "Nothing wrong with fat. Men love it."

"You know what I mean." There was that lower lip again. I hoped Dominus Bernard had enjoyed it in his season, for I was ready to yank it off. "Baby fat. A belly."

"Then I suggest," I said, "you eat like a cow, starting now, and pray you'll grow nice and round all over to hide that baby longer."

Her face fell. "You hate me, don't you?" she said. "You think I deserve this, for my sin."

There it was—the gleam of ordinary humanity, the window through which I could pity her. Was she toying with my sympathy on purpose? Or was she sincere?

"Astruga," I said, "if you knew how many of Dominus Bernard's pregnant *enamorat* I have led to that priest's very own altar, you'd know how little I judge anyone for succumbing to him. I am not in the business of troubling over other girls' sins. My job is to clean up the—"

"How many?"

"Hm?"

"How many girls has he . . ."

Santa Sara! "You're hopeless, Astruga."

She twisted away from where I could see her face. "He . . . he told me that I . . ."

I took her face between my hands and made her look at me. "Of course he did," I said. "He's a scoundrel, and that's what they all say."

Her eyes grew red.

"Oh no," I said. "You're not still fond of him, are you?"

She broke away and rubbed her eyes angrily with her sleeve.

"Astruga," I said. "I don't care a nut for what you did. I will find you a groom. But you act like I'm not to eat another bite of bread until you've picked your wedding flowers."

She watched a handful of wet sand fall in indifferent lumps through her fingers.

"I'm driven mad by the fretting, Botille," she said softly. "I need something to do besides wait for the secret to get out. Anything."

Church bells tolled midday prayers. They reminded me of Felipa.

"Then get yourself to the de Prato home," I said, "and look after those poor motherless children. Their father can barely see straight, much less tend to their needs."

Her eyes grew wide with horror. Out came the lower lip. The old Astruga was back.

"I meant, what do I do to find a husband?"

I hitched up my skirts and headed up the slope. "I know what you meant," I said. "Leave that to me, and go help those children."

She ran after me. "But what do I *do* with them?"

"Feed them," I said. "Clean them. Scold them. Don't let them hit each other."

"I know nothing about tending children!" she cried.

I stopped so suddenly, she collided with me, then glared at her belly.

"I . . . Oh," she said. "*Oc.* I see."

"Have you noticed," Plazensa asked me that evening, one of the dozen times we collided behind the bar, serving supper guests, "how busy the tavern has been ever since—"

"My journey?" I supplied.

"*Oc,*" she said. "Your journey."

It was true. We cooked three times the dinner and supper to feed the customers who now showed up regularly. Before, we often had days when no one joined us at all. True, the weather brought more ships into port, and harvest labor kindled appetites, but we'd never seen this.

"It's her," I whispered. "I saw this on the road. Blessings follow wherever she goes."

"Ow!" Plazi burnt her hand on a hot turnip. "Listen to this, Botille. At noon we ran out of ale. All I had were batches fermenting. The soonest any would be ready was a week from now."

I watched as she poured a foaming glassful from the jug in her hand. "So . . . ?"

"So, if you're patient, I'll tell you. Ordinarily, I would never do this, because ale needs its time. But something told me to try this jug. So I pulled the stopper. It was perfect."

I sniffed the jug. It certainly seemed as ripe as any ale Plazensa had ever brewed.

"*And,*" she whispered, "I've been pouring from this jug all day."

We stared at each other. Plazensa nodded solemnly. All day. No jug held that much. It was a miracle.

She placed another log on the fire and poked at the ashes. A second batch of turnips was already roasting in a pan buried in the coals, and she fretted over whether they would cook in time to feed her customers. "Oh, Botille, I need you to run to Na Pieret's and buy more wine off old Garcia." She grinned. "Too bad I don't have wine aging in the cellar, but I suppose even miracles have their limits."

If Plazensa was pleased about the increase in traffic at the tavern, Jobau was not. A full tavern disturbed his drunken reverie up in the loft over the great room. He slid down the ladder at dinner, to the wonderment of the guests, and limped down the hall to an extra room. Plazensa only just managed to steer him away from Dolssa's.

The door opened then, and Sazia appeared. Astruga had kept her word and released my sister from her self-inflicted penance. She sat down on the one empty stool at the bar.

"I," she said, "will never, ever, ever have children."

Plazensa watched her with an amused expression. "Here, *sorre*," she said, "have some salmon." She flaked off a generous portion onto a dish, added a turnip and a dollop of oil. "Tell us all about it as you eat."

Sazia looked around at the floor for her usual welcome, but didn't find it. She looked pale and worn tonight, and her face fell when she couldn't find her cat. "Where's Mimi?"

I nodded toward the back. "With her."

Though Sazia would die before admitting it, I'd have sworn she envied Dolssa her place as our cat's new favorite.

Sazia picked at her food, ate a few bites, and pushed her plate away. "I'm worn out," she said. "Those children took all my strength. I feel awful. I'm heading to bed."

Plazensa's eyes flashed. "And leave my cooking to go to waste?"

Sazia ignored her. I reached for her abandoned dish. "I'll eat her fish, Plazi."

"She's leaving all the cleanup to us tonight," Plazensa fumed.

"Never mind," I said. "Leave her alone. I'll take her share of the work." Sazia was often gloomy, but this wasn't like her, to look so blue. She must still feel guilty about Felipa's death, after the fortune she'd given her. Stubborn girl! We'd told her a dozen times it wasn't her fault. Whatever troubled her, the last thing she needed was a furious Plazensa vexing her.

Plazensa stayed in a foul mood long after Sazia shuffled off to bed. She made sure to leave two-thirds of the dishes and mess to me. After such a busy day at the tavern, the pile was enormous. Plazensa made a point of heading to bed when her pile was done.

Finally I was free to undress and climb into bed beside Sazia. She slept, but uneasily, moaning and muttering to herself. What dreams, I wondered, could upset her so? She quieted down after I lay next to her, so I soon went to sleep myself.

I woke in the night to find Sazia's hot arm splayed across my body. In pushing her away, I felt her skin. She burned with fever.

I called to her to wake her up, but she wouldn't rouse. I called again, and still no answer.

I screamed for Plazi. I fell to my knees next to Sazia and prayed.

Plazi was there in an instant. She felt Sazia's skin.

"She's burning up," she said. "I can't see anything. . . . Get candles. It's her hand that's hotter than anything. Sazia! Wake up!"

Her hand? I stumbled down toward the tavern and attacked the banked ashes with a candle from the mantel. The sleepy embers wouldn't do their work. I puffed at them and watched them scatter.

Finally the lazy candle lit, so I lit another and hurried back down the hall. By their light we saw our little *sorre*'s pale, damp face and dry, cracking lips. Her hand had swollen like a rising lump of dough. A dark red splotch appeared in the corner of skin between finger and thumb. She wouldn't wake up.

"What happened?" Plazi's voice was barely a whisper.

I stared at the horrifying hand. "I don't know."

"What do we do, Botille?"

I shook my head. If Plazi didn't know . . .

I hurried for a bucket and a cloth, and began wiping Sazia's face and neck with cool water. I was sure it would rouse her, but she was too far gone.

We were losing her.

Then I remembered. "The cat," I told Plazi. "She said the de Prato's cat bit her yesterday."

"*Mon Dieu*," Plazensa wept. "I can't bear it. A cat? A devilish cat could do this?"

"*Mon Dieu, mon Dieu*." I chanted Plazi's lament over and over. God in heaven. Hear me. If anyone could help our sister . . .

Dolssa.

I ran across the hall and burst into her room. Dolssa sat up and blinked in confusion at the candlelight. I wasted no time on explanations, but dragged her to her aching feet and across the hall to the room where Sazia lay.

She gazed in sleepy horror at the sight that met her eyes. Then she looked at us. "I'm so sorry," she whispered. She backed away from the sickbed. "She looks close to the end."

"Then do something!" I hissed. "You're the holy one who talks to God all day. You're the maker of miracles. Heal our sister."

Dolssa shrank back with each word. She clutched her night-shirt to her throat and shook her head. "Who said I . . . ?"

I went back to cooling Sazia with my damp cloth. "You are," I told Dolssa. "The ale in the tavern. The bread and cheese in the bag. I *know* that was you!"

Her eyes were wide as moons. She shook her head vehemently. "I'm sorry, Botille," she said. "I'm so, so sorry. But I don't know what you're talking about. I can do no miracles."

Plazensa seized fistfuls of her own hair and wailed.

"You can," I insisted. "I've seen you do them."

Dolssa shook her head. "I am nothing," she insisted. "I have no gifts, no power. I have never done anything like what you ask."

I gathered Sazia's lifeless body in my arms and held her close. "Then start."

But my only hope, my holy woman, stood there like a limp and skinny ghost.

I could not, could not lose Sazia. I could *not* lose my own *sorre*, my flesh, my little baby child whose food I once spooned into her rosebud mouth. How would I sleep without her? How would I go on?

Foolish hope, to think this stranger could alter nature!

"Try, Dolssa," I pleaded. "Ask. I know you can."

Dolssa took a timid step forward. "My beloved could heal your sister," she whispered. "If he were here, I could ask him."

Plazi's face was frantic. "Your beloved is a *medicus*?"

"No, Plazi." I watched Dolssa's face. "Her beloved is Senhor Jhesus."

Dolssa stared at me. *How did you know?* Her face demanded an answer. I wasn't sure how I knew. It came to me. Just as thoughts had done when I first met Dolssa by the Aude.

"God in heaven, it's true." Plazensa's eyes, watching Dolssa, were wide as moons. She shook herself. "What do you mean, if he were *here*, then . . . ?"

Dolssa's face was full of pain. "Once, he was always with me," she said. "Since my mother died, and I fled Tolosa, I've not seen his face."

"You saw Jhesus's *face*?"

Dolssa nodded. "I did, then. I told others of it. It's why the friars hate me so." She wiped her eyes. "But I don't see him anymore."

"Why not?" asked Plazensa.

Dolssa's fists were full of nightgown cloth. "I don't know." Her voice sounded like a young child's. "Perhaps my fear, my anger, or my grief displeased him. My cowardice."

Tears dripped off my face onto Sazia's burning cheeks and melted away from her heat. Dolssa would do nothing. My anger roiled. Her beloved was nothing. My last hope was nothing.

"Nonsense." I wept. "If so, your precious beloved is a monster."

Dolssa took a step back. "Am I asleep? Am I in a dream of hell?" Her mouth hardened. "How dare you speak such words to me?"

"He is!" I said. "What kind of love is so fickle, so cruel as that?"

"Botille, you blaspheme," Plazensa said. "At such a time as this, when we need a miracle, must you offend God?"

"Not God," I snapped. "Just this princess, who's never known a day's suffering, who's too fond of her maiden weakness to do something to help."

"How dare you?"

Dolssa's nostrils flared. Her lip curled in noble disdain. No more the fragile, dying bird at my feet, she'd become the lordly maiden once more, and I the peasant at *her* feet. It was a punch in my gut. And all the while, Sazia wilted in my arms.

"Watch your mother burn," Dolssa cried. "Be hunted like a wild pig across the countryside. Then speak to me of suffering."

I should've been ashamed. I didn't care. My words had fangs, and I was glad of it.

"You listen to me, Donzęlla Dolssa. Fair damsel, crying for her love." I bit each syllable. "No knight rides in to rescue you. You stand before me today because *I* found you fading, but I would not let you die. And I will not let my sister die, either."

We stared at each other. Plazensa, watching us both, threw up her hands, then fell at Sazia's feet to pray. I watched her curls sway as she shook with crying.

Oh *Dieu*. What was the point? Why terrorize this girl? She couldn't do anything. No one could. All was lost, and trying was pointless. A weary heaviness fell over me.

I watched Dolssa. *She's not really so proud,* I thought. *She's just afraid*. And I'd been a beast.

"Dolssa," I said more gently. "Dominus Bernard says Jhesus is everywhere. Whether you see him or not. So ask. Please."

Dolssa stood deathly still.

"Ask!" I shrieked.

Dolssa's eyes slid shut. Her lips began to murmur soft words. Sazia's weight pressed heavily into my arms as we waited, waited, waited.

Her words unceasing, her eyes still closed, Dolssa reached

forward and enveloped Sazia's puffy hand between her own frail hands. My sister's swollen flesh seemed taut between her finger-tips. Her breathing became more shallow. Her skin went cold. I pressed my face against hers and wept.

I opened my eyes and saw a man's shape in the doorway. *Dolssa's beloved.*

Then I realized. It was Jobau, watching his daughter die.

Plazensa cried out. I looked. A creeping flood of foul discharge burst from Sazia's hand, from the dark red cat's bite. Plazi stood back in horror, but Dolssa never moved, though the putrid filth flowed across her fingers as well.

Sazia shuddered in my arms, then inflated like a bellows as she drew a gulping breath. The last of the blood-tinged fluid left her hand. My baby *sǫrre* opened her eyes.

Plazensa shrieked and plastered Sazia's face with kisses. I held her close and rocked her back and forth.

"Get off me," grumbled Sazia. "What are you all going on about? Can't a body sleep?"

Plazi and I sobbed, and laughed. We sobbed some more, then beamed at each other, and at Dolssa. She backed away awkwardly. Plazi hurried over and knelt at Dolssa's feet to bathe her hands.

"Dolssa de Stigata," Plazensa whispered. "Never till we die will we forget this gift."

It was a moment when words were demanded of me, but I had none to give. Dolssa's eyes lingered on me, but I couldn't speak.

I lay in bed that night, listening to Sazia breathe. My morbid mind still churned through all that could have happened, what might have been. Sazia dying in my arms. Her precious heart gone still. Her fevered skin grown cold. What would I say? What would we do? Who would dig my sister's grave?

But *non*, praise the *bon Dieu*! She was here. She had not died. Her death was the fevered work of waking terrors. She was well and whole. Rescued by the mercy of my poor little bird's beloved.

I thought of Dolssa, across the hall. Did she sleep? What does one do after working a miracle? Go look for something to eat?

I thought of her wounded feet and her wide, dark eyes.

How I'd mistreated her. I ought to have been ashamed of myself.

She was just one girl. Yet the Lord God Almighty was in her fingertips.

Did I truly believe that?

God in our tavern, hearing Jobau curse! We'd be struck down for certain. Almighty God, entering our lives by pure happenstance. I, who peddled in ale, and wine, and brides—how could— why would—such holiness cross paths with *me*?

LUCIEN DE SAINT-HONORE

ucien pressed through a dark and clawing wood, fleeing a voice that called his name. Fear filled his veins. His breath, too loud in his throat, would surely betray him.

She came to him tonight, not as the hunted one but as the hunter. He quickened his steps, yet on she came, finding him by scent and not sight.

Now she was behind him, in a clearing. Her gaze prickled on his skin while the moon pulsed overhead.

He turned and saw her slowly approach him, step after step.

She had come to him in a soft robe of black and red. It fell open, and he gazed unwillingly, then willingly, into the whiteness of her breast. Her hair slipped from its confinements and blossomed over her shoulders, her hips, sliding over her face like clouds obscuring the moon.

As her face drew nearer to his, her hair parted, and her red lips opened and reached for his.

She stripped him of whatever possession he could once claim over his own flesh. She robbed him of his vows, his very will. She compelled him to reach forward and kiss and touch.

And in the taste of her kiss was a sweet liqueur. The wine of desire, the elixir of falsehood. This was the spreading of untruth, from lip to loins to heart. A warning.

The devil laughed, but Lucien—the flesh—succumbed.

Lucien woke in the dark on his mat of straw in the monks' dormitory at the Convent of the Brotherhood of Sant Esteve, drowning. He feared for his soul. He felt he might vomit. What he'd done could never be undone. Once lost, his innocence was lost forever. The shame, the stain—how could he ever look Prior Pons in the face? And what of his holy calling? He'd betrayed Christ's love for him—Christ, whose all-seeing eye penetrated the heart.

Around him the brothers of the convent of St. Stephen slumbered, some noisily.

Sleep. Oh, praise the *bon Dieu*. He'd been asleep. None of it had happened.

It was only a dream.

Sweet relief flooded his limbs. He was as pure as ever.

No stain could be affixed to him by the phantasms of sleep. He clutched his innocence about him as a cloak.

But that girl, that unholy *femna*, that cursed heretic who kept slipping through his clutches! Even now, wide awake, he felt her slim, carnal fingers unbutton his cloak of innocence and worm their way inside to the unruly flesh beneath. Their touch burned his skin.

Stop it, he told himself. *The dream is only metaphor.*

She symbolized all that would ruin Christendom. Ruin *him*. Consume *him*. Devour him with her blood-red mouth of lies and lusts and burnings.

He *would* be clean, even if the struggle killed him. So *she* must be the one to die.

He breathed deeply to calm his mind. He would remain with the Brotherhood of Sant Esteve until Prior Pons's letter arrived. Though the trail had all but gone cold—though he'd lost days when that lying Jew had sent him south along the Aude, instead of east— though Satan's servants thwarted him at every turn—the sea, he felt sure, would lead him to the heretic. But he'd been gone so long, perhaps too long, chasing a bird on the wing, and he needed approval from his prior to continue his search for Dolssa de Stigata. He would wait for it more vigilantly now.

More awake to danger.

PRIOR PONS DE SAINT-GILLES

Bishop Raimon de Fauga waited in the empty vestibule of the magnificent Romanesque basilica of Sant Sarnin in Tolosa after vespers. During the ending processional, he had seen Prior Pons de Saint-Gilles seated like a mere parishioner in a bench at the rear of the sanctuary. The bishop waited for him to exit, but he remained in his seat, so finally the bishop joined him.

"Pons?"

"Raimon."

The bishop waited for some further revelation, but none came.

"What brings you here tonight?"

"The choir."

Bishop Raimon's back troubled him, and these benches

weren't helping at all. He watched as minor canons snuffed candles, one by one, throughout the nave.

"Count Raimon's knight," said the prior. "Hugo de Miramont. Do you know if he's returned yet from his search for the runaway heretic?"

The bishop turned toward his friend, which sent a popping pain running up his spine. He gasped, then, to his surprise, felt some improvement.

"I haven't heard of him returning," he answered. "If there was news of her, Count Raimon would have let us know." The bishop twisted the other way in hopes of the same loud miracle, without luck. "You're sending out another band of inquisitors soon, aren't you? Perhaps they'll do better in the countryside."

Pons nodded. "Yes, I am. But they're not the reason I came." He reached inside his habit and withdrew a folded piece of paper. "I've just had a letter from Lucien."

"From whom?"

"Lucien de Saint-Honore." The prior searched for recognition on the bishop's face. "My young friar? The one who prosecuted the Stigata women?"

"Oh yes." The bishop looked to see if anyone was watching, then stretched his arms high over his head. "That was weeks ago now. Has he found her?"

Prior Pons shook his head. "He's been gone much longer than I had wanted. He writes wondering what to do next. He believes that where he has failed to find her by land, he can find her by sea."

Raimon shrugged. "The experiment failed. No matter, bring him home."

Pons folded the note and tucked it away. "I have already written to him at the convent where he is staying in Narbona to instruct him to return at once." He paused. "Don't you find it odd, though, Raimon, that two searchers have hunted in vain, so long, for this young woman? How has she eluded both of them so thoroughly?"

Bishop Raimon rested a hand on his companion's shoulder. "She's probably dead in a ditch. It is time to do what we should have done from the first: send out a raft of circulating letters to the bishops and parishes throughout the river valleys, probably along the Roman road—everywhere she might be. Warn them of her danger to the fold; instruct any with knowledge of her to contact us immediately."

Pons considered this suggestion. "Couriers will be costly," he said, "but not more than sending errant friars and men-at-arms to find her."

Bishop Raimon clapped a hand on the prior's shoulder. "We'll smoke her out, Pons, dead or alive. Most likely dead. Meanwhile, bring your friar home. And now, come have a drink with me. Are you hungry at all?"

Pons shook his head. "*Non, grácia.* I must get back." He smiled ruefully. "I didn't even tell anyone I was going out this evening."

"Authority," Bishop Raimon said, rising to his feet, "is a weighty burden. Even our Lord craved solitude at times. As a bishop, well do I understand your pain."

In the gloom of the old church at night, Prior Pons glanced heavenward and bit a reply off the tip of his tongue.

DOLSSA

Botille's rude words were a revelation. The night my beloved healed Sazia's hand was the first time I'd truly seen myself.

I'd been a child. A weak and whining, petulant child, crying out to my beloved that he should fix all my troubles. Spare me any pain, and run at my summons. Deliver me from dark roads and vulgar sinners and crude peasants.

How could I have been so blind?

Whose prayer did my beloved answer? Botille's, not mine. Whose hands did he send to help me? Peasants'. Botille's. Plazensa's. Even the whore Jacotina's.

To love as my beloved does, I must love all those whom he loves. In heaven, there are neither nobles nor peasants. Only children of God.

I saw my pride and vanity stripped bare. With shame I remembered that my bitter cup, though bitter indeed, was nothing to his. It was time to rise up and become a true woman, a worthy and courageous bride. Rise up, o my soul!

Yet in spite of my resolve, I could only pine for him, only wish him there with me.

I sat in my room long after the sisters had gone to sleep. Maybe, I thought, tonight he would come to me. Hadn't he heard my prayer? Wouldn't he now break his silence, part the curtains that had so recently hidden his heaven from my view? Wasn't Sazia's healing a sign that our estrangement was at an end?

I waited hours to hear his voice. All I heard was the wailing infant across the wall.

Come back to me, I pleaded. *If ever my love pleased you, let me see your face and hear your voice.*

Stillness. Nothing but the baby's cry.

Why would you heal her, I pleaded, *and not visit me? I who long for none but you!*

And then, this chilling thought: What if I never saw or heard my love again? Could I love him still? Could I prove my heart faithful in endless isolation?

Hadn't my beloved done the same, until his lonely, bitter death? *My God, my God, why hast thou forsaken me?*

All I had ever done was seek gifts from my beloved. It was time to offer them in return.

My love, for my love you will always be, what, I pray, would you ask of me?

MARTIN DE BOROC

Martin de Boroc sat in a chair, his daughter draped, asleep, over his long bony legs, looking more like a parcel of washing than like a human child.

His *filha* was hungry, and so was Martin, but they neither of them even thought of food that night, nor had they since yesterday, when Botille Flasucra, one of the sisters from the tavern next door, had brought them a pot of eel stew.

Martin's boat had not left port in days. Other fishermen were bringing in legendary catches, but not Martin. He could only sit and stare as his wife, Lisette, held their dying *enfan*.

Once Martin had thought the baby's cries would drive him to

distraction, but its moans grew feebler. *Cry, enfan,* he told the child silently, without hope. *Scream, and yell, and eat!*

The only light in the room came from dying embers. As always, the faint smell of spoiled milk hung in the air. Martin's father-in-law slept in the cellar amid his goat cheeses to escape the child's noise, and Martin couldn't blame him, though he hated him for having a place to flee to avoid this sadness.

Lisette's cheeks, once so round and soft, hung limp from her bones. Her eyes could hold no more tears, and her breast, no more feelings, and no more milk. She could only wait and watch with a slow, sustained terror for the end.

Every time she had tried to feed the child, it had tried to suckle, then given up. When Lisette squeezed milk onto his tongue, it arched its back and screamed. Other wet nurses were called. Goats' milk was offered. But nothing could induce this child to survive.

How many hours had passed since the sun went down, Martin could not tell. But tonight, he was sure, would finish the matter.

His tongue was dry. He needed to relieve his bladder. His left foot had gone numb from the press of his little *filha*'s bony hip. But these didn't seem like reasons enough to disturb her peaceful sleep upon his lap.

Martin didn't hear the door open. He heard no footsteps. But a *femna* appeared where there was not one before. Slim and pale, like a ghost in the firelight, dressed only in white, and leaning on the wall as she walked. Martin could see little of her face except for her large, dark eyes. He watched her like one in a dream. She made his skin prickle.

"It is the angel of death," gasped his wife, and she clutched the infant closer. But the young *femna* made no move toward the child. Instead she set to work building up the fire. She was slow. Each movement seemed hard for her. Gradually, she filled a pot with water and set it in the cinders, then draped a blanket over a peg close to the fire. She moved a chair nearer to the hearth. She gestured to Lisette, who sat in the chair as if in a trance.

Martin watched as the young woman reached her arms toward Lisette, asking for the child. She did not seize it, nor exert any compulsion. She simply held out her arms and waited.

Lisette wavered. She swayed from side to side in her chair.

"Are you living flesh?" she whispered.

"*Oc*. I am."

Still Lisette rocked. Martin had to strain to hear her next question.

"Will the child live?"

The *femna*'s outstretched arms never faltered. "If God wills it."

Lisette's breath came in shallow pants. Not for the first time, Martin feared his *enfan filh* was not the only member of his family preparing for the next world.

"What is your name?" she asked the mysterious *femna*.

Martin watched the *femna*'s face. Even from across the dark room, her eyes pulled at him, leaving him longing for something,

something he'd tasted once, or heard, or dreamed. He couldn't re-member what.

"My name," said the phantom, "is Dolssa."

Lisette seemed to struggle to think. "Where are you from?"

"I have no home," was the reply. "Here is where I live now."

Slowly, fearfully, Lisette surrendered her child.

As soon as Dolssa had the *enfan*, she enfolded it in her arms, cradling it close to her face. Martin blinked in the darkness. What was she doing? She was talking to the *enfan*, murmuring, singing, even laughing. And between every word, she kissed it, over and over. Kissed its cheeks, its nose, its forehead. Kissed its chin, its neck, its eyelids, its soft ribs and distended belly. Kissed its feet and knees and arms, uncurled its tiny fingers with her lips to kiss its little hands.

The child was not crying, Martin realized. He sat up with a start. Had it died? Had this Dolssa kissed it to death? His *filha* whimpered as his movements startled her. She shifted and nestled back into his lap to sleep.

The young woman poured a stream of soft words and kisses over the child as Lisette sat crookedly in her chair, with her limp hands hanging down. Before Martin realized how she'd reached his side, Dolssa was handing the baby to him.

He cradled the *enfan* in his rough hands and held it close to peer into its face in the dim light. It made no more mewling cries, but lay calmly, poking out its tiny pink tongue, which left its rose-petal lips wet and shining in the firelight.

Martin had never held his infant *filh* before. Why would he, with no milk to offer it? But as he watched the babe's eyes open and shut, its tiny nose pulling in air, its little mouth searching for something to drink, he yearned for the child.

He brought the baby close and kissed its downy head. He drank the scent of new skin through its shock of thick black hair.

The baby kicked its little foot.

Martin kissed the head again, and kissed one smooth cheek, then the other. He kissed up and down the fragile arms, the round loaf body. The child swung an arm and poked Martin in the eye, and he laughed and realized he was crying, streaming wet tears onto his son's head and chest, where they ran down into the crease of the neck. He kissed the tears away, only to add more.

"Live, little one," he told the child. "Live, *mon filh.*"

And his heart broke, for the child would not live, could not live, and now he loved him. He would have to bury that love along with his *filh*'s small body. And what use would he be to Lisette, in the days to come, a shattered man comforting a shattered woman?

Lisette. He had forgotten about her. And the strange visitor.

Lisette's back was still toward him, but where before she had sat lifeless and inert, now she leaned forward intently. Her elbows spread outward like bird's wings, and her hands were busy doing something. Martin couldn't tell what. The young *femna* knelt before her on the hearth, helping her, encouraging her.

The child stirred in his hands. Little squashed nose, a jutting, wrinkled forehead, and long twiggy fingers. This had to be the ugliest infant in Christendom, but for all that, he was much, much too perfectly formed to die. Martin kissed his nose, then nuzzled it with his own.

Lisette let out a cry. Was she hurt? Was the strange *femna* doing her an ill?

Then Lisette called to him. *"Lach!"* she cried. "Martin! *Lach*!"

Milk.

The woman appeared again beside Martin, wide-eyed and smiling, reaching for his son. He hesitated. If he parted with this peaceful, breathing child, would he ever see him again? Would this fairy, this specter, restore to him what she now demanded he relinquish?

"Martin," Lisette urged. "Hurry. Give him to me."

So he poured his tiny son into the woman's waiting arms and watched as she brought him to Lisette. She knelt and adjusted him upon a pillow on Lisette's lap. She fussed over him and murmured to his wife.

Martin couldn't bear it any longer. He scooped his unconscious *filha* into his long arms and arranged her bony limbs upon the bed in the corner. She moaned and stretched. He hurried to his wife's side.

Her eyes shone as she smiled up at him. "It's *lach*, Martin." She couldn't tell whether to laugh or cry. "This Dolssa has recovered my *lach* for our son."

Martin de Boroc's thoughts moved as slowly as the tide. It

was no wiser, thought he, to plunge into hope than into love.

"But, *galineta*," he said, "you had *lach* before, and he wouldn't drink it. What he drank, he didn't keep."

The woman named Dolssa ceased her fussing and stood back to display her handiwork. There lay the child, his mouth latched firmly on to his mother's breast. His cheeks and neck pulsed with his suckling like the rhythmic throbbing of gills on a sea bass.

Little *tozet*. His little *filh*.

The stillness of the room filled with the whiffling, snorting, smacking sound of the child's breathing and swallowing. He kicked and grunted in his eagerness to eat. Martin knelt and took the child's wrinkly foot and kissed it.

"What's come over you?" teased his wife. "Next thing you'll be playing nursemaid to the wee babe." She beamed down at her infant. "Little swine," said she. "My greedy baby pig."

At last the child relinquished his hold, and Lisette patted his back over her shoulder until she was rewarded with a fruity belch. She offered him more to drink, and he settled in eagerly.

"I don't know, Donzella, how we can ever thank you," said Martin. His throat would not cooperate, and his words squeaked. He turned in embarrassment toward where the mysterious *femna* sat watching.

But she wasn't there. She wasn't anywhere. As silently as she'd come, she'd gone.

BOTILLE

f I dozed the rest of that night, it was only to rest my eyes.
I watched over Sazia, but my thoughts were on Dolssa.

Dawn was not far off when I thought I heard footsteps from
Dolssa's room. I stole out of bed, took my still-lit candle, and
poked my head inside her chamber.

She glanced up in wide-awake surprise. She was sitting upright in her bed, adjusting her blankets as though she were just now
settling down for the night.

"Haven't you slept either?" I asked her.

She seemed unsure of what to say. "Not yet."

I couldn't bring myself to meet her gaze. All my rudeness and
ingratitude barred my way. But I had to fix it. "May I come in?"

She watched me strangely. "It's your *maison*."

A reminder of my coldness. "It's yours now, too." I sat at the foot of her bed. "If the food ran low, Plazi would kick me out and keep you."

Laugh, Dolssa. Relieve my guilt. But she didn't.

"I'll try not to eat much," she said.

"No! Eat all you want," I stammered. "It was a stupid joke. I didn't mean . . ."

Her wide lips smiled, a little. "I know."

Then neither of us knew what to say.

"Does the food run low sometimes?" Dolssa asked.

"Not since you've been here," I told her. "But, *oc*, of course it does. That is life. That's why we love harvest time."

She watched me curiously. "Yet you would bring me here and share with me what you have, when you don't always have enough."

Who would not do the same? I wanted no praise for that.

"And you expect nothing from me. No payment. No service."

No prostitution, I almost said. I stifled a smile. "Oh, I don't know," I said. "We may eventually have you slice a carrot or two. Chop an onion. But only when it's safe to come out of hiding." Then I remembered that she had probably never done either thing in her comfortable former life. "Never mind. I didn't mean that. You don't need to—"

"I would be most honored," Dolssa said with a smile, "to chop an onion with you." She laughed. "If you'll teach me how."

"There's nothing like a good onion," I said, then wished I hadn't. But Dolssa didn't seem to mind, nor think me a fool.

We sat in silence. Dolssa nestled down into her bed. Her eyes closed, and she began to drift toward sleep. The sight of her feeling safe and peaceful reminded me of the shivering, muttering, frightened creature we'd carried back from San Cucufati.

A nightingale poured out its morning joy, not caring that most of Bajas was still abed and wishing to remain there for another hour.

"I had a nightingale near my home in Tolosa."

Dolssa's voice came from far away. I was surprised she was still awake.

"He lived in some trees that grew by the river. I would lie in bed and imagine he was a fair knight, coming to sing to me outside my window."

She opened her eyes to find me watching her, and blushed.

"I came to know his song so well, I fancied I could tell him apart from other *rossinhols*." She laughed. "You must think I'm ridiculous."

I patted her knee. "A lover knows her beloved's voice."

She smiled. "That is right."

"And *your* beloved," I told her, "knows yours."

She looked at her hands. Her eyes shone wet in the candlelight.

I took a deep breath. "Dolssa," I said. "I was wrong. My words were not only unkind, but untrue."

She looked at me strangely. "Oh no," she said. "You were right."

I shook my head. "You're not here because *I* wouldn't let you die. You are here because God would not. You owe me nothing. He sent me there. He kept me from telling the friar about you." In that moment, I realized that if I had, Sazia would now be dead. It left me cold. "I nearly did tell the friar, you know. I was sure a man of God could help you."

She shuddered. "Not that one."

She cocked her head to one side. How like a bird she often was. And those bright, dark eyes.

"I understand you," she said. "But I also know there were many people who passed by me on my journey. And none of them were called to hear and help me. Or if any were, they did not stop. But you, Botille. You did."

It was my turn to stare at my hands.

"My beloved knows you, too, Botille."

I wasn't sure what I thought of that. But I couldn't resist teasing her. "Are you jealous?"

She laughed. "Terribly." Then she grew more serious. "You said exactly what I needed to hear. Don't apologize."

I refused to be pardoned so easily. "It was cruel. It's not how I see you. Not at all."

Dolssa watched me thoughtfully. Then an idea seemed to strike her. She moved over on her bed, and patted the space beside her. "Lie down," she said. "Let's get some rest."

I felt shy. I should get up and go back to my room. I should check on Sazia. But she was fine, and I knew it. Better than fine, with God watching over her.

So I joined Dolssa. She nestled down under her blanket, tucked it over me, and rested her head against my shoulder. Her breath soon settled into a long, slow pulse, while her warmth spread to cover my legs and feet. There was nothing more to hear but her quiet breath, and the plaintive song of the *rossinhol*.

If I'd encountered Dolssa in her old life, we would never have spoken. Someone of her rank would have no use for one of mine. The same could be said of my sort, as we looked with contempt or envy upon our betters.

Yet here we lay, we two, after all we'd been through, after all she'd suffered, and all my eyes had seen. I'd needed her, that night, to heal Sazia. Perhaps, for a moment, Dolssa had needed me, too. How curious. How rare. How little we ever know anyone.

Between the shutters, I caught a glimpse of one bright morning star.

Oh, Dieu, I prayed. *I have never assumed you thought much of me. Nor would I expect you to. But you've brought me here to help your beloved. I don't know how, but you walk with her. My little bird I found. Show me what you want me to do for her, and I'll try. I'll do all I can to keep her safe. For Sazia's sake. And for Dolssa's.* I paused a moment. *And for mine. Amen.*

BOTILLE

W e slept late. I crept from Dolssa's room with the morning sun high in the sky and found Plazi still in bed. We lay there together, drunk on joy. Dolssa had snatched our *sǫrre* back from certain death. Heaven itself had come down to our little tavern.

We let Sazia and Dolssa sleep even longer. But once we'd explained to Sazia what had happened to her, she fell at Dolssa's feet and kissed her hands. Plazi and I eyed each other. Never in our lives had we seen our surly *sǫrre* behave like this. From then on, Sazia's gaze followed Dolssa adoringly. Dolssa glanced at me in helpless desperation. I only laughed.

Plazensa cooked Dolssa and Sazia such a breakfast as Bajas

had never seen. She sent me running, bartering here and there for bacon, hunting through our chicken coop for eggs, even pulling two onion beauties from my special patch for the morning feast.

We crowded into Dolssa's room to eat it. Even Jobau came. Poor Dolssa nearly died of fright. She had no idea who he was. Jobau ate some food. Sazia tolerated him. More miracles.

After breakfast I ventured to Na Pieret's vineyards in search of Garcia to haggle for more *vin*. It was a perfect autumn day, with sea breezes off the lagoon cooling the warm sunshine of late September. All nature, I felt, celebrated my joy with me. Blue, blue, blue were the sky and the sea, golden the hazy sunlight. Leafy vineyards chattered in the wind, but not as much as the army of Na Pieret's harvesters did as they sliced fat clusters off the vines.

I found Jacme and Andrio lounging in the shade under an old stone wall and gave them the tongue-lashing I knew Na Pieret would wish them to have. They paid my scolding not a chestnut's worth of attention. Perhaps I was too glad to truly harangue them.

"Find me a wife, Botille," said the great bushy-bearded Jacme. "One who cooks fit for a queen, with an *aze* fit for a king!"

"Take your foolish talk away from me, Jacme," I retorted. "I'll find you a wife when you have more than two shillings in your pockets to feed her with. What's your cooking wife to bake her dainty dishes with, fish bones and lizards' heads?"

"Can you cook?" said that reprobate. "After half a pitcher of *vin*, even you'd be pretty."

A shadow fell over my shoulder. I looked up to see Symo standing there listening to their insults.

Lovely.

He carried a long knife for slicing the woody grape stems, but now it looked like a weapon in his hands. But that may have just been his usual dragonlike expression. He said nothing, but leveled a look at the two wastrels—his own servants now. They rose to their feet and slunk back to work, muttering to each other when they thought he could no longer hear.

Symo's glare in my direction was no more friendly than that he'd given to his hired hands. No salutation, no kindness to a *femna*. No courtesy whatsoever.

At least one of us bowed. "*Bonjǫrn* to you, too, Symo," I said.

If those glowering eyebrows were any thicker, they'd sprout leaves. When he was an old man, I'd wager, it would require a blade like his grape trimmer to mow them into submission. If he reached old age, that is—if someone didn't murder him for general orneriness first. I preferred to avoid the brows, and their owner, so I resumed my walking along the path that wound through farm plots and vineyards, up to the high lookout over the lagoon.

"What do you want?" He jogged to catch up.

"Nothing from you," I said. "I'm on my way to see Garcia. The tavern's out of wine."

"You can't see Garcia," said my sour-tempered companion. "He's sick abed."

"Sick?" I said. "Garcia? He's never sick."

"I suppose your word makes me a liar," said Symo. "He hasn't come to work today."

"Poor man." I looked about. "Which of Na Pieret's servants can sell me wine?"

He paused in his tracks and stuck out his chest, the peacock. "You don't need to ask a servant," he said. "You can ask me."

"Oh, can I deal directly with the heir to the estate? How fortunate I am today!"

It was fascinating, the way his features bunched up when he was angry. And he was so often angry that I never lacked for opportunity to behold this marvel.

"Get off with you, then," he snapped, "and find your *viṇ* somewhere else."

I'd prodded him too far. This wouldn't do. There was no one else whose wine Plazensa wanted. A thorny burr was this new son of Na Pieret's. And worse, now I must placate him.

"Pay no heed to my teasing," I said in a sweeter voice, though it choked me. "It's just our way here in Bajas."

He marched onward, but since we were heading in the direction of Na Pieret's cellars, I took this as a good sign.

"I'd be grateful," I said, "if you would sell me your wine. It's what Plazensa prefers, and there's no crossing Plazensa."

He favored me with an answering growl. "Hurry up, then. I can't be all day about it."

I quickened my footsteps to keep pace with him, and when a

few minutes had passed with no further sarcasm, I risked combining two errands into one.

"All the young maidens are aflutter at your arrival in Bajas," I said. "Now that you're so well settled, with such good fortune in your prospects, and by all report, such an able vintner, it's certain you'll be thinking about marrying."

Sarcasm returned in full measure. "Oh, so you read the future?"

"Not I," I said. "That's Sazia."

"Then you read minds?"

"Still Sazia." I smiled. "Though Plazensa also does a fair job of knowing what I'm up to."

We reached the cellars, which were really a cave that had been excavated deeper and framed by a small hut. Symo pulled open the door and disappeared into the darkness. I followed unbidden and watched as his head vanished into a hole in the ground.

His voice echoed up through the cave. "Your sister this, and your sister that," his ghost voice said. "Don't you ever think on your own? Don't you do anything besides meddle?"

"Meddling is my special skill," I bellowed down the hole. His head poked up before I'd finished, which left me bawling into his left ear.

"Sorry," I said.

Symo hauled two large jugs of wine onto the floor of the hut, then hoisted himself up to my level and counted my shillings.

"The money's all there," I said. "I'm no cheat. But tell me, what do you think of Astruga? Remember, I introduced her to you yesterday, at Felipa's burial?"

He only gave me a look, then loaded the jugs onto a small one-wheeled barrow. "Can you push this yourself, or shall I send a lad to help you?"

"You can't deny she's pretty," I said. "What a figure! Longest, thickest hair in all Bajas." Excluding Plazensa, but we needn't quibble.

Symo pushed the barrow, and with it, me, out the door. "You can take her hair, and her figure, elsewhere. Be off with you. An-drio!" He beckoned to that young *ome* to come help me.

"I don't need Andrio," I said. "Leave be. But you should think more on Astruga. She's—"

Symo set down the barrow. "If I had to listen to that"—no word seemed sufficient to contain his contempt—"that *female*, prattling and simpering every day of my life, I'd jump into the lagoon and float wherever the tide took me."

"Well!" I said. "Look well to yourself. With your temper, Lord knows how difficult it will be ever to find you a wife in Bajas who suits you."

His face reddened. "The day I need *you*," he said, "to find me a wife, is the day I—"

"Is the day you realize just how far your savage manners will take you here!" I cried. "You've got no cause to come here, Senhor

Nobody from Nowhere, and think that just because your rich *tanta* has become your *maire*, and given you her all, suddenly you're too good for everyone and everything."

His face was inches from my own. His eyebrows were poison-tipped darts.

"You pestilent wench!" he hissed. "Don't meddle in my affairs."

"I won't," I snapped, "and you can die a lonely bachelor." I seized the barrow and lurched down the hill with it.

"Better to die alone," he shouted after me, "than to live with a prating female!"

"Better a prating female," I retorted, "than a man who's a devil!"

I rattled all the way back into town feeling particularly pleased with myself. For planting a first nuptial suggestion, I thought, it had gone well. Symo's type always resisted loudly at first, but I'd bet the coins still jangling in my pocket, he'd pay closer heed from now on whenever Astruga walked by.

BOTILLE

I returned to find the tavern fragrant with freshly baked *fogasa*, and Plazensa haggling with Focho de Capa over the price of four plump pheasants.

"Botille!" cried that fat and jolly man. "Na Pieret bids me tell you and your sisters to come as honored guests at Saturday evening's feast to celebrate her nephews' arrival."

Focho de Capa did a little of everything, and a whole lot of nothing, but whenever there was a party, there he was, lord of the revels, master of drink, player of *fidel* tunes, and caller of dance steps. There was no feast in Bajas without Focho. If there were, we'd sit and stare at one another without knowing what to do. Today, though, poacher was his trade.

"Never mind that," Plazensa said, chopping carrots with fury. "It's robbery what you think to charge me for these fowl. So be it. I don't need roast pheasant. I've got plenty of beans, and Botille's onions, and I can always go to Amielh Vidal for a pair of nice fatty ducks."

I kissed Focho's whiskery cheek and left them to their argument, and took two flat loaves of *fogasa* without Plazensa's notice, not that she would have minded.

One was for Lisette and Martin next door. I hadn't heard the baby fuss all morning, and I was worried. I entered the house, and my heart sank. No fire burned on the hearth. Nothing moved at all. There on the bed lay the still forms of Martin, Lisette, and the baby. At midday, in sunshine such as this? I hurried over.

They were all so still. I was sure something terrible had happened. I opened my mouth to call their names.

Then the baby made a soft murmuring sound and twisted its head slightly. Lisette, without waking, moved a protective hand toward the child and patted its belly. Martin snored.

I realized then that I was not alone. Their young daughter stood beside me, watching me through dark, serious eyes.

"Are you all right, Ava?"

No response.

"Are you hungry? Are you frightened?"

She didn't even blink. I sighed and reached out my hand. "Come with me, then," I said. "We have things to do." I broke off a chunk of their *fogasa* and handed it to her, then left the rest on the table. She gnawed on it as we climbed up the hill toward the town. Crumbs and dribble spread in a slow patch down her dress front.

Next we went to the humble de Prato *maison*, and knocked.

Astruga opened the low door and ducked out, looking ready to bite the ear off anyone there, until she saw it was me. Then she looked ready to bite both my ears. From behind her came the sounds of children squalling. Peering past her, I saw Joan de Prato sprawled upon his bed, snoring drunk.

"So it's you," she said.

"*Bonjǫrn*, Astruga," I said. "Ava, say '*bonjǫrn*' to Astruga."

Ava said nothing.

"A fine *sǫpa* you've stewed me in, Botille," Astruga said through clenched teeth. "Easy enough for you to say, 'Go help those children.' I don't see you here, bruising your ears on their noise, pinching your nose at their filth."

I handed her the *fogasa*. "Some bread for the children," I said. "God reward you."

"That little *tozęt* wets himself," she hissed. "At three! And you knew it before you sent me here, didn't you?"

I clutched Ava's hand tighter and backed away. "I swear I didn't, Astruga."

"I'll never forget how you tricked me into doing this," she said. "I'll finish the day, because someone's got to get to the bottom of this reeking mess, and then I am *through*. Done. Going home. Do you hear? Find someone else to come look after the little beasts."

"Astruga," I whispered. "Hush your voice. They've lost their mother."

"If I stay here another hour," she cried, "I'll lose my head!" She ducked back through the low door and slammed it shut.

Ava's bread-crumbed face regarded mine, as though she expected a comment.

"Come on," I told her. "Let's go home."

Those poor children. Were they more unfortunate than they'd been before Astruga appeared to inflict her care upon them? Perhaps my instincts had steered me wrong this time.

I brought Ava back to the tavern and sat her in a chair at the bar with an apple. Plazensa made a welcoming fuss over her while I slipped away and headed for Garcia's *maison*. If illness was in the air, I had no right to bring a child there.

I found Na Pieret standing outside the door to Garcia's home.

I bowed. "*Bonjorn*, Na Pieret. Should you be here? You mustn't get sick."

Na Pieret took my hand. "At my age, Botille," she said, "I can get sick if I want to."

I wrapped my arm around her waist to support her. "Bajas would be lost without you."

"*Non*. I have my sons. I can go in peace when the *bon Dieu* calls me." She squeezed my hand. "That is why I can afford to wait here for news of my faithful Garcia."

I didn't like the way Na Pieret spoke, as though she were already choosing her burial clothes. Inside, Garcia's wife moved between two beds. *I should go in,* I thought, but I was not eager to catch an illness.

"Have you felt ill at all?" Na Pieret asked me.

I was surprised. "Me? Not a bit."

"I have wondered," she said, "if this illness is something Garcia and his son caught in their travels." She turned my face toward the light, and I blinked against the sun. "But of course you and your sister are well, and so are the *tozets*."

"It will pass," I said. "Garcia wouldn't miss Saturday's feast."

She looked worried. "Ah. The feast. I told Focho to announce it yesterday, before I knew about Garcia."

I wondered if Dolssa could help. But I mustn't bring her out of hiding. "We will pray for them," I said.

Na Pieret smiled a little. "Really? That's kind of you."

"You sound surprised," I said. "Why is that?"

She leaned against me once more. "Some people pray for the sick," she said, "while others bring them dinner."

"And some, my dear Na Pieret," I said, "do both."

"If Botille has begun to pray, I'm sure the angels are smiling." She winked. "I'll make sure they have plenty of food and drink, Botille," the good lady said. "I know you normally tend to these things, but I will look after Garcia's family."

I nodded. "You are wrong, Na Pieret," I told her, "if you think those new sons of yours can ever replace you in Bajas."

She turned a worried look my way. "What? Don't you like them?"

I thought of the veins bulging in Symo's neck this morning, and coughed to hide a laugh. "Well enough, well enough," I said. "But no one could ever replace you. Not for Garcia, nor for your other servants." I squeezed her tight. "Never for me."

She returned the embrace. "There's my girl." She placed a hand over her heart. "Here, Botille, is where you'll always be." She smiled. "I need you to like the *tozęts*. Who else will tell them what to do when I no longer can?"

That afternoon a groggy and awkward Martin stumbled next door to collect his little Ava, and he disappeared before we could ask him how Lisette and the baby fared.

Plazensa and Sazia spent the day doting on Dolssa as though she were *comtessa* of all Provensa. They bathed her nicely mending feet and rubbed them with olive oil and lavender. Dolssa seemed embarrassed at the attention, but also pleased.

The sun had just begun to set in glorious pink and violet behind Bajas when Plazi summoned us to follow her into Dolssa's room. "I want you to try something on," she told Dolssa. She helped her out of her nightshirt, then pulled a gown from her basket. "From Sapdalina." She draped it long for us both to see. Together we helped Dolssa feed her arms into the sleeves and button it up.

The linen fabric was a rich woad-dyed blue. The bell-shaped sleeves fluttered gracefully past Dolssa's hands, and the yellow sash we tied around her waist bunched up excess fabric.

Plazi frowned. "We must feed you more and fatten you up," she said, "but I'll still need to tell Sapdalina to take these seams in before she finishes the trim. You're too thin by half."

I patted Dolssa's shoulder. "You look beautiful."

Sazia chimed in. "Don't let Plazensa make you feel bad."

Dolssa smiled and ran her hands over the gown. "It's fine, indeed," she said, "though here in my little cell, I have no need for clothing this fine."

Plazensa took a step back for a better look and sighed. "Ah, such a dress," she said. "You could get married in a dress such as this."

Dolssa's eyebrows rose. "Is this . . . is that why you've had this dress made?"

"No!" said Plazensa, then quailed under Dolssa's gaze. "Well, it was."

Sazia and I gaped at each other. Was this our Plazensa, cowering at Dolssa?

"When you first arrived," Plazi pleaded, "we thought marriage was your best safety. And Botille, she is good at finding husbands for young *femnas*."

Not lately. I kept my thoughts to myself.

"We thought you might be a fit for our Senhor Guilhem." Plazi was actually squirming.

Senhor Guilhem!

Santa Sara, *Dieu* help me, but I had never sent word to Bajas's lord that the fabled lady would not be coming to Bajas tonight! A thousand curses on my sorry head!

"But now," Plazensa went on, "we vow not to speak of it again. Our home is humble, but you are welcome here forever."

Sazia poked me with her elbow. *What's the matter?* her eyes asked.

"After what you've done for us . . ." Plazi wiped her eyes on her sleeve.

Dolssa blushed at my sister's gratitude. She squeezed Plazi's hands. "*Grácia.*"

"Then you'll stay?" asked Plazensa. I'd never seen her so eager, so nervous. I confess, I felt the same.

Dolssa smiled. "For as long as it pleases God."

Plazensa let out a squeal and threw her arms around Dolssa. We all joined in, encircling the girl who lived in Jhesus's embrace, who, with her beloved, had saved our sister.

Down the corridor we heard the tavern door bang, and footsteps on the floor. "Suppertime," I said, and my sisters and I hurried to the front room.

Sazia cornered me behind the bar. "What's the matter, Botille?"

I buried my face in my hands. "I told Senhor Guilhem, days ago, that a noble lady with a broken heart would pass through Bajas tonight. That he could meet her in Na Pieret's woods." I wanted to tear out my hair. "And that you had prophesied her to be his one true love."

Sazia shook her head. "You never know when to stop, do you?"

I hoisted a pan of turnips out of the coals. "You're no comfort at all."

"Do you think he'll go to meet her?" asked Sazia.

A glimmer of hope at this thought. "You're the seer. You tell me." I burnt my finger and stuck it in my mouth. "He acted uninterested. Maybe he'll forget about it."

Sazia reached for my pan and spoon. "Go now," she said. "Give him the message. Make something up, since you're so good at that."

I pulled off my apron and kissed Sazia's cheek. She waved me away.

I was out of breath from running by the time I reached Senhor Guilhem's home, straight up the hill near the church of Sant Martin. A servant boy answered. He told me Senhor Guilhem was not at home.

"Is he away from Bajas?" I begged.

"No." The youth eyed me strangely. "He was here earlier today, and will sleep here tonight. He asked us to prepare a special supper for him and a guest."

I was so dismayed at this that I ran off without thanking him. A great discourtesy.

I ran through the streets in the deepening twilight, uphill and down, searching for any sign of Senhor Guilhem, and found none, reproaching myself all the while. A pretty web I'd been weaving ever since Dolssa had come here. Now I'd lost count of its threads.

The trap I'd spun to catch my runaway a noble husband had worked too well.

Full darkness fell. The moon rose, glimmering in the sky. I had failed to find him. Nothing for it but to head to the woods and intercept him there myself.

Nightingales called to one another overhead as I made my way toward Na Pieret's woods. Twice today I'd traveled this way, but now darkness swallowed the path. Creatures of the night with pale eyes filled the skies—owls and bats and spirits of the dead. I gave myself a good shake.

These woods were a small grove, only a bit larger than one of our small peasant's plots. I passed through grassy vineyards, taking one neat row all the way up a slope to the thicket of trees. But I balked at penetrating the wood. I was too skittish. So I skirted around it and picked a large chalky rock to sit upon, just uphill from the vineyards and the trees. From here, I thought, moonlight would give me the best view of the road, the woods, and the path to it. I perched upon the rock, hugged my knees to my chest, and waited.

How angry would Senhor Guilhem be? Would he even come? Could some kindly saint in heaven have intervened on my behalf and made him forget my yarn about the virtuous noble maiden? Might his mysterious supper guest be someone else altogether?

I waited.

What a dunce I was to think I could make a match for a nobleman! What a price I'd pay for his anger. Foolish, foolish!

This would be the end of my matchmaking altogether. It would be a blow to the goodwill we held in Bajas. That worried me most. I made matches not solely for the money, though the *bon Dieu* knew we needed that, too. But all my weaving and winding of ties between the townsfolk and our family were meant to keep us safe. To allow us to fit, and not just fit but be welcome and needed. Even after four years here, with Plazensa's exotic ale and cooking mingling on the tongues of these wine-drinking Provençals, we were still out-of-towners. A whore's daughters, charges of a drunken vagrant whose brawling days weren't gone from memory, with Sazia playing soothsayer, and Plazensa playing a bit of the whore herself. So long as we were liked and helpful, we got on, but if not, may the *bon Dieu* help us.

Bats swooped overhead. I hunched my head down into my body. Why wouldn't Senhor Guilhem come, so I could catch him? Yet I prayed he would not come. I strained to see and hear.

And then I heard footsteps along the path. It was Senhor Guilhem, dressed in a surcoat, hose, cape, and tall feathered hat. He'd even taken my bait about dressing fine! Oh, if only I could slither off this rock, crawl into a hole, and disappear.

The time to approach him was now. But I couldn't bear it. So I waited and watched.

Having reached the wood, Senhor Guilhem seemed unsure of what to do next. He stood uncertainly upon the path.

He ventured a pace or two into the trees, only to return just as quickly.

He leaned against a stout tree, then decided it wasn't to his liking.

I swallowed. What to tell him? I lured him here with a lie. What lie could I now invent to salvage his pride?

"Donzęlla," he cried softly. "You can come out, Donzęlla. There is no need to fear."

Sazia would have died laughing at our nobleman made the fool. I'd die of mortification.

I decided to cut through the vineyard some distance away, then make myself appear to run along the road. I could tell him that I'd only just had word from the noble lady. That she was delayed by, oh, sickness, or discovery of her plans by her jealous parents. Something like that. The time was now. I rose from my perch, then halted.

Voices floated up from the woods. A woman's voice, mingling with Senhor Guilhem's.

What in the name of heaven?

My skin prickled. Had the tale I'd spun come true?

I crept down through the trees for a closer look.

"Don't be afraid, noble lady," I heard Senhor Guilhem say. "No harm will befall you. I swear upon my *onor*."

"No harm?" answered a dusky voice. "Not even to one such as I?"

Senhor Guilhem bowed and swept his hat off his head.

"Never, so long as I live," he said. "Come, dine with me in my home. I know your sufferings, and I long to assist you."

The voice hesitated in replying. "But that God himself should have shown them to you," she replied, "how could you begin to know my sufferings?"

"Come out to the path." Guilhem grew more eager by the minute. "I will lead you from here to safety. You shall be under my protection."

The woman's dusky voice wove a spell around the night. "You sound like an honest man," she said. "I'll come."

Footsteps crunched through the undergrowth. I ventured forward.

A dark figure left the wood and stepped onto the path.

Senhor Guilhem moved closer.

We both saw her. Senhor Guilhem stepped back.

She was rumpled and worn. Branches clung to her black clothes. She drew back her hood. Moonlight lit the streaks of white in her hair. Her bearing was tall and proud, but her eyes were sunken, and her cheeks hollow with age and hunger.

"A heretic," whispered Senhor Guilhem.

"Blessings on you," said the woman.

"No!" Senhor Guilhem's cry was shrill. "Do not bless me! I do not ask you to bless me!"

What had I done?

The *bona femna* slipped her hood back over her hair. "But, gracious Senhor," she said, her voice laden with hurt. "You promised me protection!"

"Not for you!" cried our nobleman. "Never for you. I thought you were someone else."

"So I shall be then, if needs must," pleaded the woman. "Only keep me safe from those who hunt me."

He shook his head. He stepped back, and back again. He was almost in full retreat. "Leave here!" he cried. "No one saw me here. I shall tell no one I saw you. That is all the protection I can give you."

The woman genuflected. Once, her holiness would have caused him to kneel before her.

"Then I accept such protection," she called after him, "in God's name."

"In any name," cried the retreating form, "but his!" He ran until I could hear his footsteps no longer.

The woman returned to the privacy of the trees. I blessed the dark for hiding me from her. She passed by close enough for me to hear the fugitive *bona femna*'s final malediction upon our young lord Guilhem.

"*Coward.*"

BOTILLE

I crave your pardon, Senhor, most humbly," I told the stone floor. "I myself only received word that the beautiful noble lady's plans had changed last night."

I stood in the open courtyard of Senhor Guilhem's home. It was morning. The servant boy had ushered me in and bidden his master to receive me. I'd had a sleepless night to worry myself into a lather over what had happened in the forest. Now I needed to make the best of a bad mess.

"Why didn't you send me word?"

He *was* angry. Not that I'd dared hope otherwise.

"Senhor, I came to your home last night," I said, "but you were not here."

The servant boy would already have told him this. It would give my story credence.

"Did you travel to the forest," he asked slowly, "to give me the message there?"

Oh no.

I raised my aching neck and looked at him. "No, Senhor," I said, trying to sound surprised. "A maiden like myself? Alone in the woods, after dark?"

I'd give a cask of Plazi's ale to know what passed through his mind then. We sisters did not have the most maidenly reputations.

"So you did not go to the woods."

I shook my head.

His frown became a smile too broad. "Fortunately for you, neither did I," he said. "Did you think I would believe a tale such as yours?" He laughed for all Bajas to hear. "When I go courting, I don't go in the woods, searching for phantom *domnas*."

I bowed. "Of course not. I beg forgiveness for ever troubling you."

He rose and walked me toward the door. "No forgiveness is needed," he said, "for I was never in the woods last night."

I heard the blade on the edge of his voice.

I bowed once more and fled for home. If he was afraid, then so was I. The less I saw of Senhor Guilhem for weeks to come, the better.

Garcia was worse. But Lisette's *enfan* was better. She and her husband were overjoyed at the turn he'd taken. They showed their baby to anybody who would see him, and soon a parade of visitors came and went to the goat-cheese man's house. Plazensa didn't mind, for many of them stopped in at the tavern for a drink afterward, but I was puzzled. Glad news though it surely was, what could attract so much curiosity about a baby deciding to eat?

And then I smelled the first whiff of the rumors, breathed out by customers quenching their thirst at the tavern.

Martin and Lisette's baby boy was healed in the night by a visit from an angel.

An angel named Dolssa.

I barged through the door to Martin and Lisette's house. There sat Lisette like the Virgin herself, clasping the naked *enfan* to her breast.

It was Lisette holding court to a rapt audience that frightened me. True, it was only her kinsmen, Martin's elderly mother, his cousins, and their closest friends. In short, half of Bajas.

"Then, two nights ago," she intoned, "an angel appeared in the night. A woman in a white gown. With eyes like eternity, and hair like the sea at midnight!"

A thrill of wonderment went through the listeners. An angel, in this very room? And why should they doubt? Good Christians did not speak lightly of angels. And there was the plump, peaceful child to prove it.

"What did she do?"

"She kissed the child and prayed over him," she said. "Then she helped my *lach*, which had run dry, to flow down once more and feed him." Lisette kissed her infant's cheek. "He's been drinking ever since. Day and night, the greedy little piglet!"

"Dolssa," someone said. "I never knew anyone named Dolssa."

"Is she a saint?" wondered a third. "One of the blessed martyrs?"

I snuck out the way I'd come.

I pulled Plazi and Sazia away from the bar and told them what had happened. Sazia instantly comprehended the danger, but Plazensa was only rapt with awe.

"She healed Lisette's baby," my older sister whispered reverently. "God's miracles abound!"

I took her by both shoulders. "*Oc*, but don't you see?" I said. "The fame of this miracle will spread all the way to Tolosa. We won't be able to hide her anymore. It won't take the friars long to hear and to guess who this 'angel Dolssa' is."

Plazi's face fell. We stood together in an anxious huddle.

"What was she thinking?" I moaned. "How could she have done this?"

Sazia lifted my face by the chin and made me look at her. "You wouldn't speak this way, Botille, if you were the *enfan*'s mother."

"How could God allow her to suffer harm for such good deeds?" wondered Plazensa.

I thought of the *bona femna* in the woods last night, and the ones we'd seen on the road. I thought of Carcassona, our first home, in our mother's childhood days, before the crusaders came and expelled every man, woman, and child. All the burnings, and the blood. Holy wars fought because the Church thought our holy men and holy women were heretics. And now our Dolssa was their target.

"Because this is Provensa, Plazi," I said. "God does not shield the good from dying cruelly here."

I left my sisters and went to Dolssa's room. She looked up at me with such a glad smile of welcome, my mouth went dry. After all she'd been through, after coming to trust me, must she now be punished for her kind deeds?

"Dolssa," I said, "there is a rumor spreading throughout the village that the neighbors' failing *enfan* was cured by an angel visitor named Dolssa."

Her face fell, just as my heart sank. She rose and paced the floor. At least her feet were mending. Pray the *bon Dieu* she would not need them to take flight again.

She stopped. "The child is well, then," she said. "That is the important thing."

Not to me, it wasn't. I confess it. How could she be immune to fear? "But, Dolssa," I cried, "don't you see? They'll find you now."

She resumed her pacing. "They were always going to find me."

"How can you say that?" I clasped both her arms in mine. "You've been safe here. You've been mending. You could have stayed here forever with us." My face grew hot, and I knew I would cry. "Dolssa, do you want to die?"

I thought I saw a struggle in her eyes, between calm trust and fear.

"No more than your neighbors wanted their *enfan* to die, Botille."

I sank down onto the bed.

"To leave, then?"

We looked up to see Plazi and Sazia standing in the doorway to Dolssa's room. Plazensa hid her face in her apron. Sazia wrapped her arms around our sister.

I couldn't bear it. Not losing her, not seeing her so calm about it, not seeing Plazensa cry. Too much precious blood had already soaked into our dry southern ground.

"We will fight it," I said. "We will fight this rumor by proving there is no angel Dolssa. She's flesh and blood like the rest of us." I reached for Dolssa's hand. "We will bring you out to meet them, and destroy this rumor before it takes root."

Sazia stared at me in horror, and my stupid error became plain. A holy woman and healer was less astonishing than an angel, but not by much. News could spread either way. And once she was known, what would happen to her?

"No." I retracted my earlier speech. "Never mind, it's too risky—"

"I will go."

We gaped at her.

"Botille is right. My concealment is past. Let us go meet the village."

Voices called us from the tavern. Customers would be helping themselves to the ale and wine in another moment if we didn't return.

"Are you sure," Sazia said slowly, "that this is what your love bids you do?"

Dolssa took Sazia's hands in her own. "It is what he would do, and did do," she said. "That may be all I can ever know about his will for me from this point onward."

"I don't understand," I told her.

"Once, he walked with me each day, and talked with me each night," she explained. "Once, we were joined as two lovers with one heart. If those days are ended, and I never see him again, I will still remember them. If I only hear his voice now in the cry of an *enfan*, I can still come when he calls. If his call cannot reach my ears, I can still follow his feet."

I wished to heaven I'd never spoken aloud the idea of going out. It was madness, and Dolssa had caught the infection from me. But she was determined.

"His feet, I am certain, would walk out that door to where the people were."

And so it happened. Dolssa de Stigata greeted Bajas.

She walked out the front door. She entered Martin and Lisette's home. I worried Lisette might drop the baby.

Dolssa held out her arms and bid Lisette and Martin to touch her and prove her real.

She was not an angel, she told them, but someone who had devoted her life to prayer.

It was not she who had healed their child, but God.

Children ran at their parents' bidding to fetch *tantas* and *oncles*, *mimas* and *paps*. Whole streets returned with them. Lisette's house overflowed, so Dolssa went outside to be seen. I stayed close beside her, lest Bajas tear her to adoring pieces.

She stood there in her blue robe, with a simple white cap over her dark hair. And even if I'm called a liar for it, I swear this is true: clouds over *la mar* parted, letting a beam of golden sunlight pierce through and illuminate the spot on which she stood.

We told them she was our friend from far away, come to visit. That they must not speak of her as an angel. We wished they would not speak of her at all, but allow her to live a quiet life of prayer, here in Bajas, and bless us with her silent presence.

But Bajas, I feared, would not be so easily fooled. She was an angel in blue, halo and all.

At the top of the hill appeared a face I knew well. Saura, wife of Garcia the elder, and mother to his namesake. She had heard of the holy woman, and she came running.

The crowd was a barrier now, but the look on her face told everything. She was about to lose her husband and her son, to become a childless widow in one fell day. Na Pieret reached Saura, and linked her arm through her elbow. The concern on their faces smote my heart.

What else could I do? I leaned in to Dolssa and whispered in her ear. She nodded, and together we pushed a path through the crowd toward the grieving women.

We climbed the hill with all Bajas following, speaking to one another in hushed tones. It was Felipa's burial in reverse: uphill, not down; raising the dead, God willing, not lowering them into the ground. Through it all, I watched Dolssa. She who was so afraid of being seen by the friar had no fear now, though all the world watched her.

We reached Garcia's small *maison*. Saura's neighbor woman came out, shaking her head.

My heart sank, but Dolssa did not pause. She entered the *maison* with me at her heels. I asked Na Pieret, whose trip up the hill had tired her badly, to keep the others out and let Dolssa have peace. Na Pieret nodded and planted herself in the doorway.

In the dark of the sickroom, I could not see at first. Garcia and his son lay stretched out on two cots. They were still and pale. I couldn't bear to look. Just last week, they'd been our protectors, our cheery traveling companions. Young Garcia was far too young to die, with all his brainless jokes, vexing Sazia.

Saura slumped in a corner. I didn't know what else to do, so I sat and cried with her.

Dolssa laid a hand on the elder Garcia's chest, then rested her other on his forehead.

"He is not dead," she said.

Saura stiffened. She looked up, but Garcia lay as still as ever.

Dolssa moved over to young Garcia and rubbed his chest and belly. "He lives as well."

"If you can do anything," came Saura's strangled voice, "in God's name, help us quickly, before their spirits have fled this world."

Dolssa pulled a short stool in between the two cots, and sat. She took each of the Garcias by the hand and held both hands in hers, then closed her eyes.

I wished I could know what words she sent up to her beloved, if she was indeed praying. I could no more count on God to hear and bless me than I could count on the winds off *la mar* to consider my wishes and grant me my needs. Some days the wind was a friendly breeze at my back. It might just as likely blow the roof off the tavern.

Saura's prayers, on the other hand, I could hear. She rocked back and forth on her hips on the ground, with her bowed head resting upon her hands. As she rocked, she murmured her prayer.

"*Mon Dieu, mon Dieu*, oh God, blessed Jhesus, mother Maria, save my husband, my only son. Oh, God, if it is not too late, if I have not angered you too much with my sins, please God, save the child and his father, or I will go with them to the grave. How can I live? Why spare me? Has this holy woman come to mock me? Why does she do nothing? You can heal them, whether or not she can. Hear my prayer, holy Paire, my prayer for all these long days and nights, for I can pray no longer, nor even stand upon my feet. Grant me my son. Take me in his place. I'll go gladly. But spare me my boy, and if you will it, his father to watch over him."

I looked up.

Dolssa no longer held the two Garcias' hands. She had joined them together. She slid the cots closer until they made one bed, and father and son lay alongside each other, their fingers entwined. She crouched down at the head of their cots, her chin resting between the two. She talked with laughing eyes and a smile on her face, as though she were telling a charming story or a wonderful joke. She talked as if to someone beside her whom I couldn't see, so naturally that I began to imagine I could see the face that held her gaze.

Saura ran out of words to pray. She wiped her face on her sleeve and looked up through bleary eyes. Dolssa beckoned her over. She rose and took one uncertain step, and then another. Another still, and then she froze.

Garcia's eyes opened and searched for his wife's face. In a

moment she was at his side, weeping into his neck. And Garcia the son, the reed-thin youth whose hand was still clutched tightly in his father's, stirred in his sleep.

All my heart magnified the joy of the miracle. The looks in Saura's eyes, and in Na Pieret's, were everything to me. To see those two feeble hands, the father's and the son's, grasp each other and pull each other back to strength—I will never forget it if I live to be seventy. For one sweet chiming moment, heaven was all around us. All things were possible, and kindness and love could conquer any sorrows, any fears.

Then I left the *maison* and saw the crowd as Na Pieret proclaimed the news. I saw their wonder and amazement. I saw the way they whispered Dolssa's name in reverent, hushed tones. I saw how their ranks had swelled to include every one of us, young and old, every fisherman and merchant and traveler from the port and from the roads. Plazensa's eyes, aglow with pride. Dominus Bernard's face, rapt with awe. Sazia's face, drawn with worry. Symo's, inexplicably, looking murderous.

May God forgive me for what I thought then. Almost, I confess, I wished Dolssa had failed.

DOLSSA

y own dear love, gone so long, returned! He found me there in the house where father and son lay dying. He placed his hands upon their hearts and bid them live, in answer to their wife and mother's prayer.

While the town rejoiced, their attentions elsewhere, he took me in his arms. He had never been far from me, he said. It pained him to see me grieve without him, but it served to grant my prayer to be made worthy to taste the sorrows he had tasted. I was sent here to learn to see him, and to love him, in the faces of those around me.

These weeks were my own wilderness. My forty days to

purify my soul. My sufferings, for my sanctification, as so many saints now in heaven have taught.

But he had returned to me at last. Never, he promised, would he leave me again.

A glorious future opened before me, of friendship, belonging, service, and joy. This place would become my home. Botille and her sisters, my new family. This town, Bajas, my new people. Once again, with my beloved near, I could become a window, to shine his love into a darkened world.

BOTILLE

t twilight, two days later, a stranger arrived at the tavern.
If only he had been a stranger.

They had been two long days for Dolssa, but her sweetness never
flagged. From morning till night, people brought her their illnesses
and woes. She sat and spoke with them all. She was never in a
hurry, and strangely, those who waited in line to meet her did not
seem to grow impatient. They did grow thirsty, however, which
kept Plazensa happy.

"How does she endure it?" Sazia watched Dolssa patiently

listen to person after person. "People are nothing but vexation. I avoid them."

Dolssa had changed. Gone was any trace of fear, any focus upon herself. She shone. Each visitor felt it. They sat as long as they could in the orb of her light.

As each suppliant left her, I followed them to the door and said, "Please, for Donzɛlla Dolssa's sake, do not tell others outside of Bajas that she lives here." They all nodded soberly. They remembered the crusades, and knew about inquisitors. I thought I was doing some good, until Sazia pulled me aside and told me that if I wanted to ensure that word of Dolssa reached París, Londres, and Roma by next week, I should keep doing what I'd been doing.

At suppertime, that second night, Plazensa finished a lesson in womanly graces with Sapdalina, one which left Sazia seized with ill-concealed sniggers. Plazi ordered everyone out, fed us a stew, and sent a grateful Dolssa to bed. Then she opened the door to the tavern once more, and let the usual crowd come in. The great room was full to bursting, but everyone was strangely quiet. A holy woman on the premises must have damped their appetite for carousing and song. Even Jobau, who had returned to his loft the prior day with a torrent of abuse for our noise, poked his head over the edge to see what had happened to the tavern.

One by one our customers left, until only old Plastolf de Condomio sat at the bar, mumbling toothlessly and nursing a cup of wine. Sazia went to bed, and Plazensa disappeared down into her brewery to check on another batch of ale, leaving me to tend the tavern. I wiped the tables and chairs and swept the floor. I spread ashes around and over the coals so the fire couldn't grow but the embers would still kindle in the morning.

I rose from the ashes, turned, and jumped to see a man standing there. He was dressed in knight's clothing and armed with a sword, so I bowed. Quickly.

"How can I help you, Senhor?"

Then I looked at his face, and he looked at mine.

He was the man from the road. From our journey back from San Cucufati to Bajas. The one who had stopped to stare me down not long after we'd found Dolssa.

I swallowed. What if he'd been searching, not for a lass to tumble with in the tall grasses, but for one specific *donzɛlla*?

"*Bon sɛr*," I whispered.

He knew me. There was no doubt. He remembered.

"Do you offer lodging?"

His voice was deep. His accent was like Dolssa's. Tolosan. His bearing was erect and strong, though trim. He was no brawny man of war, but someone lithe, I thought, and deadly.

"Our rooms are full," I lied. "But you, Senhor, would prefer a place more fitting than our low quarters. Our lord in Bajas, Senhor Guilhem, would gladly receive you in his home."

"Our *low* quarters?" Plazensa rose from the wine cellar and turned her most bewitching smile upon our guest. She planted herself close beside me, behind the bar, where she could give my bottom an angry pinch. In reply, I softly ground my heel into the top of her foot.

"Fair enough for most folk," I said through smiling teeth, "but since our rooms are *all full anyway*, this noble *senhor* would do far better if he were to present himself to Senhor Guilhem."

His gray eyes watched us both. We'd failed to fool him; that was plain. My backside would be purple from Plazensa's pinching. I eased off her foot.

"Perhaps, then, I will simply take some wine."

My hand shook as I poured it. "With our compliments, *bon senhor*."

Plazi shot me a venomous look. I was pouring him our best vintage, for free, and there was no doubt this man could pay full price for it.

He sat at the bar and sipped his wine. I offered him *fogasa* and olives and soft goat cheese to go with it, then slipped down the corridor. I didn't have to call to know Plazensa would follow.

"How dare you?" she fumed, while Sazia snored, unawares, on our bed.

"Trust me, *sorre*," I whispered. "He's from Tolosa, and he's looking for Dolssa."

Her face changed, but she would not give up a golden fare easily. "Just because someone is from Tolosa doesn't mean—"

"We saw him on the roads," I said, "not long after we found her. He stopped and stared at us." My heart raced. "I assumed he wanted a roll in the hay. Now I'm sure he was hunting her."

"But you said it was a friar looking for her," Plazi whispered. "How also this knight?"

I shook my head. "I don't know. But I'm sure he is."

Plazensa looked toward the corridor. "Go down to the waterfront and ask for Litgier. He sleeps on his boat. Tell him to wait out of sight until I come out. I will escort this knight to Senhor Guilhem's house, but I want him to follow me, unseen and unheard."

Anxious dread settled in my belly. I'd never known Plazi to fear any man.

We returned to the tavern. Plazensa effortlessly fell into conversation with the stranger, but I could barely hear them for the buzzing in my brain. I passed through the tavern as though nothing in the world were wrong, then hurried down through the darkness toward the water.

Finding Litgier, whoever he might be, was quickly sorted. He turned out to be the large fisherman I'd seen come for Plazi. He accepted the instructions without a word. We returned to the tavern, but by the time I'd reached the door, he'd vanished into the waiting dark. I passed by the silent figure of the knight's horse, tethered to a post, laden with bags as though it had taken a long journey, and went inside.

Plazensa still chatted winsomely with our noble guest. Plastolf de Condomio had left her alone with him. She wasted no time, when she saw me, and pulled a shawl over her arms.

"Let me show you the way to Senhor Guilhem's, *bon senhor*," she said prettily. "In the dark it could be hard for you to find."

He made no objection but followed her outside. I soon heard the horse's hooves clopping slowly up the hill toward town.

She came back before long, and offered her large companion a drink, but he declined, so she bid him *bon sęr* at the door, then came inside and sat down.

"Did he say anything?" I asked. "Did you find out anything more about him?"

She shook her head. "His name is Hugo de Miramont, and he is from Tolosa."

I nodded. "I knew from his voice."

"He asked if we ever see friars here in Bajas," Plazensa said, and we looked at each other. "Or many visitors from the lands of the count of Tolosa."

I buried my face in my hands. "He's looking for Dolssa," I moaned. "I knew it."

"He'll find her, too," said Plazensa. "Yesterday made certain of that."

BOTILLE

e did not tell Dolssa about Senhor Hugo de Miramont when she woke the next morning.

The day was overcast and heavy. We waited in the silent gloom for Dolssa's downfall. Plazensa turned away all petitioners at the door of the tavern.

Hour after hour crawled by, yet the rain never came, and neither did the knight. As the afternoon began to tip toward evening, I wondered if I could have been mistaken. Perhaps he did not seek Dolssa. Perhaps he wasn't even the man I'd seen on the road.

Except I knew he was.

Waiting became unbearable. Finally we agreed Plazensa should venture up to Senhor Guilhem's. Casually, unobtrusively, she would ask servants about Senhor Hugo's movements. Sazia and I picked pebbles and dirt out of a sack of dried beans and waited for information.

Plazi returned with her hair tousled by the rising wind, but there was a smile on her face.

"He's gone," she said. "He left town this morning. Only passing through."

I sagged with relief, but glum Sazia would not surrender so easily. "What if he's gone to send word that he's found Dolssa's hiding place?"

"Tchah," scolded Plazensa. "What on earth should make him think he had? *Oc*, if he'd seen her, I'd say your idea had some sense, but you go too far, *sorre*. He's gone."

It was easy to be persuaded. We turned our attention to our daily work, which was a relief.

"There's nothing for it, then, *sorres*," cried Plazensa after the last lunchtime dish had been washed and stacked, "but for us to dress ourselves for Na Pieret's feast. Come on. We'll close the tavern and make a night of it."

Sazia and I stared. Close the tavern? Never since it had opened had Plazi suggested such a scheme. Another of Dolssa's miracles. We threw the latch, then ran to find more interesting clothes than our daily dresses. I poked my head into Dolssa's room to ask her if she'd join us.

I found her lying on her side, still in her nightdress at this late hour, on her mat on the floor, her head propped up on her elbow. Once again, she'd been talking to someone I couldn't see. She wore a scarlet blush on her cheeks and a sparkle in her eyes.

"*Bonjorn*, Botille." She smiled but made no move to rise.

"*Bonjorn*," I told her. "Na Pieret di Fabri holds a feast tonight to celebrate her nephews' arrival. It will be a great to-do, with food and music and dancing."

She smiled as I spoke, and I realized it was not I, but her beloved who held her gaze. She remembered I was there, though, and glanced back at me. "That sounds very pleasant."

It was like stumbling upon two lovers kissing. Only here, the second lover was the Lord Jhesus.

Plazensa appeared at my side and peered over my shoulder at Dolssa. "You should come with us tonight," she said. "It would do you good to have a bit of rest and amusement."

Dolssa's eyes grew wide. "Oh," she said, "I can rest better here." She smiled knowingly at the figure that lay beside her. "I think I'll be most comfortable at home. But *grácia*."

Plazi plucked me away by the cloth at my back. "As you prefer." I shut the door.

"What's come over her?" I whispered to Plazi.

"She's in love, silly," Plazensa said. "Can't you, of all people, recognize the signs?"

I halted in the doorway to my room. "If that's love," I began, "it will never tempt me."

My sister gave my nose a friendly pinch. "Nonsense," she said. "You're just jealous." Plazensa called up into the loft, "You'll have to run the tavern yourself tonight, Jobau. We're going to a party."

Our lord and master sent us a grunt by way of a reply.

The sun had gone all the way down behind Bajas, and clusters of lights twinkled up the hill at Na Pieret's home. Dark massy clouds still shifted overhead, and stirred the lagoon, but we were determined not to let them mar the celebration. Already, strains of music wafted down toward the waterfront. Plazensa insisted we take a detour to rap loudly, three times, upon the door to Sapdalina's father's little *maison*. She didn't wait for an answer, but hurried onward.

"What was that for?" Sazia muttered to me.

I shrugged. "We'll soon find out."

Na Pieret's party spilled out her front door and onto the street. In the courtyard, Focho de Capa sawed at his *fidel*, with others joining on flute, dulcimer, and drum. Jacme and Andrio were already bowling spectators aside, energetically swinging each other about by the elbows while women laughed and clapped. Torches blazed from every window, sending shadows leaping like featureless nighttime revelers.

Everyone in Bajas was invited, and most had never seen so much to eat in their lives. Na Pieret's great room overflowed with food. Her hired cooks had roasted a gigantic boar, and piled rafts high with baked salmon and boiled clams. There were squashes and turnips and potatoes and (oh heaven!) melting sweet onions; cheeses, and bits of tongue bobbing in sauces; breads and sweetmeats; goose liver and chicken liver and truffles and other kinds of savories; and tarts of every fruit ripening just then. And wine! Wine flowing from dozens of pitchers. Peasants' eyes popped to see such bounty. It was a hard grind, eking out a living from a tiny wedge of chalky soil, even in the most fertile of years. This must have cost Na Pieret a fortune. To feed all Bajas? It was unheard of. Bless her generosity. All this to celebrate her nephews. I hoped they were worth such a fuss.

The fragrance of roasting food, sweet wine, and women's lavender-scented hair put me into a party mood. After all our worries, it was high time for some merriment. A cup of wine sent me tripping merrily along that path. Think of the blessings and miracles we'd seen! Knights and friars, friars and knights. We were in God's hands, so who could harm or threaten us?

Senhor Guilhem, who'd been talking with Lop the *bayle*, cornered Plazensa and led her into the dance. A second cup of wine made me think of dancing too. I went in search of Na Pieret, to bid her *bon sęr*, and thence to find a partner. Dominus Bernard, I thought, would do nicely. No one would ever think I was one of his lovers.

To my surprise, I came across Astruga clutching one of the de Prato children in each hand. With their free hands, they stuffed their faces with pork. She squawked at them to wipe their chins. Joan de Prato lurked behind, utterly cowed by imperious Astruga.

"*Bon sęr*, Astruga," I said, and kissed her cheeks. Someone had refilled my empty cup, and suddenly Astruga was my long-lost and dearest friend.

"*Bon sęr*, Botille," she said. "I haven't time to talk with you now."

"As you wish," I told her retreating and celebrated backside. "Any other time will do."

It took some maneuvering to reach Na Pieret, thronged as she was, but I finally did.

"You're late," she said by way of greeting.

I bowed deeply, and only wobbled a little. "*Bon sęr, ma domna.*"

"You're drunk," she observed.

I took another long gulp. "*Non*. I'm just a little thirsty."

She shook her head and smiled. "Tell me, Botille," she said, "don't my sons look handsome tonight?"

I followed her pointing finger to locate these paragons of young manhood. There was Gui, intercepting Plazensa from Senhor Guilhem just as a song ended and asking her to dance. Senhor Guilhem looked none too happy about it. Gui, I thought, had better learn the proper order of things in Bajas, and soon. Rank was rank, and he'd best be careful.

"Now where is Symo . . . ah. There he is." She pointed over to a corner, where Symo stood looking miserable in a tightly fitting velvet coat and tunic. A pair of older *omes* stood talking close by, and Symo pretended, badly, to attend to their conversation.

"Aren't they handsome?" Na Pieret asked.

"Gui has a pleasing way about him." I took another sip. "Symo's clothes are very fine."

Na Pieret twitched my ear with her finger and thumb. "Oh, go on about you, then," she said. "Give him time, and Symo will grow on you."

"Like a fungus," I thought. Then I realized that, thanks to the wine, I'd thought my thought aloud. But Na Pieret only laughed. She breathed in deeply, savoring the tingling party air as if she'd drunk a thirsty draught of excitement.

"This takes me back, Botille," she said, "to the old, old times when I was a little girl. Such parties we had then! And dancing. Such colors, all the ladies' skirts like flowers, and the cuts of the young men's coats—ah, me! To be young again." She closed her eyes, lost in remembering. "At feasts at Senhor Guilhem's grandfather's house, the *jocglars* would sing the songs of the *trobadors*, and we danced and danced and danced. I was a new bride, and the world was pink." She looked like a dreaming child. "Those were happy times."

I smiled around me at the festivity. "Has it changed so much, then?"

Her face became serious. "The war changed it all, Botille."

I squeezed her hand. "But we're happy tonight. You brought the old times back."

Her eyes were sad. "Only a shadow of them." She gave my hand a return squeeze. "But you're right. No sense moping. I'm just an old woman reminiscing. Let us indeed be happy tonight."

"That's the spirit." I planted a kiss on her cheek. "Would you like a drink, *ma domna*?"

"Not from the looks of you," she teased. "I will get myself something to eat. Run along, and dance off some of that wine."

It occurred to me then that I hadn't eaten. It occurred to my stomach, too, which began to feel wobbly. I made my way to a serving table and took some bread and a wedge of cooked onion, and ate them together, then a piece of fish and some cheese. After a few moments I began to feel a bit better, so I ventured back outside for some fresh air.

I found Sazia surrounded by farmwives, who loved her fortunes. She stood near the musicians, tapping her toes to their song.

"How goes it, Sazia?" I bawled.

She clapped a hand over her head and glowered at me. "Well enough without your popping my ears."

"Sorry."

Just then we saw Plazensa approach Focho de Capa and gesticulate wildly to him.

"What's she doing?" I made sure to speak more normally.

Sazia shook her head. "I don't know. But you missed a great fuss. You should have seen Plazensa, tongue-lashing Gui for being too friendly with her. He barely knew what hit him."

I steadied myself against the wall. "Plazi?" Maybe I still needed more food. "Why would she do that? She's never, ever—"

"I know." Sazia was behaving as though it took me too long to finish a thought. How rude of her. "From what I could tell, he wasn't doing anything out of line."

I looked over to where Gui stood watching Plazensa and

looking forlorn. Perhaps it was just as well that she'd snubbed him. But why? Was it for her huge fisherman? Litgier? Was that his name?

There was a break in the music. Focho looked at Plazi, who glanced up the street, then back at Focho with a nod. The musicians struck up quite a different tune then, one that drew all eyes at the party. Plazensa looked, then Focho looked, then all the musicians and all the revelers beheld the apparition approaching them from down the street.

It was a lady. As she entered the orb of light near the torches we saw that she was dressed in a flowing gown of the most delicate green, with fluttering sleeves and a sapphire sash tied about her waist. Her bodice shimmered with exquisite embroidery, mermaids and seashells. Her hair was piled high in a knot, then trailed down her neck from that peak, entwined with ribbons and beads.

My phantom noble lady had found us.

I looked to see Senhor Guilhem take a step forward. His face was flushed. He looked unsure of what to do with his hands.

The lady hesitated at the edge of the party. Almost, it seemed, she wanted to pull back. And no wonder. She couldn't be real. She was just my fanciful story come to life. In the morning, like a fairy, she'd be gone.

Plazensa appeared at her side, took her arm, and brought her into the circle. She nodded at Focho to pick up the tempo, which he obligingly did, and then she led the strange lady straight past Senhor Guilhem and into Gui's arms.

He led her forward for a step of the dance, then back again. The strange lady followed, and smiled at him. Other dancers stepped into the form, and I lost sight of them. I blinked, and blinked again. Had I imagined the whole thing?

"Well?" A smug Plazensa appeared between Sazia and me. "Admit it: Dolssa isn't the only miracle worker. Did I or did I not perform a wonder tonight?"

"What are you talking about, Plazi?" I said. "Who is that *femna*?"

Plazi's eyes bulged. "You mean you don't know?" Her laugh trilled over the music and dancing. "You actually don't know?"

Sazia stared at the couple as they whirled by. "It couldn't be!"

"But it is." Plazi was playing with me now, like Mimi with a cornered rat.

Sazia tugged my sleeve. "You'd better hang up your matchmaker's bonnet, Botille," she said. "That's Sapdalina out there, rapidly making Gui fall in love with her."

My jaw, I knew, lay on the cobblestone square. Sapdalina?

"Now, now." Plazi smiled. "Botille is still the matchmaker. This case needed my expertise."

I watched Sapdalina's lips move. They were talking. She was smiling. Gui was laughing. His great teeth gleamed in the torchlight. I marveled at the sight. How could Sapdalina—squashy, nervous, sticky Sapdalina—ever hold herself so well?

"Does Gui know," I asked my sisters, "that he's dancing with his seamstress?"

Sazia shook her head. "If you couldn't tell, how could he?"

"But how did you do it?" I said. "In so short a time?"

"Easiest thing in the world." Plazi wrapped her shawl around her shoulders. "Sapdalina's quite a wit if you get to know her. Once she stopped being so nervous, it was just a matter of teaching her how to behave, and to wipe her nose, for heaven's sake. And fixing her clothes, of course. The poor thing has no mother."

"Neither do you," observed Sazia.

Plazi grinned. "I'm extraordinary." She gave each of us a kiss on the cheek. "Well, girls, I'm off. I only came to see Sapdalina and make sure she danced with Gui. My work is done."

I tugged on her arm. "Stay, Plazi," I pleaded. "No one will visit the tavern tonight. Not with free wine here."

My *sorre* shook her head firmly. "I've left Dolssa too long unguarded," she said. "You two, stay and enjoy yourselves."

Her words made me feel fuzzy and confused. "I should come home too, then."

"Not on your life," said Plazi. "Stay and drink and dance and laugh. Kiss a *tozet*."

"Ugh," said Sazia. "I'm going for some plum tart." They both left before I could object.

I danced with Dominus Bernard. I danced with Focho de Capa, who managed to match my steps while playing his *fidel* all the while. I even danced, to my great surprise, with Giacomo Arbrissi, the Italian merchant.

"What are you doing here?" I demanded.

"I just arrived in port tonight, from Narbona," he said.

"Storm's brewing. I wasn't planning on stopping, since I was just here, but I had a passenger who insisted on taking shelter in Bajas. And anyway, I didn't like the looks of the weather."

I hitched up my skirts and skipped round him with the dance. "Lucky for us, then," I said. "Stay a day or two. Did you pick up any good wares in Narbona?"

"A few things," he said. "But tell me, what's the occasion? What are we celebrating?"

I explained about Na Pieret's nephews, and danced another round with my jovial merchant friend until I could barely keep to my feet. I found a dim corner of the house with a stool to sit on, and another cup of wine, which I sipped much more slowly this time, and munched on a piece of raisin cake. It was a wonder there was any food left at all, with swarms of hungry peasants invited to help themselves, but Na Pieret's cooks kept on producing dishes from an apparently limitless store.

I slowly became aware of a pair of feet stationed a short distance from me. I looked up to see Symo towering over me, watching me with a bored expression.

"Oh," I said. *"Bon ser."*

"Bon ser."

Having gotten that out of the way, I wasn't sure where else to take the conversation. I wasn't feeling at the peak of my verbal abilities just then.

"What are you doing here?" I asked him.

"I live here."

I favored him with a scathing look. "I know that," I said. "I mean, *here* here."

"What are *you* doing here, then?" he asked me.

I held up my cup and my wedge of cake. "This," I told him with great hauteur, "is what I am doing."

"Have you had enough to drink?" he asked in his most sneering tone. "Because I could always get you some more."

"I'll have you know," I said, "that I don't usually drink much at all."

"Is that so?"

"Yes, it is so." I nodded. "No sense drinking up all the profits at the tavern."

Symo pulled over a chair and seated himself. "Makes more sense to drink all of ours."

I raised my cup. "To your health." I took a sip. "It's a party, isn't it?"

He shrugged. "So they tell me."

"Don't be sour." I took a bite of raisin cake, but some of it crumbled onto my lap. "It's a party for you."

"I didn't ask for one," said my surly companion. "It's a great waste if you ask me."

"Nobody asked you." I eyed his fancy clothes. His head seemed to bulge from his tight collar. "If you're so uncomfortable, you could loosen your top button."

He fidgeted with the button, then left it as it was to spite me. "Who says I'm uncomfortable?"

I took another sip of wine. "You look like the fatted hog, all trussed up for roasting."

It might have been the wine, but I thought I saw thunderbolts shoot from his eyeballs at me then. He peeled off his velvet jacket and loosened his shirtsleeves.

"There," I said. "That's better. Don't you think that's better?"

In answer, he merely folded his arms across his chest. I took another sip.

"You've done a fine job," he said, "keeping your runaway hidden."

My body tightened in spite of the wine. "I'm not the one who—"

"How long will it take for all Provensa to know her name and her fame?" He was ruthless. "The Comtessa of Tolosa is probably hearing a report of her tonight as she takes her supper."

"She's in God's hands," I told him. "Would you rather Garcia and his son had died?"

He said nothing then.

I leaned in closer to him and tapped his knee. "Tell me this," I said—*tap-tap-tap*—"why does your tanta Pieret like you?"

He glared at me. "You're drunk."

"Possibly," I admitted. "But just a little."

"You should go home."

I thought about it. "That's not an altogether bad idea," I said. "I think, though, that I'll just wait here a bit. Before I go."

He shrugged. "Suit yourself."

"You still haven't answered my question," I said. "Why does Na Pieret like you?"

He snorted. "I should ask the same of you."

I sat back. "Why, we're friends," I said. "Everybody knows Na Pieret and I are friends."

He said nothing. I call that being a poor conversationalist.

"You make sure," I said, "that you always treat Na Pieret with great courtesy. Because if you don't"—here I rose to my feet, and found them rather shaky—"all Provensa's not big enough to hide from me." I leaned against the wall to steady myself. "Want to dance?"

"No."

"Too bad," I said, "because I don't want to either."

He watched me. I wondered if maybe my withering snub hadn't landed quite where I thought it would. I decided it was time to go home.

"Botille . . ." he began, but I needed no more of his sneering. I left Symo simmering in his own sauce, and wandered outside. Where the music was, Sazia wouldn't be far away. A pair of farm-wives had coerced her into reading their palms. She rose immediately when I told her I wanted to leave. She threaded her arm through my elbow tightly.

"Come on, Botille," she said. "I've got you."

"No need," I protested, then tripped on my skirt.

Past the shelter of the houses on Na Pieret's street, we felt the gusting wind whip our faces, stronger now by far than when we'd arrived. The air was heavy and thick with dampness from the sea. Giacomo Arbrissi had said there was a storm brewing.

"We'd better hurry," I told Sazia.

She shook her head and kept my footsteps even. "Not in your state, we won't." We carefully picked our way downhill, hitching up our skirts in one hand and holding on tightly to each other with the other, until we reached the welcoming shuttered light of the tavern windows.

We found Plazensa seated behind the bar. Something was wrong. She was still and white. She didn't turn to look at us. For a horrid, drunken instant I thought she was a bled corpse.

"What's the matter?" Sazia cried. "Plazensa, what's wrong?"

Slowly, my older sister placed a warning finger over her lips. "It's the friar," she whispered. "He's come. Tonight, to rent a room. He said his name was Lucien de Saint-Honore."

ESCLARMONDA DE MONSOS, SECOND TESTIMONY

Witness Testimony recorded by Lucien

City of Narbona

Friar! *Grácia* for coming. I see that young oaf Pascaut *did* find you at the convent. *Bon.*

I'll tell you why I've summoned you. I didn't bring you all this way *not* to tell you.

Friar, God is kind to you. Here you were, days ago, so despondent, searching for your runaway. Is she the daughter of a pious nobleman?

But hear this! My sister, my own sister, Friar, has sent me a message. She sent a nephew all this way to bring me word. She lives in Bajas. South, along the coast of the lagoon. She's a widow, my sister is, but her son, the fisherman, is good to her. They had a baby, the fisherman and his wife, and it wouldn't thrive. It happens, God knows, and watching young mothers pine will break your heart. How many times I've seen it!

Oc, I'm telling you. The baby was healed by a woman who appeared in the night. Be she flesh or be she spirit, they could not say. But her name was Dolssa. A name you don't often hear. My sister knows how crippled I am, and my poor husband, how weak in his wits. She sent her messenger to say, *Come to Bajas and be healed*. I thought, *That young friar was looking for a Dolssa*. This one clearly belongs to God. Could be they're the same. So I sent for you.

I can't make the journey. I'm far too weak. But I can rejoice in God's miracles, and pray this Dolssa might send a healing my way. Would you ask her, for my sake?

Go to her there, Friar, in Bajas. Go, and may God's will be done in her, and in you.

DOLSSA

woke in my beloved's arms to the sound of that voice, naming his dreaded name. I told myself I lay caught in the snares of a hideous dream. I was sure I could nestle back down into the warmth of sleep, but I looked into my beloved's eyes and saw his tears.

Tears for me.

Tears for Mamà.

Tears—how could I bear it?—for Lucien de Saint-Honore.

The rescues, the miracles. My beloved's return. His promise never to leave me. I had hoped they meant the dawn of a new day for me. A new life in my own new promised land.

I know better now.

GUILHEM DE BAJAS

enhor Guilhem watched the glistening stranger at the party dance with the newcomer, one of the nephews of the widow Pieret. Snubbed! By some fairy *femna*, whose dress and bearing bespoke rank and position, yet he'd never seen her before. He would never have forgotten a creature such as she. And now she danced with that showy upstart from out of town, that nephew of Na Pieret di Fabri's. He'd better watch whom he offended, new as he was to Bajas. But where had this bewitching creature come from?

Plazensa Flasucra had something to do with it. Now *there* was a face and figure to leave even this fairy creature in the pale, but there was no marrying a public tavern keeper.

Was this the woman Botille Flasucra had spoken of? The mysterious and beautiful stranger? Or had she played a trick, a prank designed to make a fool out of him with that wretched crone in the woods? He wouldn't have thought it of her.

"Senhor."

He turned to see his young page standing at his side, holding a letter.

"What now?" He rubbed his eyes. It was late. Many of the older folks had already gone home to bed. A letter at this hour?

"Pardon, Senhor," said the page. "The letter just arrived. The messenger said 'urgent.'"

Guilhem sent the boy home. He tucked the letter into his belt and resumed brooding over the dancing *femnas*, then thought the better of it, went inside the house, and opened the letter.

Lop, the *bayle*, detached himself from a conversation and approached the young lord.

"Trouble, Senhor?"

Senhor Guilhem roused himself to answer Lop. "Why should there be trouble?"

Lop bobbed his head in acceptable contrition. "You looked concerned, Senhor. And there is the late hour of the letter."

Guilhem tucked the letter back into his belt. "It's from the bishop of Tolosa," he said, "warning us of a fugitive heretic roaming abroad. One who somehow escaped her burning. If we hear of her, we are to let them know."

He thought of the woman in the woods. But there was no reason to suppose she was the heretic they sought. These last few *bonas femnas* and *bons omes*, they were everywhere throughout Provensa. An open secret no one wanted to think about. Like lepers. He would say nothing about her. There wasn't a chestnut's chance it was she.

"That is a curious thing," said the *bayle*. "I just spoke with Giacomo Arbrissi."

"The Italian merchant?"

Lop nodded. "*Oc*. He tells me he stopped in port tonight with a passenger bound for Bajas. A friar. An inquisitor. One who came, he said, looking for a heretical woman believed to be in Bajas."

Senhor Guilhem's eyelids fell shut. In Bajas? The noose was pulling tighter. That woman in the woods—she was no prank. She would prove his downfall. If they hunted for her, and found her, the inquisitors could say he, Guilhem, harbored heretics, and strip him of his lands and name. And if they ever knew he'd spoken with her—and she'd tell them—that would damn him even more. Until now, with lax Dominus Bernard at Sant-Martin, and no one making noise about *bons omes* and *bonas femnas*, Guilhem had figured heresy was a problem for other, larger landowning lords— not him. But if the war had taught Provensa nothing else, it had finally, and brutally, taught its nobles this lesson: keep heresy far from your borders, far from the souls of your subjects, or pay the price on earth and in hell.

Life had gone from tranquil to deadly practically overnight. And all because he'd listened to some petty matchmaker's tales.

Senhor Guilhem opened his eyes. Lop was watching him strangely. That wouldn't do.

"*Dieu*, I'm tired." Guilhem affected a casual pose. "Too much wine. I'm going to bed."

"I'll walk with you."

Outside, the whipping wind cleared the young lord's head somewhat.

"Tell me, Lop," he asked, "did Giacomo tell you the name of the heretic they're seeking?"

The shaggy-whiskered *bayle* shook his head. "Why, did the letter name the woman?"

Guilhem climbed the dark streets toward his *castrum*. "Dolssa," he said. "Unusual name."

Lop stopped in his tracks.

"What's the matter?"

"Dolssa," Lop said, "is the name of the *medica*, the healer woman all the village speaks of."

"Blood of Christ." Senhor Guilhem rubbed his hand over his face. "Here, in Bajas. It would have to be here. Of all the forgotten corners in Christendom . . ."

I shall tell no one I saw you. That is all the protection I can give you.

"You say this inquisitor is here now?"

Lop nodded. "According to what the merchant told me, *oc*."

"Where is he?"

Lop shook his head. "I don't know."

They resumed their climb. Wind blasted through their clothes.

"Do you want me to arrest her, Senhor?"

Guilhem hesitated.

"Quickly," he said, "gather wood. We will execute her ourselves, before morning. Then when the friar begins his questioning, we can show our hands clean before the Church. They cannot fault us for exterminating heresy on our own, when first we find it. They must praise us for it. They cannot strip my lands from me for that."

He'd said too much. Exposed his fear to the older man. He might be young, but he was a lord, and he must never betray weakness. He hated Lop for catching him so exposed.

"Execute her," Lop repeated slowly. "On the Sabbath. With all the people venerating her as a holy woman."

"That is what we must stamp out," Guilhem said, "before the friar observes it. Do it tonight, before dawn."

Lop held out a hand. "There's rain coming."

"I don't care about rain."

Lop's silence irked Guilhem more than any response he might have made.

"So, I will build the fire . . . ?" The *bayle*'s unspoken question dangled in the night air.

"*Oc*." Senhor Guilhem tried to swallow, but his mouth was dry. "I myself will bring you the heretic."

BOTILLE

here is he now?" I cried. "Has he taken her away?"

"Hush," Sazia hissed. "Plazi, is the friar here?"

My elder *sǫrre* was too shaken to speak. Sazia laid her hands on Plazensa's shoulders. Plazi took a slow breath.

"He's here now. In the back bedroom, alongside Dolssa's."

The room tilted.

Here.

Plazensa threw a log onto the fire. She took a broom and pretended to sweep, making noise to cover our conversation. Her whispers shook.

"I told him we had no suitable room." Her speech was no louder than breath. "He offered to sleep on the hearth of the tavern. I told him he should stay at the church, in Dominus Bernard's quarters. But he didn't want to show up at a late hour, unannounced, with a storm on the way. He wanted to pay to sleep here tonight, then make what plans he would, tomorrow."

But, Plazi, I wanted to scream, *why did you let him stay? No man can ever get past you. You're more cunning than them all.*

She knew my thoughts.

"He was determined, Botille," she whispered. "I'd attract his attention more by refusing than by simply renting him a room. It's just until tomorrow morning."

"Until tomorrow," whispered Sazia, "when we must lead him up the streets of a town where her name is on every tongue."

I ventured a step down the hall. From his room came the sawing sounds of the friar snoring. How dare he snore, like any man, like Jobau, or some peasant, when awake he was malice and murder roaming abroad?

"All the inquisitor needs to do," Sazia whispered, "is ask anyone if they know a Dolssa. All Bajas would tell him proudly, 'The holy woman at the tavern.'"

I was falling, sinking, drowning in the pit of my stomach, in the hungry, howling waves of *la mar.* Cold terror poured down my throat like salt water.

"They will seize her by morning," Sazia said. "They will burn her before midday."

"That isn't all," I said. "They will take and burn us, too."

I couldn't speak. I couldn't think. My young, vibrant sisters. Snuffed out like smooth new candles.

We pretended the words hadn't been said.

Sazia spoke. "How did he find her?"

"The knight," Plazensa said. "He must have ridden off to send a message to the friar."

"Botille," whispered Plazi, "are you all right?"

She put her arms around me. The sea of grief inside me parted, and I cried into her neck.

"I did this to you," I said. "I brought the danger here. Sazia warned me."

"Don't," said Sazia.

"You did what a Christian ought to do," Plazensa whispered.

"Even if," added Sazia, "it was exactly what the friars say a Christian ought not do."

I remembered my talk with Dominus Bernard. "Inquisitors," I said, "punish those who help heretics just like the heretics themselves."

We sat there in the red glow of the dying embers on the hearth, leaning against one another.

"We could take a boat," I said. "We could all make our escape by *la mar*."

"We'd have to go to Egypt or Araby," said Sazia, "for anywhere in Christendom, they could find us."

"*Mon Dieu*," whispered Plazensa. "We are all dead."

A movement at the back caught my eye. We froze, then looked

up to see Dolssa venturing into the firelight from the corridor to our rear chambers. Her gaze took in each one of us, with eyes that overflowed with pity.

"Get back in your room," I whispered. "You're not safe here."

Dolssa did not react. "I know the inquisitor is here," she said. "I heard him."

Plazensa closed her eyes.

I wanted her to say, *Protect me. Hide me. Please.* Just to know she was human, and afraid, as we were. What she said instead was this:

"You have been so kind to me."

I took Sazia's healed hand in mine. "A kindness," I protested, "you have more than repaid."

"But you would have helped me," insisted Dolssa, "even if none of God's miracles had followed." She took a brave breath. "I have endangered you all by staying here. I never should have yielded to your kindness as I did. It was unforgivable of me. I will leave you now."

We rose in alarm, but stifled ourselves before waking the friar.

I reached her first, and threw my arms around her. "Never, never leave us," I whispered. "Unless we can take you to safety ourselves."

"They'll catch you if you flee tonight," Sazia said. "Any moment now, it will storm."

Tears coursed down Dolssa's face. "I watched my mother die for me," she whispered. "I can't allow them to hurt you, too."

Plazensa wiped Dolssa's face with a cloth. "Dear friend," she said, "your leaving now would only get you wet. They know you live with us. What will come, will come. Don't go."

Dolssa sank onto a barstool. She buried her face in her arms and wept.

After a while she raised her tear-stained face. "God knows, I am weary enough of the hunt," she said softly. "But why must I always bring harm to those who are kind to me?"

Sazia rubbed her shoulders.

Dolssa raised her head. She blinked at us like a sleepy child.

"Know that I am praying for each of you. And your Jobau."

And our Jobau.

She wiped her eyes with her sleeve, and rose to her feet. "My love asks me to tell you: don't be afraid."

My sisters and I felt one another's thoughts. Fear lay curled to strike in the back bedroom.

"Does he offer you the same comfort, Dolssa?" I whispered.

She who'd saved our Sazia—could she not save us now? Couldn't her beloved shield us under his wings?

She had prayed for her own mother, too.

Outside, the sky wrenched in half, sending a cracking boom across the lagoon.

We were dead already.

That night, while the rain lashed at Bajas, Sazia and I climbed up and down every street and knocked on every door. Our townsmen looked murderous when they opened the doors, but we told them anyway.

Our Dolssa's holiness has angered the inquisitors.

They call her a heretic. They don't understand.

They have sent an inquisitor here to Bajas to hunt for her. Staying, if you can believe it, at the Three Pigeons.

They plan to execute her.

Tell your children to forget her name.

Please, do not betray our holy woman, or she and we will die in the flames.

What will we do? We don't know yet. Pray for us, and do not tell.

Martin and Lisette de Boroc were the first people we visited. Lisette broke down weeping. She offered to hide Dolssa in her home. She volunteered her husband's fishing boat to take Dolssa anywhere. But Martin understood. He put his arm around his wife's waist and tugged her back inside. He had mingled enough with the larger world to see the danger more clearly. They'd find no mercy, no sympathy, no understanding in the inquisitors. Their baby's saved life would not excuse them for praising a heretic as a holy woman, nor for helping her escape.

We warned Dominus Bernard. He had an overnight visitor, and was none too happy to be disturbed by our knock. When we told him to prepare himself to host an inquisitor tomorrow morning, the mood for love left him, more pity to his unseen companion. We pleaded with him not to betray our Dolssa.

"What do you think I am, Botille, a monster?" he said.

What I knew him to be was a survivor, and that was what I feared most.

Saura, Garcia's wife, was devastated by the news. She was as devoted to Dolssa as she was to God and his church. They were one and the same for her. Who else but God could have allowed Dolssa to perform her mighty works? How could God burn God?

I hated to wake Na Pieret, but she came immediately to the door, on the heels of the serving woman who answered our knock. She bid us come in out of the rain. We dripped upon her threshold. Symo appeared behind her in a nightshirt and cap.

We told our tale, and Na Pieret leaned against the doorjamb, and thought.

"You are sure that *la donzẹlla* Dolssa has been convicted by the Church?"

"I have only her account of things," I said, "but that is enough to leave me terrified." I looked to Symo. "You were there when we found the friar hunting for her."

I wished Na Pieret would take the problem under her capable wings. With her wisdom, her wealth, her influence, could she not bring to pass a miracle of her own, one that protected Dolssa and all of us from danger?

But she had her sons to think of now. If she became involved with Dolssa, she could lose all she possessed. All her lands and wealth. And I knew she wanted, more than anything, to leave a legacy to her nephews. She had brought them here to love them and to give them everything. So she would not die unloved and alone.

"I will think on this, Botille," said Na Pieret. "I will pray for you. In the meantime, though, be careful."

A gap appeared between us as she pulled the door shut. I saw it in her eyes. I stumbled back as though she'd slapped me.

Not only could inquisitors seize, convict, and burn, they could slice through long ties of loyalty with the double-edged blade of fear.

"This cannot work," Sazia spoke through chattering teeth. Her hair hung in wet ropes down her face.

We stood before the *maison* of Lop, the *bayle*. Guilhem's official, the sword of the law in Bajas. What to do? Ask him not to tell *himself* about our Dolssa? Of course he would know of her. No one in town could fail to. His position exposed our folly to us. All our trudging about and rousing the villagers had been for nothing.

We went home.

The rain relaxed its fury and settled in as a steady drizzle. The storm moved south, and left off lashing through the tree branches. We were nearly home, when Sazia noticed it. A light in the woods. No, through the trees, down toward the beach, not far from the tavern, on the patchy knoll that separated the waterfront from the useful soil of Bajas.

We crept closer and hid behind the tall trees.

"*Mon Dieu.*" I leaned against a tree.

It was Lop, building a pyre.

Sazia ran home to tell Plazensa, and to check on Dolssa. I stayed to keep watch.

A dark shape approached the tavern. They were coming for Dolssa. Should I scream to warn my sisters?

Then the shape veered off course and picked its way down through the trees.

I sagged in relief. "Thank God," I whispered. "It's only you, Symo."

"What's happening?"

I pointed to where Lop moved about before his smoldering, hissing fire. "He's building a pyre."

Symo watched the *bayle* work. "He's having a deuce of a time in all this wet."

"But the fire still grows."

Symo fingered my dripping sleeve. "Have you been out all night?"

"Begging." I shivered.

Lop paused and looked toward us. We hid ourselves behind two trees. Finally the *bayle* went back to work.

"They're going to kill her," I said, "then kill us."

He said nothing.

"Symo," I said, "stay away from this. Disappear. The friar will forget about you. If he wonders where my brother is, the villagers will tell him I have no brother. But if you get involved, you'll die for no reason."

The glint of firelight reflecting off his eyes was all of him that I could see.

"Go home," I said. "I can't bear to think of how Na Pieret would grieve for you."

Footsteps from up the road made us both freeze. Footsteps, and a struggle. And the muffled cries of a woman's voice.

"Dolssa," I said. "They've got her."

"Hush!"

I couldn't. "I have to do something!"

"Don't!"

Symo clamped his hand over my mouth. I struggled against him, but he wouldn't budge. I tried to bite his fingers.

"Be still," he hissed into my ear, "or they'll have you."

The tavern still sat quietly. A little light peeped through the shutters. Shadows passed before the light but never paused to go inside.

Lop's flames mounted higher. They cast enough light now that I could glimpse the man and his captive as they drew nearer where I stood.

It was Senhor Guilhem, pulling a woman with him. A woman in dark dress, with gray hair streaked with white. A once-proud woman, hunched with age, gagged and shaking.

Not Dolssa.

The *bona femna* from the woods.

Oh no. No, no, no.

Yet she was not Dolssa. Was my gladness sin?

It wasn't gladness.

My knees gave way. Symo caught me and kept me from falling. The wine and hearth-fire scent of him filled my lungs, while Lop threw another log.

Guilhem dragged the struggling woman toward the fire. She fought, but the frail thing was no match for a hearty man. A dirty cloth was wound around her mouth. Lop spoke to the lord of Bajas, and the woman got in the way, so he threw her down upon the ground.

She lay there like wet washing. They conferred, like men debating how best to plow a field. Dawn began to peer over the horizon.

Finally Lop drove four stakes into the ground, two on either side of the fire, barely a body's width between the two poles on either side. So she couldn't roll away.

"Who is she?" Symo's grip on me relaxed.

"An old *bona femna* who hides in the woods," I whispered. "We should do something."

"You can't."

"We have to."

His lips pushed his murmured words straight into my ear. "Botille," he said, "if you try, they'll kill you next. And your sisters. And Dolssa."

Leaping, dancing flames. Would all I loved be next to burn?

"There's nothing you can do for her," he said. "There is a chance, though, that this woman's death could save Dolssa, and you."

They hoisted the woman's limp form into the air, and awkwardly, straddling the fire, they laid her down between the stakes. The posts, they'd become, of her final bed. She struggled and fought. A pitiable sight. Her dress was so wet that for a moment I thought she had put the fire out.

Lop fanned the flames and loaded more wood.

Then her hair flamed bright. Her clothing next caught fire. Even the gag burned at last, leaving her free to scream. And they, her murderers, dared demand that she be still.

The stench of burnt hair and cloth reached my nose, and I vomited.

Then scorching meat.

Sizzling blood.

And still the heretic screamed.

I hid my face against Symo's. He wrapped his arms around me and pressed his bristly cheek into mine.

I thanked God for the comfort of a human presence, any presence, any beating heart.

The tavern door banged open. We turned our heads to see someone hurry out. Too tall for one of my sisters.

The friar Lucien de Saint-Honore. The sight of him drained the last dregs of life in me.

He stood, smelling the air. His gaze went straight to the fire. He hurried down the slope toward the beach.

We separated, Symo and I.

In that moment, the *bona femna*'s screaming stopped. The fire and smoke had overcome her lungs at last.

Men's voices reached us, but I could not bear to hear. We crept back to the tavern.

LUCIEN DE SAINT-HONORE

ucien de Saint-Honore ran down to the pyre on the beach. When he collided with the full wave of odor from the burning body, he ducked his head to the side.

"What is happening here?"

The two men standing by turned to study him.

"So young," observed the younger of the two men, more finely dressed.

"Who are you?" Lucien demanded.

The speaker of the pair regarded him. His eyes were wide open, and horrified. As though the dead had been his own beloved. "I should ask that question of you."

Lucien moved uphill from the smoke. He looked at the

scorching remains atop the fire, and grimaced. Unlike some of his older associates in the convent at Tolosa, he was still unused to this sight.

"You laid this person in the fire," he marveled, "like a roasting animal."

The other man, with thick whiskers protruding from every side of his face, like a lion's mane, spoke. "Finishes the job faster," he said. "Merciful."

"Who was executed here?"

The younger man folded his arms across his chest. "You still haven't stated your name."

Lucien gritted his teeth. "I am Lucien de Saint-Honore, inquisitor, and friar of the Dominican convent at Tolosa. I have traveled here in pursuit of a heretic, Dolssa de Stigata. My authority comes from Pope Gregory himself." He held himself tall.

The two men looked at each other. Then the younger of them extended his hand to Lucien.

"Well met, inquisitor," he said. "I am Guilhem de Bajas, and this is Lop, my *bayle*. Bajas is my holding, and you see before you all that remains of the heretic you seek."

Lucien forgot his companions. He took a step closer to the fire. There they were, the blackened, leering, smoking limbs, the bits of graying bone. How could they be she? He closed his eyes and saw her soft, living flesh, her red lips, the dark mark above them, reaching forward to kiss him. . . .

His eyes flew open. "You are certain it was she?"

The wiry man's eyes went to the younger lord.

"We are a small community," said Senhor Guilhem.

The bushy man went silently back to the fire. He shifted logs around to speed the burning. Some, he placed over the corpse, obscuring it from view.

Dolssa de Stigata. His heretic, his great mission, was now mere matter, like any other log in the fire.

"Why did you execute her?" Lucien heard his voice ask. "I heard she was reputed a holy woman."

Senhor Guilhem turned to stare at him. "Was she, then?"

Lucien stepped back from the heat of the fire into the cool dawn air. "No, she was a heretic. A great deceiver. I . . . I had heard, though, that she had grown a large following here."

"We don't harbor heretics," the young lord said too quickly. "Not here in Bajas."

The gray man watched.

Dolssa de Stigata was gone from his sight now. Now and always. Lucien shivered. A welcome distraction appeared in his thoughts.

"I saw a *toza* just now," he told the others. "I met her once before. Her name is . . . Botille."

"The matchmaker," said the gray man.

"Matchmaker?" asked Lucien.

Senhor Guilhem shot his companion a look. "Most meddlesome, fast-talking, lying little slut you could meet."

Lucien turned this intelligence over carefully. This sounded nothing like the half-witted girl he'd met.

"And her brother . . . ?"

The young lord looked to the *bayle* and shrugged.

"Botille has no brother, Friar," he said. "She and her sisters run the tavern. You're staying there?"

Lucien nodded absently. "That's right." *No brother.* Of course. The embrace he'd seen hardly looked brotherly.

The sun was fully risen now, and up the hill villagers began to stir. The smoke from the pyre began to attract curious eyes, but the presence of the *senhor*, the *bayle*, and a holy stranger kept on-lookers at a distance.

"Make it known, Lop," said Guilhem, "that the *heretic* has met her death."

The *bayle* nodded and left.

"Well, friar," the lord said, "how can I serve you? Will you need supplies or funds for your return to Tolosa?"

Lucien returned the lord's gaze. "Not just yet," he said. "The heretic's death does not necessarily kill the poisonous flower she has planted here. I have more inquiries to conduct. For now, as it is Sunday, I'll take myself first to the church."

BOTILLE

ord of Dolssa's death and the friar's coming brought everyone to Mass.

We stood toward the rear of the nave at Sant Martin's—Plazensa, Sazia, Symo, and I. All Bajas sat before us. Some were crying. Most were stiff and still. All of us, waiting.

Friar Lucien de Saint-Honore sat in the wings to one side of the altar, also waiting.

The *bona femna* who'd died filled my thoughts.

How old was she? Which village had been hers? What was her name? Who had been her friends long ago? How many men and women, boys and girls, had bowed to her daily, seeking her blessings, long ago, before the Church and the French won their wasting war and drove the friends of God into hiding?

Dominus Bernard chanted the liturgy, but his Latin was clumsier than usual, with Friar Lucien watching. He elevated the host, and we all bowed our heads. Senhor Guilhem approached the altar to receive it. Lucien de Saint-Honore, Na Pieret, and a few others received the host, while the rest of us adored the Savior's body and blood from our places. I saw Na Pieret's gaze move quickly to Symo, standing with us, and just as quickly back down to the floor. She was worried. She didn't like his choice of place. I wondered about it myself.

Dominus Bernard seemed done with the Eucharist, when, to our astonishment, another man from the back strode down the aisle to receive it.

Plazi, Sazia, and I exchanged a glance as he passed by. It was the knight, Senhor Hugo de Miramont. He cut through the chapel like a blade.

"He's here," Plazi said.

"I *knew* it," moaned Sazia. "They were allies from the first."

I watched as the knight approached the friar, searching for a hint of comradeship. Had Senhor Hugo, in fact, summoned the inquisitor?

Their eyes met. That they knew each other, no one could doubt. A flush rose in Lucien de Saint-Honore's cheeks. He held his head high. They'd won. Or so he believed.

The sight of Senhor Guilhem and Lop filled me with loathing.

Symo watched me sideways. The memory of his appearance last night, and of my embarrassing display of weakness before him, left me sick. I'd embraced him. A woman had been dying. A woman who wasn't Dolssa. But dying, cruelly, all the same.

"Why are you here?" I whispered in Symo's ear.

He looked at me as though I were the greatest idiot in Christendom. "Because you're my half-wit *sorre*," he said. "That's what we told the friar. So now we're stuck with it."

"It's what *you* told the friar," I said.

His forehead furrowed. "Both of us," he said, "if we knew then what we know now, might have made different choices."

"I'd never have gone to San Cucufati," I said, "if I'd known what trouble I'd find there."

Sazia eyed us both malevolently and held a finger over her lips.

Dominus Bernard finished the Eucharistic celebration and carefully wiped and placed the sacred vessels, then turned to Friar Lucien de Saint-Honore.

"Today," said our priest, "we will be favored by a sermon from a member of the Order of Friars-Preachers, Lucien de Saint-Honore. He brings us a message from Tolosa." With that unceremonious introduction, Bernard sat down.

Friar Lucien rose. He had retonsured his head so that his white crown poked out from his ring of dark hair like the sun-bleached homes on Bajas's hill. His black cloak and white habit hung over his tall frame. He spoke not in Latin but in our tongue, though his northern French accent colored his voice. And what a voice! He seemed to sing. His voice filled the sanctuary and rippled off its walls. It danced with the starry motes of light drifting down in the morning air.

"My friends," he began. "I greet you in Our Lord's name, and on his errand. I bring to you the salutation of the Lord Bishop of Tolosa, Raimon, and all the brotherhood of the chapter in Tolosa of Sant Dominic's Order of Preachers."

The friar produced a sheaf of parchment leaves emblazoned with a red seal. "I come with the authorization of the Holy Father, who, as Apostle and head of the Church, and in great concern for the safety of your souls, before his death asked the friars of my order to assist the Church in conducting inquisitions throughout Provensa." He paused to read straight from the leaves. "'All princes, lords, knights, and nobles, magistrates, rulers, royal officials, and officers of law are hereby enjoined to assist this effort, and to lend their authority, and the full might of law, to the care and protection of the Church.'"

Senhor Guilhem sat tall and proud. *The care and protection of the Church* sounded so right, so worthy and necessary, rolling off Friar Lucien de Saint-Honore's golden tongue.

"'Any who are slack in their duties as princes and rulers in Christendom must face interdict, excommunication, anathema, and loss of lands and holdings, as needs may dictate.'"

Senhor Guilhem still sat tall, but his jaw now worked as though he chewed on a tough chestnut. Dominus Bernard's face was ashen.

"Heresy has run rampant among you." Friar Lucien tucked away his papers. "Many of you were deceived by the wonders demonstrated by Dolssa, the so-called holy woman."

Quiet crying echoed in the sanctuary at the mention of her name.

"So much so that you weep at her loss," said the indignant friar, "rather than exulting in God's victory over error."

The mourners grew still.

"To finish the work that God's crusading army began in this corner of the Lord's vineyard, and to root out the pernicious influence of this heretical impostor, I have come to investigate this area, to ascertain what errors still lurk in Bajas. We begin tomorrow. Your priest, Dominus Bernard, shall supply me with your names, and from these I shall issue summons. I shall speak with each of you, in turn. *Tozets* from ages fourteen and up; *tozas*, twelve."

Santa Sara. Fourteen? Twelve? Fathers and mothers cast anxious glances at their older children. No one seemed enraptured by the friar's honeyed voice now.

My sisters and I knew one another's fears. We would be named by every half-grown child in town as Dolssa's protectors. I took Sazia's hand—that same hand that would have killed her—in mine. She would not be with us today, were it not for Dolssa.

"Take comfort," the friar said. "Heaven stands ever ready to welcome the sinner who repents. I am authorized to offer full clemency and pardon to any who come forward of their own free will and confess to their errors, whether in thought, in deed, or in association. Not to those who knowingly teach heresy, of course, for their lot is fixed, but for those who have succumbed to falsehood. If they come to me with a penitent heart, cooperate fully in our investigations, and reveal all that they know, they shall be pardoned. Any who come to me today, at the church of Sant Martin, will find me ready to hear their confession."

Thus he drew the noose around us. How was it done so neatly, with no weapons but words and a letter with red wax?

Many would seize hold of such an offer. All it would take was one.

The smell of incense made it hard to breathe. My legs twitched to run out of the church.

Their lot is fixed. Poor, sweet Dolssa. The feet we washed and anointed with oil—had we healed them so they could walk more ably into the flames?

I gazed at the cross above the altar, and the figure of Christ dying there. Could it ever be true, what this friar said? Was Dolssa an affront to our Lord's holiness?

Oh, Johan the Evangelist, I cried in my heart to the shrine where days ago I'd prayed. *You who were also called by our Lord, "Beloved." Plead for us, and help us.*

I didn't realize I was crying until dark spots splashed onto my bodice. Symo elbowed me and frowned. I didn't care. Let him despise me, the unfeeling monster.

A movement from the back startled me. Footsteps from the rear, striding down the aisle again. It was the knight, Senhor Hugo, once more. The friar seemed as surprised by this interruption as I was. My sisters and I held one another's hands. I realized I'd taken hold of Symo's hand, too. I shook it off like contagion.

The knight halted a few paces before the friar.

"Yes?" asked Lucien de Saint-Honore.

His bearing as a man of war seemed to discomfit the preacher. They watched each other until Senhor Hugo went down on one knee and bowed his head.

"Friar Lucien," he said loudly, "I offer myself and my sword to your service in this part of Christendom, to carry out God's work."

Lucien de Saint-Honore closed his eyes and took a deep breath. He rested a hand upon the knight's shoulder.

"Bless you, soldier of the cross," was his reply. "I gratefully accept your service in God's name."

When his eyes opened, they gazed heavenward, rapt with adoration and gratitude.

LOP

Lop the *bayle* returned home to his small *maison* after mass and pulled off his shoes.

The old woman who cooked and cleaned for him a few times a week had left a pot of something on his hearth. He poked at the fire and threw on a few more sticks. It reminded him of last night's execution, and he shuddered.

It was a good living, acting as Guilhem's *bayle*. No one troubled him, and he got his money. The mighty must acknowledge him, and the peasants must fear him. So long as he was strong and able, it was a good life, if dull sometimes for want of friendship. But friendship doesn't fend off starvation in winter, nor shelter anyone from the deadly winds of political and religious conflict that had raged throughout Lop's lifetime.

Still. That burning woman. She hadn't stopped burning, behind his eyelids, since this morning. All through breakfast. All through mass. He never took this job wishing to throw old gray *femnas* in the fire. A woman of the same age as his own mother, were she still alive. Who wanted to do that?

But he'd done it. Lop would never be found lacking in his job. *Dieu*, he was tired.

There was a knock at the door. He pulled on his shoes and rose. His sleepless night haunted him now. He opened the door to find the Tolosan knight, Senhor Hugo, standing there.

Lop, as a rule, did not show surprise. He genuflected, befitting the nobleman's rank.

"Senhor de Miramont," he said, "how may I serve you?"

"Your name is Lop?"

"*Oc*." He bowed again. "Would you care to come inside my home?"

"*Grácia*." Senhor Hugo pulled his cloak about his sides and ducked through the door. He was a much taller man than stocky Lop. He sat upon a stool next to the fire.

The *bayle* pulled a pitcher of wine and some cups from a shelf, but the knight waved the offer away. Lop put them back.

"Good *bayle*," the knight said. "What can you tell me about the woman executed last night?"

Lop ran his hand over his wiry whiskers. Danger tingled in the air. He must choose his words carefully.

"She did not much welcome death," he said. "I can say that much."

"Who among us does?"

Lop met his gaze. "There are some," he said, "who seem to court it."

"What else?"

Lop watched the man's face. "Her name was Dolssa."

"Did she state that as her name?"

Lop shook his head. "*Non*. It's what Senhor Guilhem said."

"So he was with you, then, last night?"

"For much of the time, *oc*."

Lop wondered to what these questions tended, but he knew not to pry. This knight betrayed no urgency, no desire, but pressed his questions coolly upon him.

"Where was the woman found?"

Lop rubbed his beard. "I don't know," he said. "It was Senhor Guilhem who found her and arrested her. Somewhere outside of the *vila*, I think."

The knight sat and watched Lop until even he, veteran of trouble, broke his gaze and looked away. He looked back. Another question seemed to hang in the air.

Lop went on the offensive.

"Did you know the woman, Senhor?"

Nothing could ruffle Senhor Hugo. "I was there when she was sentenced in Tolosa. *Oc.*"

"And she escaped?"

He nodded. "She did."

No credit to you, thought Lop. A low laugh rumbled in his throat. "Some trick that must have been," he said, "for such an old crone to slip through the Bishop of Tolosa's chains."

Senhor Hugo watched Lop. "Heretics," he said slowly, "can be cunning."

"Or have cunning friends," added Lop.

The knight's eyebrows rose. "That is also true." He stood and placed a coin upon the table. "For your good help," he said. "I'll see you again." He left before Lop could rise to show him to the door.

BOTILLE

e have to hide you."

My sisters and I crowded into Dolssa's bedroom. Her face was pale as she listened to all that had happened in the night and in the morning at mass.

"There is only one place we know of," I said, "where searchers ought not to find you, and that's down in Plazensa's ale cellar."

Dolssa thought a while. "If they think me dead," she asked, "will they still search?"

Sazia answered in low tones. "They will search for any shred of you," she said. "Any clue as to whom you influenced, what you did, what you left behind."

"Until Lucien de Saint-Honore leaves town," I said, "you are not safe."

She wrung her hands. "Let me leave you!" she begged. "Let me carry my danger away from this place."

I knelt down and took her hands in mine.

"Dolssa, that time is past," I said. "We will face this together."

A tear ran down her cheek.

I spoke as gently as I could. "What does your beloved tell you?"

She looked up at me. "My mother asked me the same question the night she died."

"And what did you say?" asked Plazensa.

Dolssa shook her head. "I had no answer." She rose slowly to her feet. "I will go to the cellar. May . . . may I have a candle?"

Plazi looked sad. "Only if you want to watch the rats. Better not to, *galineta*. Someone could glimpse the light or smell the smoke. And it's not the cellar itself. It's a long box within the cellar where jugs are stored, built into the foundation, so it's not often seen. Searchers could well pass over you and not know to look."

Dolssa looked green. "Not a cellar, but a coffin."

We nodded. We felt awful.

She swallowed. "When must I go down? At night?"

I turned to Sazia. "What do you think, little *sorre*? When will danger come?"

Sazia shook her head mournfully. "Exactly when is unknown to me, but that it's coming soon is certain."

Dolssa rose unsteadily to her feet. "Take me to my grave, then," she said. "Perhaps, with practice such as this, I'll come to fear it less."

We settled her as best we could into the ale cellar. It was a gruesome place to hide a human soul. I felt miserable doing it, and even more so as I saw how humbly she submitted to it, though it terrified her. Her chamber was indeed a coffin, damp, with pale roots snaking through the walls.

My sisters went back upstairs to prepare the next meal for the tavern, and to receive the inquisitor when he returned. I should have joined them, but I lingered a few moments before closing the lid over Dolssa's sham tomb.

We sat together on the slab lid of the box that would hide her from view, and together we watched the small light from my little candlestick. I wished I could do something to comfort her.

"We'll get through this," I told her. "Your beloved would not have spared you this far for nothing."

Dolssa took so long in answering, I wondered if she'd heard me. Breathing, down in that musty gloom, took all the courage she had.

"My beloved," she finally said, "ought to be enough for me."

She was scolding herself. Poor girl.

"What's he like?" I asked her.

She turned to look at me curiously. "Don't you know?"

I leaned against her shoulder. "Not as you do," I said. "I've heard Dominus Bernard's sermons, of course. He's a shameless old rascal, but I know he loves Jhesus. That's not what I mean. You say he's your beloved. If you were any other girl with a beau, I would ask you, what's he like?"

"Oh." I wondered if she were blushing.

"I like Jhesus myself," I said. "I wish he were one of the customers at the Three Pigeons." I nudged Dolssa. "I suppose, thanks to you, he has been here a good deal lately."

I got a smile from her then, in spite of her melancholy.

"Don't lose heart, *galineta*," I whispered. "You can trust us."

"Have you ever had a beau, Botille?"

I laughed. "Not I! I've no time for that. Nobody courts the matchmaker."

Dolssa looked puzzled. "I was sure that you and that young *ome* . . . What was his name . . . Symo? From our journey . . . ?"

I snorted with laughter. "You may be a holy woman, Dolssa de Stigata," I told her, "but you're no prophetess."

Plazensa opened the door to the cellar. I saw her feet and heard her voice. "Best come up now, Botille."

I wiped my eyes. "I'll come see you again, as soon as it's safe," I told Dolssa.

Dolssa kissed my cheek. "Do that, please," she said. "But for your sake, I pray, not until then."

I settled her into the stone box and lowered the lid over her.

Like a burial, indeed. Like rolling a stone over a garden tomb.

God in heaven, I prayed, *hide her here.*

I left Plazi and Sazia to their task of plucking two fat ducks, and returned to Dolssa's room to remove from it any shred of evidence that a woman had stayed there.

I couldn't think. My hands shook at the simplest of tasks. Every rush of sea wind at the shutters, every sound of man or beast, left me jittery and sick. If I pitied myself my troubles, I needed only to think of poor Dolssa.

We sent Mimi down to keep her company, and sometimes we heard the squeal of a dying rat from below. I wondered which was worse—hearing Mimi kill them, or knowing they were silently, sniffingly there.

We prepared dinner as though there would be tavern guests, stuffing ducks with chopped onions and mushrooms, and roasting them in a hot oven.

"No one's coming tonight at all, it seems," noted Plazensa.

Sazia poked her nose in the oven. "More for us."

We actually looked up with anticipation when the door opened. But it was not a customer. It was Lop the *bayle* and Senhor Hugo the knight. Following at their heels was Friar Lucien de Saint-Honore.

While my heart stopped beating, Plazensa, that wondrous

femna, pulled a crackling brown duck from the oven and presented it to her treacherous audience. "Just in time, my good men," she said. "Dinner for three?"

"I'll pour the wine," offered Sazia, "unless ale is your pleasure tonight?"

Friar Lucien de Saint-Honore seemed to have noticed Plazensa's smile for the first time. I would have enjoyed watching him struggle, any other day but this. Senhor Guilhem seemed to have noticed it too.

"We're not here to dine," the senhor said after an awkward pause. "Search the building."

Dieu, help us. Hide Dolssa.

Lop led the charge, room by room through the tavern, with Senhor Guilhem at his side. He poked his staff under and behind all the furnishings and beds. He made no effort to spare our things. We sat and waited numbly in the tavern. When they entered Dolssa's room, I held my breath, as if they might smell her lingering echo there.

"For what do you search, my lords?" Plazensa asked the friar and the knight.

Senhor Hugo was the only one who bothered to respond.

"My report," he said, "which I will take back to Bishop Raimon of Tolosa, requires me to reconstruct the heretic's final days and weeks. There seems to be some confusion. Some believe"—he glanced at Senhor Guilhem—"that she made her home in the woods, while others"—here he stared straight at me—"say she made her home at this tavern."

"*Did* the heretic Dolssa make her home here at this tavern?" asked Lucien.

Oh, sisters, what do we do?

I dared not speak. Plazensa rose to the challenge.

"Many travelers stay here at the Three Pigeons for a time," said she. "It is the nature of a public house such as ours."

Friar Lucien de Saint-Honore pressed his hands together. "Did the heretic Dolssa make her home here at this tavern?"

"We had a Dolssa here," she said, "for a few nights. We took pity on her. She was poor and weak when she arrived."

"When did she arrive?"

Plazensa turned to Sazia. "Do you remember, *sǫrre*?"

Sazia shrugged. "Some days ago. A week? I can't be sure."

"How did she get here?"

Sazia replied again. "She had neither mule nor horse."

"When did she last leave?"

The hardest question of all. The woman who died needed to be Dolssa. She needed to have left here in order to be found in the woods last night.

I held up two fingers. "Two?" I babbled. "Two nights, good-bye, *femna*."

Senhor Hugo de Miramont's eyes narrowed, but he said nothing.

Plazensa and Sazia glanced at me. They didn't understand that I must play the half-wit. Not yet.

Lop returned to the front room. Friar Lucien pointed up to the loft over the bar.

Plazensa sighed. "Jobau," she called upward, "lower your ladder."

A boar's grunt was our answer.

"Jobau," Plazi persisted, "we have men here who think you might be a holy young maiden. Lower your ladder."

Jobau told us, and all within earshot, which precise anatomical parts of a jackass he thought we were.

"Drop your ladder, you drunken swine, or you'll get a flogging that'll smack you sober," called Lop.

The ladder came down with a crash and a shower of insults. Lop climbed up, prodded the fetid heap of straw and blankets Jobau called a bed, and came back down. Jobau kept a steady torrent of abuses hurling down upon us for a good while after, and I'd never liked him better than I did just then.

"Satisfied?" Plazensa's eyes flashed.

"That's it, then," said the knight, but the friar held up a hand.

"Where do you store your wine and ale?" he asked my older sister.

She blinked at him. "In the cellar."

"I thought so."

Plazi wordlessly rose and slid aside the wooden slab that guarded the opening to her precious stores. Lop held a candle and descended the ladder. He disappeared, leaving us with the knight and the friar watching us.

Keeping our faces still. That was the hardest part.

"Did you venerate Dolssa as a holy woman?" asked the friar.

Plazensa didn't flinch. "We knew there were those," she said calmly, "who called her a healer. A *medica*. To us, she was just another boarder at the tavern."

She made me proud.

A piercing scream met our ears. Lucien de Saint-Honore jumped. From down below, we heard Lop swear. Mimi shot up the ladder and into the tavern. She disappeared under the bar, hissing at us.

I crouched down for a look at her. "Are you all right, cat-cat?" I asked in my infant voice.

"Why would there be a cat in an empty cellar?" demanded the friar.

"Tending to the rats, of course," Plazensa said haughtily. "I run a clean establishment."

We waited longer. And longer still. Finally the *bayle* appeared from out of the ground. He had a nasty gash running alongside his nose, beading angry drops of blood.

"If I ever see that cat of yours again," he told us, "I'll skin it alive."

"Where's my candlestick?" Plazi asked him.

The *bayle* headed for the door, with the knight and friar following. "Fetch it yourself," he said. "Your devilish cat made me drop it."

I think I was still shaking that night, when Symo arrived, and we told him what had happened. He might as well know all, since he'd become our brother.

He kicked off his boots and stretched his foul-smelling feet onto a nearby chair.

"It was bound to happen," he said. "You're lucky they didn't find her."

Mimi strutted by and arched her back—a Mimi who had just feasted on her own specially caught raw fish. Plazensa had told me to buy one from Litgier, but he refused payment.

"We've fixed a room for you," Sazia told Symo. "The room that used to be Dolssa's."

"And just like that, I'm banished to bed?" He stretched his burly arms, cracking several joints in the process. "Where's my dinner?"

Taking advantage of Plazensa just isn't done. My older *sǫrre* bit her lip and sliced him a plate of duck and turnips with murderous efficiency.

I couldn't abide conversation, nor the stench of his feet. I left the bar and sat in a low chair by the wall, peering out at the darkness of the lagoon through the shutters.

More low clouds had rolled in on sea breezes, blocking any gleam from the night sky.

I couldn't bear to think of Dolssa, alone in her darkness all night. She must be terrified. After the men had gone, I went downstairs and sat with her for a time, but we none of us dared stay long. Should anyone return, all must seem as usual.

And would they return?

Might the *bayle* recall that he had not, blessings upon our mangy cat, searched the wine cellar as well as possible? Where else could we take Dolssa where she could hide in peace? For she could not stay here forever. Nor could she ever return to the open in Bajas.

We needed time to think, and a good space to hide.

All was quiet in the tavern, save for the unpleasantly moist sounds of Symo's chewing.

I laid my head in Plazi's lap. I needed to hide my melancholy from Symo's unfeeling eyes. Plazi rolled her bracelets like cartwheels across my back.

Symo rose to his feet. "Let's move Dolssa somewhere safer." We stared at him. He pulled on his boots. "Dinner, by the way," he said, "was fairly good."

"Ignore him, Plazi," I said. "He's an ape, not a man."

The ape peered through the shutters. "It's good and dark tonight," he said. "Let's go."

"Go where?"

He pulled on his coat. "Get your holy *femna*," he whispered, "and let's be off."

I folded my arms across my chest. "Not until you speak sense."

"Just get her and come." His voice was dangerously low. "Walls have ears."

Plazi and I retreated behind the bar to confer.

"What should we do?" I whispered. "Should we trust him? Could this be a trap?"

"Any hiding place is better than this one," she said, "but I don't like it."

The door shut. We looked up to see that Symo had gone. What? Plazi and I stared. What could it mean? Would he now betray us?

I ran after him, out the door and out into the street. Only the faintest sound of footsteps told me he was heading uphill toward town. I flew after him until we collided in the dark. We both stumbled. Symo only barely caught me before we fell.

He clutched me by my arms and forced me to look at him. He was nothing but darkness, and a gleam upon eyes and teeth.

"Why did you leave?" I asked him.

"Why did I come, is the question!"

He was so angry. Symo was always angry, but this frightened me.

"You came because you had to, you bungler," I reminded him. "You invented the lie, and you're seeing it through."

"Did I have to, Botille Flasucra? Did I?"

Oh, *Dieu*. With my sisters and Dolssa in mortal peril, must I appease Symo's temper, too? Heaven help me! But the brute demanded I face him.

"No," I said.

He relaxed his grip.

"You didn't have to. Now let me go."

He released my arms. I almost stumbled again, I was so off-balance, but I righted myself this time.

"I didn't have to come, but I came. And still you do not trust me. You stand there, asking your sister, 'Should we trust him?' 'Is this a trap?' *Mon Dieu!*"

Could people hear us?

The thought of Dolssa, huddled in the cellar, gave me strength. "I hardly know you," I said. "I have Dolssa's life to think of, and my sisters'. And now the friar's here—"

"Sssh." He took my elbow and led me back down the hill toward the water.

We stood alone on the dark beach. The air smelled of salt and sand and fish. As though all was peace, and harvesttime, and autumn nights. Not the end of everything.

"'Now the friar's here'?" He prompted me to continue.

"*Oc.*" I breathed in the wet sea air. "Now the friar's here, and I have no answers. Only fears, and danger everywhere I turn."

Symo kicked at the wet sand. It splashed in clumps into *la mar*. "You hate me, don't you?"

"No." My answer surprised me. Didn't I? "No, I don't hate you. I just don't like you much."

He looked out over the water. He laughed a little, a dry, bitter sound. The first time I'd ever heard him laugh. Then he stood a while. There was only enough light to see the glint in his eyes, and the stirring of the wind through his dark hair.

"You can hate me if you like, Botille," he finally said, "but you've got no choice but to trust me. I should have thought you'd have the sense to see that."

I wanted to be far from here. Long gone, with my sisters and Dolssa close by me. *Carry me away,* I begged *la mar, far away to safety. Then bring me back home to the Bajas I knew before.*

"Come on, then," Symo said. "It's dark enough. Let's pack some food and lead your Dolssa to my wine cellar, out in the vineyards. She'll be far more comfortable there."

LUCIEN DE SAINT-HONORE

"State your name."

The scrawny lad across the table from Lucien mumbled something.

"One more time, my son?"

"Garcia." The boy licked his chapped and peeling lips.

"Garcia." Lucien wrote the word on a piece of parchment. They had experimented, first with the notary, then with having Bernard, the parish priest who'd brought the boy in, take transcription, but neither was quick enough. The priest's writing was full of errors. Ignorant provincial clerics. No wonder the people were susceptible to error, with an *illiteratus* expounding scripture to them.

"Surname?"

The boy gazed at him blankly. They sat in the dusty sacristy of Sant Martin's church. Barely more than a closet, it was filled with candlesticks, censers, vessels for wine and oil. The youth sweated in his seat as Lop, Senhor Hugo, Bernard, and Lucien looked on.

"Family name," suggested Lop, seated on a short stool in one corner.

Lucien looked expectantly at the boy.

"What is your father's name, son?" asked Senhor Hugo, who stood against the back wall, watching like a vulture on a bare branch as each person was examined.

"Oh. Garcia."

Lucien decided to let it pass. He wrote "de Bajas" after the boy's name. "How old are you?"

The boy sighed with relief. Finally a question he could answer. "Fourteen."

"Garcia," Lucien said. "Do you now, or have you ever at any time, known, spoken to, bowed to, adored, venerated, given gifts, food, shelter, or aid to, or otherwise succored a heretic, one of the so-called *amicx de Dieu*?"

The boy turned to Dominus Bernard in a plea for help. "I . . . pardon?"

The priest just stared at the floor.

This boy was clearly slow of mind. But that could be useful. Lucien smoothed his pile of parchment leaves. No hurry, no hurry at all.

"Have you, my son, ever seen any people called *bons omes* or *bonas femnas*? The good men and the good women, sometimes called the 'friends of God'?"

The boy frowned. He seemed relieved; this wasn't the question he'd been fearing. "There used to be an old lady, a few doors down. Esmerelda. Folks would bow to her, and she would bless them. Mamà would have me take fruits to her sometimes."

E-s-m-e-r-e-l-d-a. Lucien wrote the name carefully. "Do you know her family name? Any other names by which she was known? No? No matter." He dipped his quill in the ink. "Is she still alive?"

The boy shook his head. "Been dead for years."

"And do you know where she is buried?"

The boy's expression said this was a daft question. "Churchyard," he said. "Same as everyone else."

"I see." Lucien laid down the quill and looked more closely at the boy. "Now, Garcia," he said, "did you think Na Esmerelda was good?"

Garcia blinked at this. "Mamà and Papà said she was." He thought a moment more. "Sometimes she would give me bread."

"So your answer is yes?"

The boy nodded.

"How often did you eat her bread?"

The lad squirmed in his seat. "When she baked enough to spare. She was poor, so it wasn't often."

Lucien wrote this carefully. "Did you ever bow your head to Esmerelda? Did you ask her to bless you?"

The boy scratched his head. "Probably," he said at length.

"Probably?"

He squirmed. "At least a couple of times," he said, "as Mamà showed me to do."

Lucien wrote this carefully. "Your *mamà*, is she still alive?"

Young Garcia grinned. "*Oc*. Papà says Mamà never gets sick."

"Excellent." Lucien smiled at the boy. "What is her name?"

"Saura."

Lucien wrote this. "Now, Garcia, I want you to think. How old were you when you last bowed to Esmerelda?"

The youth did a bit of work upon his fingers. "Nine?" he ventured. "I think that's how old I was when she died."

"I see. And up until she died, how many times would you say you brought her fruits?"

A slow-dawning suspicion materialized in the youth's eyes. "Should I not have taken fruits to the *bona femna*?" he inquired. "My mamà told me to. She said it was alms. Aren't alms a good thing?"

The priest, Bernard, rose abruptly and began pacing the floor.

"Christian charity given to those who are worthy is always the right thing," said Lucien smoothly. "Now, think. On how many occasions did you bring fruits?"

The boy shrugged. "Ten times," he said. "At least."

"Ten times bringing fruits," Lucien narrated aloud as he wrote, "and several bows." He laid down the quill once more. "Now, Garcia. Did you know a woman named Dolssa de Stigata?"

Garcia's look changed. His eyes lowered.

"No," he said. "I never met any woman by that name."

Lop leaned back on his stool. "But everyone in town is talking about her."

"Good *bayle*," Lucien said, "allow me. Garcia, do you mean to say that you have never laid eyes on a *femna* named Dolssa de Stigata?"

The boy shook his head fervently. "Never. I've never seen her."

Lucien bit his lips to hide a smile. The lad had been coached, then. The way the youth became so much more anxious when the fugitive's name was mentioned was extremely interesting. Was it a flat-out lie? Or was there more to it?

"It seems that many people in town saw her," Lucien said softly. "How could an active boy like you miss out on that?"

The boy hesitated. He was piloting his own boat now, without his parents' preparation to guide him. "I was sick," he explained. "I was in bed with a fever a few days ago."

"Hm." Lucien reinked his quill. "Up and about again so soon?"

He nodded. "I'm all better now."

Lop, the *bayle*, watched with his hands folded across his chest. "Did they tell you, son, who made you better?"

Lucien made a note to himself to tell Senhor Guilhem to have the *bayle* removed. His brash way of interceding might work in everyday village lawsuits, but an inquisition into heretical depravity was a delicate exercise. In the future, Lop could remain outside. Civil authorities were only needed to carry out the sentencing. The knight, Lucien reasoned, could stay, but only to provide a witness, and protection.

"It was the woman, wasn't it? Na Dolssa, who made you better?" Lop was at it again.

The boy knew he'd lost. He nodded.

"God made you better," Lucien said. "Always give the glory to God, and not to man. You may go."

Young Garcia jumped up from his chair. "I'm done, then?"

Lucien gave him a grave look. "You may wait outside the door until we come out to speak with you."

The boy drooped and slunk away. Senhor Hugo watched him go with a look in his eyes that Lucien could not read and did not altogether like. He reviewed his notes and began issuing orders to Lop.

"Two yellow crosses marking him as a heretical sympathizer, to be sewn upon the shoulders of his clothing and worn for life," said Lucien. "Exhume the bones of Esmerelda for posthumous burning, but first, let us learn more about who her other associates might have been. Summon the parents, Garcia and Saura, for questioning. House arrest, lifelong, a probable outcome in their case, but first we must inquire of them, though with this testimony against them by their own son, who clearly bore no malice against them, we can convict even if they deny any connection to the heretical woman."

Lop's eyes narrowed. "All this, over Esmerelda? The crosses and house arrest?"

Lucien nodded.

"The lad'll have no more playmates," the *bayle* said. "No girl will marry him. No man will hire him. No one will dare."

Lucien de Saint-Honore interlaced his fingers and gazed back at the *bayle*. He had all the time needed to correct this official's misunderstandings about his mandate.

"Without a son to work and bring in food, the parents will starve to death on house arrest," Lop said. "The entire village would have bowed to Esmerelda and others like her."

"Which is why firm measures are needed," said Lucien, "in a region mired in falsehood."

Lop turned away, but Lucien heard what he muttered under his breath. Perhaps he was meant to. "There'll be nothing left of Bajas when you're done."

Lucien coughed slightly. "Would you like to be relieved of these duties, if they displease you?" The gray-eyed *bayle* made no response. "I can speak to Senhor Guilhem about it."

The *bayle*, who was easily twice the friar's age, was unmoved by this threat. "Why haven't you brought in the sisters from the tavern yet? Why are we wasting our time on children?"

Lucien liked being asked. "I am weaving my net, good *bayle*," he said. "One careful thread at a time. Method is the key. Not haste. Method."

Lop stood and shook out his stiff shoulders. "And you mean to take this much time in questioning every man, woman, and child in Bajas?"

Lucien smiled calmly. "I do," he said. "If the proceedings are tiresome to you, Senhor Hugo and I can manage them ourselves. By all means, you may resume your normal activities. At the end of each day we shall compile the sentencing and pass it along to you to carry out."

Lop sat back down. "I'll stay," he said. "I can endure as much boredom as you can."

Senhor Hugo looked away just then, and Lucien saw, to his great annoyance, that the knight was silently laughing.

HUGO

---

enhor Hugo de Miramont sat on a rock on the grassy slope leading down to the waterfront. He watched *la mar* as peaceful waves curled and broke upon the sand. What a day this would have been to strum his gittern and think gentler thoughts. In another world, another age.

His senses tingled. Someone was watching him. He turned about slowly, to betray no concern, but found nobody in sight other than some fishermen at work at the wharves a long ways away, and harvesters in the distance who were nothing but specks.

Odd.

Then his eyes caught his observer, and he jumped. A sleek

gray cat sat watching him from atop a small rock. Its cool, unblinking eyes examined him without apology.

The tavern cat. The one that scratched the *bayle*. Hugo blew out his breath and laughed.

"Honor to you, Grimalkin," he murmured. "Shame upon me. You've bested a knight of the count of Tolosa with nothing but your silent paws."

At the sound of his voice, the cat's ears pricked. It rose from its sunny rock, stretched its spine, then picked its way across the grass toward him, and stood expectantly at his feet.

The knight reached down and stroked the cat. It purred and arched its back.

"What secrets you could tell me, little cat," said Senhor de Miramont, "if you could talk."

But the cat was through with conversation. It sauntered up the hill and ventured out toward the countryside, where the harvesters wielded their stem-cutting blades and sang as they hauled in the last of the season's crop.

BOTILLE

he next day was a blur.

Dolssa had become our peace, our concern, our consolation. We tasted her absence like a missing tooth.

By the docks, in the streets, we heard rumors of children and youth rounded up for questioning. With each hour we were glad they hadn't come for us, but we couldn't understand it. The waiting was almost worse.

No one came to the tavern.

That night, a knock at the tavern door roused me from where I sat with my *sòrres* in a stupor of silent fear.

I unlocked the door and opened it to find Dominus Bernard. His face was gray. He wouldn't look me in the eyes. My stomach sank.

"You've come to take us in, haven't you?"

He came inside and closed the door.

"Botille," he said, "hear me quickly. You must leave here. You and your family. Go as far as you can, as fast as you can."

Plazensa rose from her seat and stirred behind the bar. Mimi mewed at the priest, then rubbed herself against his ankles.

"I can't stop this," Dominus Bernard went on. "You're in grave danger."

"We can't flee with Jobau," I whispered. "We wouldn't leave someone behind. You know that." He must know who else I meant by *someone*.

My old friend's mouth hardened. He took a slow breath, and spoke, no longer to the living, but the dead. "Then my coming here was wasted. Far better, had I stayed at home."

Plazensa approached and pressed a cup of wine into our village priest's hand. "We thank you, Dominus," she whispered. "Is there nothing you can do for us?"

Bernard refused the wine as though it were bitter. "I came tonight to warn you."

Without another look, he turned and left.

I roamed about in the afternoon, needing something to do. I headed out toward Na Pieret's vineyards, thinking I might find a chance to peek in on Dolssa, but Symo, seeing me, gave a shake of his head and sent me back. Harvesters were everywhere. It wouldn't have worked. I knew Symo was bringing her food and water, and even, at her request, some candles, parchment, and ink. What she needed most was company. I wondered what she was writing. I missed her.

I thought of visiting Sapdalina, but she wasn't home. Her father told me she was out walking with Gui.

Well.

Nor was Astruga at home. Her father told me she was still tending the de Prato children. I headed over to see her there.

She ducked out through her open door, then frowned at the sight of me.

"What do you want?"

"*Bonjorn*, Astruga," I said, and kissed her cheek. She backed away from me.

Over her shoulder I could see the small *maison* had smartened up considerably under her care. A noise erupted from the children, and she ordered them to leave off whacking each other. They obeyed. Joan de Prato passed by outside, pushing a barrow of wheat sheaves. He glanced at Astruga, and she back at him, and something passed between. Not a smile. Not quite. But something near.

"What have you come for, then, Botille?" asked Astruga.

"Oh, nothing," I said. "Just to see how you were getting on. Shall I send someone else to relieve you from watching the children?"

"Do I look like I need relieving?" She swelled with indignation.

"Not at all."

"There's no one else who could just step in and manage them, anyway," she said. "She wouldn't know them as I do."

I nodded. "You've done right by them. It's plain."

"*Oc*. Well." She stepped back inside. "I won't be needing your help anymore, Botille," she said. "You shouldn't come back here." She closed the door.

That night I defied what Symo had told me, and I snuck out to the vineyards after dark to go sit with Dolssa. I had to know she was all right. I could make the journey in the dark.

But I didn't get far. Halfway along the path leading to Na Pieret's wine cellar, I heard voices. I stopped alongside the path to listen. I didn't want to reveal my presence to anyone.

It took no time to discern that the voices belonged to Jacme and Andrio, Na Pieret's farmhands. They weren't quiet. They were roaring drunk.

"It's that friar," Jacme said. "He's the one. The others are all talk."

"Him with his *French* accent," said Andrio's voice. "He's younger than we are! Who does he think he is?"

I could picture them lying in the damp grass, with their legs splayed out before them, and pitchers of stolen wine clutched in their great hammy hands.

"Do you know what he did?" asked Jacme.

"What?"

Jacme's throat took a long drink. "He put my *maire* on house arrest. My blessed *maire*! For *heresy*."

"He never!" exclaimed Andrio. Knowing this pair, I was certain Andrio had heard this outrage a dozen times already, but he would always oblige his friend.

"Because when she was a small *toza*, not even six years old"—Jacme slurred his *s*'s—"her parents brought her to be raised up by an aunt who was a *bona femna*."

"My mother grew up that way too," said Andrio. "Every *toza* did. Back then."

"He's a jackass."

"A jackass from Fransa," said Andrio, "which is the worst kind."

Jacme took another swig. "They don't know us at all."

Andrio burped. "They've sentenced dozens to wearing yellow crosses for life."

"My own *maire*!" cried Jacme.

"The jackass."

They ruminated on injustice for a time. Then Jacme spoke again.

"D'you know what we should do?"

"What should we do?"

A drink. "We should drive him out of town."

"*Oc*," cried Andrio. "Teach him a lesson."

"I have a few questions," said the other, "that I'd like to ask *him*."

I knew what the rising pitch of those voices meant. One didn't run a tavern for years without learning to recognize when ne'er-do-wells were whipping themselves up for a brawl.

"We'll be heroes," said Jacme. "Na Pieret and Senhor Guilhem will thank us."

"Heroes. *Oc*."

The stupid, stupid *tozets*! What could be more dangerous than such stupidity?

"He walks by the water in the evenings," said Jacme. "We could surprise him right now."

"*Oc*. Send him packing from Bajas."

Jacme's voice dropped dangerously. "Or maybe not."

Andrio considered this. So did I. But they mustn't. If they threatened or wounded the inquisitor, their deeds would be trumpeted all the way to Roma. If they thought we were seeing the Church's full wrath now, they were mistaken. Those two must be stopped.

"They're murderers, you know," Jacme said.

"That's true," replied Andrio.

"Making the *bayles* burn innocent people," said Jacme. "They'll burn us all before they're through. Come on. Let's go."

They climbed to their feet and lumbered off.

I waited for their sounds to fade. Jacme and Andrio wouldn't listen to me even if they were sober. Dolssa, my poor bird, would have to wait alone in the dark a little longer. I had to find Symo before those drunken fools found the friar.

I raced blindly down the lanes of the vineyard, not daring to take the traveled path, lest I overtake Jacme and Andrio alone. Tall grasses tugged at my shoes, and the uneven ground made me stumble. Finally my feet found a small footpath, and I flew along it until I'd reached the road that passed by the tavern. I ran inside.

"Symo?"

My *sorres* looked at me blankly. He wasn't there.

I turned and pressed up the hill toward town. Most of the village was tucked in for the evening, digesting their suppers. I encountered no one, worse luck.

I knocked at Na Pieret's house.

She answered the door herself. "Yes, Botille?"

"Is Symo here?" I gasped.

I couldn't bear the disapproval in my old friend's eyes.

"Haven't you seen plenty of him lately?"

Now she resented his time with us. Or feared what it might do. Oh, Na Pieret, *ma maire*, why have you rejected me?

"I need his help," I said. "Jacme and Andrio are drunk. They plan to go beat up the inquisitor, Lucien de Saint-Honore. To repay him for the punishments."

"Jacme and Andrio often do the things the rest of us wish we could do," she observed.

"Na Pieret!" I cried. "Surely, you can see what the outcome would be. They'll kill him!"

"Not Jacme," she said. "He's all bluster. He's no murderer."

"Whether they kill him or no," I cried, "if they assault him, the Church will crush Bajas. They'll bring down armies upon us. The Crusades started over just such an offense. While we stand talking, the chance to stop them dwindles." I filled my lungs and cried out, in case her nephew was inside the house. "Symo!"

He appeared beside me. He'd been somewhere on the street. "I'm here, Botille," he said quietly. "What do you want?"

His expression was grim, and so was Na Pieret's, watching us. They'd quarreled over me. Over Dolssa. I could taste the bitterness.

I quickly told Symo what I'd heard. He turned and ran to the waterfront. Na Pieret called after him. His only reaction was to stop at someone's shed along the way and commandeer a sturdy rake.

We reached the row of trees. There was no sign of a struggle anywhere. Perhaps the friar had not chosen to walk tonight. Or perhaps we were too late. I prayed that the two ruffians had not gone to find their victim elsewhere.

A slim crescent moon shone over the lagoon. It would have been a lovely night, but for this.

"I should go looking for them," I whispered.

"Ssh." Symo placed a finger over his mouth, then pointed.

A figure descended the grassy slope toward the water. It was the friar, Lucien. He looked around, apparently to see if he was alone, then knelt and scooped up a handful of ashes. He rose and let them trail through his fingers onto the sea breezes.

Once more he knelt to scoop the feathery ash. *Almost*, I thought, *like a mourner.* What could he be thinking?

There was no time to wonder. Jacme and Andrio ran out from behind a hillock and struck his bare head with their wine pitchers.

He toppled face first into the fire pit.

His assailants were upon him in an instant. Symo burst from his hiding place and cleared the beach. He dealt ferocious blows to Jacme and Andrio's tailbones with the handle of the rake before they could even turn around to see who was there. They rolled over, cursing and yelping, then staggered to their feet.

"Time to go home, lads," said Symo.

But Jacme and Andrio, rubbing their sore *azes* and shouting insults at Symo, apparently did not agree.

I ran to the friar to see what was left of him. *Please, Dieu in heaven above, let our enemy live, or we are standing corpses.*

He was alive and breathing, but only just. I rolled him out of the ashes and onto the sand. Then I turned to see what had become of the others, and my own heart nearly stopped.

Jacme and Andrio weren't good thinkers at the best of times, but one thought had made its way through their wine-soaked heads. There were two of them, and only one of Symo.

They each took a step closer.

"*Get back*," Symo yelled. He brandished his rake. "If there's to be murder tonight, it'll be by my hands, not yours."

And still they came closer.

"Jacme, you fool!" I screamed. "Go home! You'll see all Bajas burn for what you've done, you stupid swine!"

"You're next, Botille," Jacme called. "After I deal with this son of a jackass who thinks he's lord over us."

They fell into crouch positions. Symo was strong, I knew, and brave enough, but the other two passed their time, when they weren't lazing or singing, by wrestling each other and all challengers. They could slaughter him. And they'd found the deadly shards of their broken pitchers.

Andrio circled around behind his prey, and now they had him surrounded.

"Symo!" I cried. "Watch out!"

I heard voices from the direction of the *vila*, so I cried out for help. The friar's eyes were fluttering. But I didn't dare take my eyes off the men.

It might have been a dance. They circled around Symo, while he twisted and turned to keep them both in his sights. Jacme would feint for his front, then skip back while Andrio lunged for the backs of Symo's knees. Jacme's pains were rewarded with the butt of the rake handle punched into his gut, and Andrio got a rake head crashing over his skull.

But these blows didn't stop the pair. They only made them angrier. Their broken weapons forgotten, both charged Symo, but he shoved the rake handle under Andrio's armpit and used it to swing him around bodily, levering him straight at his friend. They collided like battering goats, their force striking each other instead of Symo.

"Go home," Symo said, "or I'll feed your feet to the sharks."

Behind me, the friar moaned. A trickle of blood from his sooty scalp dribbled down into his eye. Before me, Jacme and Andrio rose to their feet, snarling like wounded bears.

Two women appeared from up the road. Praise the *bon Dieu*. It was my *sorres*.

"Find help," I called to them across the beach. "They'll kill him!"

Sazia hitched her skirts and ran up the hill, while Plazensa ran across the sand to me.

She took one look at the friar. "Is he alive?"

"Let's pray he is."

I heard wood crack on bone, and a shout of pain. Jacme fell on his *aze* in the sand, but Andrio saw an opening and tackled Symo to the ground. In no time he'd pinned him. Symo's legs thrashed but found no hold. Andrio looked like a rabid dog ready to bite Symo's throat out.

Plazensa's eyes flashed. "Come on, Botille," she said. "What I'd give now for my rolling pin."

She seized a sturdy limb of unburnt wood from the rim of the pyre, and I followed her lead. She swung her beam wide and brought it crashing down onto Andrio's head. He fell limply onto

Symo's neck like a drowsy lover. I saw that Jacme was beginning to rouse, so with a well-aimed blow, I sent him back to sleep.

Running footsteps and shouts came down the slope. Sazia had dragged out Martin de Boroc. Seconds later Gui ran into view. He halted at the sight of his brother, bent double and heaving gasps of air; he took in the sight of three bodies on the beach.

"What've you done now, brother?"

"It wasn't me," croaked Symo. "It was those crazy *femnas* who finished the business."

"Carry the friar to the tavern," ordered Plazensa, "then get these two back home to their mistress. Lock them up and dump cold water on them if they give you any trouble."

Gui and Plazensa carried the friar back to the Three Pigeons along with Sazia, leaving Symo and me to recuperate and supervise the farmhands with Symo's rake. Sazia and Plazensa stayed to tend the friar. Gui returned to the beach and heaved Jacme and Andrio into Na Pieret's cart with Martin's help, then let her mule carry them home.

Symo and I returned to the tavern in silence.

We'd failed. We'd stopped them from killing him, but we hadn't kept him safe, and now hell itself would swallow us. I had tried to do right, but once again my best efforts had led to disaster.

Symo limped.

"Are you badly hurt?" I asked him.

He didn't answer.

"You'll be bruised in the morning," I said.

Still nothing.

We were nearly home. Since my conversation was so odious to him, I debated saying anything at all, but even as dejected as I was with the outcome, it had to be done.

"*Grácia.*"

We were at the door. Instead of opening it, he stopped and looked at me so intently that it made my skin crawl. Was he ever anything but angry? Was my *grácia* so trifling as to insult him, after the price he'd paid?

It grew awkward to wait for him to stop glaring, so I pushed past him and opened the door.

I didn't get far. Plazensa and Sazia stood over a bed they'd formed from two tables, whereon the pale, still form of Lucien de Saint-Honore was spread.

Sazia's eyes met mine. "He's fading, Botille."

Dieu *in heaven, help us.*

I turned to Symo. "You know what I must do."

Symo dragged a hand down over his face. "I'll help you bring her."

LUCIEN DE SAINT-HONORE

Lucien was dreaming.

He lay in a dark wilderness, dying of thirst. His body had already lost strength; he could no longer attempt to crawl on in search of water.

The people from the tavern appeared, the sisters and the brother—was he a brother?—but when he asked water or wine of them, they shook their heads. *No, no, none for you.* They mocked his thirst and his need.

Then the heretic appeared.

Now Lucien understood that he was dreaming indeed, for the heretic was dead already. But the thirst, the thirst was real. It sucked him down into a waiting grave.

Was he dead already? Was that why the heretic was there?

He struggled to rise, to fight and crawl on once more for water, but the tavern sisters pushed him down. They laughed at his desperation.

Then the heretic appeared by his side, and the sisters departed. She held in her hands a vessel of water. Lucien tried to ask her for some, but his tongue was swollen. He couldn't speak. Could he, should he petition a child of error for any favor? Would doing so offend God?

The heretic looked at someone Lucien couldn't see. "I cannot do it," she told that someone. "Forgive me, but I cannot plead for him."

Lucien tried to reach for the vessel, but his fingers were fixed to the ground. His life slipped from him. *God help me,* he tried to say, but his lips refused to move.

The heretic looked down at him. She rested her hands upon his head and his ribs. Her eyes filled with pity. A single tear formed and fell from her cheek and landed upon his face.

Lucien felt the tear soak in. It was water. It filled his lungs with air, and his veins with strength.

She uncorked her vessel and held it at his lips.

"Bless this man," she said aloud. "Bless this living, breathing child of creation, fearfully and wonderfully fashioned by your own hands."

Lucien de Saint-Honore slid into blackness.

BOTILLE

_____

Symo and I hurried Dolssa back to her hiding place long after midnight. Symo led the way, while Dolssa held my hand. She did not know the path as well as I.

We were close to the end, to Symo's cave, when a nightingale's cry rang out through the darkness.

"Hear how the *rossinhol* bids me good-bye," she said. "Of all the things to miss underneath the ground, I think oftenest of his song."

Sweet Dolssa. What cheer could I give her now? "Your handsome knight has not forgotten you," I told her.

I felt, more than saw, her smile. "No indeed. A heart ever

faithful. He has followed me here." Her smile passed. "Could he follow me, I wonder, to where I'm going next?"

We reached the cave, but neither of us could bear to enter just yet.

"I must thank you, good Symo," said Dolssa, "for the parchment and candles. Writing has been a tremendous comfort."

Symo nodded, then faded into the darkness. I knew he wasn't far.

I held both of Dolssa's hands in mine. "I don't know how you did what you did tonight," I told her. "To bless that friar!"

She hung her head. "Not I, Botille. I did nothing."

Not true, but I let her denial pass. "You're the bravest person I'll ever know."

"As are you." She stroked my cheek with her fingertips. "And the most loyal friend."

I couldn't help crying then. I embraced her and wept upon her shoulder.

"Botille," she whispered. "Pray for me. I still don't want to die."

"You shall not die," I vowed. "We'll find a way."

She wiped her eyes. "If anyone can, dear friend, it is you."

I embraced Dolssa one more time.

"After Mamà died, Botille, I swore I would not love another living soul, only to lose them again. I was certain my beloved was more than enough for me," she whispered into my ear. "But you, Botille, have been my *medica*. You've mended my wounded feet and heart." She squeezed me tightly. I knew my heart would burst. "I will not lose you now."

I couldn't speak. I kissed her cheek.

"Botille." Symo's low voice reached me in the darkness. "We need to go."

PRIOR PONS DE SAINT-GILLES

It was midmorning when Prior Pons and Bishop Raimon, and their retinue of friars, clergy, soldiers, and servants, ascended Bajas's hill and reached the church of Sant Martin. They had left at dawn from the Abadia de Fontfreda, and made good time.

"I trust we will not find we have made this trip in vain." Bishop Raimon wheezed as he dismounted his horse.

"Lucien's letter was urgent," Pons reminded him. "Not only reports of the heretic in this little *vila*, but of her poison spreading rapidly and taking root. He's young. He could never prosecute so many on his own."

"Certainly not," answered the bishop. "But my back will never recover from such an insult."

"Smell the sea breezes, though!" A young friar from their company flung out his arms and drew in deep breaths. Bishop Raimon only rolled his eyes.

A priest opened the door to the sanctuary to greet them. A handsome man, though shabby, his face fell at the sight of the senior clergy.

"My lords," said he, and bowed. "You come from Tolosa?"

"*Oc*, that is right," said Prior Pons. "And you are?"

"Bernard, your honor," said he. "Priest of Sant Martin's and the *vila* of Bajas."

"I presume, then, that our brother, Friar Lucien de Saint-Honore, has made his abode with you?"

The parish priest licked his lips.

"Good sirs," he said, "I fear you will need to come with me."

The local lord, Guilhem, poured a torrent of words upon them, and Bishop Raimon had ears to hear what was said, but Prior Pons could only stand at the bedside of young Lucien, his own charge, in some dismal tavern, and trace the line of the gash in his forehead, back and forth. They were sons to him, his young recruits to the Order of Friars-Preachers. Lucien was not many years past boyhood. Zealous, true, and ambitious, but so were all those destined to be great in the realm of the Lord. Time and experience would temper him. He was keen of mind, yet not so wedded to his studies, as some were, that he would not go and do God's work in the world. He did not deserve to die—even if, as a true martyr, he would bypass the angels at the gates of heaven.

Pons placed a hand on Lucien's heart, and rejoiced to feel it move.

Bishop Raimon had anger enough for the two of them.

"Think you," the bishop snarled to the young lord, "that Christ's church will stand idly by while unholy men assault the Lord's servants? Think you that brutality like this will be tolerated *for one instant?"*

The young lord, Guilhem, quailed. "No, my lord," he said. "Not for one instant. Nor should it. The rogues who did it, they are wastrels and brawling drunks. The *bayle* has them in custody, and they shall be flogged this afternoon. After that we shall assist you in making of them whatever example you see fit."

A serving wench, and a comely one at that, appeared with a tray of cups of wine.

"Refreshment, my lords?"

Prior Pons finally spoke. "How came he to be in this place?"

Bernard, the priest, spoke up. "He was assaulted on the beach," he said. "Near where the heretic was burned. These three sisters came to his aid and brought him in to tend him."

Bishop Raimon considered the three sisters. "God bless you for your kindness."

They bowed. Then the middle one pointed toward young Lucien.

"He wakes," said Pons. "Fetch him wine! Bring water!"

The sisters hurried to comply, while Prior Pons bent closer to his young friar's face.

"No need to speak," he told Lucien. "Rest."

"Do not let the bishop bless them," was Lucien's thin reply.

Prior Pons let this pass. The poor fellow must still be disoriented from his injury.

It did not stop Lucien from speaking again. "I will come to the whipping."

Prior Pons straightened up. "By no means!"

In answer, the friar struggled to sit. He rose before other hands could prevent him.

"I am well enough," he said. "I must be there. Seeing them punished will help me to forgive them. Jhesus has healed me to bring this moment to pass."

Prior Pons watched a dazed look pass over the young friar's face.

"Jhesus has healed me," he repeated. "Jhesus has done it. It could only have been he. . . ."

BOTILLE

enhor Guilhem read out the charges late that afternoon.

"For most violently and with premeditated and murderous intent assaulting a man of God, the friar Lucien de Saint-Honore of the Order of Preachers, in a vile and cowardly manner, lying in wait, attacking him unawares, entirely unprovoked, I sentence you to forty lashes." He swallowed and glanced at the bishop and prior from Tolosa. "And, to teach you to remember to honor the Savior's church, I sentence you to branding by hot irons on the forehead with the mark of the cross."

The people of Bajas gaped in horror. We expected the flogging. Never this.

A fire crackled between the accused and their accusers. Small, but hot, and hungry, fed from a pile of wood and a bellows by one of the bishop's servants. Now I understood its purpose.

Waves rocked soothingly at the sand, making gentle music to accompany the torturing of Jacme and Andrio. Both stood, with bound wrists tied high to a pole, on the very same beach where they had thought to teach the inquisitor a lesson. They were a sight less menacing-looking now, and sadly sober. Stripped all but naked, and terrified. Still, after what they'd done, I found it hard to pity them. A cleric's murder could have cost us all our lives.

But now, the clergy believed our Dolssa had already been executed. After today, they'd all go home. We could get on with our lives. We would find her a new hiding place to live out her life in peace. I reached out and took my sisters by the hand. The image swam unbidden into my mind of each of them with cross-scarred foreheads.

Poor Jacme and Andrio. Poor, poor, stupid creatures.

We all stood to behold the pageantry of justice. Lop had led the accused down the hill and into the public ring. The nobles, the friars, the bishop and his priests, and their retinue of soldiers formed a wall of righteousness to withstand the teeming threat of our drunken, heretical, rural peasant vice.

In the midst of the clergy, seated in a chair and sheltered on either side by other tonsured friars, was a frail Lucien de Saint-Honore. Even from afar, the red wound on his scalp cried out for retribution.

Lop practiced a few strokes with the whip upon the sand. On the second test it cracked. The third made Lop confident. The fourth caught Andrio across his left shoulder.

The lash's bite left a mark, and soon a thin line of blood.

Jacme was next to cry out.

The whip cracked and stung, cracked and stung, and before long they were sobbing, broken, their feet scrabbling in the sand as they tried to fall, pleading for an end, cringing before the lash. Drops of blood sprayed off their skin at each stroke.

Jacme and Andrio had been prepared to kill a man in cold blood. Or so they'd said. And they nearly did. They were lucky to walk away with their lives. But it was a pitiable thing to watch a human soul treated worse than one would ever treat a donkey. It always was. No matter how many times I'd seen it before.

Lop left them there, drooping, crying, no longer caring who saw them so. He knelt and winced before the fire's heat. With both hands he wrapped a hot iron handle in leather and thick cloth, then raised a red-hot poker high. Its thick cross glowed bright as poppies.

It happened so fast. Two knights in the bishop's retinue wrapped broad leather straps around Jacme, and pinioned his limbs to the pole whereon he was tied. A third clamped his hands on either side of Jacme's head to hold it still. Lop brought the poker to Jacme, and Jacme spat at him. Lop pressed the hot brand onto his victim's forehead. Crookedly.

His searing skin hissed. Jacme screamed. Smoke billowed, floated away on the breeze. Lop pulled the brand away, then carefully pressed it back again, to cauterize the mark.

Piss darkened the cloth tied around Jacme's middle and ran down his legs.

I couldn't bear to watch Andrio's turn. Sazia hid in my arms. "Poor fools," Plazi whispered to herself. "So young."

It ended. Lop stopped. The poor maimed ones' pitiable cries keened on the wind off the sea.

We exhaled, and waited. Please, *Dieu*, put a stop to this.

Let someone speak. Let something release us all from this horror. Let lightning from heaven strike these churchmen who even now triumph over such mad cruelty.

There was a stir. We all watched as Lucien de Saint-Honore rose, guided by his helpers, and approached the blubbering, bleeding men. They stopped their whimpering and waited. I imagine they wondered what more he could do to them.

He stood over them, beholding their faces with grave and sober concern.

"I forgive you," he told them.

"You're a fool," was Jacme's answer.

The clerics looked aghast at this irreverence. Lucien de Saint-Honore's hand fluttered to his wounded head.

A burnt cross leered at the friar from above Jacme's swollen-shut eye. The other eye found Symo in the crowd. He spoke, though, to the friar. "You think you've burnt your heretic," he said, "but you've been duped. If you want to know where your Dolssa is, follow the tavern cat."

BOTILLE

---

y sisters and I clutched one another's hands.

Jacme. How could you?

God in heaven, show me what I must do. Was there time? Could I run and warn Dolssa?

Shocked murmurs ran through the assembled villagers. Among them were many sounds of joy. Lisette de Boroc. Saura Garcia. Discovering their angel was not dead.

A figure slipped away from the clergy. I watched in horror as the tall form of Senhor Hugo strode up the hill toward the village and Na Pieret's fields beyond. My heart sank. That man was deadly. He'd surely find her.

Senhor Guilhem hurried toward Jacme and Andrio. "Get them

away from here," he told Lop. "Drag these beggars out."

Lop untied Jacme from the post and began pulling him up the hill.

"The ruffian thinks to surprise me with this revelation about Dolssa, the heretic," cried Lucien. "But it was already plain to see that this town is steeped in a conspiracy of silence. They've sworn a pact not to reveal the heretic's whereabouts. She lives, I'll swear it, concealed away by the tavern sisters."

"My sǫrres," I told them in tears. "I—"

"No, Botille." Plazi stopped my apologies with a kiss. "No need."

The older Dominican friar, the one who seemed to be Lucien de Saint-Honore's superior, hurried to his side and tried to persuade him to come back to his seat.

"And the woman you burned," the friar told Senhor Guilhem, "was never Dolssa de Stigata. Isn't that right, Senhor Hugo?"

But the knight was gone. The churchmen looked about for him in confusion, but it didn't matter. Now they all knew.

"I swear to you, my lords of the Church . . ." began Senhor Guilhem, but I had no ears for his feeble protest.

"We've failed." I could barely speak. "I couldn't save Dolssa, my sisters, and now I've killed you."

From somewhere, Symo appeared beside us. The young friar fixed his eagle eye on us.

"Those two." Lucien pointed to Symo and me. "*They* did it. I met them on the road. They pretended to be sister and brother, but they aren't. Fornicators! Secret lovers. Sinners, heretical conspirators, posing as kindred and thinking to fool the Lord by it!"

The Dominican prior, the bishop, and Senhor Guilhem eyed one another.

Symo's eyes met mine. Fornicators, lovers? Any other day I would have laughed. The look in Symo's eyes, though, made me want to weep.

"Of course they're not siblings," said Senhor Guilhem. "I told you that."

"They brought her here," Lucien said, "and hid her in the tavern. Then they taught the village to adore her as a holy woman, by tricking them into thinking she had healed their false ailments."

"Symo," I whispered. "I'm sorry."

He made me look into his eyes.

Lop returned from hauling Jacme, and deputized others to take Andrio away.

"Lucien," said the older Dominican, "what do you *mean*, Dolssa de Stigata has not been executed?" He looked about him. "Everyone told us she'd been burnt days ago."

"I don't know who that was. Some vagabond, perhaps. But it wasn't she." Lucien's expression was triumphant. "I'm certain of it. Even without the brute's admission. Else, why so many lies?"

I had underestimated Friar Lucien's cunning. We all had.

"Why burn the woman all the *vila* adored? Everything smells wrong here. Like the stench of rotting fish." A high flush colored

Friar Lucien's cheeks. "It wasn't Dolssa de Stigata. She's still alive."

"If that's true," said Bishop Raimon, "then it will soon be remedied. And this time, the entire village will witness her execution."

A wail went up from the crowd. The bishop's sharp eyes turned to find the offender out.

"Woman!" he cried. "Step forward, and explain this outburst."

Lisette de Boroc stepped forward with her infant in her arms. He'd grown fatter. Martin de Boroc held his daughter in his long arms and watched his wife in horror.

Bishop Raimon surveyed her appearance.

"You wish to defend the heretic, Dolssa de Stigata?"

Lisette genuflected. Poor simple creature. Her face was full of trust.

"Honored bishop," she said, "spare her life, I beg you! Dolssa helped my baby eat when he wouldn't. She saved his life. It was a miracle."

She tried to slip back into the crowd, but Bishop Raimon would have none of that.

"State your name," he said.

Martin de Boroc closed his eyes.

"Lisette de Boroc," she replied.

"Your age?"

"Twenty-five," said she. One of the younger Dominican friars who had accompanied the clerics from Tolosa produced parchment and ink to write her words.

"How many children do you have?"

I think it was then that Lisette caught the first scent of danger.

"Two," she murmured softly.

"*How* many?"

"Two."

"Two young children. What is your husband's name?"

"Martin, Lord bishop."

People began to stand apart from Martin. He had caught the disease they feared.

"His trade?"

She turned and faced him. She realized what she'd done, poor creature. *I'm sorry,* her face said.

"His trade?"

Martin nodded to his wife, whose face grew red.

"I'm a fisherman," he called out.

Lucien de Saint-Honore had some words with the older Dominican friar, the one who seemed to be his superior. At length he said, "Present yourselves at church tomorrow morning."

Martin pulled Lisette close to him and wrapped his arms around his entire family.

Saura stood, pale and stricken, at the forefront of the crowd. She crept forward in the sand, and hesitated, but when she opened her mouth, she poured out her words like water.

"Please, holy friars, pardon me, a poor ignorant woman. I am a mother and a wife, and my husband and son were ill, ready to die of fever, and this *femna*, Dolssa, healed them. The fever parted, and they got better. Please don't hurt them. They were asleep when she came, and they didn't know anything about it. It was I who asked her to come help them if she could. I know you will learn this anyway as you question people, for the whole town was there, and they saw it happen. We rejoiced together. Dozens came forward afterward to be healed and helped by her. She healed them all. And they know it is true. I know you will question me soon for saying all this. But I must tell it now. *Please* do not kill her. Dolssa de Stigata has the spirit of God in her."

Bishop Raimon and Prior Pons recoiled at her last statement.

Martin de Boroc stepped forward, and did the bravest, most foolish thing he would ever do. "What Saura says is true," he said loudly. "Only God could have healed my son. Na Dolssa does God's work, and who can deny God?"

A breeze off the lagoon ruffled the assembly. We all, it seemed, held our breath.

"Do you hear her, my brethren?" the bishop cried. "How many souls has this creature infected already? The whole *vila* is reprobate. The damage is far worse than we'd feared. These people convict all Bajas with their damning testimony."

The clerics huddled once more. Their wall of soldiers closed ranks around them. The churchmen whispered together for long, torturous moments, while seagulls cawed across the beach, and bells tied to fishing boats chimed a lullaby.

Then the circle broke.

"We have reached a decision," cried Friar Lucien de Saint-Honore. "We recommend to Senhor Guilhem that he implement these sentences, to demonstrate that he is a true lord of the Christian faith." Senhor Guilhem all but shook. "The heretic should be found, and struck through with an arrow, then burned. You three sisters, and the young *ome*, will lead the *bayle* to her, then share her fate." He gestured wide with his arm, taking in the sweep of the assembled Bajas. "This entire village is guilty of fostering and concealing heresy, so the entire village—the houses, all the property, and those persons identified as believing her words—must burn."

A cry went up from the assembled crowd. The clergy turned sharply to find the offenders, and the soldiers' hands went to their scabbards. Then all was still. We couldn't even mourn our homes, much less our friends or our lives.

Senhor Guilhem and Lop looked gray. The lord of Bajas could not impose such a sentence and keep his lands, nor his people's obedience. Neither could he ignore the churchmen and their soldiers and keep his lands, much less his immortal soul.

The prior sent friars up the hill to ring the bells at Sant Martin. To smoke out any remaining villagers who might still be in their houses.

Soldiers were sent to ransack our barns, strewing hay around each *maison*, ready for burning. A few were left to keep a close watch on us.

The canons returned with a stack of candles and a glowing lamp. One by one they lit the candles, one for each of the church-men. From the bishop down to the lowest monk, each in his own orb of holy light, they bowed their heads and prayed, asking God to bless them in their sacred work.

"I told Litgier to stay away at all costs." Plazensa's whispering voice shook. "He's out fishing. Didn't want him mixed up in the whipping." She wiped her eyes. "Now I'll never tell him good-bye."

Oh, Plazi. To hear my sister admit what she never had before cut my heart.

On the beach, husbands and wives huddled together. They clutched their children against their breasts.

Behind me, Symo stood with his head hung down. My sisters, drained of hope, held each other.

Somewhere, in the darkness, Dolssa sat in her cell, and if her beloved kept watch over her, perhaps Senhor Hugo would not find her.

I had one last chance to try anything. But what? God in heaven, what?

My gaze fell upon Dominus Bernard, watching me. I remembered his words. *They even convict and execute the dead.* Who could hope for mercy from such monsters?

They dig up heretics' bones and burn them.

There it was. My chance.

I stumbled forward and fell down upon my knees in the sand at the churchmen's feet.

"Good bishop," I cried. "Good prior. Good friar." I licked my lips with a dry tongue. "Spare this village, I beg you. These people are innocent. The victims of my falsehoods. The heretic will mislead the village no more after this moment. Teach them, explain to them the error of their ways, and they will listen. They are ignorant, and they believed my lies. Correct them, and they will repent. But you need no longer fear the heretic, for she is dead."

The churchmen continued their chanting prayers, but Bishop Raimon conferred with Lucien de Saint-Honore and the prior.

"Explain," demanded Lucien.

I took a deep breath. If ever I'd lied my way out of trouble before, oh, Mamà's magic, don't fail me now.

"I found Dolssa de Stigata by the side of the road, nearly dead from starvation, on a journey, weeks ago. I brought her home and nurtured her out of pity, and nothing more. She told me she feared you, so I shielded her from you."

"Hear how by her own admission she damns herself!" Lucien pointed accusingly at me.

What to say? My beautiful sisters. Could I not find a way to help them?

"All this was my own doing," I said. "My sisters, and this young man, who fear God and his church, warned me against it."

"They were complicit with you from the very start," insisted Lucien.

I shook my head. "Only for kindness's sake. After Senhor Guilhem burnt the *bona femna*," I said, "I was content to let that story stand, that she had been Dolssa, so that we could all have peace. Because Dolssa de Stigata died of fever two nights ago. She caught it from the sick Garcia family."

I heard a cry in the crowd. Saura.

Felipa, forgive me for what I am about to do.

"The heretic Dolssa is the last person buried in the church-yard," I said. "Go look for yourself, and see. Spare these who have been victims of untruth. Give them a penance, but let them live. If you must burn Dolssa de Stigata, you'll find her in the graveyard. Burn her, and me along with her. Take my life for both our crimes."

The sun sank behind Bajas. The sky was soft, a heavenly shade of lavender.

"Lop," called Senhor Guilhem. "Bring more wood for the fire."

"It isn't so!" cried a loud, familiar voice.

My heart sank. Astruga.

"The last woman buried in the churchyard is the good Christian wife of Joan de Prato, may she rest in peace," Astruga said. "Botille lies, not caring if she damns an innocent *femna*."

Astruga, you stupid creature! You who once called yourself my friend. To please your new love, and guard his wife's bones, you have robbed Bajas, and me, of our last hope.

"Botille lies," repeated Friar Lucien slowly. "Again and again, Botille lies." He approached me, cautiously, as if I might bite. "But why? It is curious, is it not? Even as she offers her own life, she lies. She is desperate to make us believe the heretic Dolssa is dead. Why? Because she is not dead. And Botille is so far gone in the service of Satan that she's willing to die to shield the heretic."

He was practically upon me now. The friar's face swam before my tear-filled eyes.

"I pray you, man of God," I begged. "Have mercy. We showed you pity last night. We saved your life, as the blessed Samaritan did, when you were left for dead."

A confused look passed over Friar Lucien's face. He raised a trembling hand to his forehead. "We?" he repeated. "We?"

I did not dare answer. God in heaven, did he remember Dolssa?

Friar Lucien towered over me now, yet he came closer still.

"Did you . . ." He bent over to speak to me words no one else would hear. "Did you summon the heretic to pray over me?"

His wild eyes burned into mine. Sea breezes ruffled his fringe of hair, and sweat shone on his brow.

I shook my head. An instant too late.

"You did." His fingers shook. "You let her touch me. Her cursed hands were upon my flesh!"

In all that crowded beach, it was only we two.

And then I understood. He feared me. He knew who had healed him. He remembered now. And he knew I could tell it. How the heretic had infected him with her poison touch.

If I were willing to betray Dolssa.

Prior Pons appeared at Friar Lucien's side. Lucien backed away from me, stumbling in the sand in his haste.

"The *toza* lies!" he cried. "The heretic lives. Find her!"

While Prior Pons tried to soothe Friar Lucien, the jowly bishop of Tolosa conferred in low tones with Senhor Guilhem, who argued heatedly with him. Finally the bishop spoke.

"People of Bajas, your lord Guilhem has pled for you tonight. You will all do a heavy penance for your sins and errors, but your lives and homes will be spared. You must renounce heresy and those who spread it. You will watch as the Lord's avenging fire burns these four, who were clearly all confederates in this deception. And you must lead us to the place where Dolssa de Stigata lies hidden. People of Bajas, do you accept the mercy offered you?"

No one moved. Then Astruga and Joan de Prato came forward, knelt, made the sign of the cross, and added a log to the fire. Focho de Capa came forward and did the same. Garcia the elder came with his son, leaving his wife weeping behind him. Dominus Bernard took a pathetic stick. With tears streaming down her cheeks, unwilling to look at us, Na Pieret walked forward and took a piece of wood, supported by Gui and Sapdalina on either side.

Symo groaned behind me. I reached for his rough hand and wrapped my fingers around it.

There was one crumb of comfort to be found. I did not see the de Borocs anywhere. I prayed they had slipped away in the gathering dark to hide on Martin's boat. *May it carry them far from here, to safety. May Saura find an escape of her own, whether her husband and son join her or not.*

Bishop Raimon nodded in triumph as each person bowed before him. "Now, bring us the heretic," he said, then pointed to us. "These four shall join her in hell."

Rossinhol, el seu repaire

M'iras ma domna vezer,

E digas li·l mieu afaire

Et ilh diga·t del sieu ver.

Nightingale, oh, ease my cares.

Swift to my lady's side, take wing.

Bring back word of how she fares,

Tell her my heart-sick suffering.

—Peire d'Alvernhe,
twelfth-century *trobador*

HUGO

nce out of sight of the gathering at the beach, Hugo de
Miramont ran. He didn't know where. He only knew
what direction he'd seen the cat go. Uphill, toward the countryside.
He didn't know where the cat's journey had ended. But moments
were all that were left now. Unless the tavern wenches had moved
the girl out of his reach.

There was only a little light left in the sky. Speed, stealth, and
cunning must lead him to his prey. It had to be tonight. It had to
be now.

He scanned the horizon as he mounted the vineyard slope.
All was murkiness now the landscape and woods, and far below,
the dark, brooding sweep of the sea. From a limb he could not

see, a nightingale's song pierced the gloaming. Hugo stopped and calmed his breathing, then strained his senses for a sign, for a sound, a whisper.

A shadow moved. He turned and waited. It moved again. Toward him. He crouched along a leafy grapevine and watched it approach.

It *was* her. Triumph. A miracle. He waited until she was almost there, then rose to block her path.

She startled, then stepped back. "Oh," she said. "Oh."

"Dolssa de Stigata," said Hugo, "you may not remember me, but I—"

"I do," said she. "You're my kinsman. From Papà's funeral. You came and heard me preach. Then stood by and watched as they burned Mamà."

She remembered him well. He wished she hadn't. "But I—"

"It's all right," she told him. "I understand their power, and I understand fear." She paused. "I can forgive you, now."

Hugo seized her arms. "I don't need forgiveness," he said. "Come with me. This way."

"No need for force," she cried, then composed herself. "I will follow you. My Lord told me you were coming."

Hugo halted. "He did?"

She nodded. "To bring me to the flames."

Hugo paused to listen for other feet. "Then it wasn't me he spoke of," he said. "And we must hurry."

"What do you mean?"

What to do? He knelt down before the young woman, pulled something from a pouch, and held it toward her.

In the twilight, Dolssa was forced to touch, more than see, what he held. He'd bought the fruits from a farmer in Bajas just the day before. Her fingertips brushed the velvet skin of two soft apricots.

"Oh."

Her fingers rested upon the fruit, and upon Hugo's skin. He caught his breath as the feel of her touch filled his body. Her scent was lavender and linen and the warmth of candlelight.

"Fly with me," he whispered. "Maiden most pure. I can carry you far from danger."

Her wide eyes beheld him in the darkness. Like lamps, they captured the glow of the rising crescent moon. Hope filled his breast. Every rushing breath fired him with strength and courage. She was here. Safe. He'd found her. If she would come with him, he could conquer all enemies. If she would be his, their souls together would enter paradise.

"All this time," she said softly, "you . . ."

He nodded. His body was on fire with her closeness. "All this time."

All the miles, all the hours, watching, waiting, hunting, pretending. God had heard his prayers and brought him to this moment. Here, with her, before their foes could find them.

Church bells rang from the distant tower of Sant Martin. What could they mean?

"Good Senhor," Dolssa said gently, "my Lord delivered me from the flames in Tolosa, to bring me to this place and time, for purposes I don't know. My time has come. He has called me to rise from my hiding place and face my enemies."

No, no! Above all other foes, must he persuade her, too, to value her life?

"Donzęlla Dolssa," he whispered. "It was I who cut you free that night."

He heard the intake of her breath. Her confusion and disappointment filled the air between them.

He had dismayed her. *Beast, to boast in this way!*

"Surely delivering you was the will of God," he went on, "as much as it was the deepest wish of my heart." He bowed his head. "I could only save one of you. This was the choice she would have wanted me to make."

They paused to hear voices ascending the hill, and with them, torches. In the distance, the glow of a large fire began to glimmer through the trees.

"I've watched you grow," he pleaded. "Years before you were aware of me. Your father spoke often of you to me, and I grew to love you before I'd even seen the young woman you became. I've heard you teach. I see what light surrounds you. Holy maiden, you do not know what you are to me."

He longed to embrace her, but dared not move.

She gazed back at him. "What do you want?"

"Only your happiness," he said, "and safety. I can take you to

Anglatèrra, where I have an estate. I can take you to the ends of the earth."

Her eyes closed. She struggled.

He whispered. "Don't be afraid."

"Afraid?"

"Of me." He took a deep breath. "It is no use for me to pretend," Hugo's words rushed out, "that I would not wish for a chance to offer you my heart. But whether you would have me or no, I swear to you, maiden, that I would give my life to serve you, and to defend your right to live as you choose."

Her lips parted. She turned aside slightly, and spoke. "Is this your will?"

She wasn't talking to him.

Lights approached. Hugo didn't fear them as much as he feared the answer Dolssa might receive. To have her safe in his reach at last, and fail . . . It couldn't be borne.

Dolssa took Hugo's hand and pulled him to his feet. "Tell me," she said, "how do my friends fare tonight? The sisters from the tavern. Are they in danger?"

Hugo's heart broke.

She must ask him that.

Just one lie.

The trusting spirit at his side rested her arm upon his. Somewhere near was one who loved her even more than Hugo could, and whose eyes could read his heart.

He had come this far, so far to taste the bitter gall of defeat.

So be it, then. If he would keep his vow to serve her, then deliverance must belong to her beloved now.

"They are in danger, Donzęlla," he said. "When I left, the bishop had learned you were yet alive, and that the sisters had lied to conceal you."

She threaded her arm more tightly through his. "Then you must lead me to them," she said. "Would you do me the courtesy of bringing me there yourself, instead of this mob that's so keen to find me?"

Hugo's jaw set in a grim line. "With pleasure."

Though that, God knew, was another lie.

BOTILLE

he bishop's sentence echoed in my ears. I melted into the arms of my dear ones.

Before they came and took us, one moment, and one embrace more, for my Plazi, my Sazia, my darling *sǫrres*.

And Symo.

He wrapped his arms around me.

"Never mind, Botille." He spoke into my ear, and kissed it gently. "I knew from the first you'd be the death of me."

I pulled away to look into his eyes, but he wouldn't let me. He turned his face away, while his words sank down into my skin. *Symo?* Stubborn, surly Symo. Always vexing, always helping. Always there.

Mon Dieu.

What I might have felt, after the shock of it? All that might have been, there wasn't time to know. He held me tight, and I wet his shirt with tears, until Lop returned with his load of wood, and rough hands pulled us apart.

How quickly does a fire fanned and fed by friends grow tall.

Dieu, bless Dolssa, and Jobau. Bless Mimi, my little cat.

And kill us quickly, for I can't abide the thought of fire.

The sky slipped from lilac to purple to blue to black. The fire grew higher and higher.

The churchmen sang,

> *Accende lumen sensibus,*
> *infunde amorem cordibus,*
> *infirma nostri corporis,*
> *virtute firmans perpeti.*

It meant something like:

> *Lighten our senses,*
> *fill our hearts with love.*
> *Make our weak bodies*
> *forever strong.*

A voice I knew from a lifetime ago sang out from beyond the darkness.

"Hey ho, hey hum, see the churchmen come. And whom shall they slaughter today?"

My *sorres* and I stared at one another.

A figure wandered into the firelight. Hobbled right up to the bishop and spat upon him. A servant cuffed his jaw, but the figure only laughed, spraying the clerics with some of the brew in the jug he carried.

It was none other than our Jobau.

"Take the babe, take your wife, and run for your life from the men who love to pray."

"Who is this offensive creature?" demanded a bristling Bishop Raimon.

"What's the fire for, boys?" Jobau took a swig. "Hot enough to wake even a damned soul like me. I look out the door, and see everyone gathered around a blaze, and I say to myself, 'Oho, either it's a party, or the holy men have come to town.'" He wandered over to Bishop Raimon. "I'm a drunk," he told him, "since you asked. The vilest sinner in all Provensa. Death to the king of Fransa! And you men"—another drink—"are the murderers who made me this way. What do you think of that?"

The bishop beckoned to Lop. "Get this refuse out of here, and flog him."

"Not"—Jobau took a swig—"until I tell you a story."

"Drag him away!" cried the bishop. But Jobau—the bizarre wonderment of this reeking, shriveled man cursing at the bishop—had already hooked the curious ears of the soldiers. They could wait a few minutes.

"I'll tell you the story"—there was an edge to Jobau's voice—"of a young man in Fransa who loved the Church and dreamed of adventure. He wanted to take up his cross. Just like Jhesus. He answered the call to go on crusade and drive filthy heretics from the count of Tolosa's lands. Worse than infidels, the heretics were. More dangerous than Mohammedans."

"Bayle," ordered the bishop. "Remove him." But Lop was held sway under Jobau's spell.

"So this young man left his mother and father and joined an army marching south. Tens of thousands of us there were, singing songs and dreaming of our mansions in heaven.

"But do you know what happened?"

"No one heeds you, foul creature!" cried Lucien de Saint-Honore.

Everyone did.

"Besièrs happened." Jobau's voice lashed like Lop's whip. "We wiped it off the map. We didn't leave a rat's *aze* alive in all Besièrs. Not even a curly-haired baby girl. All gone. Burnt up like bacon that falls in the fire. That's holy war."

Never had I heard this tale before. My own Jobau's life, and I never knew.

"And on from there, and on, throughout the south, for years. Every town that would surrender to Simon de Montfort, 'God's own prince,' we would spare the town and kill the *bons omes* and *bonas femnas*. Sear them with hot irons. Toss them alive into flaming pyres. Chop off their ears and noses. Throw them in wells. Strip them, stone them. That's what we did in the good *vilas*. In the bad *vilas*, we got to kill everyone."

"What's he doing?" Sazia whispered.

Jobau was determined to have his say. "Did you ever trip on the bodies of young boys, with their guts ripped open and gushing out, you men of God? That's holy war. Did any of you fight it?"

He searched their expressionless faces. He dropped his jug in the sand and cackled. Then he approached Bishop Raimon. All his mirth was gone now.

"You murderers, you killed God for me. You kill everything. And you never need to lift a sword to do it. You just lift your god, and poor souls run to do your killing for you."

His entire audience listened, as if in a trance.

"One day I just walked away. I could never go back to Fransa as the murderer I'd become. So I wandered around the south, the enemy's terrain, for years. I saw nobody harming anybody's faith but you. I drank in search of sleep without dreaming, but the dreams of what I'd done found me all the same.

"I ended up in Carcassona. I lived with a woman and her two daughters. We had a child together. The woman brewed ale to keep me from dying too quickly on wine. But she died first. After some trouble with debts and fights, the *tozas* and I ended up here in Bajas.

"And one day a *donzẹlla* showed up at the tavern with the true God in her fingertips. She healed my baby girl. And you can't bear it.

"So kill us. Kill us all. Kill my daughters, kill me, kill and kill and kill until all that's left is to kill each other. And when you do, the *bon Dieu*, if he's really there, will be your judge."

The villagers stared at Jobau. A month ago, had Jobau told this tale in the tavern, he'd have met with cheers. Now no one dared to make a sound.

The fire crackled. Bishop Raimon trembled with fury. He leveled a quivering finger at Jobau.

"Seize this blasphemer," he cried, "and bind him with his wicked daughters."

Jobau laughed. He laughed as two soldiers seized him by the arms and dragged him away from the clerics, toward us.

The pyre raged in its full heat. It scorched us, but not, I knew, as it soon would.

What would it be like to die? When the torment and the pain were through, would my soul go to God? Or be trapped, doomed, damned in an exile of darkness and pain?

Lord God whom Dolssa loves, I prayed, *receive our souls unto you.*

"The fire is ready," said Lop.

"Take the beauty first," said the bishop. "Take them one by one. Leave the lying, talkative one for last, so she may watch them all."

They dragged Plazi toward the fire.

I opened my mouth to scream, to plead, to bargain one last time for her life. But something made me stop. A voice, a feeling that silenced me.

I turned. We all turned. What made us all turn, there in that inferno of noise and heat?

Standing in our midst was Dolssa.

She came, to help us. Nothing forced her to come. Now we would all die together.

Unless her beloved had one more miracle.

The men clutching Plazensa's arms let go.

"Release them." Dolssa faced the bishop and the friars. They stared at her.

She glowed, not from the firelight, but as if lit from within. I wondered if she were already a ghost.

"Let them go," said she, "and I yield myself to you."

The churchmen looked at one another.

Friar Lucien's face had gone gray at the sight of her. He said, "We don't need you to yield. We have them, and we have you."

Dolssa's voice was calm but piercing. "Let them go," she said once more. "My beloved has protected me thus far, and he will protect me forever. You have no power over me but what he grants you."

"*Your beloved*," cried Lucien, "has granted *all* power to us. The keys of the kingdom. The power of Sant Peter, to bind on earth that which shall remain bound in heaven, to loose—"

"*Lucien.*"

The senior friar's voice rang with warning and alarm. Lucien paused. Only then, it seemed, did he realize the danger—the heresy—in what he'd said, in who he'd admitted Dolssa's beloved to be.

"Release my friends," Dolssa said, "with a binding oath that no harm may come to them, that they may live out their lives freely, and I will yield myself to your flames. God in heaven is our witness, and he will be your judge."

Lucien de Saint-Honore panted in frustration. "My lord Bishop," he cried, "do not succumb!"

"You fear me," Dolssa said, "for my beloved is with me, and he will speak for me. Bishop, how fares your back? Friar, how mends your head?"

Bishop Raimon's hand went to his lower spine. He stood straighter, and a look of relief crossed his jowly face. The friar's hand went to his scalp. His angry red wound was gone. He stared at the hand as though it were not his own. Then at Dolssa, as if he'd never seen her before.

The bishop consulted with the other churchmen. Dolssa waited calmly, with her head bowed and her hands crossed, for their answer.

Bishop Raimon stepped forward. "These five aren't important," he said, gesturing to my sisters, Jobau, Symo, and me. "Let them go."

The soldiers surrounding us stepped away.

Symo was at my side in an instant. "Run," he said. "We'll all run together—"

But before he could finish his thought, Dolssa spoke.

"Botille."

I ran to her.

"Oh, Dolssa," I cried, "what have you done?"

She smiled. "Remember me."

"Can't we fly from here?" I begged.

"Remember me," she said.

I kissed her face and hands. "Always."

I gazed into her eyes until hands pushed me away, until Lop seized my fragile friend, picked her up tenderly, like a daughter, and set her on her feet upon a wide stone slab next to the fire that lifted her head and shoulders just above the flames.

"People of Bajas," the bishop cried, "in fear for your immortal souls, do you consent to this?"

No one spoke. One by one they bowed themselves down, lowering their faces toward the dust.

It is a mercy, they say, to kill quickly those souls bound for the pyre. A mercy that also ensures the job gets done. Sometimes the marksman's arrow finishes the task. Sometimes it's done by strangling.

A soldier braced himself and loaded his crossbow. He cranked back the lever and aligned the bolt, then squinted along the length of the shaft, finding the line that led straight to Dolssa's beating heart.

His fingers flexed.

Lucien de Saint-Honore stretched forth his hand, almost as if to stop him.

Dolssa stood and waited. If she felt fear, it didn't show. She turned to where, I knew, she saw her beloved, and kept her gaze fixed on him.

I could barely watch for tears.

The crossbow thumped.

A figure leaped.

The bolt twanged.

A gray cloak snapped.

The bolt spun straight and true and buried itself in Senhor Hugo's back.

Dolssa's mouth hung open.

The knight slumped, and she caught him in her arms.

Lucien de Saint-Honore's scream rang across the beach.

"Run with me," Symo pleaded.

Dolssa staggered under the weight of her prize. Hugo mustered strength to stand upon his feet, then buckled once more.

Dolssa encircled his neck with her arm, then gently kissed his lips. A look passed across the dying man's face that human words cannot describe. Dolssa held him tightly to her, then fell with him into the flames.

Friar Lucien de Saint-Honore gaped at the sight. "*Non!*" he cried. "*Non, non, non!*"

Prior Pons and other clerics struggled to push the raving friar back into his seat. He relented at last, but still strained to turn his gaze toward the fire. He watched, forlorn, like a lost soul, as his heretic and her knight were consumed together in the hellfire he had lit.

He toppled from his chair and vomited into the ashen sand.

Again and again I saw them both. Like two butterflies. Their capes, like fluttering wings.

So gently did they fall, like feathers gliding on a breeze. They disappeared, like foxes slipping into their holes. There, and then not there. My nose smelled the stench of burning cloth and hair, but my soul breathed in a sweetness, as if a heavenly perfume had been released into the sky.

Dolssa's beloved had taken her straight to him.

"Seize the conspirators," cried the bishop.

A roar broke from Symo's throat. "You promised to release us!"

"All contracts with the dead are broken," said His Excellence. "Throw them in together."

Soldiers picked their way across the sand toward us. I took my sisters' hands. But Jobau, that reprobate, whispered under his breath.

"I can only give you seconds, my daughters," he said. "Use

them well." He chucked his finger under Sazia's chin. Then, without any pause, he plowed into the line of soldiers, taking two of them down in a jumble of arms and legs.

Symo snatched my hand in his, and Sazia's in his other. Plazi missed nothing. She took Sazia's other hand, and we bolted for the shallows, splashing through them, then up behind the tavern into the swallowing dark of scrub pines and tall grasses.

BOTILLE

e ran.

That is all I can remember.

We ran, stumbling over murderous ground, blind, tripping on roots, sinking in bogs. Climbing the hillside, sucking air into our burning lungs. Racing for dear life, and trying to stay together.

Branches and weeds whipped our faces. We were coneys fleeing from the wolf. Coneys, though, had holes to hide in.

We ran. Each step was hope. But there wasn't much. In no time at all, they were after us.

Symo dragged me along. Sazia shook off his hand, but we held tightly together.

We were losing. My *sǫrres* couldn't keep Symo's pace. The

soldiers' cries reached our ears. I stopped. Symo's pull almost knocked me over.

Separate yourselves.

The thought came so suddenly, I paused and turned to look for Dolssa. It felt like her voice. Or, rather, like the sense I'd had of where to find her, and how to help her, that night we met. I didn't question it.

"Together we're no match for them," I told the others. "We must separate and hide. It's our only chance."

I felt Plazi and Sazia nod, but Symo would not have it.

"No!" He tugged harder on my hand. "We'll never find each other."

"We will," Plazi said. "We sisters can always find each other."

"Daybreak," Sazia said. "The cove, near where the wild grapes grow."

"Where's that?" Symo demanded. My sisters had already gone, opposite ways, quiet as cats.

"A league or more, south of town," I said, and took off.

He followed me. "I'm not leaving you, Botille."

"You must, you great ox!" I hissed. "You'll get us both killed!"

He let out a growl like an angry dog, then disappeared into the shadows.

I ran while I could, then dropped to my knees and crept forward. I listened for any sound. Terrifying noises filled my head. Were they coming closer? Had they caught one of my sisters? I couldn't tell what was real and what was my own fright. I crawled on.

My knees were raw, my hands bleeding. I came to a rocky patch and found a gap underneath where two chalky boulders rested against each other. I climbed into the narrow tunnel and lay there, listening to my breath and my heart. Far away, and farther still, searchers crashed about and called to one another, but I never heard a shout of triumph. With that sliver of comfort, I flung one prayer out upon the nighttime breeze.

Oh, sisters, oh, Symo. Be safe tonight, and hide well, until we meet in the morning.

Senhor Hugo's fall, and Dolssa's kiss. Jobau the hero, now surely dead. Symo's whispered words to me. Jacme, Andrio, and Astruga's betrayal. Saura's tears, and Na Pieret's firewood.

Dolssa, descending into the flames. For us.

I clutched Mamà's crucifix between my finger and thumb.

Life, love, neighbors, belonging. Friend, father. Town and home, peace and good name. All smoke and ashes.

BOTILLE

rocked to sleep in my mamà's arms.

"Who's my girl?" whispered she. "Who's my pretty girl?"

I nestled down into her comforting lap, and let her put me to sleep.

I woke in the expectant dark just before dawn. Small creatures smelled the morning coming, and as their bellies woke them, they woke me.

Time to go find Sazia, Plazensa, and Symo.

No hunters, no soldiers, disturbed the early peace. Each footfall that went unanswered by a pursuer's chase made me bolder. I followed the scent of *la mar* and picked my way carefully over low paths toward the coast.

My sisters would find me at the cove, I felt absolutely sure. Perhaps it is strange that I felt no fear, but truly, I did not. The sense we had of each other, that we'd always had, from Mamà, knowing each other's thoughts, each other's hearts, blazed full force. My sisters were alive and well. We would find each other and run away together. *Oc*, we had lost all we'd worked to build in Bajas, and we would mourn our Jobau. But we'd be together.

I picked my way down a small gully where rainwater trickled into the sea, and found myself at the shore. From there it was a walk of some distance, hugging close to trees and other conceal-ments near the waterline, until I reached Sazia's cove.

The sun began to lighten the eastern horizon. I looked about for any sign of the others, but made no sound. I sat and concealed myself among the snarled, wild vines, and watched and waited.

Dawn was a long time. It could be they still slept. I waited and watched the sun climb the sky through the cool shelter of wild grape leaves.

Morning birds pipped at one another. They pecked at snails in the shallows. Insects buzzed around my feet. Small fish broke the water's surface to snap at bugs. If Mimi were here, I thought, she'd catch one.

I slurped water from trickling gullies, and picked at wild sour grapes.

Perhaps they, or I, had found the wrong spot. I ranged up and down the beach, defying enemies to find me, hoping my sisters and Symo would. Fishing boats passed by now and then, but I hid from view. Word spreads quickly from port to port, and I needed no spies telling tales of me.

Symo. The things I had to say to him! How dare he, for one thing, and where did he come off, for another, and what made him think he had any right, for thirds. What rich delight I would take in telling him what I really thought of his bad temper, his thick eyebrows, and his nerve.

But he never came. Nor did my *sǫrres*. I waited there for three whole days.

What if they were somewhere near? Hurt, stuck, afraid? At night I roved as far afield as I dared, softly calling out their names. No one ever answered, though dogs would bark, and creatures scuttle. More than once I was almost discovered by peasants, but the *bon Dieu* kept me hidden from view. Not only was I removed from my own people. Now I was invisible to them.

I searched but found no sign that any of them had ever come. I dozed and dreamed, and woke thinking I'd heard Plazensa's bracelets. Sazia's low voice. Symo chewing on a plate of dinner.

The fourth morning I rose up and walked away, heading south and inland, far from the spying eyes of the sea.

BOTILLE

Nights grew colder. I had only my dress. I stole a shawl that an old woman had hung to dry on a bush. I felt bad for her sake, but not enough to return it. Back to thieving again.

At first I found food. Harvesttime meant gleanings and pickings could be had in any garden plot. I slept at midday, when it was warmest, then traveled by twilight and early morning. I searched for my family, and I hid from passersby. If my family were still alive, they, too, would be hiding from the eyes of strangers, blending into their surroundings. We might pass one another on the same road and never know it.

Every footstep made me nervous, but none more than the tread of a clergyman. What I feared most of all were the black-and-white friars. Two by two, they made their way everywhere.

Outside Perpinhan, a group of Franciscan brothers offered *sopa* to the poor. I was dirty and desperate enough to stand in line. I drank down the hot soup they offered me.

An older friar gazed into my eyes. "Bless you, my daughter," he said. "You are very young to look so hungry and cold."

His kind eyes lured me in, made me long to trust him. Did they always feed the hungry? Might my sisters or Symo have passed this way? I guzzled the soup as fast as I could.

"What is your name, child?"

A few gulps more, and I returned the bowl, bowed my thanks, and ran away. No churchman should ever hear my name. I hadn't yet thought of another to give.

I picked my way across the Pirenèus Mountains, stealing clothing and begging food as I went. Where I could, I slept in barns, huddled next to calves and goats. The mountain air was cold, and winter was fast approaching. I had to get to warmer Aragón, or perhaps Catalonha, south of the mountains. The language was different there, but not so different that I couldn't manage. The church would be there, too, but perhaps word of a runaway heretic girl would be slower to reach this way.

For I was the traveling heretic now. I was Dolssa. The fugitive running from the Church, bereft of family and friends.

Every night I prayed for Plazensa, for Sazia. For Symo, too, wherever he might be. I prayed for Jobau's soul, for Mamà's, and for Dolssa's, too, though it lay safe in her beloved's arms.

Sweet and pure Dolssa, who willingly gave up her life for ours. And that knight, who died trying to help her! Had I known he was an ally, what might have been?

She need not have died. The world would have been better served by letting us die and preserving her gifts. She was a shining light. The world needed lights like hers more than it needed a soothsayer, a tavern keeper, and a failed matchmaker.

I missed my sisters. Whenever I lay down to sleep, I felt as though Plazensa and Sazia were my lungs, robbed from me, and I couldn't breathe. When finally I slept, Symo appeared in my dreams, without a word, holding me in his arms as he'd done before, resting his head upon my shoulder.

I began telling fortunes for pennies, or for food, for travelers I met on the road. I was a fraud, of course; I didn't have Sazia's gifts. But I could make things up. I knew well from watching Sazia what people liked to hear. I could often learn a good deal about them just by listening to their chatter and studying their appearances. I told them things about themselves that they hadn't told me, and they hailed me as a true fortune-teller. It was thievery of me, but less so, I thought, than stealing food and clothes outright. I gave some entertainment for my pay. I began to have the means to feed myself and buy from peasant women some of their warmer secondhand clothes.

I was the fortune-teller now. I was Sazia.

When asked, I told them my name was Astruga.

I crossed the Pirenèus and kept my journey pointed south, deep into the kingdom of Aragón. Here the land was different, drier and warmer. I missed above all the call of the seagulls, and the murmur of *la mar*. But ports, I knew, were places where stories were told, where churchmen came and went. Better safety, I thought, could be found inland.

Their language was different, but not so much that I couldn't keep pace. An accent was not a drawback for a fortune-teller; it made me exotic. But I worked to imitate the local dialects so I could blend in as much as possible.

One cold night I pooled my pennies and begged of an older woman a low price for a bed for the night. She let me in and fed me. I told her my name was Maria and that I came from Tolosa. This far from Provensa, she wouldn't recognize my false dialect.

She seemed glad of my company, and I was glad of hers. She told me to call her Mima. I helped her clean her cottage after supper, and brought in wood for her in the morning. I paid for my room and made to leave, but she told me if I wanted to, I could stay.

Trust her.

Bonjọrn, Dolssa.

I lived with Mima for two months. She never asked where I came from. She gardened, she took in washing and boarders and sold supper. I helped her. She was a widow, she told me, with a son she hadn't seen in years.

I watched Mima watch her neighbors pass by, and in time I began to see one particular man hold her gaze more than any other. A grizzled cobbler who often bought her suppers and who lived just up the street.

One night I followed him out the door.

"Do you like her cooking?"

He looked at me as though I'd gone daft. "I eat it, don't I?"

"Marry her," I told him.

His shoes ground a hole in the red dusty path. "How's that?"

"Marry her," I repeated. "Eat her food for the rest of her life, without price."

So he did.

Mima asked me if I'd look after her house for a while. As a favor, she put it, but I knew it was her gift of gratitude. It was the first time I'd ever lived truly alone. I planted her garden in the spring. I took special care to plant many onions.

The cobbler grew fat on Mima's cooking and made more shoes than ever. He made special shoes for Mima's aching feet, and that was more love than her tired bones knew how to receive. I hadn't utterly lost the old matchmaking magic.

I took to telling fortunes in my little cottage. Mima sent people to me, and they brought silver pennies, and sometimes bits of meat or fish, in return for my predictions. When my customers were young and unmarried, I predicted spouses for them with special accuracy.

I had to play up the part of the fortune-teller, so I hung curtains around a corner near the door, where I placed a small table and two chairs. When someone wanted a fortune, they dropped a coin in a slot in my outer wall. It clinked in the bowl on my table, which signaled me to veil my face, don my earrings, and assume my role. I blew out the candles, ushered them in, and let the charade begin. It didn't yield enough money to support me, quite, but with the garden and Mima's help, I managed.

Mima worried about me, so she brought me little gifts of grain or vegetables, or wool to spin. When it came time to pay tribute money to the local senhor, Mima paid mine without a word.

One day she brought me a sack of barley. I studied it and wondered to myself. Could I recreate Plazensa's brew?

Good luck smiled upon me. In a few weeks I had four jugs of foaming ale. I sold it by the glassful to Mima's neighbors, earning enough to eat for a while and buy still more barley. These Aragónese enjoyed the novelty of my brew. I hoped it would stay that way.

I talked to Plazensa as I did my work. I'd become her, also.

In the steady sunshine of Aragón, it was hard to know when one season bled into another. I woke one day to realize that a year had passed since I lost my old life. I woke another morning, and found it had been three. I was Maria now. My life in Bajas seemed so far behind me, though the events of my final day there were forever etched in daily memory. I still prayed each night for Symo's and my sisters' souls, wherever in this world or the next they might be found.

Sometimes, in the night, I thought of all the ways life could have been different. What if I'd heeded Sazia's warnings and avoided the trip to San Cucufati? What if I'd passed by Dolssa's spot on the riverbank a moment before, or after, and heard no sound at all? What if I hadn't told our group to separate when hunted by the soldiers?

I'd be dead, in the latter case, along with my sisters and Symo. For Dolssa's and Jobau's sake, I tried not to wish that it were the case.

These thoughts were blades, and there was no point reopening cuts.

If I'd never met Dolssa, who would I be today? What if I'd never known the girl in love with God?

And Symo. I had all the time in the world to wonder what might have been possible there. He was the most infuriating *tozęt* ever to make me want to twist his ears. I hoped he'd survived. Even if he slept in another *femna*'s arms and counted his blessings at being rid of that dangerous Botille. I hope he lived long and fat and contentedly, growing his own chickpeas and tying his own grapes in some safe, hidden corner of the world.

I went through the quiet motions of my days. I carried water from the spring to water my vegetables. I came in time to be fond of my neighbors. But life was muffled. Muted. Even my lightest moments were wrapped in relentless grief and loss, pressed down by the anxious taste of waiting for hopeful news that would never come.

BOTILLE

pringtime came, and Mima pined for a pilgrimage to Barçalona. There was a monastery there, Sant Pau del Camp, where an uncle of hers had been a monk, and she longed to see it before she died. Not that death was anywhere near her, as robust and cheery as she was now. But she was determined, and her cobbler would not leave his trade, so she begged me to accompany her.

I resisted. I wanted no part of monks or friars or churchmen. Barçalona worried me, that seaport town. Sant Dominic's Order of Preachers was sure to have a foothold in such a busy place, even if not at the abbey at Saint Paul of the Countryside.

But Mima pressed me. She didn't dare travel alone. A trip

would be good for me, she said. I'd been too melancholy for too long, she said. Who knows, I might find a little romance on a journey such as this, she said.

I wanted romance as much as I wanted Lucien de Saint-Honore to knock at my door. But after all she had done for me, I didn't have the heart to keep saying no to Mima. *Go,* said the familiar voice.

Perhaps a journey would do me some good. I was Maria now, and nobody knew my face. I could keep to myself and attract no danger.

So I journeyed with Mima to Barçalona from our tiny settlement on the outskirts of Balbastro. Outside Barçalona, we sought shelter from rain at a women's convent and passed the night in the dormitories. I hesitated at first, but Dolssa's voice said, *Go without fear.*

I listened to the sisters chant their nighttime prayers. How lucky they were to have each other.

In the morning, I rose before Mima, and couldn't return to sleep, so I went outside to look at the rose gardens. I knelt to admire the showy yellow blossoms. Beyond them were pinks and whites, all swaying together in the dim morning haze.

I noticed a movement farther off in my line of sight. Two young sisters of the convent—novices, I supposed—sat talking in secret behind taller shrubs. I watched as they whispered back and forth. Soft sounds of laughter met my ears. Were they breaking rules? Was there a vow of silence? Their covert friendship among the roses made me smile.

I lost track of time, soaking in the blossoms while the sun climbed in the sky. What a thing, to tend and grow not food, but splendor. I quickly cut a small branch with a swollen bud from the yellow shrub. I would see if by chance I could keep it moist and alive this whole journey home, and plant myself a rosebush.

The secret friends arose and parted from each other with kisses on their cheeks. The shorter one ran inside, while the other headed my way, toward the garden. I tucked my guilty rosebud under my dress and felt a thorn prick tender skin. The girl saw me then and froze. She made to turn back toward the convent and escape my prying gaze. But I saw her eyes before she recognized mine.

"Sazia."

She turned back, and we ran into each other's arms.

My Sazia. Alive and whole and warm in my grasp. My baby *sorre*.

She was taller than I was now. Leaner. Her hair, hidden behind her wimple. Her eyes, her teeth, her very own nose and cheeks, like no one else's could ever be. They were hers, and she was mine. I wouldn't have believed that after so much pain, my heart could still hold this kind of joy.

Grácia, *Dolssa, for bringing me here*. Grácia *for this miracle*.

Her story was soon told.

She'd been caught. Not the night of the burnings, but early the morning after. Soldiers brought her back to Bajas. The terror she endured was beyond imagining. Friar Lucien, Prior Pons, and

Bishop Raimon had already left for Tolosa. They were worried about Lucien, whose wounds had healed astonishingly, but who now seemed possessed by a fit of melancholy. They left other friar inquisitors to clean up the mess Dolssa had left in Bajas.

Soldiers brought her to Sant Martin, where the churchmen stayed, and Dominus Bernard bargained for Sazia's life. If she would join a convent, she would be spared. Sazia agreed, and the presiding friars, who did not share Lucien de Saint-Honore's animosity for Dolssa and her helpers, rejoiced over her as a lost sheep regained into the fold. So off to a Dominican convent in Narbona, Sazia was sent.

"Did you learn anything of Plazensa?" I asked her, there among the flowers. "Or . . . Symo?"

She shook her head. A painful silence filled the space between us.

"So, you went to the convent."

"I raged against it at first," she told me. "I was so sick with grief and anger that I could barely eat. I thought of trying to flee, but if they caught me, my old sentence of execution would return. I spent miserable months in the hospital wing. There I became friends with one of the older women named Sister Margarethe. We were both ill together. She taught me to read."

As Sazia recovered, she fell into the new rhythms of life. She found a taste for study, especially under Sister Margarethe's tutelage. She made friends with other sisters. After a year there, Sister Margarethe was offered a position as abbess at the convent outside

Barçalona. She invited Sazia, now under the name Sister Clara, to come with her.

"Sister Clara," I repeated. "It's so strange to think of you with a new name. But I have one too. I'm Maria."

Sazia grinned. "An excellent choice."

I told her about my little home in the country. "You shall come live with me," I told her. "We'll be together again. No one will know where or whom you are. We'll be safe."

Sazia was slow to reply.

"Do you still fear that if you leave, you'll be punished?"

She shook her head. "No. Sister Margarethe cares for me. She is not like the friars."

I squeezed her hand. "Then it's settled! Come back with us in two days' time."

I waited for an answer, until I realized silence *was* her answer.

"It's so good to see you, Botille," she said.

"Maria." My hurt wouldn't keep silence.

She stroked my cheek. "How I have prayed for you."

I wiped my eyes on my sleeve. "And I for you."

"Praise God for bringing you here to me!"

I'd never heard Sazia speak so before. Who have you become, little *sorre*? What happened to my teasing, mocking, ungovernable girl?

Bells in the convent began to ring. To find her, and not keep her, pierced my heart.

"I like my life here, Botille," she said. "I'm learning so much. The sisters . . ."

She was my sister, still, and I knew her thoughts. She was worried I'd be vexed with her. Something new had found a hold on her affections. My Sazia could never return to me.

"It's all right."

She took courage. "It's good to be one of the sisters." She took a deep breath. "It is good to belong here."

But you belong with me.

The old Botille would have scolded her mightily and marched her out by the ear.

But I was Maria now, and Sazia—Clara—was grown up.

"May I visit you again?" I asked.

She beamed. "I hope you will."

I nodded. "I will see what I can do. I don't much like the thought of spending time at a Dominican convent."

Her cheeks colored. "They're not *all* like the inquisitors in Tolosa."

Hear her, defending them! The order that tried to kill us!

Bells rang again. Sazia began to be anxious to go. "It's time for prayers."

"I never would have predicted, oh, soothsayer, that you would one day be a nun," I told her with a smile. "You never had any use for holiness before."

Her eyes grew wide. "Oh, *sorre*," she said earnestly. "That was before I knew Dolssa."

BOTILLE

ima and I returned home and fell back into the rhythms of our lives. Summer came in, with heat enough to melt any desire I felt to live. I toiled all day in the garden and in my little brewery. Local farmers had less time for fortune-telling during the dry season of the year, when water must be hauled from streams backbreakingly far away, so I had to work harder to feed myself. The blistering air never moved, and I gasped as Mima and I tilled her plot. If my sweat could have watered my garden before the sun baked it off me, it would have been a mercy to me and to my onions.

Bajas had plenty of summer heat, but nothing like this. Grateful as I was for the safety of my hidden life, I was reminded so often of who I was—an alien in a strange land, far from the world that worked as I wished it would.

I thought often of Sazia in her cloister. If I'd had to spot her solely on the life she led, I never would have recognized her. Would those who knew me ever recognize me? I couldn't recognize myself.

One scorching evening before the sun set, when the day's work was done, I collapsed onto my cot. Too hot to eat, too thirsty to live, but too limp to trudge to the stream for a bucket for drinking and washing. What I'd give to dip my feet in *la mar* tonight. Scoop up a bucket of oysters and eat them cold. Instead I lay panting atop my covers, feeling the dusty red soil of Aragón cling to my weary skin. If the heat would've let me, I'd just go to sleep, but in the stale air of the cottage, sleep wouldn't find me for hours.

The sun was nearly set. I loosened my dress.

A coin clinked in my fortune-teller's bowl.

I moaned. What, now? At this hour, when I was so filthy and spent?

I rolled slowly upward and reached for my scarf, which I wound around my hair. I attached my earrings, made an attempt at dusting myself off, then opened the door.

A tall man entered in a cleric's dark robe and hood. *Lucien de Saint-Honore.*

No, it wasn't. It was only my fevered imagination. Every clergyman was still Lucien to me. This man wasn't quite tall enough. He walked with a limp.

I took a step back. In the fading light, I couldn't make much of the hooded face. But I never read fortunes for churchmen.

"I'm sorry, good sir," I told him, "but I am not giving fortunes at this hour."

The man regarded me, though what he saw in the dim light, I couldn't guess. Hopefully, not my dirty face.

"A pity," he said. His voice rasped like a sick person's, but he did not seem ill. "I have come a long way. Word spreads of your fortunes."

A new fear gripped me. I did *not* want a reputation. Was it time to move on and begin anew? Had I stayed here in Mima's hut outside Balbastro too long?

I peered more closely at the stranger. Again I thought back to the Dominican friar, but I knew it couldn't be him. He frightened me, though. I needed to get him out of there.

"I don't give fortunes to holy men," I told my visitor. "I can't afford to offend the heavens."

"But you can afford to offend me?"

I handed him his coin back. "You're not from Aragón."

"Neither are you."

"Provençal?"

"As are you, or so my ear tells me."

"You know," I said, "you sound terrible. Truly. Do you want a drink of water?"

He coughed. "I wouldn't mind."

I frowned. "Too bad my bucket's empty."

He shook his head, then pushed the coin back. "Please," he

said, as though the word were foreign to him. "A favor. From your native countryman. I've come all this way with a question pressing heavily. They said you could lead me to the answer."

He would not go away. I might as well keep his coin. It was the first I'd seen in more than a week. "Hold a moment."

I stirred up the ashes in the fireplace enough to kindle a small blaze, just enough to light a candle. I set it on the table.

"Sit," I said. "Hold out your hand."

I took his palm and began to massage it. The Sazia I remembered had taught me well, even if Sister Clara would never touch a man's hand again. A small sigh escaped his lips. It worked every time.

"You have traveled long," I began.

"I already said that."

"Who says you didn't?" I snapped. "Be still, or the spirits will not speak to me."

I rolled the fleshy thumb in its socket. "You're troubled in mind." I racked my brains for more to say. His dusty cloak and covered face gave me little to work with. Then I remembered his limp. "You've been wounded . . . in body and spirit." I felt rather proud of that last little touch.

"As anyone could see," said he.

I was tempted to bend his thumb back the wrong way. "You'll not get your money back for your rudeness," I said. "Be quiet and wait."

The night air was stiflingly hot. I knew better than to let this arrogant creature in my door, then I'd gone ahead and let myself be persuaded.

"You should not give up hope," I said at length. It seemed like a promising direction. "What you seek is nearer than you think." Everyone, I found, was seeking something.

The stranger made a little snorting sound.

"Are you laughing at me?"

"*Non*, pardon." He coughed. "Dust in my nose."

I shifted my attention from his thumb to his fingers. I noticed how his cloak shadowed his features. "You are also, I think, hiding from something. Or someone."

He didn't object. A good sign.

"You have lost a loved one." Everyone had. "They watch over you."

"What is your name?" he asked me.

The interruption peeved me. I was just getting going. "What does that matter?"

He waited.

"My name's Maria."

"Do you live alone here, Maria?"

My gut turned to water. "Not so alone," I said, "that others won't hear me if I scream." Clergy or no, he might be forming some plans for me tonight.

He held up both hands. "Peace." The hands rested again on the table. "I must say, I'm disappointed," he rasped. "You were praised to the skies. But you've told me nothing to answer my question."

The end of my scarf came loose and clung to the back of my sticky neck.

"Why don't you quit wasting my time and tell me what

your question is?" I said. "Then perhaps I can help you."

He thrust his hand at me. "Aren't you supposed to guess it?"

"Aggravate me too much," I told him, "and the spirits may anger and punish you." I rubbed his hand. I may have also tugged on the hairs on the back.

"I wouldn't want angry spirits after me." He mocked me, the pig. How quickly could I get him gone? Even a sleepless, sweaty summer night was better than his irksome company.

"The question is, where have you been so long, Botille?"

I couldn't find breath. The raspy voice was gone. The voice I knew had come back to me.

He took my hand in his.

With my free hand, I reached over and snatched off his hood from his head.

"Why didn't you wait for me to come find you?"

Symo's face in the candlelight. Here, in my home.

I can't be certain of what happened next. The chair Symo sat in did not survive it.

I stood up, embarrassed, wiping tears off my face. He clambered to his feet and stood before me.

A terrible thought struck me. I remembered Sazia, and asked, "Are you a *monk* now?"

He grinned. "Are you mad?" He pulled off his robe to show peasant's clothes underneath. I sagged with relief. It was him. That thick, strong build I remembered, though it was cut leaner by hunger.

"What happened to your leg?"

"One of the bishop's soldiers."

Mon Dieu. My poor Symo. Lame and hurting for so long. "How did you ever manage to escape?"

For the first time I saw fear in his eyes. Then I understood.

"You wear the cloak," I whispered, "to avoid being caught. You're not just a heretic now."

His eyes never left mine. I backed away. A little.

"They would have killed you, Botille, if they could," Symo whispered. "And me. And your sisters."

I closed my eyes. I remembered that night. I remembered the bishop. I remembered the flames.

What must the struggle have been like? What would I have done if I'd been there?

"If you want me to go, I will, Botille." He stroked a lock of my hair that had escaped my scarf. "I'm just glad to know you're all right."

I opened my eyes to see him resigned. Backing away. Making no demands.

My vision blurred through my tears. He'd killed a soldier. They would have killed us. I needed to think of something else.

"How did you find me?"

He made a wry face. "I've never stopped walking or asking people questions. A nameless girl in hiding is no easy thing to find."

Impossible boy. Back from the dead, breathing the stale air of my tiny home, with candlelight playing over his dusty face, after faithful years spent searching. For me.

"I thought I'd never find you. You were dead, or lost forever." He looked away from me. "But then, these last months, I felt something was guiding my steps to you."

Dolssa.

"I had to know if you lived, Botille."

My eyes stung. Sobs welled up inside me. I could not allow it. Think of all he'd carried since that terrible night. Pain, and fear, and scarring memories. What he'd done, and what he'd seen.

I took his hand and held it. "I should never have left you that terrible night, my friend."

Symo's head hung down. His eyes went to his cloak, and to the door. "*Oc.* Your friend." He blinked several times. "That is good." He pulled the door open and turned toward the road.

"Where are you going?" I thrust forward my chair, the only one left. "Sit."

He paused, then slowly sat.

"Show me your leg."

He pulled up his clothing to show me his wounds. All around the knee and thigh. The soldier had been skilled with a dagger. It was a wonder Symo had survived. I traced my finger across the livid scars, and he winced.

He watched me closely, as if dreading my verdict. I wanted to kiss his wounds then, but feared I'd hurt him.

"It's a wonder you're alive," I told him. "We'll get to work mending you." I poked and prodded and examined his ribs, and raked my fingers through his shaggy hair. I needed to know all the damage his hungry years of roaming had done to him, for my sake. "Feed you up, too. Put some meat on your frame. Give you a bath. Heaven knows you need one."

Liar! Mine was not the examination of a healer. Like Thomas who doubted, I wanted to thrust my hand into his side and satisfy myself he was no ghost. I needed proof I wasn't dreaming—that his living flesh had truly reappeared, in my home, tonight.

Symo's eyes were bright in the candlelight, but his scowl was the same old scowl. "Will you *ever* stop bossing and pecking at me?"

"Pah!" I planted my fists on my hips. "Not till I'm pleased with the results. You're a wild boar that needs taming."

"And you," he said, "are the most vexatious, obstinate, cussed female ever to draw breath."

I began pulling off his shoes.

"What are you doing?"

"Do you know what you need, Symo?" I said.

"What?"

"A wife."

He unwound the scarf from my hair. "You're not still match-making, are you?"

"A little." I perched on his lap, on his good leg. "We've got good, tough *femnas* here. Just the sort to please you."

He pulled me close, nearly bursting my lungs, and stopped me from speaking further in a manner most impertinent.

I'd had enough of his talking, myself.

1267

BOTILLE

The priest married us as Pedro and Maria. We were married just the same.

We worked our little plot of ground, and Symo brought the dry soil to life. It pained me to see him limp back and forth with his yoke of buckets, but he did it daily, and his leg grew stronger. His help freed me to do other things to feed us—buy a little goat, and then another. Brew more ale, tend chickens. Sell the best onions in the county.

We had a son, whom we named Bertran. Just the one, though I prayed for more. Loving him made me rich in ways I'd too long been poor. Tending him brought my mamà back to my side to share with me each new discovery. Watching Symo love Bertran healed my open wounds.

We remained in Balbastro until Mima died. Seven years. Then both of us felt it was time to move on. We'd had no threats, no close calls, but if I'd learned one thing from Dolssa, it was to listen to those feelings. So we gathered our son, our animals, and our things, and packed for the trip. We went to Barçalona to inquire after Sazia, and show her nephew to her.

She was a grown woman now, with duties in the abbey. She trained novices in their studies. My little *sorre*, not just a reader, but a teacher! She made me feel proud. And rough, and ignorant. But mostly proud. She kissed Bertran and gave her love.

Something was different about her, though. Her Sister Margarethe had died. There was fear in her eyes. She advised us not to visit for a time, until she found a way to send us word. Word never came, until now.

I never again saw my Bajas by the sea, though I dreamed of returning for the rest of my life. My Symo pined for his brother, Gui, and I, for news of Plazensa.

Here is how my tale ends. It's a bitter ending, but I do not complain. Sorrow finds us all, and the *bon Dieu* has been more than kind to me.

My Symo one day could bear it no more, the yearning for his brother. He took the journey over the Pirenèus, and back into beautiful Provensa. He had to see Gui.

He never returned.

Bertran, who had grown to be a man, traveled back to learn what had become of his father. He avoided Bajas, but went to the

Abadia de Fontfreda. There, staying in the strangers' quarters, he learned of the old, crippled man who had returned to Bajas after twenty-five years away, and was executed for heresy and murder.

The shock left us weak. I thought my heart would break. At least I'd had my Symo for many years. Bertran made it home and took to his bed. My precious son could not take comfort. I recovered to tend to my ailing *filh*, but he was not so blessed. My only son.

Now I am all alone. My only comfort is my sweet little cat. I'm just an old woman, waiting to die.

BOTILLE

nd now I have told you my tale, *bon* friar. You were a patient one to listen so well. I rather fancy you enjoyed it. I didn't think inquisitors usually took the time. But you traveled all the way from Barçalona to hear me. That would make any man patient.

Well, I think you are right to preserve a record of the account of the maid Dolssa. I wonder, though, why do you want to? To warn Christians not to be deceived?

This story will give them plenty of warning.

I'm not surprised that it took our priest a while to figure out which middle-aged woman you were looking for. I don't feel as old as I look, I'll have you know. And here I thought he was looking for alms for the poor when he came to my lonely little home!

Tell me, what will happen to Sister Clara, at the abbey? Will she be pardoned, because she told you about me? I pray the *bon Dieu* she will.

She doesn't know you traced me here? *Oc*, that is a pleasing thought. How, then, did you learn of me from her?

I see. Of course. Confession.

1290

FRIAR ARNAUT D'AVINHONET

The Convent of the Jacobins, Tolosa

Botille's narrative interested me in several persons, some of whom I knew a little about. Other cases required additional inquiry on my part. Here is what I learned:

Soon after Dolssa's death, Gui found parchment and ink in his wine cellar. He brought it to Dominus Bernard, who recognized in Dolssa's writings a great treasure. Poems and love songs to her beloved, rivaling the *trobadors'* own ballads, were scribbled in the margins of her narrative. He set the words to music and performed them as his own sacred songs in churches throughout Provensa, to wide acclaim. He died a celebrated psalmist of the faith.

Prior Pons de Saint-Gilles served as prior in other cities, and eventually returned to serve in Tolosa before his death. He passed into eternity decades after the strange business in Bajas.

The duty of ordaining a successor to the priory fell to Bishop Raimon de Fauga. He chose Lucien de Saint-Honore, the fame of whose hunt for the fugitive heretic Dolssa de Stigata had spread throughout the Order of Preachers. After not many more years, at Raimon's death, Lucien ascended to the office of bishop.

Bishop Lucien was known as a sensitive, gentle, almost fragile preacher, giving special pastoral care to children, the simple, and the sick. Only in matters of heresy was Bishop Lucien de Saint-Honore unyielding, though he, himself, never attended another burning in his life.

Na Pieret di Fabri died within a year of Symo's disappearance. Gui and his new wife, Sapdalina, nursed her kindly during her ailing months and inherited her vineyards.

Plazensa Flasucra was not seen in Bajas again. Neither was the fisherman, Litgier.

Thus I conclude my record. I imagined reaching an ending would bring me rest. But Bishop Lucien de Saint-Honore bequeathed to me more than his story. He has infected me with his own unease about the matter of Dolssa de Stigata, that strange, rebellious maiden.

Now I, like he, must burn her.

As Botille did, I began to feel my efforts were being led along by Dolssa's urgent voice inside my head. Or perhaps, across the decades, the persuasiveness of Botille's stories simply tricked me into believing it so. Yet the number of times I felt led to just the place, within these cavernous vaults, where a useful record might be found is too great to count.

I should fling this volume into the fire that even now lights my study, and no one would ever be the wiser. But I find my heart urging me to reconsider the matter. In the interim, I shall search out a safe place to hide it, and make the fate of this record the subject of prayer.

2014

THE WRITER

Boston, Massachusetts

What answers Friar Arnaut may have found through prayer, in his private corner of the convent archives, we'll never know.

The Dominican convent in Toulouse was a collection of shabby buildings during Friar Lucien's younger days, but by the time Friar Arnaut was piecing together Botille's and Dolssa's stories, the Dominicans had erected a magnificent church, called the Convent of the Jacobins. The great theologian St. Thomas Aquinas is buried there. Still, to this day, if you visit, you can admire its most notable feature, a soaring column made to look like a palm tree over the main vault of the nave, with arching ribs fanning out upon the ceiling like palm leaves. It's dizzyingly grand and gorgeous.

This distinctive palm structure was still being built in 1290, and Friar Arnaut d'Avinhonet had the bad luck to pass underneath the scaffolding as a worker dropped his chisel. Friar Arnaut met his eternal reward. I hope it was a good one.

We would probably have no record of when an obscure Dominican met his death, except that his fellow friars were so troubled by the accident that one of them noted it in an official journal on 22 November. The year 1290, it appears, was a busy one for Arnaut. He wrote a book, hid it, and died.

At some point, probably long afterwards, when the concerns of the thirteenth century were a distant memory, someone must have found the forgotten volume's hiding place. I picture a friar stumbling upon it, not bothering to read it, and shelving it in the archives without a second thought.

Old books tend to be shuffled around, stolen, loaned, sold to collectors, transferred to different churches or to universities. Though too many disappear forever, some have an uncanny way of popping up. Arnaut's record, I'm glad to say, popped. It wasn't my discovery, but I was fortunate to have gone to college with one of the scholars asked to translate the pages. He invited me to read the translation and offer style corrections to make the writing more accessible to modern readers. That's how I met Arnaut, Botille, Lucien, and Dolssa.

As I sifted through and marked up each day's new pages, one question kept running through my mind. *Do I believe this?*

Normally, I would read a medieval religious text to understand how past generations thought, and what they believed. I would look for clues and details to round out my understanding of the past. The question of belief—my personal belief—would never even enter into my thoughts.

By the time I'd reached the book's end, the question had changed. What's more, the urgent voice asking it was clearly not my own, but a young woman's, hopeful and trusting.

Do you believe me?

I wondered if I needed a little time off.

The night I finished Frair Arnaut's translated account, I mourned. I remember the night was hot and muggy, as Boston summer nights can be. I sweltered in the dark and thought about Dolssa and Botille, and the cost of their friendship in human blood.

I must have finally slept, for I vividly remember waking up. A voice called my name, and a hand shook my shoulder. I snapped on the light; no one was there. I couldn't shake the feeling, though, that someone was. Someone whose touch on my skin smelled of candlelight, ink, and lavender.

I went to my small desk, opened a notebook, and wrote the following pages. Only a few, but I wrote them without pauses or corrections. I had no intention of doing so. I didn't know what words to use until my hand wrote them, though as I wrote, I saw every color, heard the singing bird, and tasted the dry Spanish dust.

The next morning I wondered if it had all been a dream, but there on my desk were the pages. Believe them or not. For those like me who can't bear not knowing how stories end, I offer what follows after, though I admit it won't give full satisfaction.

For any who may wonder, I do believe her.

FERNANDO DÍAZ

ernando Díaz sat in the shade of the village church in Polinyino, Aragón, and dumped his pouch of polished stones into his hand. His father was inside the church, but Fernando, age eleven, had disrupted mass enough times that his father was content to leave him outside.

A stone slipped through his fingers and rolled in the dust. Fernando crawled after it. It stopped near a hole, the size of a brick or two, in the church's wall.

"Little boy," called a voice.

Fernando froze. He looked about and saw no one. The voice came from the church. Was it an angel, sent to chasten him for not attending mass?

"Little boy," called the voice again. It came from below him; a movement through the gap in the wall caught his eye.

"Are you in the dungeon?" Fernando whispered. "They keep you there to burn you."

"You're a smart boy," said the voice. "Do you fear God?"

Fernando's eyes grew wide. What if this *was* an angel, in disguise, sent to test him? "I do," he declared. "Of course I do."

"Then, in God's name, will you do a good deed for a woman about to die?"

Fernando scuttled back away from the church wall. People about to be burned were wicked, he knew. He shouldn't talk to the woman. But he couldn't even see her. And she was, after all, soon to die. Fernando hated the burnings. He pitied the poor sinners.

But this woman didn't sound forlorn.

"You must keep this a secret. Never tell a living soul. Do you promise me that?"

Fernando had no intention of ever telling anyone he was talking to a convict. "I swear it."

"Good boy." The woman poked her fingers out through the hole. "Listen closely. Do you know the little house outside of town, on the winding road heading east, where Pedro and Maria live with their son, Bertran? Sturdy fellow, dark eyebrows? The old man has a limp, and their mean black cat has but one eye?"

"I know it," said Fernando. "That's the meanest cat in Polinyino."

"You speak the truth. Can you go to that house, without anyone knowing, and give Bertran a message?"

That would be easy enough. "I can," the boy said.

"Blessings on you, bright child," said the old woman. "Tell him, 'They're coming. Go quickly. I gave you an hour, at most. Take good care of Papà. Go with God.'"

"'Go with God,'" repeated Fernando. He hoped he could remember it all.

"He will be terribly sad to hear your message," the old woman said. Fernando caught the catch in her voice. "Only that grieves me now. But tell him I said *all shall be well*." She paused. "Unless he forgot to thin my onions this morning, and then I'll haunt him when I'm dead, forevermore."

Fernando felt sorry this friendly voice had to die. Would she really haunt her son over onions?

"Most of all, dear child," it said, "never, ever tell a living soul I spoke to you, nor you to me. Once you give the message to the young man, he will vanish, and no one else in the wide world ever need know."

Fernando promised. As a child, he understood secrets. He could run and deliver the message, and be back before the end of mass.

"And remember to never tell lies," she called after him. "Liars are always found out in the end."

He shivered. Why had she said that? *Did she know?* Perhaps others also knew about his lying to Mamà, that very morning, about the dropped basket of eggs?

He headed out of town toward the one-eyed cat's house. The heat of the day bore down upon him. Imagine, building a fire to execute a sinner on such a day as this! Was he wrong, he considered, to have made a promise to a wicked person? Should he try to forget it, and stay far away from where sinners made their dwelling? But he'd promised. Breaking promises was lying. That must be why she'd given that strange warning. But which was the greater sin? To lie, or to help a heretic?

Somehow, in spite of the heat, a nightingale found the will to sing. Fernando sat down under a shady tree to hear the tune, and wondered what to do next.

Dramatis Personae

Ages given for the year 1241, unless otherwise noted.

Principals

Dolssa de Stigata, eighteen: a young noblewoman raised in the city of Tolosa

Botille Flasucra, seventeen: a peasant girl, tavern wench, and matchmaker in the seaside village (*vila*) of Bajas

Friar Lucien de Saint-Honore, twenty-five: a traveling friar of the newly founded Dominican Order of Friars-Preachers, from the Dominican convent in Tolosa

Botille's Family

Plazensa Flasucra, twenty-one: Botille's older sister, head tavern wench and brewer at the Three Pigeons

Sazia Flasucra, fifteen: Botille's younger sister, of a fortune-telling and prognosticating persuasion

Jobau, fifties: a drunkard, and Sazia's father, who makes his home with the three sisters

CHURCHMEN

Prior Pons de Saint-Gilles, middle-aged: head of the Order of Friars-Preachers in Tolosa, supervising the daily living, preaching, and inquisitorial activities of a group of Dominican brothers

Bishop Raimon de Fauga de Miramont, middle-aged: Dominican friar and bishop of Tolosa, originally from the city of Miramont

Dominus Bernard, forties: parish priest of the Church of Sant Martin, Bajas

Friar Arnaut d'Avinhonet, fifty-four at the time of his writing; a Dominican historian working in the archives of the Convent du Jacobins in Tolosa in 1290

TOLOSANS OF RANK

Count Raimon VII, forty-four: the count of Tolosa, with lands extending far throughout the region; the most powerful and influential lord in Provensa, in spite of heavy losses suffered when Pope Innocent III declared a holy crusade against his father, Raimon VI, and excommunicated him for harboring heretics

Senhor Hugo de Miramont, thirty-eight: a knight from Miramont who makes his home in Tolosa and serves as man-at-arms for Count Raimon VII

VILLAGERS OF RANK IN BAJAS

Senhor Guilhem de Bajas, late twenties: Lord of Bajas, and of its *castrum*, or grand fortified house

Na Pieret di Fabri, sixties: noble in origin, the childless widow of a prosperous vintner, owner of many of the vineyard plots in the countryside surrounding Bajas

Symo, twenty-two: Na Pieret's nephew, originally from San Cucufati

Gui, twenty-one: Symo's brother and Na Pieret's nephew, also from San Cucufati

Lop, forties: the *bayle* (bailiff), an officer to Senhor Guilhem

Peasant Villagers

Martin de Boroc, thirty: a fisherman, husband to Lisette, and father to Ava

Lisette, twenty-five: daughter of the goat-cheese man, wife to Martin de Boroc, and mother to Ava

Ava, two: Martin and Lisette's daughter

Paul Crestian, fifties: Lisette's *papà*, the goat-cheese man

Joan de Prato, thirty-one: farmer, husband to Felipa, and father

Felipa de Prato, twenty-eight: wife to Joan and mother to two young children

Astruga, nineteen: an unmarried young woman in search of a husband, known for her beauty

Sapdalina, twenty-two: another unmarried young woman in search of a husband, a skilled seamstress

Focho de Capa, fifties: a musician, jack-of-all-trades, and master of revels at village celebrations

Azimar de Carlipac, forty-six: a shipbuilder

Amielh Vidal, thirty-three: raises and sells, among other things, ducks

Litgier, twenty-seven: a fisherman

Plastolf de Condomio, seventies: the oldest man in the village

Jacme, Andrio, and Itier, twenties: unmarried peasant farm-hands to Na Pieret di Fabri

Garcia the elder, fifty: a trusted and experienced servant on Na Pieret di Fabri's farm

Garcia the younger, fourteen: Garcia the elder's only son

Saura, forty: Garcia the elder's wife, the mother of Garcia the younger

Peire, thirty-three: a fisherman, Rixenda's husband

Rixenda, twenty-nine: a fishwife, Peire's wife

Author's Historical Note

The Passion of Dolssa is fiction, but the historical setting is real. Some characters are borrowed from history: Count Raimon VII, Bishop Raimon de Fauga, and Prior Pons de Saint-Gilles (I took some liberty with the dates of his tenure). Dolssa de Stigata's story is based on the lives of several medieval female mystics, set against one of medieval Europe's most violent and disturbing conflicts.

Faith, Femininity, and Mysticism in the Middle Ages

In the twelfth and thirteenth centuries, a movement emerged within Roman Catholic Christendom to imtitate Christ by living in simple poverty as Jesus and his apostles did. Monasteries reformed, and new orders of monks and friars formed, most notably, the Franciscans, founded by St. Francis of Assisi, and the Dominican Order of Friars-Preachers, or the Dominicans, founded by St.

Dominic de Guzmán. Both orders rejected life in wealthy monasteries and devoted themselves to traveling and preaching.

Christian writers including Bernard of Clairvaux began to describe Jesus in terms of his compassion, empathy, humility, and suffering, as opposed to, say, his role as Judge, or Captain of the Hosts (armies) of Heaven. This was a Jesus anyone could admire and imitate—especially women. Bernard also wrote extensively in praise of the Virgin Mary. This was new. Mary as Christ's pure and loving mother made a much more hopeful feminine role model for women to embrace than sinful Eve, Delilah, or Jezebel.

These changes, coupled with increased literacy and Bible reading, brought women flocking to religious lives, taking vows in convents or forming private religious houses. Many sought to know Jesus through prayer and meditation, seeking visions and visitations. Some claimed to receive them. Complete union with the divine was their goal, and it involved a path of sacrifice and self-denial. Such seekers, male or female, are called *mystics*.

Clare of Assisi, Catherine of Siena, Theresa of Avila, Mechthild of Magdeburg, Marguerite Porete, and Julian of Norwich are among the medieval women mystics upon whom Dolssa is based. These women lived startling lives, attracting followers and reportedly performing miracles. They practiced seclusion or acts of charity. Most insisted on lives of chastity, wanting no husband but Jesus. This was a bold, defiant choice in a society that offered women few prospects other than marriage. They took the idea of

Jesus as their husband or lover quite seriously; in fact, many spoke of Jesus in passionate, sexual terms that would make modern readers blush.

Those mystics who could write seemed compelled to record their experiences, but for a woman to claim divine inspiration and publish her visions could be seen as usurping authority belonging to the Church. Some were embraced by the Church and sainted after their deaths. Others were executed.

Names and Places

Specific local religious controversies plagued the lands between the Garonne and Rhône Rivers during the twelfth and thirteenth centuries. Now present-day southern France, the region was called *Provincia* ("the countryside") by Latin churchmen, and stretched well beyond what we now call "Provence." The region's famous troubadour poets called it *Provensa*, which I use in the novel, though most people thought of themselves more as belonging to their town or city (or its lord) than to a broader region.

After these lands became part of the kingdom of France in 1271, they were known as Languedoc, after *langue d'Oc*—the language (tongue) of Oc. ("Oc" was their word for "yes.") The region was ruled by counts and lords, large and small; the most powerful were the counts of Toulouse.

Cortezia, the Friends of God, and Heresy

In the twelfth and thirteenth centuries, Church intellectuals became alarmed about heresy, and the dangerous influence of false beliefs on the faithful.

Any unorthodox, unsanctioned religious idea or practice is a *heresy*; a person professing such beliefs is labeled a *heretic*. Heretics exist within their own faith; for example, Muslims and Jews can't be considered Christian heretics. Wherever religious innovators appear, some are embraced as welcome new voices, but others are seen as dangerous to the faithful, particularly ones that challenge the authority or conduct of the leaders. Francis of Assisi's humble poverty and charity earned him sainthood; Peter Valdez's earned him excommunication. Peter's followers vocally criticized the clergy; Francis's did not.

Christian theologians in the rapidly growing universities were especially concerned about heresy. They studied arguments written by early Church Fathers against third and fourth century heresies and grew convinced that the same false doctrines had leapt across a thousand years and as many miles, with Satan's help, to poison Christendom. And Provincia, they were certain, was a hotbed of heresy.

Provincia's language was distinct from its neighbors', and so were its local customs. Its traditions centered around *cortezia*, meaning courtliness or courtesy (though it reaches far beyond polite manners). *Cortezia* dictated certain rituals for greeting, bowing to, helping, and giving gifts to others, according to the *onor* (honor and/or wealth) of all involved. A person might be called a good man (*bon ome*) or good woman (*bona femna*) for being noble or rich, landowning or influential, but a life of known holiness could also merit the label. These holy men and women were known collectively as the friends of God (*amicx de Dieu*). They lived in every village, dressed and ate simply, and performed certain prayers, greetings, and rituals to cultivate and spread their holiness. Specific practices and beliefs varied locally, but the holy good men and women were widely respected, routinely asked for their prayers and blessings. They weren't a church; they embodied a way of seeking everyday holiness that was specific to Provincia.

The friends of God saw themselves as pious Christians, but to Catholic clergy passing through Provincia, they looked like a secret organized religion, and an offshoot of ancient heresies. Ignorance of another culture undoubtedly contributed to these suspicions. Also, the friends of God's humble ways, with little appearance of hierarchy or priesthood, differed sharply from Catholicism. The Church was already concerned about critics who protested its wealth and ostentation, and wary of groups that protested them via alternate lifestyles. The respect in which the good men and women were held suggested that holiness could be found in one's neighborhood, without a priest's help, despite the Church's claim to be the only valid source of sacraments essential for salvation. Furthermore, as mentioned, Church clerics' university training predisposed them to believe ancient, sinister heresies threatened the Church already. The friends of God, therefore, were the demons they'd been searching for.

The Murder of Peire of Castelnau and the Start of the Albigensian Crusade

Dominic de Guzmán visited Provincia in 1204 and was horrified. He founded his Order of Friars-Preachers in Toulouse in 1215 specifically to combat heresy. Pope Innocent III, meanwhile, pressured Raimon VI, count of Toulouse, to purge his lands of heretics. He sent a legate, or papal ambassador, to meet with Raimon in January 1208. When discussions ended badly, the legate, Peire of Castelnau, left. The next morning a squire charged into Peire's camp and skewered him with a lance by the Rhône River.

Historians believe Raimon never ordered Peire of Castelnau's death, and think the assassin was from Raimon's court, acting stupidly and alone, hoping to impress his lord. But Peire's murder was all the provocation Innocent III needed to proclaim a crusade into Raimon VI's lands in 1209.

It was the first holy war where Christians were guaranteed salvation for killing other Christians.

Soldiers "bearing the sign of the cross" were promised salvation, spoils of war, and debt relief. Compared to a Jerusalem crusade, a march into the sunny south looked easy. By summer 1209, tens of thousands of "pilgrims" had gathered near Lyon to journey down the Rhône into Count Raimon's lands.

The first great battle at Béziers was a heartbreaking massacre. Thousands of servant boys tagging along with the crusaders charged the city, climbing walls and sneaking through drains, killing everyone they met, until French knights finally joined them. The boys in their fury heaped corpses on street corners and torched them. The city became an inferno, burning to the ground, incinerating anyone who survived the initial slaughter. Arnauld Amalric, abbot of Cîteaux, papal legate and leader of the crusade, supposedly said, when asked how the crusaders could tell who was a heretic and who was not: "Kill them all! Truly God will know his own." (Soon after the September 11, 2001, attacks, I saw the same idea repeated almost verbatim on a bumper sticker regarding Muslims, and how to tell which were terrorists.)

The crusade, now called the "Albigensian Crusade" after a nickname northern Frenchmen used for southerners, raged for twenty years. Soldiers ravaged Provincia each summer, butchering and mutilating entire towns of people who wouldn't surrender. Provençals battled bravely, and both sides suffered tremendous losses. The war's grim conclusion, with the Treaty of Paris in 1229, established terms that eventually annexed the county of Toulouse into the kingdom of France.

"The Albigensian Crusade ushered genocide into the West," writes historian Mark Pegg, "by linking divine salvation to mass murder, by making slaughter as loving an act as [Christ's] sacrifice on the cross. . . . A crusader not only cleansed his soul by cutting the throat of a pestilential baker from Toulouse, he cleansed the very soul of Christendom" (*A Most Holy War*, page 188).

Inquisition as an Innovative Solution

Cleansing the soul of Christendom remained an unfinished task after the crusade. The friends of God and their sympathizers still lived in hiding. Inquisition arose as a way to smoke them out. The Dominican Order was commanded by Pope Gregory IX to carry out this work. The friars pursued their task with zeal.

Anyone who had ever associated with the *amicx de Dieu* faced likely punishment. Excommunication meant eternal damnation, and it wasn't the inquisitors' only tool. A common sentence was wearing two large yellow crosses on one's clothes for life. This might seem benign, but it visibly marked those to be shunned in Christendom. Pope Innocent III had already proclaimed in 1215 that Jews and Muslims must dress differently from Christians. (Not unlike during World War II, when Germany required Jews to wear yellow stars on their clothing.) Branding people as alien and dangerous barred them from society, friendship, employment, and trade, as though they were infectiously ill. In the eyes of inquisitors, as "doctors of souls," heresy was indeed a disease, a spreading contagion.

The inquisitions "into heretical depravity" sliced through communal loyalties. When persecution became a way of life, fear made neighbors betray neighbors, and turned kin against kin. *Cortezia* dissolved forever, giving way to suspicion.

Inquisitors could only issue religious punishments. (In 1252 they were granted permission to use torture to obtain confessions—a privilege also granted to civil courts). Inquisitors never burned anyone. They recommended civil sentences, then "relaxed" the guilty into the custody of lords and their bailiffs (*bayles*), who carried out the punishments. These lords, still smarting from the wounds of war, had no wish to offend the Church by indulging heretics. Most cooperated.

Inquisitors wrote manuals, trained others, and kept detailed records. They were nothing if not efficient in the "business of the faith." In some cases their inquisitions saved lives. In a post-crusade climate where lords were frantic to avoid the stain of heresy, which could cost them their lands, some lords became reckless butchers. The inquisitors brought a form of due process to the sentencing.

While crusading clergy were often ruthless and bloodthirsty, most churchmen believed they performed a necessary service for God. Some inquisitors rejoiced in destroying heretics; others mourned them as lost souls. Nevertheless, historical records show a clear pattern of the charge of heresy being wielded disproportionately against those who stood in the way of the pope's or the monarch's ambitions; against those who criticized inquisitors; or against those with treasures worth confiscating. It was an effective tool for silencing and looting an enemy, and it remained so for centuries in Europe.

It is this tension among faith, violence, and self-interest that I struggled with most in my portrayal of churchmen. While their deeds may have been monstrous, it is too simplistic to portray them as monsters. Humans have the greatest capacity for evil not when they act alone but in committees, bureaucracies, and board-rooms, carrying out agendas they can justify as their painful duty for the greater good.

The Myth of the Cathars

Search anywhere for information about the Albigensian Crusade, or heretics from southern France, and you'll find them called "Cathars"—in encyclopedias, tourist literature, even academic works. A full description of Catharism's doctrines and hierarchy will follow, claiming a centralized structure, a missionary program for obtaining converts, and a vocal objective of toppling the faith of Rome.

There never was an organized church of Cathars. Historical descriptions of so-called Cathars were written decades later, almost all by Italian Dominican inquisitors. No friend of God in Provincia was called a Cathar, least of all by the "heretics" themselves.

It's not just the name that's wrong. The entire story surround-ing them as a unified and organized religion, with coherent beliefs and a mission to destroy Catholic Christianity, is pure fantasy.

The label "Cathar" is found in the fourth century in the writings of St. Augustine and the Council of Nicea. No link exists between fourth-century Cathars and the good men and women of Provincia. Where thirteenth-century Church intellectuals saw similar ideas, they presumed shared origins. So they described the *amicx de Dieu* in language that sometimes copied verbatim Augustine's descriptions of his Cathars.

In reality, many of those interrogated by inquisitors couldn't explain what the good men and women believed at all. Their impact may have had less to do with doctrine, and more to do with tradition, or family and friendship ties. The good men and women were part of the fabric of life in Provincia, just as farmers and fishermen, priests and prostitutes were. None of them needed a religion to explain its presence.

In the nineteenth century, however, European and American scholars, studying the records of the Cathars written by Catholic scholars, presumed without question that they were a church. They proposed the paradigm that remains popular: that Catharism was the most famous heresy of the Middle Ages, that it was the instigator of both reform and repression within the Church, that it was an early but crushed form of proto-Protestantism. This deeply romantic image of the tragically pure, martyred Cathars still lingers in some academic publications, and in plenty of popular fiction. Cathar legends, castles, and tourist attractions thrive today.

Dolssa is not one of the good women. She is a Catholic mystic. But her fate is wrapped up in that of the friends of God, since she was born in the waning years of the crusade, and the dawn of the inquisitors. In the aftermath of the Albigensian

Crusade, even deviance as pious as hers could be deadly.

The annihilation of the good men and women, the vanishing of *cortezia*, and the success of the Cathar myth serve as reminders that the victors in the belief wars will always be the chroniclers whose testimonies last, the historians whose interpretations spread, the writers of the books that are not burned. The best way to squash an inconvenient idea is to not to combat it but to quietly burn its records, discredit and suppress its voices, and deny their existence. Where denial is impossible, fabricating a new story about them and their origins will work just as well.

This is why Holocaust deniers frighten me, as do those who overlook genocide, and those who use legislative means to rewrite textbooks. If truth matters one iota, we can't be content to write history as we'd like it to have gone. We must tell it, to the best of our biased and hampered ability, exactly as it was.

Church chroniclers may have pointed a false trail, but the inquisitors who transcribed the testimony of every peasant or noble interviewed did us a tremendous, if accidental, service. Even in the act of silencing heresy, they preserved the voices and values of a world on the brink of extinction. Though people answered questions in fear for their lives, and often agreed to answers inquisitors supplied for them, their passionate, flawed, vibrant humanity echoes through dusty parchment pages, perceptible to those modern historians willing to devote the time and study, as my Friar Arnaut did, to examining what the sources actually said. This novel is dedicated, with deep affection, to two of them.

GLOSSARIES

About the Use of Foreign Words in This Novel

Occitan is the name used today for the Romance language still spoken in southern France, Monaco, and parts of Italy and Spain. It descends recognizably from a language used during the Middle Ages that scholars call Old Provençal. It was the elegant, poetic language of the troubadours whose songs were sung in courts throughout Europe.

In France today, Occitan stubbornly survives, though the number of speakers continues to decline. I chose to use Old Provençal words as linguistic reminders of a once-flourishing language and culture that gradually succumbed to war, oppression, and annexation.

Finding authoritative sources for a language spoken in the thirteenth century was difficult, especially for an English speaker with limited French. Old Provençal had many different dialects and no standardized spellings. I drew from several sources mentioned in the bibliography, prioritizing those that seemed oldest and most authoritative. Ultimately I chose to codify my own lexicon for use in this book, and occasionally I did borrow a word or two from modern Occitan. I also used some words from

Latin, with smatterings from other European languages then in use, since trade, church, and legal matters took place in a multilingual context then, as now.

To me, Old Provençal read strangely at first, but its strangeness became its beauty.

OLD PROVENÇAL WORDS USED

abadia: abbey.

Abadia de Fontfreda: loosely, the Coldspring Abbey. Known by its French name, L'Abbaye de Fontfroide, it is not far from Narbonne (Narbona) and Bages (Bajas). It still functions as a museum, vineyard, winery, restaurant, and hotel.

acabansa: finished, done.

amic/amicx: friend (singular/plural).

amicx de Dieu: the friends of God. See *bona femna* and *bon ome* for more information.

amor: love.

an: year.

aze: buttocks, bottom.

bastida: bastide, a new type of walled market town built throughout Provensa according to the terms of the Treaty of Paris that ended the

Albigensian Crusade. Count Raimon VII of Toulouse was allowed to build such towns for economic and political purposes, provided they did not have military fortifications. In this way he attempted to rebuild his lands following the devastation of the crusade. Over the next century some seven hundred were built.

bayle: bailiff; an officer of a count, a lord, or the king.

bon/bona: good (masculine/feminine). Plural, bons/bonas.

bona femna/bonas femnas: good woman (singular/plural). The term could mean generally a woman held in esteem or respect. In the specific context of the practices deemed as heretical by the pope and the inquisitors, it meant those women who practiced certain localized rituals of courtesy (*cortezia*) and holiness, and received honor (*onor*), respect, and gifts in their community for their holy status, or at least they did before the Albigensian Crusade of 1209–1229. Men who held the same status and observed the same practices were called *bons omes*. They were also, as a group, referred to as the *amicx de Dieu*, or friends of God.

bonjọrn: good day (greeting). From *bon* (good) + *jọrn* (day).

bon ome/bons omes: good man, the masculine counterpart of bona femna (singular/plural).

caçolet: there is no English name for this dish; we call it by its French name, *cassoulet*. It was a peasant dish that originated in Provensa, made from dried beans, bits of meat and fat (typically salted duck and pork, or mutton, goose, partridge), slow-cooked in a clay bowl (a *cassoule*) to form a succulent and hearty stew. Three cities that feature in our story—Toulouse (Tolosa), Castelnáudary (Castèlnòu d'Arri), and Carcassonne (Carcassona)—have a friendly dispute today over which of them originated the cassoulet.

castęl: castle.

comtessa: countess.

cortezia: courtesy, courtliness. An elaborate set of rules and rituals for how all members of society showed deference and respect to one another, through words, actions, and gifts. In the thirteenth century, in this area of Provensa, courtesy was far more than mere social politeness. It permeated all social relationships, and defined the "courtliness" of the age for which southern nobles were known.

devina: soothsayer, witch (feminine).

Dieu: God.

domna: lady; term of address used for women of noble origin.

donzęlla: Miss, maiden, young woman (suggesting nobility).

enamoratz/enamorat: lover, (singular/plural) .

ęnfan: infant or young child.

faidit: a term for southern nobles displaced from their lands (and thus their honor or *onor*) by the crusade. It disparagingly implied that one was an outcast, a rebel, a sympathizer with heretics, a fugitive, and a criminal.

femna: woman.

filh: son.

filha: daughter.

flamenc: flamingo.

fogasa: flatbread cooked on a hearth, a common staple of diet in Provensa (modern spelling, *fogassa*). Similar, though not identical, to the Italian *focaccia* or French *fouace*.

galineta: sweetheart.

grácia: grace, mercy; also thanks.

Jhesus: Jesus.

jocglars: the performers who sang the songs written by troubadours; in French, *jongleurs*.

lach: milk.

legums: vegetables.

luna: moon.

maire: mother.

maisoṇ: home, dwelling, domicile, usually of someone not noble.

mar: sea.

merda: fecal matter.

mima: term of endearment for grandmother.

moton: mutton; sheep or goat's meat.

mujọl: mullet; an edible fish found in the Mediterranean.

Na: (short for domna) lady; term of address used for women of noble origin.

ome: man.

ọncle: uncle.

onor: honor; it could also mean a gift, or the title or inheritance to a piece of property, as these were, in this society, related ideas.

paire: father.

pap: term of endearment for grandfather.

pọl: chicken, rooster.

polẹt: young chicken, young bird; can also be a term of endearment: "My little chicken!"

poma: apple.

pọrta: door or gate.

Pọrta Narbonesa: the Narbonne Gate, a major gate entering the city of Toulouse (Tolosa) from the south.

Provensa: a term used by troubadours to describe the region of present-day southern France where Occitan was spoken.

rossinhol: nightingale.

sant/santa: saint (masculine/feminine).

senhor: lord.

ser: evening.

sopa: soup.

sorre: sister.

tanta: aunt.

toza: girl.

tozet: boy.

trobador: troubadour, one of the poets of the twelfth and thirteenth centuries, who originated in Provensa. They are largely credited with establishing the foundations of Western poetry and romantic literature and, in some sense, romance itself as we now understand it, through their songs and ballads of courtly love.

vila: village, villa, town.

vin: wine.

Latin Words Used

castrum/castra: fortified farm or village (singular/plural).

Dominus: Lord. Latin, not Old Provençal, was used to designate a priest. Hence Bernard, the village priest, is "Dominus Bernard" not "Senhor Bernard." (The tradition of referring to priests as "Father" emerged later.)

friar: brother; used to refer to members of various male religious orders who viewed one another as brothers, including the Dominicans and Franciscans.

illiteratus: illiterate. Friar Lucien, trained in theology using Latin, would have felt superior to less educated country priests and used this Latin slur, which he would have heard in his university studies.

medicus/medica: healer (masculine/feminine).

Provincia: the Latin name for the region referred to elsewhere in the novel as Provensa. Churchmen and scholars, such as Friar Arnaut d'Avinhonet, would certainly have referred to it by its Latin name.

socii: partner, associate. Each Dominican friar was assigned a companion, to remain with him at all times. They were supposed to work in pairs.

OTHER TERMS

Albigensian: a French term used to describe the "heretics," as the good men and good women were accused of being. The term was coined by northern Crusaders and the monastic intellectuals who wrote about and argued in favor of the Crusade of 1209–1229. In time, the Crusade came to be known as the Albigensian Crusade, but the people living in and around Provensa, the term I'm using for present-day Southern France, would have been unlikely to use this term during the war— and prior to the war, would have been extremely unlikely to consider the good men and good women anything other than good Christians.

fidel: a stringed musical instrument played with a bow, also called the *vielle* or *viuola*. Considered a precursor to the violin or viola.

Place Names

The Occitan name for places in the book, and what we call them now.

Place Name (Occitan)	Place Name Today (In French, Spanish, or English)
Anglatèrra	England
Avinhonet	Avignonet
Bajas	Bages
Balbastro, Aragón	Barbastro, Spain
Barçalona, Catalonha	Barcelona, Catalonia
Basièja	Baziège
Besièrs	Béziers
Carcassona	Carcassonne
Castèlnòu d'Arri	Castelnaudary
Florença	Florence (Firenze in Italian)
Fontcobèrta	Fontcouverte

Londres	London
Narbona	Narbonne
Perpinhan	Perpignan
Polinyino, Aragón	Poleñino, Spain
Roma	Rome
San Cucufati	St. Couat d'Aude
Tolosa	Toulouse
Vilafranca de Lauragués	Villefranche-de-Lauragais

ADDITIONAL READING

On Medieval Women Mystics

Carol Flinders's *Enduring Grace* brings the spirituality, sensuality, and longings of the seven women she studied vividly to life. Dolssa is a composite of the courageous mystics Flinders portrayed, and a monument to my gratitude.

On the Albigensian Crusade, the Inquisitions into Heresy, and Daily Life in the Thirteenth Century

Mark Gregory Pegg's *A Most Holy War: The Albigensian Crusade and the Battle for Christendom* and *The Corruption of Angels: The Great Inquisition of 1245-1246* are comprehensive, compelling, and field-changing works on the Albigensian Crusade and the "inquisitions into heretical depravity" that followed it. His insistence on examining original sources strips away the myth and fallacy that have for centuries dominated scholarship on heresy and medieval Christianity. Pegg paints a colorful portrait of a society comprised of memorable names and voices, then shows with unflinching candor how war, interrogation, and persecution ripped that society apart. Most strongly recommended.

On Other Aspects of Medieval Community Life

R. I. Moore's highly influential work, *The Formation of a Persecuting Society: Authority and Deviance in Western Europe, 950–1250* tells the story of how persecution became a way of life in Latin Christendom beginning in the twelfth century. Quite simply, it wasn't always the case, and Moore convincingly pinpoints its surprising origins. A highly rewarding read. His more recent *The War on Heresy* elaborates on and clarifies in a sweeping narrative this "persecuting society" from the eleventh to the thirteenth centuries. Leah L. Otis's meticulous work, *Prostitution in Medieval Society*, dives deeply into a marginalized yet indispensable aspect of medieval community life. Prostitution touched community, family, marriage, sex, politics, religion, and money. Thus her work, which, fortunately for me, focused on the very corner of Europe I was most interested in, was a treasure trove of detail.

On the Language of Old Provençal and the Songs of the Troubadours

For a work that presents troubadour writings in faithful and lyrical English translations by poets including Ezra Pound, alongside the beauty of the original Occitan (or, to be precise, Old Provençal), I recommend *Lark in the Morning*, edited and translated by Robert

Kehew, Ezra Pound, and W. D. Snodgrass. For anyone wishing to closely study Occitan as spoken during the Middle Ages, I recommend *An Old Provençal Primer* by Nathaniel Smith and Thomas Bergin.

On All of the Above

The audio course, "Terror of History: Mystics, Heretics, and Witches in the Western Tradition," published by The Great Courses Company, and taught by Professor Teofilo Ruiz of UCLA, provides an engaging and far-reaching overview of the ideas presented here.

Selected Bibliography

Adamson, Melitta Weiss. *Food in Medieval Times*. Westport, Conn.: Greenwood, 2004.

Ames, Christine Caldwell. *Righteous Persecution: Inquisition, Dominicans, and Christianity in the Middle Ages*. Philadelphia: University of Pennsylvania Press, 2009.

Bennett, Ralph Francis. *The Early Dominicans: Studies in Thirteenth-Century Dominican History*. Cambridge, England: Cambridge University Press, 1937.

Brunn, Emilie, and Georgette Epiney-Burgard. *Women Mystics in Medieval Europe*. New York: Paragon House, 1989.

Cheyette, Fredric L. *Ermengard of Narbonne and the World of the Troubadours*. Ithaca, N.Y.: Cornell University Press, 2001.

Flinders, Carol. *Enduring Grace: Living Portraits of Seven Women Mystics*. San Francisco: HarperSanFrancisco, 1993.

Furlong, Monica. *Visions & Longings: Medieval Women Mystics*. Boston: Shambhala, 1996.

Kehew, Robert, Ezra Pound, and W. D. Snodgrass. *Lark in the Morning: The Verses of the Troubadours*. Chicago: University of Chicago Press, 2005.

Levy, Emil. *Petit Dictionnaire Provençal-français,*. 3rd ed. Heidelberg: C. Winter, 1961.

Moore, R. I. *The Formation of a Persecuting Society: Power and Deviance in Western Europe, 950–1250.* Malden, Mass.: Blackwell, 1990.

Moore, R. I. *The War on Heresy.* Cambridge, Mass.: Belknap of Harvard University Press, 2012.

Otis, Leah L. *Prostitution in Medieval Society: The History of an Urban Institution in Languedoc.* Chicago: University of Chicago Press, 1985.

Pegg, Mark Gregory. *The Corruption of Angels: The Great Inquisition of 1245–1246.* Princeton: Princeton University Press, 2001.

Pegg, Mark Gregory. *A Most Holy War: The Albigensian Crusade and the Battle for Christendom.* Oxford: Oxford University Press, 2008.

Ruiz, Teofilo. "Terror of History: Mystics, Heretics, and Witches in the Western Tradition." Chantilly, Va.: The Great Courses Company, 2002. Audio recording.

Sibly, W. A. and M. D. Sibly, eds. *The Chronicle of William of Puylaurens: The Albigensian Crusade and Its Aftermath.* Woodbridge, Suffolk, Eng.: Boydell, 2003.

Smith, Nathaniel B., and Thomas Goddard Bergin. *An Old Provençal Primer.* New York: Garland, 1984.

Wakefield, Walter L. *Heresy, Crusade, and Inquisition in Southern France, 1100–1250.* Berkeley: University of California Press, 1974.

Acknowledgments

The colorful, messy, flesh-and-blood humanity of those who died on either side of the thirteenth century turmoil over heresy weighed upon me during the two years I worked on this book. This book is for them. So much needless loss must impart a sense of reverence, and, for the writer, a humbling obligation to get the story right. Yet there will be errors, and for them, I apologize.

For all the scholars, medieval and modern, who took pen to paper or parchment to record and analyze the history of the turbulent thirteenth century, and the plan to expunge heresy from the soul of Europe, thank you for your devotion to your life's work.

This book wouldn't exist without Teofilo Ruiz, Distinguished Professor of History at UCLA, who first pointed the way. It *couldn't* exist without Mark Pegg, author and professor of history at Washington University in St. Louis. Mark lent his expertise, his enthusiasm, and a year of his life to this project. I'll miss our collaboration. I can never repay his kind generosity.

Alyssa Henkin, my agent, and Ken Wright, my publisher, were unanimous in their passion for this idea. Their belief kept mine afloat. Kendra Levin's tireless editorial efforts deserve a gold star and a lifetime supply of Wonka chocolates. I can't thank her enough for her wisdom nor her kindness. Others at Penguin Young Readers Group showed tremendous support. I'd be lost without the brilliant Janet Pascal. To Kim Ryan, thanks the world over. To Jennifer Loja, my gratitude for your faith in me. My publicist Marisa Russell's energy and creativity are amazing. To the marketing, publicity, and sales teams, you're the real thing. Thanks for all you do. To Lindsey Andrews, Cara Petrus, and Jim Hoover, thank you for making this book so lovely.

The Passion of Dolssa is immensely richer for the thoughtful contributions of early readers Nancy Werlin, Ammi-Joan Paquette, Deborah Kovacs, and Ginger Johnson. I'm deeply grateful.

Finally, to Phil, whose belief and insights I prize above all—here you remain, after all these years, a man for all seasons, a faithful heart for the ages.

Questions for Discussion

1. Both Dolssa and Botille become fugitives at some point. In what ways do their escapes and journeys parallel each other? How does hiding from a threat influence their beliefs and actions?

2. Botille, her sisters, and Dolssa are all young women making their way through a heavily patriarchal world without the support of parents or a husband or the Church. How does their independence affect perceptions of them? In what ways does the community reject or support them because of their gender and familial status?

3. Who are the villains of the story? What makes them a villain? What sympathetic or redeeming qualities do they have, if any? To what extent should people who do evil things be viewed as sympathetic?

4. Dolssa's mother says "For my sake, guard your tongue to guard your life, my daughter" (p. 10). Would it have been better for Dolssa to remain silent instead of speaking out? Why or why not? At what other points in the story does the dilemma of silence vs. standing up for one's beliefs play a role for any of the characters?

5. *The Passion of Dolssa* is rooted in historical events and uses Old Provençal words to develop the setting. What aspects of the book do you find the most relatable today? Do you see any parallels between our world and the one Botille and Dolssa live in?

6. There are many narrators throughout the book, from the main characters like Dolssa and Botille to minor characters like Hugo to the villagers whose testimony Lucien records. What do these perspectives add to the story? How would the book be different if we did not hear the words and voices of these multiple minor characters?

7. How does Dolssa's presence cause the village community to develop or fragment? Is her influence for the better or for the worse? What do you think she should have said or done differently after her arrival in the village?

8. Compare Dolssa's actions when she is separated from her beloved and her mother to Botille's actions when she is separated from her sisters and Symo. How do Dolssa and Botille react to loss? To reunion?

9. Botille and her sisters each have a specific gift or calling: matchmaking, fortune-telling, or hospitality. How do these gifts impact the sisters' influence on one another and on their community? What significance do the gifts have to Botille once she is separated from her sisters?

10. At the very end of the book, Fernando wonders, "But which was the greater sin? To lie, or to help a heretic?" (p. 446). How does this moral dilemma show up throughout the book for different characters? What might Fernando himself decide to do after the book ends?

11. At the end of the book, Botille says of her sister Sazia, "If I'd had to spot her solely on the life she led, I never would have recognized her. Would those who knew me ever recognize me?" (p. 420). How do the values of and choices made by the characters change over the course of the book? Are the changes for the better or for the worse?

12. What happens to the story if you consider each of the three main characters (Botille, Dolssa, and Lucien) as antagonists to the other two? What does each pair of enemies fight over?

13. Botille and her sisters go from homeless outcasts to valued contributors to their community; Dolssa, who once lived a privileged life, travels the opposite way. What is significant about this reversal of character arcs?

14. The good intentions of minor characters often produce disastrous results for the main characters in the story. Is this a reflection of reality? Why or why not?

Discussion questions contributor: Luisa Perkins

TURN THE PAGE TO READ A
SAMPLE FROM JULIE BERRY'S NOVEL—

JULIE BERRY

ALL THE
TRUTH
THAT'S
IN ME

Her words could ruin him, but her silence will destroy them both.

"A distinctive novel that includes a powerful
message about the value of women's voices
and what is lost when they are silenced."
—*The New York Times Book Review*

We came here by ship, you and I.

I was a baby on my mother's knee, and you were a lisping, curly-headed boy playing at your mother's feet all through that weary voyage.

Watching us, our mothers got on so well together that our fathers chose adjacent farm plots a mile from town, on the western fringe of a Roswell Station that was much smaller then.

I remember my mother telling tales of the trip when I was young. Now she never speaks of it at all.

She said I spent the whole trip wide-eyed, watching you.

After

BOOK ONE

I.

You didn't come.

I waited all evening in the willow tree, with gnats buzzing in my face and sap sticking in my hair, watching for you to return from town.

I know you went to town tonight. I heard you ask Mr. Johnson after church if you could pay a call on him this evening. You must want to borrow his ox team.

But you were gone so long. You never came. Maybe they asked you to supper. Or maybe you went home another way.

Mother chided me ragged for missing chores and supper, and said all that was left for me was what had stuck to the stew pot. Darrel had already scraped the pot bare, but Mother made me wash it in the stream anyway.

There's nothing so bright as the stream by day, nothing so black on a moonless night.

I bent and drank straight from it. It was all I had to fill my belly. And maybe, I thought, you'd be thirsty, too, after a scratchy day of haying, and before retiring to bed you'd dip down into the same stream and drink the water I had kissed. You've cooled off here most summer nights since you were a boy.

I thought how, in the darkness, I would feel like any other girl to you. Beneath my dress I have no cause for shame.

I thought how, if you knew, you might look twice at me, bend your thoughts my way and see if they snap quickly back, or linger.

But you don't know.

And you never will.

For I am forbidden from telling.

II.

This morning I was in the fringe of woods beyond your cabin long before you were up. I had to circle around a tree so you wouldn't see me when you passed by on your way to the outhouse.

Something occupies your thoughts today. There's a spring in your step, and you hum as you walk. You seem in a hurry to get on with something.

Jip didn't notice me. He hovered at your ankles and rubbed his side against your boot. He's half deaf and blind, with little left of his sense of smell, but still you keep him. He's an old friend.

I watched your cabin as long as I could before I had to hurry back, lest Mother notice me missing.

III.

Darrel knows. He caught me in the woods outside your house. He threatens to tell Mother, if I don't do his chores for him in the chicken hut and bring him berries and nuts and first cherries whenever I find them. He and his great mouth need my constant feeding in order to stop their constant talking.

IV.

Tonight the moon came out, and I went out with it, to watch it rise over the treetops. So silent, the moon.

I remember. Night after night, its silence would comfort me. How dark the nights when it went away. But it always came back.

It was my only friend in the years with him.

It is still my consolation.

V.

You are not like him.

No matter what anyone says.

VI.

Father used to say my singing could charm the birds down from the trees. Loving fathers will say anything, but I used to dream one day my song would bring you to me.

It was always you. When you gathered nuts in the forest with the other coltish boys, I liked your smiles and jokes the best. I swelled with pride when your slingshot brought down a big tom turkey.

Do you remember me digging worms for you when you were twelve and I was eight?

I would meet you at the creek with my little sack of soil and present you with the fattest crawlers I could pluck from pulling weeds in my mother's kitchen garden. You called me "Ladybird." It was Father's name for me. He meant "sweetheart." You meant "girl worm-catcher." I was still pleased.

You'd do somersaults when you knew that only I could see

them. You pretended not to hear me clapping, and we'd both laugh when you toppled on your rear.

You left a basket of apples for me at my willow tree once. I saw you sneak away after.

In time, you became a man, and all at once, I became this.

VII.

Do you remember the Aldruses' logrolling? I can never forget it, though I suppose it must be just another day to you.

It was four years ago. I was just fourteen, and growing.

It was a hot day in late summer. A young couple had recently arrived in Roswell Station from Newkirk, up north, and they wanted to set up housekeeping east of town, where the last forest overlooks the marshlands. Clyde Aldrus had staked out a lot and asked the town to come clear away the timber he'd felled. His young wife, Joan, was near to delivering her first.

You must remember the day's work. You left your ripening wheat fields and toiled under the hot sun all day with your hatchet and ax, in company with the men and older boys and the oxen and their chains.

But do you remember the food? And what you said to the girl who prepared and served the hominy pudding?

I hope you do not remember my hominy pudding. I would rather forget that. I chose it because I'd heard you say once, after church, that it was one of your favorite suppers.

Our whole family came: Mother, Father, Darrel, and me. Father whistled all the way through town, driving Old Ben hitched to our apple cart. Mother sat beside him and shook her head, laughing at him. I held on tight to the hominy pudding cradled in my lap.

Mother sat with the women and sewed gowns and bonnets for the new baby. The young ladies presided over the table in their absence. We were all so nervous, we girls, about presenting our cooking to Roswell Station for the first time.

I stood slicing pears with Abigail Pawling when someone tugged me aside.

"Can you keep a secret?" Lottie Pratt whispered under her bonnet brim into my ear.

"Of course I can," I said. "What's the matter?"

She led me behind the pile of logs already gathered by sweating men. Back at the table, Maria Johnson and Eunice Robinson eyed us. Maria's new dress was blood red, with a white scalloped collar and black ribbons on the sleeves and bodice. Earlier, when Maria was out of hearing, little Elizabeth Frye said her father thought the dress dipped dangerously close to vanity. And if beauty wasn't enough, while the rest of us girls struggled with our puddings and hotchpots, Maria Johnson had brought three golden-brown plum tarts.

Lottie, who'd done all her father's cooking since her mother's death many years ago, had no reason to fear being outshone by Maria. Her yeasty rolls could rival even Goody Pruett's baking. She pulled my ear close to her mouth.

"I've got a fella," she whispered.

I pulled away to see her face. She must be joking. But her cheeks were flushed, and her eyes were bright.

"Who?" I breathed.

"Sssh! Tell you later," she said. "Watch me tonight and guess. But swear you'll never speak a word of it."

My head spun with this information. From the corner of my eye, I saw you fasten a chain around a log and wave to Leon Cartwright, who led the ox team.

"What do you *mean*, you've got a fella?"

Lottie's chest swelled with her importance. "Says he's gonna marry me," she said. "He's given me ever so many kisses."

"Kisses!" I gasped. Lottie pressed her pink finger over my lips.

You turned then and saw us whispering there, and straightened up and grinned. I had to take a deep breath.

Lottie missed nothing. Her eyebrows rose. In a terrible instant I realized: you might be her fella.

"Is it Lucas, Lottie?"

She giggled. "What if it is?"

Eunice and Maria were openly frowning at us now. Mrs. Johnson approached the food table, and Maria pointed her mother's gaze our way.

"I've got to know," I begged.

"Why, is Lucas *your* fella?"

I prayed my weakness wouldn't show. "Don't tease me, Lottie," I said. "Just tell me."

A shadow passed over us both, and we looked up to see Mrs. Johnson's arms folded across her ample bosom. "Hadn't you young ladies best get back to your tasks?" she said.

Lottie hurried off, but I trotted meekly back to the table.

"There's a good girl," Mrs. Johnson said, and patted my back. "Lads'll want food soon, and you'll want to show off your pretty face *and* your pretty dish."

I turned to Mrs. Johnson in much astonishment, but she only winked back. Her daughter, Maria, was less patient with me.

"Run and fill these from the well." She handed me two large tin pitchers. I didn't mind an excuse to step away, so I headed toward the new well Clyde had dug.

I dropped the bucket down and listened to it splash. When I was sure it had sunk deep enough to fill, I leaned all my weight against the crank to pull it up again. This pulley was more stubborn than some, and I struggled to complete each turn.

"Let me help," said a voice. Someone beside me took hold of the crank.

It was you.

I wanted to run, but I had pitchers to fill, and how would that look if I bolted away? I hesitated with my hands still on the wooden handle, and you smiled at me.

"Here, we'll do it together," you said. With your hands overlapping mine, you rotated the well-pull effortlessly. My arms followed the motions to no useful purpose. I was sure my cheeks must have gone cherry red. You were almost a man now. It had happened to you so suddenly.

You brought up the bucket and poured water into my pitchers. Then you offered me a cold drink from the cup hooked to the bucket rim, and there was your boy smile in a broader, more angular face. I was so nervous, my arms shook to hold the pitchers. You took one of them and carried it back with me to the table.

"You've grown taller, Ladybird."

"That's what Mother says," I managed to say. "She's had to make me a new dress to fit."

I wanted to die of shame. Mentioning the fit of my dress to any young man, and worse, to you!

I floundered for rescue. "She . . . made me do a great deal of the stitching myself."

You glanced sideways at my gray dress, then up at me. "Looks like you've made a handy job of it."

We reached the table and set the water down. Maria Johnson saw you and twined her bonnet strings between her thumb and finger.

"Dinner's not for an hour yet, Mr. Whiting, so you'll have to come back then," she said. "We can see you're working up an appetite."

Your gaze lingered on Maria's dark curls poking out from under her starched white bonnet. Then you tipped your broad hat at all the girls and strode off to the log-pull. Maria and Eunice both watched you go. I let out a long breath and leaned against the rough-hewn wall of the Aldruses' new home. Lottie caught my eye and smiled, and I sighed in great relief.

I knew then that you were not her fella.

That was the last conversation you and I had, and the last time I saw Lottie smile.